A Silent Witness

A Dr. John Thorndyke Story
By R. Austin Freeman

Originally published in 1914

A Silent Witness

© 2010 Resurrected Press
www.ResurrectedPress.com

Published by Intrepid Ink, LLC

Intrepid Ink, LLC provides full publishing services to authors of fiction and non-fiction books, eBooks and websites. From editing to formatting, to publishing, to marketing, Intrepid Ink gets your creative works into the hands of the people who want to read them.
Find out more at www.IntrepidInk.com.

ISBN 13: 978-1-935774-06-8

Printed in the United States of America

FOREWORD

In *A Silent Witness* R. Austin Freeman introduces yet another young medical doctor with a problem whose ties to Dr. John Thorndyke provides the solution. Thorndyke, a lecturer in Medical Jurisprudence at the school of St. Margaret's Hospital, is also a barrister, which is a lawyer qualified to plead cases before the bar, though his practice mostly involves acting in a consulting role on matters of forensic evidence.

On reading the Thorndyke stories for the first time one has to remind oneself that they had been written not in recent years, but at a time contemporaneous to that of the incidents in the story, that is during the first years of the twentieth century. The reason for this is that so many of the forensic techniques employed by Dr. Thorndyke seem so familiar.

None of the methods used in the Thorndyke novels and stories were made up. The techniques were all available and practical at the time the events in those stories were written. That is why it is important to remember that the author, R. Austin Freeman, is not recreating Edwardian science; he is recording it as it was occurring. Not only is there the usual meticulous use of fingerprints, but also quantitative chemical analysis of a most unusual subject, done not in the blink of an eye, but in the most believable manner.

While the elaborate disguises used in *A Silent Witness* were typical of detective fiction of the time, the attention to forensic evidence and in particular the medical details obtained from *post mortem* examinations are what set the Thorndyke books apart from other works of the period. Freeman's medical background and experience are in evidence throughout the series.

One example of this is in the ingenious method used in the first attempt on Jardine's life. Rather than using some mysterious poison gas, the murderer uses carbonic gas, carbon-dioxide, the same gas that is used to provide the fizz in "soda water" or "soda-pop." This unseen killer is every bit as terrifying as some "green mist." Even more ingenious is the use of the same gas as improvised fire extinguishers to thwart the second attempt. Freeman's use of science in this case is both accurate and realistic. Yet a third property of this gas plays a role in the crime and its ultimate solution.

About the Author

Richard Austin Freeman (1862-1943) was born in London. He studied medicine at Middlesex Hospital and then entered the Colonial Service. He was assigned to a post in Accra on the Gold Coast of Africa. During his time in Africa he contracted blackwater fever which forced him to return to London. Unable to find a permanent medical position, he decided to try his hand at writing fiction. His first stories were written in collaboration with Dr. John James Pitcairn, the medical officer at Holloway Prison, using the pen name Clifford Ashdown. In 1907 the first Dr. Thorndyke novel *The Red Thumb Mark* was published. He served as a Captain in the Royal Army Medical Corp during World War I. He continued writing up until his death, writing parts of *Mr. Polton Explains* in a bomb shelter in 1939 at the age of 77.

Greg Fowlkes
Editor-In-Chief
Resurrected Press

TABLE OF CONTENTS

1
THE BEGINNING OF THE MYSTERY

THE history upon which I am now embarking abounds in incidents so amazing that, as I look back on them, a something approaching to scepticism contends with my vivid recollections and makes me feel almost apologetic in laying them before the reader. Some of them indeed are so out of character with the workaday life in which they happened that they will appear almost incredible; but none is more fraught with mystery than the experience that befell me on a certain September night in the last year of my studentship and ushered in the rest of the astounding sequence.

It was past eleven o'clock when I let myself out of my lodgings at Gospel Oak; a dark night, cloudy and warm and rather inclined to rain. But, despite the rather unfavourable aspect of the weather, I turned my steps away from the town, and walking briskly up the Highgate Road, presently turned into Millfield Lane. This was my favourite walk and the pretty winding lane, meandering so pleasantly from Lower Highgate to the heights of Hampstead, was familiar to me under all its aspects.

On sweet summer mornings when the cuckoos called from the depths of Ken Wood, when the path was spangled with golden sunlight, and saucy squirrels played hide and seek in the shadows under the elms (though the place was within earshot of Westminster and within sight of the dome of St. Paul's); on winter days when the Heath wore its mantle of white and the ring of gliding steel came up from the skaters on the pond below; on August evenings, when I would come suddenly on sequestered lovers (to our mutual embarrassment) and hurry by with ill-feigned unconsciousness. I knew all its phases and loved them all. Even its name was delightful, carrying the mind back to those more rustic days when the wits foregathered at the Old Flask Tavern and John Constable tramped through this very lane with his colour-box slung over his shoulder.

It was very dark after I had passed the lamp at the entrance to the lane. Very silent and solitary too. Not a soul was stirring at this hour, for the last of the lovers had long since gone home and the place was little frequented even in the daytime. The elms brooded over the road, shrouding it in shadows of palpable black, and their leaves whispered secretly in the soft night breeze. But the darkness, the quiet and the solitude were restful after the long hours of study and the glare of the printed page, and I strolled on past the ghostly pond and the little thatched cottage, now wrapped in silence and darkness, with a certain wistful regret that I must soon look my last on them. For I had now passed all my examinations but the final "Fellowship," and must soon be starting my professional career in earnest.

Presently a light rain began to fall. Foreseeing that I should have to curtail my walk, I stepped forward more briskly, and, passing between the posts, entered the narrowest and most secluded part of the lane. But now the rain suddenly increased, and a squall of wind drove it athwart the path. I drew up in the shelter of one of the tall oak fences by which the lane is here inclosed, and waited for the shower to pass. And as I stood with my back to the fence, pensively filling my pipe, I became for the first time sensible of the utter solitude of the place.

I looked about me and listened. The lane was darker here than elsewhere; a mere trench between the high fences. I could dimly see the posts at the entrance and a group of large elms over-shadowing them. In the other direction, where the lane doubled sharply upon itself, was absolute, inky blackness, save where a faint glimmer from the wet ground showed the corner of the fence and a projecting stump or tree-root jutting out from the corner and looking curiously like a human foot with the toes pointed upward.

The rain fell steadily with a soft, continuous murmur; the leaves of the elm-trees whispered together and answered the falling rain. The Scotch pines above my head stirred in the breeze with a sound like the surge of the distant sea. The voices of Nature, hushed and solemn, oblivious of man like the voices of the wilderness; and overall and through all, a profound, enveloping silence.

I drew up closer to the fence and shivered slightly, for the night was growing chill. It seemed a little lighter now in the narrow, trench-like lane; not that the sky was less murky but because the ground was now flooded with water. The posts stood out less vaguely against the background of wet road, and the odd-looking stump by the corner was almost distinct. And again it struck me as looking curiously like a foot-a booted foot with the toe pointing upwards.

The chime of a church clock sounded across the Heath, a human voice, this, penetrating the desolate silence. Then, after an interval, the solemn boom of Big Ben came up faintly from the sleeping city.

Midnight! And time for me to go home. It was of no use to wait for the rain to cease. This was no passing shower, but a steady drizzle that might last till morning. I re-lit my pipe, turned up my collar, and prepared to plunge into the rain. And as I stepped out, the queer-looking stump caught my eye once more. It was singularly like a foot; and it was odd, too, that I had never noticed it before in my many rambles through the lane.

A sudden, childish curiosity impelled me to see what it really was before I went, and the next moment I was striding sharply up the sodden path. Of course, I expected the illusion to vanish as I approached. But it did not. The resemblance increased as I drew nearer, and I hurried forward with something more than curiosity.

It was a foot! I realized it with a shock while I was some paces away; and, as I reached the corner, I came upon the body of a man lying in the sharp turn of the path; and the limp, sprawling posture, with one leg doubled under, told its tale at a glance.

I laid my finger on his wrist. It was clammy and cold, and not a vestige of a pulse could I detect. I struck a wax match and held it to his face. The eyes were wide-open and filmy, staring straight up into the reeking sky. The dilated pupils were insensitive to the glare of the match, the eyeballs insensitive to the touch of my finger.

Beyond all doubt the man was dead.

But how had he died? Had he simply fallen dead from some natural cause, or had he been murdered? There was no obvious injury, and no sign of blood. All that the momentary glimmer of the match showed was that his clothes were shiny with the wet; a condition that might easily, in the weak light, mask a considerable amount of bleeding.

When the match went out, I stood for some moments looking down on the prostrate figure as it lay with the rain beating down on the upturned face, professional interest contending with natural awe of the tragic presence. The former prompted me to ascertain without delay the cause of death; and, indeed, I was about to make a more thorough search for some injury or wound when something whispered to me that it is not well to be alone at midnight in a solitary place with a dead man,- perchance a murdered man. Had there been any sign of life, my duty would have been clear. As it was, I must act for the best with a due regard to my own safety. And, reaching this conclusion, I turned away, with a last glance at the motionless figure and set forth homeward at a rapid pace.

As I turned out of Millfield Lane into Highgate Rise I perceived a policeman on the opposite side of the road standing under a tree, where the light from a lamp fell on his shining tarpaulin cape. I crossed the road, and, as he civilly touched his helmet, I said: "I am afraid there is something wrong up the lane, Constable; I have just seen the body of a man lying on the pathway."

The constable woke up very completely. "Do you mean a dead man, sir?" he asked.

"Yes, he is undoubtedly dead," I replied.

"Whereabouts did you see the body?" enquired the constable.

"In the narrow part of the lane, just by the stables of Mansfield House."

"That's some distance from here," said the constable. "You had better come with me and report at the station. You're sure the man was dead, sir?"

"Yes, I have no doubt about it. I am a medical man," I added, with some pride (I had been a medical man about three months, and the sensation was still a novel one).

"Oh, are you, sir?" said the officer, with a glance at my half-fledged countenance; "then, I suppose you examined the body?"

"Sufficiently to make sure that the man was dead, but I did not stay to ascertain the cause of death."

"No, sir; quite so. We can find that out later."

As we talked, the constable swung along down the hill, without hurry, but at a pace that gave me very ample exercise, and I caught his eye from time to time, travelling over my person with obvious professional interest. When we had nearly reached the bottom of the hill, there appeared suddenly on the wet road ahead, a couple of figures in waterproof capes. "Ha!" said the constable, "this is fortunate. Here is the inspector and the sergeant. That will save us the walk to the station."

He accosted the officers as they approached and briefly related what I had told him. "You are sure the man was dead, sir?" said the inspector, scrutinizing me narrowly; "but, there, we needn't stay here to discuss that. You run down, Sergeant, and get a stretcher and bring it along as quickly as you can. I must trouble you, sir, to come with me and show me where the body is. Lend the gentleman your cape, sergeant; you can get another at the station."

I accepted the stout cape thankfully, for the rain still fell with steady persistency, and set forth with the inspector to retrace my steps. And as we splashed along through the deep gloom of the lane, the officer plied me with judicious questions. "How long did you think the man had been dead?" he asked.

"Not long, I should think. The body was still quite limp."

"You didn't see any marks of violence?"

"No. There were no obvious injuries."

"Which way were you going when you came on the body?"

"The way we are going now, and, of course, I came straight back."

"Did you meet or see anyone in the lane?"

"Not a soul," I answered.

He considered my answers for some time, and then came the question that I had been expecting. "How came you to be in the lane at this time of night?"

"I was taking a walk," I replied, "as I do nearly every night. I usually finish my evening's reading about eleven, and then I have some supper and take a walk before going to bed, and I take my walk most commonly in Millfield Lane. Some of your men must remember having met me."

This explanation seemed to satisfy him for he pursued the subject no farther, and we trudged on for awhile in silence. At length, as we passed through the posts into the narrow part of the lane, the inspector asked: "We're nearly there, aren't we?"

"Yes," I replied: "the body is lying in the bend just ahead."

I peered into the darkness in search of the foot that had first attracted my notice, but was not yet able to distinguish it. Nor, to my surprise, could I make it out as we approached more nearly; and when we reached the corner, I stopped short in utter amazement.

The body had vanished! "What's the matter?" asked the inspector. "I thought this was the place you meant."

"So it is," I answered. "This is the place where the body was lying; here, across the path, with one foot projecting round the corner. Someone must have carried it away."

The inspector looked at me sharply for a moment. "Well, it isn't here now," said he, "and if it has been taken away, it must have been taken along towards Hampstead Lane. We'd better go and see." Without waiting for a reply, he started off along the lane at a smart double and I followed.

We pursued the windings of the lane until we emerged into the road by the lodge gates, without discovering any traces of the missing corpse or meeting any person, and then we turned back and retraced our steps; and as we, once more, approached the crook in the lane where I had seen the body, we heard a quick, measured tramp.

"Here comes the sergeant with the stretcher," observed the inspector; "and he might have saved himself the trouble." Once more the officer glanced at me sharply, and this time with unmistakable suspicion.

"There's nobody here, Robson," he said, as the sergeant came up, accompanied by two constables carrying a stretcher. "It seems to have disappeared."

"Disappeared!" exclaimed the sergeant, bestowing on me a look of extreme disfavour; "that's a rum go, sir. How could it have disappeared?"

"Ah! That's the question!" said the inspector. "And another question is, was it ever here? Are you prepared to make a sworn statement on the subject, sir?"

"Certainly I am," I replied.

"Then," said the inspector, "We will take it that there was a body here. Put down that stretcher. There is a gap in the fence farther along. We will get through there and search the meadow."

The bearers stood the stretcher up against a tree and we all proceeded up the lane to the place where the observant inspector had noticed the opening in the fence. The gravel, though sodden with the wet, took but the faintest impressions of the feet that trod it, and, though the sergeant and the two constables threw the combined light of their lanterns on the ground, we were only able to make out very faintly the occasional traces of our own footsteps.

We scrutinized the break in the fence and the earth around with the utmost minuteness, but could detect no sign of anyone having passed through. The short turf of the meadow, on which I had seen sheep grazing in the daytime, was not calculated to yield traces of anyone passing over it, and no traces of any kind were discoverable. When we had searched the meadow thoroughly and without result, we came back into the lane and followed its devious course to the "kissing-gate" at the Hampstead Lane entrance. And still there was no sign of anything unusual. True, there were obscure footprints in the soft gravel by the turnstile, but they told us nothing; we could not even be sure that they had not been made by ourselves on our previous visit. In short, the net result of our investigations was that the body had vanished and left no trace. "It's a very extraordinary affair," said the inspector, in a tone of deep discontent, as we walked back. "The body of a full-grown man isn't the sort of thing you can put in your pocket and stroll off with without being noticed, even at midnight. Are you perfectly sure the man was really dead and not in a faint?"

"I feel no doubt whatever that he was dead," I replied.

"With all respect to you, sir," said the sergeant, "I think you must be mistaken. I think the man must have been in a dead faint, and after you came away, the rain must have revived him so that he was able to get up and walk away."

"I don't think so," said I, though with less conviction; for, after all, it was not absolutely impossible that I should have been mistaken, since I had discovered no mortal injury, and the sergeant's suggestion was an eminently reasonable one.

"What sized man was he?" the inspector asked. "That I couldn't say," I answered. "It is not easy to judge the height of a man when he is lying down and the light was excessively dim. But I should say he was not a tall man and rather slight in build."

"Could you give us any description of him?"

"He was an elderly man, about sixty, I should think, and he appeared to be a clergyman or a priest, for he wore a Roman collar with a narrow, dark stripe up the front. He was clean shaven, and, I think, wore a clerical suit of black. A tall hat was lying on the ground close by and a walking-stick which looked like a malacca, but I couldn't see it very well as he had fallen on it and most of it was hidden."

"And you saw all this by the light of one wax match," said the inspector. "You made pretty good use of your eyes, sir."

"A man isn't much use in my profession if he doesn't," I replied, rather stiffly.

"No, that's true," the inspector agreed. "Well, I must ask you to give us the full particulars at the station, and we shall see if anything fresh turns up. I'm sorry to keep you hanging about in the wet, but it can't be helped."

"Of course it can't," said I, and we trudged on in silence until we reached the station, which looked quite cheerful and homelike despite the grim blue lamp above the doorway. "Well, Doctor," said the inspector, when he had read over my statement and I had affixed my signature, "if anything turns up, you'll hear from us. But I doubt if we shall hear anything more of this. Dead or alive, the man seems to have vanished completely. Perhaps the sergeant's right after all, and your dead man is at this moment comfortably tucked up in bed. Goodnight, Doctor, and thank you for all the trouble you have taken."

By the time that I reached my lodgings I was tired out and miserably cold; so cold that I was fain to brew myself a jorum of hot grog in my shaving pot. As a natural result, I fell fast asleep as soon as I got to bed and slept on until the autumn sunshine poured in through the slats of the Venetian blind.

2
THE FINDING OF THE RELIQUARY

I AWOKE on the following morning to a dim consciousness of something unusual, and, as my wits returned with the rapidity that is natural to the young and healthy, the surprising events of the previous night reconstituted themselves and once more set a-going the train of speculation. Vividly I saw with my mind's eye the motionless figure lying limp and inert with the pitiless rain beating down on it; the fixed pupils, the insensitive eyeballs, the pulseless wrist and the sprawling posture. And again I saw the streaming path, void of its dreadful burden, the suspicious inspector, the incredulous sergeant; and the unanswerable questions formulated themselves anew.

Had I, after all, mistaken a living man for a dead body? It was in the highest degree improbable, and yet it was not impossible. Or had the body been spirited away without leaving a trace? That also was highly improbable and yet, not absolutely impossible. The two contending improbabilities cancelled one another. Each was as unlikely as the other.

I turned the problem over again and again as I shaved and took my bath. I pondered upon it over a late and leisurely breakfast. But no conclusion emerged from these reflections. The man, living or dead, had been lying motionless in the lane all the time that I was sheltering, and probably for some time before. In the interval of my absence he had vanished. These were actual facts despite the open incredulity of the police. How he had come there, what had occasioned his death or insensibility, how he had disappeared and whither he had gone; were questions to which no answer seemed possible.

The fatigues of the previous night had left me somewhat indolent. There was no occasion for me to go to the hospital today. It was vacation time; the school was closed; the teaching staff were mostly away, and there was little doing in the wards. I decided to take a holiday and spend a quiet day rambling about the Heath, and, having formed this resolution, I filled my pipe, slipped a sketch-book into my pocket, and set forth.

Automatically my feet turned towards Millfield Lane. It was, as I have said, my usual walk, and on this morning, with last night's recollections fresh in my mind, it was natural that I should take my way thither.

Very different was the aspect of the lane this morning from that which I had last looked upon. The gloom and desolation of the night had given place to the golden sunshine of a lovely autumn day. The elms, clothed already in the sober livery of the waning year, sighed with pensive reminiscence of the summer that was gone; the ponds repeated the warm blue of the sky; and the lane itself was a vista of flickering sunlight and cool, reposeful shadow.

The narrow continuation beyond the posts was wrapped as always, in a sombre shade, save where a gleam of yellow light streamed through a chink between the boards of the fence. I made my way straight to the spot where the body had lain and stooped over it, examining each pebble with the closest scrutiny. But not a trace remained. The hard, gravelly soil retained no impress either of the body or even of our footsteps; and as for the stain of blood, if there had ever been any, it would have been immediately removed by the falling rain, for the ground here had a quite appreciable slope and must have been covered last night by a considerable flowing stream.

I went on to the break in the fence—it was on the right-hand side of the path—and was at once discouraged by the aspect of the ground; for even our rough tramplings had left hardly a trace behind. After an aimless walk across the meadow, now occupied by a flock of sheep, I returned to the lane and walked slowly back past the place where I had sheltered from the rain. And then it was that I discovered the first hint of any clue to the mystery. I had retraced my steps some little distance past the spot where I had seen the body, when my eye was attracted by a darkish streak on the upper part of the high fence. It was quite faint and not at all noticeable on the weather-stained oak, but it chanced to catch my eye and I stopped to examine it. The fence which bore it was the opposite one to that in which the break occurred, and, since I had sheltered under it, the side of it which looked towards the lane must have been the lee side and thus less exposed to the rain.

I looked at the stain attentively. It extended from the top of the fence-which was about seven feet high–half-way to the ground, fading away gradually in all directions. The colour was a dull brown, and the appearance very much that of blood which had run down a wet surface. The board which bore the stain was traversed by a vertical crack near one edge, so that I was able to break off a small piece without much difficulty; and on examining that portion of the detached piece which had formed the side of the crack, I found it covered with a brownish-red, shiny substance, which I felt little doubt was dried blood, here protected by the crack and so less altered by contact with water.

Naturally, my next proceeding was to scrutinize very carefully the ground immediately beneath the stain. At the foot of the fence, a few tussocks of grass and clumps of undergrown weeds struggled for life in the deep shade. The latter certainly had, on close examination, the appearance of having been trodden on, though it was not very evident. But while I was considering an undoubted bruise on the stalk of a little dead-nettle, my eye caught the glint of some bright object among the leaves. I picked it out eagerly and held it up to look at it; and a very curious object it was; evidently an article of jewellery of some kind, but quite unlike anything I had ever seen before. It appeared to be a little elongated, gold case, with eight sides and terminating at either end in a blunt octagonal pyramid with a tiny ring at its apex, so that it seemed to have been part of a necklace. Of the eight flat sides, six were ornamented with sunk quatre-foils, four on each side; the other two sides were plain except that each had a row of letters engraved on it-A.M.D.G on one side, and S.V.D.P on the other. There was no hall-mark and, as far as I could see, no means of opening the little case. It seemed to have been suspended by a thin silk cord, a portion of which remained attached to one ring and showed a frayed end where it had broken or chafed through.

I wrapped the little object and the detached fragment of the fence in my handkerchief (for I had broken off the latter with the idea of testing it chemically for blood-pigment), and then resumed my investigations. The appearances suggested that the body had been lifted over the fence, and the question arose, what was on the other side? I listened attentively for a few seconds, and then, hearing no sound of footsteps, I grasped the top of the fence, gave a good spring and hoisting myself up, sat astride and looked about me. The fence skirted the margin of a small lake much overgrown with weeds, amidst which I could see a couple of waterhens making off in alarm at my appearance, and beyond the lake rose the dark mass of Ken Wood. The ground between the fence and the lake was covered with high, reedy grass, which, immediately below my perch, bore very distinct impressions of feet, and an equally distinct set of tracks led away towards the wood-or from the wood to the fence; it was impossible to say which. But in any case, as there were no other tracks, it was certain that the person who made them had climbed over the fence. I dropped down on the grass and, having examined the ground attentively without discovering anything fresh, set off to follow the tracks.

For some distance they continued through high grass in which the impressions were very distinct: then they entered the wood, and here also, in the soft humus, lightly sprinkled with fallen leaves, the footprints were deep and easy to follow. But presently they struck a path, and, as they did not reappear on the farther side, it was evident that the unknown person had proceeded along it. The path was an old one, well made of hard gravel, and, where it passed through the deeper shade of the wood, was covered with velvety moss and grey-green lichen; on which I made out with some difficulty, the imprints of feet. But these were no longer distinct; they did not form a connected track; nor was it possible to distinguish them from the footprints of other persons who might have passed along the path. Even these I soon lost where I had halted irresolutely under a noble beech that rose from a fantastic coil of roots, and was considering how, if at all, I should next proceed, when, there appeared round a curve of the path a man in cord breeches and gaiters, evidently a keeper. He touched his hat civilly and ventured to enquire my business. "I am afraid I have no business here at all," I replied, for I did not think it expedient to tell him what had brought me into the wood. "I suppose I am trespassing."

"Well, sir, it is private property," he rejoined, "and being so near London we have to be rather particular. Perhaps you would like me to show you the way out on to the Heath."

I accepted his offer with many thanks for his courteous method of ejecting a trespasser, and we walked together through the beautiful woodland until the path terminated at a rustic turnstile. "That will be your way, sir," he said, as he let me out, indicating a track that led down to the Vale of Health.

I thanked him once more and then asked: "Is that a private house or does it belong to your estate?" I pointed to a small house or large cottage that stood within a fenced enclosure not far from the edge of the wood.

"That, sir," he replied, "was formerly a keeper's lodge. It is now let for a short term to an artist gentleman who is making some pictures of the Heath, but I expect it will be pulled down before long, as there is some talk of the County Council taking over that piece of land to add to the public grounds. Good-morning, sir," and the keeper, with a parting salute, turned back into the wood.

As I took my way homeward by the Highgate Ponds I meditated on the relation of my new discoveries to the mystery of the preceding night. It was a strange affair, and sinister withal.

That the tracks led from the lane to the wood and not from the wood to the lane, I felt firmly convinced; and equally so that the body of the unknown priest or clergyman had undoubtedly been spirited away. But whither had it been carried? Presumably to some sequestered spot in the wood. And what better hiding-place could be found? There, buried in the soft leaf-mould, it might lie undisturbed for centuries, covered only the deeper as each succeeding autumn shed its russet burden on the unknown grave.

And what, I wondered, was the connection between this mysterious tragedy and the queer little object that I had picked up? Perhaps there was none. Its presence at that particular spot might be nothing but a coincidence. I took it from my handkerchief and examined it afresh. It was a very curious object. As to its use or meaning, I could only form vague surmises. Perhaps it was some kind of locket, enclosing a wisp of hair; the hair perhaps of some dead child or wife or husband or even lover. It was impossible to say. Of course, this question could be settled by taking it to pieces, but I was loath to injure the pretty little bauble; besides it was not mine. In fact, I felt that I ought to notify publicly that I had found it, though the circumstances did not make this very advisable. But if it had any connection with the tragedy, what was the nature of that connection? Had it dropped from the dead man or from the murderer–as I assumed the other man to be? Either was equally possible, though the two possibilities had very different values.

Then the question arose as to what course I should pursue. Clearly it would be my duty to inform the police of the mark on the fence and the tracks through the grass. But should I hand over the mysterious trinket to them? It seemed the correct thing to do, and yet there might after all be no connection between it and the crime. In the end I left the matter to be decided by the attitude of the police themselves.

I called at the station on my way home and furnished the inspector with an account of my new discoveries; of which he made a careful note, assuring me that the affair should be looked into. But his manner expressed frank disbelief, and was even a trifle hostile; and his emphatic request that I would abstain from mentioning the matter to anyone left me in no doubt that he regarded both my communications as wild delusions if not as a deliberate hoax. Consequently, though I frequently reproached myself afterwards with the omission, I said nothing about the trinket, and when I left the station I carried it in my pocket.

No communication on the subject of this mysterious affair ever reached me from the police. That they did actually make some perfunctory investigations, I learned later, as will appear in this narrative. But they gave no publicity to the affair and they sought no further information from me. For my own part, I could, naturally, never forget so strange an experience; but time and the multitudinous interests of my opening life tended to push it farther into the background of memory, and there it might have remained forever had not subsequent events drawn it once more from its obscurity.

3
"WHO IS SYLVIA?"

THE winter session had commenced at the hospital, but at Hampstead the month of October had set in with something like a return to summer. It is true that the trees had lost something of their leafy opulence, and that here and there, amidst the sober green, patches of russet and gold had made their appearance, as if Nature's colour-orchestra were tuning up for the final symphony. But, meanwhile, the sun shone brightly and with a genial heat, and if, day by day, he fell farther from the zenith, there was nothing to show it but the lengthening noonday shadows, the warmer blue of the sky and the more rosy tint of the clouds that sailed across it.

Other and more capable pens than mine have set forth the charm of autumn and the beauties of Hampstead—queen of suburbs of the world's metropolis; therefore will I refrain, and only note, as relevant to the subject, the fact that on many a day, when the work of the hospital was in full swing, I might have been seen playing truant very agreeably on the inexhaustible Heath or in the lanes and fields adjacent thereto. In truth, I was taking the final stage of my curriculum rather lazily, having worked hard enough in the earlier years, and being still too young by several months to be admitted to the fellowship of the College of Surgeons; promising myself that when the weather broke I would settle down in earnest to the winter's work.

I have mentioned that Millfield Lane was one of my favourite haunts; indeed, from my lodgings, it was the most direct route to the Heath, and I passed along it almost daily; and never, now, without my thoughts turning back to that rainy night when I had found the dead–or unconscious–man lying across the narrow footway. One morning, as I passed the spot, it occurred to me to make a drawing of the place in my sketch-book, that I might have some memorial of that strange adventure. The pictorial possibilities of the lane just here were not great, but by taking my stand at the turn, on the very spot where I had seen the body lying, I was able to arrange a simple composition which was satisfactory enough.

I am no artist. A neat and intelligible drawing is the utmost that I can produce. But even this modest degree of achievement may be very useful, as I had discovered many a time in the wards or laboratories-indeed, I have often been surprised that the instructors of our youth attach such small value to the power of graphic expression; and it came in usefully now, though in a way that was unforeseen and not fully appreciated at the moment. I had dealt adequately with the fence, the posts, the tree-trunks and other well-defined forms and was beginning a less successful attack on the foliage, when I heard a light, quick step approaching from Hampstead Lane. Intuition-if there is such a thing-fitted the foot-step with a personality, and, for once in a way, was right; as the newcomer reached the sharp bend of the path, I saw a girl of about my own age, simply and serviceably dressed and carrying a pochade box and a small camp-stool. She was not an entire stranger to me. I had met her often in the lane and on the Heath–so often in fact that we had developed that profound unconsciousness of one another's existence that almost amounts to recognition–and had wondered vaguely who she was and what sort of work she did on the panels in that mysterious box.

As I drew back to make way for her, she brushed past, with a single, quick, inquisitive glance at my sketchbook, and went on her way, looking very much alive and full of business. I watched her as she tripped down the lane and passed between the posts out into the sunlight beyond, to vanish behind the trunks of the elms; then I returned to my sketch and my struggles to express foliage with a touch somewhat less suggestive of a birch-broom.

When I had finished my drawing, I sauntered on rather aimlessly, speculating for the hundredth time on the meaning of those discoveries of mine in this very lane. Was it possible that the man whom I had seen was not dead, but merely insensible? I could not believe it. The whole set of circumstances–the aspect of the body, the blood-stain on the fence, the tracks through the high grass and the mysterious gold trinket–were opposed to any such belief. Yet, on the other hand, one would think that a man could not disappear unnoticed. This was no tramp or nameless vagrant. He was a clergyman or a priest, a man who would be known to a great number of persons and whose disappearance must surely be observed at once and be the occasion of very stringent enquiries. But no enquiries had apparently been made. I had seen no notice in the papers of any missing cleric, and clearly the police had heard nothing or they would have looked me up. The whole affair was enveloped in the profoundest mystery. Dead or alive, the man had vanished utterly; and whether he was dead or alive, the mystery was equally beyond solution.

These reflections brought me, almost unconsciously, to another of my favourite walks; the pretty footpath from the Heath to Temple Fortune. I had crossed the stile and stepped off the path to survey the pleasant scene, when my eye was attracted by a number of streaks of alien colour on the leaves of a burdock. Stooping down, I perceived that they were smears of oil-paint, and inferred that someone had cleaned a palette on the herbage; an inference that was confirmed a moment later by what looked like the handle of a brush projecting from a clump of nettles. When I drew it out, however, it proved to be not a brush, but a very curious knife with a blade shaped like a diminutive and attenuated trowel; evidently a painting-knife and also evidently home-made, at least in part, for the tang had been thrust into a short, stout brush-handle and secured with a whipping of waxed thread. I dropped it into my outside breast pocket and went on my way, wondering if by chance it might have been dropped by my fair acquaintance; and the thought was still in my mind when its object hove in sight. Turning a bend in the path, I came on her quite suddenly, perched on her little camp-stool in the shadow of the hedge, with the open sketching-book on her knees, working away with an industry and concentration that seemed to rebuke my own idleness. Indeed, she was so much engrossed with her occupation that she did not notice me until I stepped off the path and approached with the knife in my hand.

"I wonder," said I, holding it out and raising my cap, "if this happens to be your property. I picked it up just now among the nettles near the barn."

She took the knife from me and looked at it inquisitively. "No," she replied, "it isn't mine, but I think I know whose it is. I suspect it belongs to an artist who has been doing a good deal of work about the Heath. You may have seen him."

"I have seen several artists working about here during the summer. What was this one like?"

"Well," she answered with a smile, "he was like an artist. Very much like. Quite the orthodox get up. Wide brimmed hat, rather long hair and a ragged beard. And he wore sketching-spectacles-half-moon-shaped things, you know-and kid gloves-which were not quite so orthodox."

"Very inconvenient, I should think."

"Not so very. I work in gloves myself in the cold weather or if the midges are very troublesome. You soon get used to the feel of them; and the man I am speaking of wouldn't find them in the way at all because he works almost entirely with painting-knives. That is what made me think that this knife was probably his. He had several, I know, and very skillfully he used them, too."

"You have seen his work, then?"

"Well," she admitted, "I'm afraid I descended once or twice to play the 'snooper'. You see, his method of handling interested me."

"May I ask what a 'snooper' is?" I enquired.

"Don't you know? It's a student's slang name for the kind of person who makes some transparent pretext for coming off the path and passing behind you to get a look at your picture by false pretences."

For an instant there flashed into my mind the suspicion that she was administering a quiet "backhander", and I rejoined hastily: "I hope you are not including me in the genus 'snooper'."

She laughed softly. "It did sound rather like it. But I'll give you the benefit of the doubt in consideration of your finding the knife-which you had better keep in trust for the owner."

"Won't you keep it? You know the probable owner by sight and I don't; and meanwhile you might experiment with it yourself."

"Very well," she replied, dropping it into her brush-tray, "I'll keep it for the present at any rate."

There was a brief pause, and then I ventured to remark, "That looks a very promising sketch of yours. And how well the subject comes."

"I'm glad you like it," she replied, quite simply, viewing her work with her head on one side. "I want it to turn out well, because it's a commission, and commissions for small-oil paintings are rare and precious."

"Do you find small oil pictures very difficult to dispose of?" I asked.

"Not difficult. Impossible, as a rule. But I don't try now. I copy my oil sketches in water-colour, with modifications to suit the market."

Again there was a pause; and, as her brush wandered towards the palette, it occurred to me that I had stayed as long as good manners permitted. Accordingly, I raised my cap, and, having expressed the hope that I had not greatly hindered her, prepared to move away.

"Oh, not at all," she answered; "and thank you for the knife, though it isn't mine-or, at any rate, wasn't. Good-morning."

With this and a pleasant smile and a little nod, she dismissed me; and once more I went my idle and meditative way.

It had been quite a pleasant little adventure. There is always something rather interesting in making the acquaintance of a person whom one has known some time by sight but who is otherwise an unknown quantity. The voice, the manner, and the little revelations of character, which confirm or contradict previous impressions, are watched with interest as they develop themselves and fill in, one by one, the blank spaces of the total personality. I had, as I have said, often met this industrious maiden in my walks and had formed the opinion that she looked a rather nice girl; an opinion that was probably influenced by her unusual good looks and graceful carriage. And a rather nice girl she had turned out to be; very dignified and self-possessed, but quite simple and frank–though, to be sure, her gracious reception of me had probably been due to my sketch-book; she had taken me for a kindred spirit. She had a pleasant voice and a faultless accent, with just a hint of the fine lady in her manner; but I liked her none the less for that. And her name was a pretty name, too, if I had guessed it correctly; for, on the inside of the lid of her box, which was partly uncovered by the upright panel, I had read the letters "Syl". The panel hid the rest, but the name could hardly be other than Sylvia; and what more charming and appropriate name could be bestowed upon a comely young lady who spent her days amidst the woods and fields of my beloved Hampstead?

Regaling myself with this somewhat small beer, I sauntered on along the grassy lane, between hedgerows that in the summer had been spangled with wild roses and that were now gay with the big, oval berries, sleek and glossy and scarlet, like overgrown beads of red coral; away, across the fields to Golder's Green and thence by Millfield Lane, back to my lodgings at Gospel Oak, and to my landlady, Mrs. Blunt, who had a few plaintive words to say respecting the disastrous effects of unpunctuality–and the resulting prolonged heat–on mutton cutlets and fried potatoes.

It had been an idle morning and apparently void of significant events; but yet, when I look back on it, I see a definite thread of causation running through its simple happenings, and I realize that, all unthinking, I had strung on one more bead to the chaplet of my destiny.

4
SEPTIMUS MADDOCK, DECEASED

IT was getting well on into November when I strolled one afternoon into the hospital museum, not with any specific object but rather vaguely in search of something to do. During the last few days I had developed a slight revival of industry–which had coincided, oddly enough, with a marked deterioration of the weather–and, pathology being my weakest point, the museum had seemed to call me (though not very loudly, I fear) to browse amongst its multitudinous jars and dry preparations.

There was only one person in the great room; but he was a very important person; being none other than our lecturer on Medical Jurisprudence, Dr. John Thorndyke. He was seated at a small table whereon was set out a collection of jars and a number of large photographs, of which he appeared to be making a catalogue; but intent as he was on his occupation, he looked up as I entered and greeted me with a genial smile.

"What do you think of my little collection, Jardine?" he asked, as I approached deferentially. Before replying, I ran a vaguely enquiring eye over the group of objects on the table and was mighty little enlightened thereby. It was certainly a queer collection. There was a flat jar which contained a series of five differently-coloured mice, another with a similar series of three rats, a human foot, a hand-manifestly deformed-a series of four fowls' heads and a number of photographs of plants.

"It looks," I replied, at length, "like what the auctioneers would call a miscellaneous lot."

"Yes," Dr. Thorndyke agreed, "it is a miscellaneous collection in a sense. But there is a connecting idea. It illustrates certain phenomena of inheritance which were discovered and described by Mendel."

"Mendel!" I exclaimed. "Who is he? I never heard of him."

"I daresay not." said Thorndyke, "though he published his results before you were born. But the importance of his discoveries is only now beginning to be appreciated."

"I suppose," said I, "the subject is too large and complex for a short explanation to be possible."

"The subject is a large one, of course," he replied; "but, put in a nutshell, Mendel's great discovery amounts to this; that, whereas certain characters are inherited only partially and fade off gradually in successive generations, certain other characters are inherited completely and pass unchanged from generation to generation. To take a couple of illustrative cases: If a negro marries a European, the offspring are mulattoes—forms intermediate between the negro and the European. If a mulatto marries a European, the offspring are quadroons—another intermediate form; and the next generation gives us the octoroon—intermediate again between the quadroon and the European. And so, from generation to generation, the negro character gradually fades away and finally disappears. But there are other characters which are inherited entire or not at all, and such characters appear in pairs which are positive or negative to one another. Sex is a case in point. A male marries a female and the offspring are either male or female, never intermediate. The sex-character of only one parent is inherited, and it is inherited completely. The characters of maleness or femaleness pass down unchanged through the ages with no tendency to diminish or to shade off into one another. That is a case of Mendelian inheritance."

I ran my eyes over the collection and they presently lighted on the rather abnormal-looking foot, hanging, white and shrivelled in the clear spirit. I lifted the jar from the table and then, noticing for the first time, that the foot had a supernumerary toe, I enquired what point the specimen illustrated.

"That six-toed foot," Thorndyke replied, "is an example of a deformity that is transmitted unchanged for an indefinite number of generations. This brachydactylous hand is another instance. The brachydactyly reappears in the offspring either completely or not at all. There are no intermediate conditions."

He picked up the jar, and, having wiped the glass with a dustier, exhibited the hand which was suspended within; and a strange-looking hand it was; broad and stumpy, like the hand of a mole.

"There seem to be only two joints to each finger," I said. "Yes. The fingers are all thumbs, and the thumb is only a demi-thumb. A joint is suppressed in each digit."

"It must make the hand very clumsy and useless," I remarked.

"So one would think. It isn't exactly the type of hand for a Liszt or a Paganini. And yet we mustn't assume too much. I once saw an armless man copying pictures in the Luxembourg, and copying them very well, too. He held his brush with his toes; and he was so handy with his feet that he not only painted really dexterously, but managed to take his hat off to a lady with quite a fine flourish. So you see, Jardine, it is not the hand that matters, but rather the brain that actuates it. A very indifferent hand will serve if the motor centres are of the right sort."

He replaced the jar on the table, and then, after a short pause, turning quickly to me, he asked: "What are you doing at present, Jardine?"

"Principally idling, sir," I replied.

"And not a bad thing to do either," he rejoined with a smile, "If you do it thoroughly and don't keep it up too long. How would you like to take charge of a practice for a week or so?"

"I don't know that I should particularly care to, sir," I answered.

"Why not? It would be a useful experience and would bring you useful knowledge; knowledge that you have got to acquire sooner or later. Hospital conditions, you know, are not normal conditions.

"General practice is normal medical practice, and the sooner you get to know the conditions of the great world the better for you. If you stick to the wards too long you will get to be like the nurses; who seem to think that,

"'All the world's a hospital, And men and women only patients.'"

I reflected for a few moments. It was perfectly true. I was a qualified medical man, and yet of the ordinary routine of private practice I had not the faintest knowledge. To me, all sick people were either in-patients or out-patients. "Had you any particular practice in your mind, sir?" I asked. "Yes. I met one of our old students just now. He is at his wit's end to find a locum tenens. He has to go away tonight or to-morrow morning, but he can't get anyone to look after his work. Won't you go to his relief? It's an easy practice, I believe."

I turned the question over in my mind and finally decided to try the venture. "That's right." said Dr. Thorndyke. "You'll help a professional brother, at any rate, and pick up a little experience. Our friend's name is Batson, and he lives in Jacob Street, Hampstead Road. I'll write it down."

He handed me a slip of paper with the address on it and wished me success; and I started at once from the hospital, already quite elated, as is the way of the youthful, at the prospect of a new experience.

Dr. Batson's establishment in Jacob Street was modest to the verge of dingyness. But Jacob Street, itself, was dingy, and so was the immediate neighbourhood; a district of tall, grimy houses that might easily have seen better days. However, Dr. Batson himself was spruce enough and in excellent spirits at my arrival, as was

evident when he bounced into the room with a jovial
greeting, bringing in with him a faint aroma of sherry.
"Delighted to see you, Doctor!" he exclaimed in his large
brisk voice (that "doctor" was a diplomatic hit on his part.
They don't call newly-qualified men "doctor" at the
hospital.) "I met Thorndyke this morning and told him of
my predicament. A busy man is the Great Unraveller, but
never too busy to do a kindness to his friends. Can you
take over tonight?"

"I could," said I.

"Then do. I want particularly to be off by the eight-
thirty from Liverpool Street. Drop in and have some grub
about six-thirty; I shall have polished off the day's work
by then and you'll just come in for the evening
consultations."

"Are there any cases that you will want me to see with
you?" I asked.

"Oh, no," Batson replied, rather airily I thought.
"They're all plain sailing. There's a typhoid, he's doing
well–fourth week; and there's a tonsillitis and a psoas
abscess–that's rather tedious, but still, it's improving–
and an old woman with a liver. You won't have any
difficulty with them. There's only one queer case; a
heart."

"Valvular?" I asked.

"No, not valvular; I can tell you that much. I know
what it isn't, but I'm hanged if I know what it is. Chappie
complains of pain, shortness of breath, faintness and so
on, but I can't find anything to account for it. Heart-
sounds all right, pulse quite good, no dropsy, no nothing.
Seems like malingering, but I don't see why he should
malinger. I think I'll get you to drop in this evening and
have a look at him."

"Are you keeping him in bed?" I asked.

"Yes," said Batson, "I am now; not that his general
condition seems to demand it. But he has had one or two
fainting attacks, and yesterday he must needs fall down

flop in his bedroom when there was nobody there, and, by way of making things more comfortable, he drops his medicine bottle and falls on the fragments. He might have killed himself, you know," Batson added in an aggrieved tone; "as it was, a long splinter from the bottom of the bottle stuck into his back and made quite a deep little wound. So I've kept him in bed since, out of harm's way; and there he is, deuced sorry for himself but, as far as I can make out, without a single tangible symptom."

"No facial signs? Nothing unusual in his colour or expression."

Batson laughed and tapped his gold-rimmed spectacles. "Ah! There you are! When you've got minus five D and some irregular astigmatism and a pair of glasses that don't correct it, all human beings look pretty much alike; a trifle sketchy, don't you know. I didn't see anything unusual in his face, but you might. Time will show. Now you cut along and fetch your traps, and I'll skip round and polish off the sufferers."

He launched me into the outer greyness of Jacob Street and bounced off in the direction of Cumberland Market, leaving me to pursue my way to my lodgings at Gospel Oak.

As I threaded the teeming streets of Camden Town I meditated on the new experience that was opening to me, and, with youthful egotism, I already saw myself making a brilliant diagnosis of an obscure heart case. Also I reflected with some surprise on the calm view that Batson took of his defective eyesight. A certain type of painter, as I had observed, finds in semi-blindness a valuable gift which helps him to eliminate trivial detail and to impart a noble breadth of effect to his pictures; but to a doctor no such self-delusion would seem possible. Visual acuteness is the most precious item in his equipment.

I crammed into a large Gladstone bag the bare necessaries for a week's stay, together with a few indispensable instruments, and then mounted the jingling horse-tram of those pre-electric days, which, in due course, deposited me at the end of Jacob Street, Hampstead Road. Dr. Batson had not returned from his round when I arrived, but a few minutes later he burst into the surgery humming an air from the Mikado.

"Ha! Here you are then! Punctual to the minute!" He hung his hat on a peg, laid his visiting-list on the desk of the dispensing counter and began to compound medicine with the speed of a prestidigitateur, talking volubly all the time.

"That's for the old woman with the liver, Mrs. Mudge, Cumberland Market, you'll see her prescription in the day book. S'pose you don't know how to wrap up a bottle of medicine. Better watch me. This is the way." He slapped the bottle down on a square of cut paper, gave a few dextrous twiddles of his fingers and held out for my inspection a little white parcel like the mummy-case of a deceased medicine bottle.

"It's quite easy when you've had a little practice," he said, deftly sticking the ends down with sealing-wax, "but you'll make a frightful mucker of it at first." Which prophecy was duly fulfilled that very evening.

"What time had I better see that heart case?" said I.

"Oh, you won't have to see it at all. Man's dead. Message left half an hour go. Pity, isn't it? I should have liked to hear what you thought of him. Must have been fatty heart. I'll write out the certificate while I think of it. Maggie! Where's that note that Mrs. Samway left?"

The question was roared out vaguely through the open door to a servant of unknown whereabouts, and resulted in the appearance of a somewhat scraggy housemaid bearing an opened note. "Here we are," said Batson, snatching the note out of its envelope and opening the book of certificate forms; "Septimus Maddock was the chappie's name, age fifty-one, address 23, Gayton Street, cause of death-that's just what I should like to know-primary cause, secondary causes-I wish these infernal government clerks had got something better to do than fill printed forms with silly conundrums. I shall put "Morbus Cordis"; that ought to be enough for them. Mrs. Samway-that's his landlady, you know-will probably call for the certificate during the evening."

"Aren't you going to inspect the body?" I asked.

"Lord, no! Why should I! It isn't necessary, you know. I'm not an undertaker. Wish I was. Dead people good deal more profitable than live ones."

"But surely," I exclaimed, "the death ought to be verified. Why the man may not be dead at all."

"I know," said Batson, scribbling away like a minor poet, "but that isn't my business. Business of the Law. Law wastes your time with a heap of silly questions that don't matter and leaves out the question that does. Asks exact time when I last saw him alive, which doesn't matter a hang, and doesn't ask whether I saw him dead. Bumble was right. Law's an ass."

"But still," I persisted, "leaving the legal requirements out of consideration, oughtn't you for your own sake, and as a public duty, to verify the death? Supposing the man were not really dead?"

"That would be awkward for him," said Batson, "and awkward for me, too, if he came to life before they buried him. But it doesn't really happen in real life. Premature burial only occurs in novels."

His easy-going confidence jarred on me considerably. How could he, or anyone else, know what happened? "I don't see how you arrive at that," I objected. "It could only be proved by wholesale disinterment. And the fact remains that, if you don't verify a reported death you have no security against premature burial—or even cremation."

Batson started up and stared at me, his wide-open, pale-blue eyes looking ridiculously small through his deep, concave spectacles. "By Jove!" he exclaimed, "I am glad you mentioned that—about cremation, I mean, because that is what will probably happen. I witnessed the chappie's will a couple of days ago, and I remember now that one of the clauses stipulated that his body should be cremated. So I shall have to verify the death for the purpose of the cremation certificate. We'd better pop round and see him at once."

With characteristic impulsiveness he sprang to his feet, snatched his hat from its peg, and started forth, leaving me to follow. "Beastly nuisance, these special regulations," said Batson, as he ambled briskly up the street. "Give a lot of trouble and cause a lot of delay."

"Isn't the ordinary death certificate sufficient in a case of cremation?" I asked.

"For purposes of law it is, though there is some talk of new legislation on the subject, but the Company are a law unto themselves. They have made the most infernally stringent regulations, and, as there is no crematorium near London excepting the one at Woking, you have to abide by their rules. And that reminds me—" here Batson halted and scowled at me ferociously through his spectacles.

"Reminds you?" I repeated.

"That they require a second death certificate, signed by a man with certain special qualifications." He stood awhile frowning and muttering under his breath and then suddenly turned and bounced off in a new direction. "Going to catch the other chappie and take him with us," he explained, as he darted out into the Hampstead Road. "Be off my mind then. A fellow named O'Connor, Assistant Physician to the North London Hospital. He'll do if we can catch him at home. If not, you'll have to manage him."

Batson looked at his watch—holding it within four inches of his nose—and broke into a trot as we entered a quiet square. Halfway up he halted at a door which bore a modest brass plate inscribed "Dr. O'Connor," and seizing the bell-knob, worked it vigorously in and out as if it were the handle of an air-pump. "Doctor in?" he demanded briskly of a startled housemaid; and, without waiting for an answer, he darted into the hall, down the whole length of which he staggered, executing a sort of sword-dance, having caught his toe on an unobserved door-mat.

The doctor was in and he shortly appeared in evening dress with an overcoat on his arm, and apparently in as great a hurry as Batson himself. "Won't it do to-morrow?" he asked, when Batson had explained his difficulties and the service required.

"Might as well come now," said Batson persuasively; "won't take a minute and then I can go away in peace."

"Very well," said O'Connor, wriggling into his overcoat. "You go along and I'll follow in a few minutes. I've got to look in on a patient on my way up west, and I shall be late for my appointment as it is. Write the address on my card, here."

He held out a card to my principal, and when the latter had scribbled the address on it, he bustled out and vanished up the square. Batson followed at the same headlong speed, and, again overlooking the mat, came out on the pavement like an ill-started sprinter.

Gayton Street, at which we shortly arrived, was a grey and dingy side-street exactly like a score of others in the same locality, and Number 23 differed from the rest of the seedy-looking houses in no respect save that it was perhaps a shade more dingy. The door was opened in answer to Batson's indecorously brisk knock by a woman— or perhaps I should say a lady—who at once admitted us and to whom Batson began, without preface, to explain the situation.

"I got your note, Mrs. Samway. Was going to bring my friend, here, round to see the patient. Very unfortunate affair. Very sad. Unexpected, too. Didn't seem particularly bad yesterday. What time did it happen?"

"I can't say exactly," was the reply. "He seemed quite comfortable when I looked in on him the last thing at night, but when I went in about seven this morning he was dead. I should have let you know sooner, but I was expecting you to call."

"H'm, yes," said Batson, "very unfortunate. By the way, Mr. Maddock desired that his remains should be cremated, I think?"

"Yes, so my husband tells me. He is the executor of the will, you remember, in the absence of any relatives. All Mr. Maddock's relations seem to be in America."

"Have you got the certificate forms?" asked Batson.

"Yes. My husband got all the papers from the undertaker this afternoon."

"Very well, Mrs. Samway, then we'll just take a look at the body–have to certify that I've seen it, you know."

Mrs. Samway ushered us into a sitting-room where she had apparently been working alone, for an unfinished mourning garment of some kind lay on the table. Leaving us here, she went away and presently returned with a sheaf of papers and a lighted candle, when we rose and followed her to a back room on the ground floor. It was a smallish room, sparely furnished, with heavy curtains drawn across the window, and by one wall a bed, on which was a motionless figure covered by a sheet.

Our conductress stood the candlestick on a table by the bed and stepped back to make way for Batson, who drew back the sheet and looked down on the body in his peering, near-sighted fashion. The deceased seemed to be a rather frail-looking man of about fifty, but, beyond the fact that he was clean shaven, I could form very little idea of his appearance, since, in addition to the usual bandage under the chin to close the mouth, a tape had been carried round the head to secure a couple of pads of cotton wool over the eyes to keep the eyelids closed.

As Batson applied his stethoscope to the chest of the dead man, I glanced at our hostess not without interest. Mrs. Samway was an unusual-looking woman, and I thought her decidedly handsome though not attractive to me personally. She seemed to be about thirty, rather over the medium height and of fine Junonesque proportions, with a small head very gracefully set on the shoulders. Her jet-black hair, formally parted in the middle, was brought down either side of the forehead in wavy, but very smooth, masses and gathered behind in a neat, precisely-plaited coil. The general effect reminded me of the so-called "Clytie," having the same reposefulness though not the gentleness and softness of that lovely head. But the most remarkable feature of this woman was the colour of her eyes, which were of the palest grey or hazel that I have ever seen; so pale in fact that they told as spots of light, like the eyes of some lemurs or those of a cat seen in the dusk; a peculiarity that imparted a curiously intense and penetrating quality to her glance.

I had just noted these particulars when Batson, having finished his examination, held out the stethoscope to me.

"May as well listen, as you're here," said he, and, turning to our hostess, he added: "Let us see those papers, Mrs. Samway."

As he stepped over to the table, I took his place on a chair by the bedside and proceeded to make an examination. It was, of course, only a matter of form, for the man was obviously dead; but having insisted so strongly on the necessity of verifying the death I had to make a show of becoming scepticism. Accordingly I tested, both by touch and with the stethoscope, the region of the heart. Needless to say, no heart-sounds were to be distinguished, nor any signs of pulsation; indeed, the very first touch of my hand on the chilly surface of the chest was enough to banish any doubt. No living body could be so entirely destitute of animal heat.

I laid down the stethoscope and looked reflectively at the dead man, lying so still and rigid, with his bandaged jaws and blindfolded eyes, and speculated vaguely on his personality when alive and on the hidden disease that had so suddenly cut him off from the land of the living; and insensibly—by habit I suppose—my fingers strayed to his clammy, pulseless wrist. The sleeve of his night-shirt was excessively long, almost covering the fingers, and I had to turn it back to reach the spot where the pulse would normally be felt. In doing this, I moved the dead hand slightly and then became aware of a well-marked rigor mortis, or death stiffening in the arm of the corpse; a condition which I ought to have observed sooner.

At this moment, happening to look up, I caught the eye of Mrs. Samway fixed on me with a very remarkable expression. She was leaning over Batson as he filled up the voluminous certificate, but had evidently been watching me, and the expression of her pale, catlike eyes left no doubt in my mind that she strongly resented my proceedings. In some confusion, and accusing myself of some failure in outward decorum, I hastily drew down the dead man's sleeve and rose from the bedside. "You noticed, I suppose," said I, "that there is fairly well-marked rigor mortis?"

"I didn't," said Batson, "but if you did it'll do as well. Better mention it to O'Connor when he comes. He ought to be here now."

"Who is O'Connor?" asked Mrs. Samway.

"Oh, he is the doctor who is going to sign the confirmatory certificate."

Again a gleam of unmistakable anger flashed from our hostess' eyes as she demanded: "Then who is this gentleman?"

"This is Dr. Humphrey Jardine," said Batson. "'Pologize for not introducing him before. Dr. Jardine is taking my practice while I'm away. I'm off tonight for about a week."

Mrs. Samway withered me with a baleful glance of her singular eyes, and remarked stiffly: "I don't quite see why you brought him here."

She turned her back on me, and I decided that Mrs. Samway was somewhat of a Tartar; though, to be sure, my presence was a distinct intrusion. I was about to beat a retreat when Batson's apologies were interrupted by a noisy rat-tat at the street door. "Ah, here's O'Connor," said Batson, and, as Mrs. Samway went out to open the door, he added: "Seem to have put our foot in it, though I don't see why she need have been so peppery about it. And O'Connor needn't have banged at the door like that, with death in the house. He'll get into trouble if he doesn't look out."

Our colleague's manner was certainly not ingratiating. He burst into the room with his watch in his hand protesting that he was three minutes late already, "and," he added, "if there is one thing that I detest, it's being late at dinner. Got the forms?"

"Yes," replied Batson, "here they are. That's my certificate on the front page. Yours is overleaf."

Dr. O'Connor glanced rapidly down the long table of questions, muttering discontentedly. "'Made careful external examination?' H'm. 'Have you made a post mortem?' No, of course, I haven't. What an infernal rigmarole! If cremation ever becomes general there'll be no time for anything but funerals. Who nursed the deceased?"

"I did," said Mrs. Samway. "My husband relieved me occasionally, but nearly all the nursing was done by me. My name is Letitia Samway."

"Was the deceased a relation of yours?"

"No; only a friend. He lived with us for a time in Paris and came to England with us."

"What was his occupation?"

"He was nominally a dealer in works of art. Actually he was a man of independent means."

"Have you any pecuniary interest in his death?"

"He has left us about seventy pounds. My husband is the executor of the will."

"I see. Well, I'd better have a few words with you outside, Batson, before I make my examination. It's all a confounded farce, but we must go through the proper forms, I suppose."

"Yes, by all means," said Batson. "Don't leave any loop-hole for queries or objections." He rose and accompanied O'Connor out into the hall, whence the sound of hurried muttering came faintly through the door.

As soon as we were alone, I endeavoured to make my peace with Mrs. Samway by offering apologies for my intrusion into the house of mourning. "For the time being," I concluded, "I am Dr. Batson's assistant, and, as he seemed to wish me to come with him, I came without considering that my presence might be objected to. I hope you will forgive me."

My humility appeared entirely to appease her; in a moment her stiff and forbidding manner melted into one that was quite gracious and she rewarded me with a smile that made her face really charming.

"Of course," she said, "it was silly of me to be so cantankerous and rude, too. But it did look a little callous, you know, when I saw you playing with his poor, dead hand; so you must make allowances." She smiled again, very prettily, and at this moment my two colleagues re-entered the room.

"Now, then," said O'Connor, "let us see the body and then we shall have finished."

He strode over to the bed, and, turning back the sheet, made a rapid inspection of the corpse. "Ridiculous farce," he muttered. "Looks all right. Would, in any case though. Parcel of red tape. What's the good of looking at the outside of a body? Post mortem's the only thing that's any use. What's this piece of tape-plaster on the back?"

"Oh," said Batson, "that is a little cut that he made by falling on a broken bottle. I stuck the plaster on because you can't get a bandage to hold satisfactorily on the back. Besides, he didn't want a bandage constricting his chest."

"No, of course not," O'Connor agreed. "Well, it's all regular and straightforward. Give me the form and I'll fill it up and sign it." He seated himself at the table, looked once more at his watch, groaned aloud and began to write furiously.

"The Egyptians weren't such bad judges, after all," he remarked as he laid down the pen and rose from his chair. "Embalming may have been troublesome, but when it was done it was done for good. The deceased was always accessible for reference in case of a dispute, and all this red tape was saved. Good-night, Mrs. Samway." He buttoned up his coat and bustled off, and a minute or so later we followed.

"By jove!" exclaimed Batson, "this business has upset my arrangements finely. I shall have to buck up if I'm going to catch my train. There's all the medicine to be made up and sent out yet, to say nothing of dinner. But dinner will have to wait until the business is all settled up. Don't you hurry, Jardine. I'll just run on and get to work." He broke into an elephantine trot and soon disappeared round a corner, and, when I arrived at the surgery, I found him posting up the day-book with the speed of a parliamentary reporter.

Batson's dexterity with medicine-bottles and wrapping paper filled me with admiration and despair. I made a futile effort to assist, but in the end, he snatched away the crumpled paper in which I was struggling to enswathe a bottle, dropped it into the waste-paper basket, snatched up a clean sheet and-slap! Bang! In the twinkling of an eye, he had transformed the bottle into a neat, little white parcel as a conjuror changes a cocked hat into a guinea-pig. It was wonderful.

My host was a cheerful soul, but restless. He got up from the table no less than six times to pack some article that he had just thought of; and after dinner, when I accompanied him to his bedroom, I saw him empty his trunk no less than three times to make sure that he had forgotten nothing. He quite worried me. Your over-quick man is apt to wear out other people's nerves more than his own. I began to look anxiously at the dock, and felt a real relief when the maid came to announce that the cab was at the door. "Well, good-bye. Doctor!" he sang out cheerily, shaking my hand through the open window of the cab. "Don't forget to keep the stock-bottles filled up. Saves a world of trouble. And don't take too long on your rounds. Ta! Ta!"

The cab rattled away and I went back into the house, a full-blown general practitioner.

5
THE LETHAL CHAMBER

A YOUNG and newly-qualified doctor, emerging for the first time into private practice, is apt to be somewhat surprised and disconcerted by the new conditions. Accustomed to the exclusively professional and scientific atmosphere of the hospital, the sudden appearance of the personal element as the predominant factor rather takes him aback. He finds himself in a new and unexpected position. No longer a mere, impersonal official, a portion of a great machine, he is the paid servant of his patients: who are not always above letting him feel the conditions of his service. The hospital patient, drilled into a certain respectful submissiveness by the discipline of the wards, has given place to an employer, usually critical, sometimes truculent and occasionally addicted to a disagreeable frankness of speech.

The locum tenens, moreover, is peculiarly susceptible to these conditions, especially if, as in my case, his appearance is youthful. Patients resent the substitution of a stranger for the familiar medical attendant and are at no great pains to disguise the fact. The "old woman with the liver" (to adopt Batson's pellucid phrase) hinted that I was rather young, adding encouragingly that I should get the better of that in time; while the more morose typhoid bluntly informed me that he hadn't bargained for being attended by a medical student.

Taken as a whole, I found private practice disappointing and soon began to wish myself back in the wards and to sigh for my quiet, solitary rambles on Hampstead Heath.

Still, there were rifts in the cloud. Some of the patients appreciated the interest that I took in their cases, evidently contrasting it with the rather casual attitude of my principal, and some were positively friendly. But, in general, my reception was such as to make me slightly apprehensive whenever a new patient appeared.

On the fourth evening after Batson's departure, Mrs. Samway was announced and I prepared myself for the customary snub. But I was mistaken. Nothing could be more gracious than her manner towards me, though the object of her visit occasioned me some embarrassment.

"I have called, Dr. Jardine." she said, "to ask you if you could let me have the account for poor Mr. Maddock. My husband is the executor, you know, and, as we shall be going back to Paris quite shortly, he wants to get everything settled up."

I was in rather a quandary. Of the financial side of practice I was absolutely ignorant and I thought it best to say so. "But," I added, "Dr. Batson will be back on Friday evening, if you can wait so long."

"Oh, that will do quite well," she replied, "but don't forget to tell him that we want the account at once."

I promised not to forget, and then remarked that she would, no doubt, be glad to be back in Paris. "No," she answered, "I shall be rather sorry. Of course Camden Town is not a very attractive neighbourhood, but it is close to the heart of London; and then there are some delightful places near and quite accessible. There is Highgate, for instance."

"Yes; but it is getting very much built over, isn't it?"

"Unfortunately it is; but yet there are some very pleasant places left. The old village is still charming. So quaint and old world. And then there is Hampstead. What could be more delightful than the Heath? But perhaps you don't know Hampstead?"

"Oh, yes I do," said I; "my rooms are at Gospel Oak, quite near the Heath, and I think I know every nook and corner of the neighbourhood. I am pining for a stroll on the Heath at this very moment."

"I daresay you are," she said sympathetically. "This is a depressing neighbourhood if you can't get away from it. We found it very dismal, at first, after Paris."

"Do you live in Paris?" I asked.

"Not permanently," she replied. "But we spend a good deal of time there. My husband is a dealer in works of art, so he has to travel about a good deal. That is how we came to know Mr. Maddock."

"He was a dealer too, wasn't he?" I enquired.

"Yes, in a way. But he had means of his own and his dealing was a mere excuse for collecting things that he was not going to keep. He had a passion for buying, and then he used to sell the things in order to buy more. But I am afraid I am detaining you with my chatter?"

"No, not at all," I said eagerly, only too glad to have an intelligent, educated person to talk to; "you are the last caller, and I hope I have finished my day's work."

Accordingly she stayed quite a long time, chatting on a variety of subjects and finally on that of cremation. "I daresay," she said, "it is more sanitary and wholesome than burial, but there is something rather dreadful about it. Perhaps it is because we are not accustomed to the idea."

"Did you go to the funeral?" I asked.

"Yes. Mr. Maddock had no friends in England but my husband and me, so we both went. It was very solemn and awesome. The coffin was laid on the catafalque while a short service was read, and then two metal doors opened and it was passed through out of our sight. We waited some time and presently they brought us a little terra-cotta urn with just a handful or two of white ash in it. That was all that was left of our poor friend Septimus Maddock. Don't you think it is rather dreadful?"

"Death is always rather dreadful," I answered. "But when we look at the ashes of a dead person, we realize the total destruction of the body; whereas the grave keeps its secrets. If we could look down through the earth and see the changes that are taking place, we should probably find the slow decay more shocking than the swift consumption by fire. Fortunately we cannot. But we know that the final result is the same in both."

Mrs. Samway shuddered slightly, and drew her wraps more closely about her. "Yes," she said with a faint sigh; "the same end awaits us all—but it is better not to think about it."

We were both silent for awhile. I sat with my gaze bent rather absently on the case-book before me, turning over her last somewhat gloomy utterance, until, chancing to look up, I found her pale, penetrating eyes fixed on me with the same strange intentness that I had noticed when she had looked at me as I sat by the body of Maddock. As she met my glance, she looked down quickly but without confusion, and with a return to her habitual reposefulness.

Half-unconsciously I returned her scrutiny. She was a remarkable-looking woman. A beautiful woman, too, but of a type that is, in our time and country, rare: an ancient or barbaric type in which womanly beauty and grace are joined to manifest physical strength. I felt that some unusual racial mixture spoke in her inconsistent colouring; her clear, pink skin, her pale eyes and the jet-black hair that rippled down either side of her low forehead in little crimpy waves, as regular and formal as the "archaic curls" of early Greek sculpture.

But predominant over all other qualities was that of strength. Full and plump, soft and almost ultra-feminine, lissom and flexible in every pose and movement, yet, to me, the chief impression that her appearance suggested was strength—sheer, muscular strength; not the rigid bull-dog strength of a strong man, but the soft and supple strength of a leopard. I looked at her as she sat almost limply in her chair, with her head on one side, her hands resting in her lap and a beautiful, soft, womanly droop of the shoulders; and I felt that she could have started up in an instant, active, strong, formidable, like a roused panther.

I was going on, I think, to make comparisons between her and that other woman who was wont to trip so daintily down Millfield Lane, when she raised her eyes slowly to mine; and suddenly she blushed scarlet.

"Am I a very remarkable-looking person, Dr. Jardine?" she asked quietly, as if answering my thoughts.

The rebuke was well merited. For an instant a paltry compliment fluttered on my lips; but I swallowed it down. She wasn't that kind of woman. "I am afraid I have been staring you out of countenance, Mrs. Samway," I said apologetically.

"Hardly that," she replied with a smile; "but you certainly were looking at me very attentively."

"Well," I said, recovering myself, "after all, a cat may look at a king, you know."

She laughed softly–a very pretty, musical laugh–and rose, still blushing warmly. "And," she retorted, "By the same reasoning, you think a king may look at a cat. Very well, Dr. Jardine. Good-night."

She held out her hand; a beautifully-shaped hand, though rather large–but, as I have said, she was not a small woman; and as it clasped mine, though the pressure was quite gentle, it conveyed, like her appearance, an impression of abundant physical strength.

I accompanied her to the door and watched her as she walked up the dingy street with an easy, erect, undulating gait; even as might have walked those women who are portrayed for the wonder of all time on the ivory-toned marble of the Parthenon frieze. I followed with my eyes the dignified, graceful figure until it vanished round the corner, and then went back to the consulting-room dimly wondering why a woman of such manifest beauty and charm should offer little attraction to me.

Batson's practice, among its other drawbacks, suffered from a deadly lack of professional interest.

Whether this was its normal condition, or whether his patients had got wind of me and called in other and more experienced practitioners, I know not; but certainly, after the stirring work of the hospital, the cases that I had to deal with seemed very small beer. Hence the prospect of a genuine surgical case came as a grateful surprise and I hailed it with enthusiasm.

It was on the day before Batson's expected return that I received the summons; which was delivered to me in a dirty envelope as I sat by the bedside of the last patient on my list.

"Is the messenger waiting?" I asked, tearing open the envelope.

"No, Doctor. He just handed in the note and went off. He seemed to be in a hurry."

I ran my eye over the message, scrawled in a rather illiterate hand on a sheet of common notepaper, and read:

"SIR,
Will you please come at once to the Mineral Water Works in Norton Street. One of our men has injured himself rather badly.
Yours truly,
J. PABKEE.
P.S.-He is bleeding a good deal, so please come quick."

The postscript gave a very necessary piece of information. An injury which bled would require certain dressings and surgical appliances over and above those contained in my pocket case; and to obtain these I should have to take Batson's house on the way. Slipping the note into my pocket, I wished my patient a hasty adieu and strode off at a swinging pace in the direction of Jacob Street.

The housemaid, Maggie, helped me to find the dressings and pack the bag—for she was a handy, intelligent girl though no beauty; and meanwhile I questioned her as to the whereabouts of Norton Street and the mineral water factory.

"Oh, I know the place well enough, sir," said she, "though I didn't know the works were open. Norton Street is only a few minutes' walk from here. It's quite close to Gayton Street, in fact these works are just at the back of the Samway's house. You go up to the corner by the market and take the second on the right and then–"

"Look here, Maggie," I interrupted, "you'd better come and show me the way, as you know the place. There's no time to waste on fumbling for the right turning."

"Very well, sir," she replied, and the bag being now packed with all necessary instruments and dressings, we set forth together.

"Is this a large factory?" I asked, as she trotted by my side, to the astonished admiration of Jacob Street, and the neighbourhood in general.

"No, sir," she replied. "It's quite a small place. The last people went bankrupt and the works were empty and to let for a long time. I thought they were still to let, but I suppose somebody has taken them and started the business afresh. It's round here."

She piloted me round a corner into a narrow bystreet, near the end of which she halted at the gate of a yard or mews. Above the entrance was a weather-beaten board bearing the inscription, "International Mineral Water Company" and a half-defaced printed bill offering the premises to let; and at the side was a large bell-pull. A vigorous tug at the latter set a bell jangling within, and, as Maggie tripped away up the street, a small wicket in the gate opened, disclosing the dimly-seen figure of a man standing in the inner darkness.

"Are you the doctor?" he inquired.

I answered "Yes," and, being thereupon bidden to enter, stepped through the opening of the wicket, which the man immediately closed, shutting out the last gleam of light from the street lamp outside.

"It's rather dark," said the unseen custodian, taking me by the arm.

"It is indeed," I replied, groping with my feet over the rough cobbles; "hadn't you better get a light of some kind?"

"I will in a minute," was the reply. "You see, all the other men have gone home. We close at six sharp. This is the way. I'll strike a match. The man is down in the bottling-room."

My conductor struck a match by the light of which he guided me through a doorway, along a passage or corridor and down a flight of stone steps. At the bottom of the steps was a flagged passage, out of which opened what looked like a range of cellars. Along the passage I walked warily, followed by the stranger and lighted, very imperfectly, by the matches that he struck; the glimmer of which threw a gigantic and ghostly shadow of myself on the stone floor, but failed utterly to pierce the darkness ahead. I was exactly opposite the yawning doorway of one of the cellars when the match went out, and the man behind me exclaimed: "Wait a moment, Doctor! Don't move until I strike another light."

I halted abruptly; and the next moment I received a violent thrust that sent me staggering through the open doorway into the cellar. Instantly, the massive door slammed and a pair of heavy bolts were shot in succession on the outside.

"What the devil is the meaning of this?" I roared, battering and kicking furiously at the door. Of course there was no answer, and I quickly stopped my demonstrations, for it dawned on me m a moment that the factory was untenanted save by the ruffian who had admitted me; that I had been decoyed here of a set purpose, though what that purpose was I could not imagine.

But it was not long before I received a pretty broad hint as to the immediate intentions of my host. A gentle thumping at the door of my cellar attracted my attention and caused me to lay my ear against the wood. The sound that I heard was quite unmistakable. The crevices of the door were being filled, apparently with pieces of rag, which my friend was ramming home, presumably with a chisel. In fact the door was being "caulked" to make the joints airtight.

The object of this proceeding was clear enough. I was shut up in an air-tight cavity in which I was to be slowly suffocated. That was quite obvious. Why I was to be suffocated, I could form no sort of guess excepting that I had fallen into the hands of a homicidal lunatic. But I was not greatly alarmed. The air in a good-sized cellar will last a considerable time, and I could easily poke out anything that my friend might stuff into the keyhole. Then, when the men arrived in the morning, I could kick on the cellar door, and they would come and let me out. There was nothing to be particularly frightened about.

Were there any men? The injured man was evidently a myth. Supposing the other men were a myth too? I recalled Maggie's remark, that she "had thought the place was to let still." Perhaps it was. That would be rather more serious.

At this point my agitations were broken in upon by sounds from the adjoining cellar; the sound of someone moving about and dragging some heavy body. And it struck me at once as strange that I should hear these sounds so distinctly, seeing the massive door of my own cellar was sealed and the walls were of solid brick, as I ascertained by rapping at them with my knuckles. But I had no time to consider this circumstance, for there suddenly rose a new sound, whereat, I must confess my heart fairly came into my mouth; a loud, penetrating hiss like the shriek of escaping steam. It seemed to come from some part of the cellar in which I was immured; from a spot nearly overhead; and it was immediately echoed by a similar sound in the adjoining cellar and then by a third. Even as the last sound broke forth, the door of the adjoining cellar slammed, the bolts were shot and then faintly mingled with the discordant hissing. I could hear the dull thumping that told me that the cracks of that door, too, were being caulked.

It was a frightful situation. The hissing sound was obviously caused by the escape of gas under high pressure, and that gas must be entering my cellar through some opening. I felt for my match-box, and, groping along the wall towards the point whence the loudest sound–and, indeed, all the sounds–proceeded, I struck a match. The glimmer of the wax vesta made everything clear. Close to the ceiling, about seven feet from the ground, was an opening in the wall about six inches square; and pouring through this in a continuous stream was a cloud of white particles that glistened like snowflakes. As I stood under the opening, some of them settled on my face; and the more than icy coldness of the contact, told the whole, horrible tale in a moment.

This white powder WAS snow-carbonic acid snow. The hissing sound came from three of those great iron bottles, charged under pressure with liquified carbonic acid, which are used by mineral water manufacturers for aerating the water. The miscreant (or lunatic) who had imprisoned me had turned on the taps, and the liquid was escaping and turning into to snow with the cold produced by its own rapid evaporation and expansion. Of course the snow would quickly absorb heat, and, without again liquefying, evaporate into the gaseous form. In a very short time both cellars would be full of the poisonous gas, and I-well, in a word, I was shut up in a lethal chamber.

It has taken me some time to write this explanation, which, however, flashed through my brain in the twinkling of an eye as the light of the match fell on that sinister cloud of snowflakes. In a moment I had my coat off, and was stuffing it for dear life into the opening. It was but a poor protection against the gas, which would easily enough find its way through the interstices of the fabric; but it would stop the direct stream of snow and give me time to think.

On what incalculable chances do the great issues of our lives depend! If I had been a short man I must have been dead in half an hour; for the opening through which the cloud of snow was pouring was well over seven feet above the floor and would have been quite out of my reach. Even as it was, with my six feet of stature and corresponding length of arm, it was impossible to ram my coat into the opening with the necessary force, for I had to stand close to the wall with my arm upraised at a great mechanical disadvantage. Still, as I have said, imperfect as the obstruction was, it served to stop the inrushing cloud of snow. It would take some time for the heavy gas in the adjoining cellar to rise to the level of the opening, and, meanwhile, I could be devising other measures.

I lit another match and looked about me. The cellar was much smaller than I had thought and was absolutely empty. The floor was of concrete, the walls of rough brickwork and the ceiling of plaster, all cracked and falling in. There was plenty of ventilation there, but that was of no interest to me. Carbonic acid gas is so heavy that it behaves almost like a liquid, and it would have filled the cellar and suffocated me even if the top of my prison had been open to the sky. The adjoining cellar was already filling rapidly, and when the gas in it reached the level of the opening, it would percolate through my coat and come pouring down into my cellar. But that, as I have said, would take some time-if the dividing wall was moderately sound. This important qualification, as soon as it occurred to me, set me exploring the wall with the aid of another match; and very unsatisfactory was the result. It was a bad wall, built of inferior brick and worse mortar, and was marked by innumerable holes where wall-hooks and other fastenings had been driven in between the bricks. My brief survey convinced me that, so far from being gas-tight, the wall was as pervious as a sponge, and that whatever I meant to do to preserve my life, I must set about without delay.

But what was I to do? That was the urgent, the vital question. Escape was evidently impossible. There were no means of stopping up the numberless holes and weak places in the wall. The only vulnerable spot was the door. If I could establish some communication with the outer air, I could, for a time at least, disregard the poisonous gas with which I should presently be surrounded.

The first thing to be considered was the keyhole. That must be unstopped at once. Fumbling in my bag-for I had grown of a sudden niggardly with my matches-I found a good-sized probe, which I insinuated into the keyhole; and, in a moment, my hopes in that direction were extinguished. For the end of the probe impinged upon metal. The keyhole was not stopped with rag, but with a plate of metal fixed on the outside. With rapidly-growing alarm, but with a tidiness born of habit, I put the probe back in the bag and began feverishly to review the situation and consider my resources. And then I had an idea; only a poor, forlorn hope, but still an idea.

There is a certain ingenious type of pocket-knife, devised principally in the interest of the cutlery trade, that innocent persons (usually of the female persuasion) are wont to bestow as presents on their masculine friends. Such a knife I chanced to possess. It had been given to me by an aunt, and sentimental considerations had induced me to give it an amount of room in my trousers' pocket that I continually grudged. However, there it was at this critical moment, with its corkscrew, gimlet, its bewildering array of blades, its hoof-pick, tooth-pick, tweezers, file, screw-driver and assorted unclassifiable tools; a ponderous lump of pocket-destroying uselessness—and yet, the appointed means of saving my life.

The gimlet was the first tool that I called into requisition. Very gingerly—for these tools are commonly over-tempered and brittle—I bored in the thick plank a hole at about the level of my mouth; and as I worked I turned over my further plans. When the gimlet was through the door, I selected a tool on whose use I had often speculated–a sharp-edged spike, like a diminutive and very stumpy bayonet–which I proceeded to use broach-wise to enlarge the hole. When this tool worked loose, I exchanged it for the screwdriver, with which I managed to broach the hole out to about half an inch in width. And this was as large as I could make it, and it was not large enough. True, one could breathe fairly comfortably through a half-inch hole, but, with the deadly gas circulating around, a freer opening was very desirable.

Then I bethought me that the magic knife contained a saw–a wretched, thick-bladed affair, but still a saw-which would actually cut wood if you gave it time. This implement suggested a simple plan which I forthwith put into execution, working as rapidly as I could without running the risk of breaking the tools. My plan was to make a second hole some two inches diagonally below the first, and from each hole to carry two saw-cuts at right angles to one another. The two pairs of cuts would intersect and take a square piece out of the door, giving me a little window through which I could breathe in comfort.

It was a trifling task, but yet, with the miserable tools I had, it took a considerable time to execute; the more since the saw-blade was wider than the holes, excepting at its point. However, it was accomplished at last, and I had the satisfaction of pushing out the little separated square of wood and feeling that I now had free access to the pure air outside my dungeon.

But it was none too soon. As I rested from my labours, it occurred to me to test the condition of the air inside. Lighting a wax match, I held the little taper so that the flame ascended steadily, and then lowered it slowly. As it descended the flame changed colour somewhat, and about eighteen inches from the floor it went out quite suddenly. There was, then, a layer of the pure gas about eighteen inches deep covering the floor, and, no doubt, rising pretty rapidly. This was rather startling, and it warned me to have recourse without delay to my breathing hole. For though carbonic acid gas behaves somewhat as a liquid, it is not a liquid: like other gases, it has the power of diffusing upwards, and the air of the cellar must be already getting unsafe. Accordingly, after carefully wiping the surface of the door with my handkerchief, I applied my mouth, with some distaste, to the opening and took in a deep draught of undoubtedly pure air.

The position in which I had to stand with my mouth to the hole was an irksome one, and I foresaw that it would presently become very fatiguing. Moreover, when the gas reached the level of my head, it would be difficult to prevent some of it from finding its way into my mouth and nostrils; and if it did, I should most assuredly be poisoned. This consideration suggested the necessity of making another hole at a lower level to let out the gas and allow me to rest myself by a change of position. But this new task had to be carried out with my mouth glued to the breathing hole; and very awkward and tiring I found it and very slow was the progress that I made. This second hole was smaller than the first, for time was precious, and I reflected that I could easily enlarge it by fresh saw-cuts, each two of which would take out a triangular piece of wood.

But it was tedious work, and its completion left me with aching arms; indeed, I was beginning to ache all over from the constrained position. Taking a deep breath and shutting my mouth, I stood up and stretched myself. Then I lit a match and looked at my watch. Half-past eight. I had been over two hours in the cellar. And meanwhile the patients were waiting for me at the surgery, and, no doubt, murmuring at the delay. How soon would my absence lead to enquiries? Or were enquiries being made even now?

Looking at the match that I still held in my hand, I noticed that its flame was pallid and bluish; and as I lowered it slowly, it went out when it was a little over two feet from the floor. The gas, then, was still rising, though not so rapidly as I, had feared, but from the altered colour of the flame, it was evident that the air of the cellar, generally, contained enough diffused gas to be actively poisonous.

After a time, the erect position began to grow insupportably fatiguing. I felt that I must sit down for a few minutes' rest, even though prudence whispered that it was highly unsafe. I struggled for awhile, but eventually, conquered by fatigue, sat down on the floor with my mouth applied closely to the lower breathing-hole. I persuaded myself that I would sit only just long enough to recover some of my strength, but minute after minute sped by and still I felt an unaccountable reluctance to rise.

Suddenly I because conscious of a vague feeling of drowsiness; of a desire to lean back against the wall and doze. It was only slight, but its significance was so appalling that I scrambled to my feet in a panic, and, putting my mouth to the upper breathing-hole, took several deep inspirations. But I soon realized that the upright position was impossible. The drowsy feeling continued and there was growing with it a lassitude and weakness of the limbs that threatened to leave me only the choice between sitting or falling. A wave of furious anger swept over me and roused me a little; a burst of hatred of the cowardly wretch who had decoyed me, as I now suspected, to my death. Then this feeling passed and was succeeded by chilly fear, and I sank down once more into a sitting position with my mouth pressed to the lower opening.

The time ran on unreckoned by me. Gradually, by imperceptible degrees, my mental state grew more and yet more sluggish. Anger and fear and ever-dwindling hope flitted by turns across the slowly-fading field of my consciousness. Intervals of quiet indifference–almost of placid comfort–began to intervene, with increasing lassitude and a growing desire for rest. To lie down; that was what I wanted. To lay my head upon the stony floor and sink into sweet oblivion.

At last I must have actually dozed, though, fortunately, without removing my mouth from the breathing-hole, for I had no sense of the passage of time, when I was suddenly aroused by the loud and continuous jangling of a bell.

I listened with a sort of dull eagerness and keeping awake with a conscious effort.

The bell pealed wildly and without a pause for what seemed to me quite a long time.

Then it ceased, and again my consciousness began to grow dim. After an interval, I know not how long, there came to me dimly and only half-perceived, the closing of a door, the patter of quick footsteps, and then the voice of a man calling me by name.

I struggled to get on to my feet, but could not move. But I still held the clasp-knife and was able to rap with it feebly on the door. Again I heard the voice–it sounded nearer now, and yet infinitely far away–and again I rapped on the door and shouted through the breathing-hole; a thin, muffled cry, such as one utters in a troubled dream. And then the drowsiness crept over me again and I heard no more.

The next thing of which I was conscious was a sounding thwack on the cheek with something wet that felt like a dead fish. I opened my eyes and looked vaguely into two faces that were close to mine and seemed to be lighted by a lamp or candle. The faces were somehow familiar, but yet I failed clearly to recognize them, and, after staring stupidly for a few moments, I began to doze again. Then the dead fish returned to the assault and I again opened my eyes. Another vigorous flop caused me to open my mouth with an unparliamentary gasp.

"Ah! That's better," said a familiar and yet "unplaced" voice. "When a man is able to swear, he is fairly on the road to recovery." Flop!

The renewed attentions of the dead fish (which turned out, later, to be merely a wet towel) evoked further demonstrations on my part of progressing recovery, accompanied by a nervous titter in a female voice. Gradually the clouds rolled away, and to my returning consciousness, the faces revealed themselves as those of Maggie, the housemaid, and Dr. Thorndyke. Even to my muddled wits, the presence of the latter was somewhat of a puzzle, and, in the intervals of anathematizing the deceased fish—which I had not yet identified—I found myself hazily speculating on the problem of how my revered teacher came to be in this place, and what place this was.

"Come, now, Jardine," said Dr. Thorndyke, emptying a jug of water on my face, and receiving a volley of spluttered expletives in exchange, "pull yourself together. How did you get in that cellar?"

"Hang' 'f I know," said I, composing myself for another nap. But here the wet towel came once more into requisition, and that with such vigour that, in a fit of exasperation, I eat up and yawned.

"I think you'd better fetch a cab," said Thorndyke, as Maggie wrung out the towel afresh; "but leave the gate open when you go out."

"Wasser cab for?" I asked sulkily. "Can't I walk?"

"If you can, it will be better," said Thorndyke. "Let us see if you are able to stand." He hoisted me on to my feet and he and Maggie, taking each an arm, walked me slowly up and down the cobbled yard, which I now began to recognize as appertaining to the Mineral Water Works. At first I staggered very drunkenly, but by degrees the drowsy feeling wore off and I was able to walk with Thorndyke's assistance only.

"I think we might venture out now," said he, at length, piloting me towards the gate, and when I had stumbled rather awkwardly through the wicket, we set forth homeward.

On my arrival home, Thorndyke ordered a supply of strong coffee and a light meal, after which–it being obvious that I was good for nothing in a professional sense, he suggested that I should go to bed.

"Don't worry about the practice," said he. "I will send for my friend Jervis, and, between us, we will see that everything is looked after. If Maggie will give me a sheet of paper and an envelope I will write a note to him; and then she can take a hansom to my chambers and give the note either to Dr. Jervis or my man Polton. Meanwhile, I will stay here and see that you don't go to sleep prematurely."

He wrote the note; and Maggie, having made such improvements in her outward garb as befitted the status of a rider in hansoms, took charge of it and departed with much satisfaction and dignity. Thorndyke made a few enquiries of me as to the circumstances that had led to my incarceration in the cellar, but finding that I knew no more than Maggie–whom he had already questioned–he changed the subject; nor would he allow me again to refer to it.

"No, Jardine," he said. "Better think no more of it for the present. Have a good night's rest and then, if you are all right in the morning, we will go into the matter and see if we can put the puzzle together."

6
A Council Of War

I AWOKE somewhat late on the following morning; indeed, I was but half awake when there came a somewhat masterful and peremptory tap at my bedroom door, followed by the appearance in the room of a rather tall gentleman of some thirty years of age. I should have diagnosed him instantly as a doctor by his self-possessed, proprietary manner of entering, but he left me no time for guessing as to his identity.

"Good-morning, Jardine," he said briskly, jingling the keys and small change in his trousers' pockets, "My name is Jervis. Second violin in the Thorndyke orchestra. I'm in charge here pro tem. How are you feeling?"

"Oh, I'm all right. I was just going to get up. You needn't trouble about the practice. I'm quite fit."

"I'm glad to hear it," said Jervis, "but you'd better keep quiet all the same. My orders are explicit, and I know my place too well to disobey. Thorndyke's instructions were that you are not to make any visits or go abroad until after the inquest."

"Inquest?" I exclaimed.

"Yes. He's coming here at four o'clock to hold an inquiry into the circumstances that led to your being locked up in a cellar, and until then I'm to look after the practice and keep an eye on you. What time do you expect the offspring of the flittermouse?"

"Who?" I demanded.

"Batson. He's coming back today, isn't he?"

"Yes. About six o'clock tonight."

"Then you'll be able to clear out. So much the better. The neighbourhood doesn't seem very wholesome for you."

"I suppose I can do the surgery work," said I.

"You'd better not. Better follow Thorndyke's instructions literally. But you can tell me about the patients and help me to dispense. And that reminds me that a person named Samway called just now, a rather fine-looking woman—reminded me of a big, sleek tabby cat. She wouldn't say what she wanted. Do you know anything about her?"

"I expect she came about her account. But she'll have to see Batson. I told her so, only a night or two ago."

"Very well," said Jervis, "then I'll be off now, and you take things easy and just think over what happened last night, so as to be ready for Thorndyke."

With this he bustled away, leaving me to rise and breakfast at my leisure.

His advice to me to think over the events of the previous night was rather superfluous. The experience was not one that I was likely to forget. To have escaped from death by the very slenderest chance was in itself a matter to occupy one's thoughts pretty completely, apart from the horrible circumstances, and then there was the mystery in which the whole affair was enveloped, a mystery which utterly baffled any attempt to penetrate it. Turn it over as I would—and it was hardly out of my thoughts for a minute at a time all day—no glimmer of light could I perceive, no faintest clue to any explanation of that hideous and incomprehensible crime.

At four o'clock punctually to the minute, Dr. Thorndyke arrived, and, having quickly looked me over to see that I was none the worse for my adventure, proceeded to business.

"Have you finished the visits, Jervis?" he asked.

"Yes; and sent off all the medicine. There's nothing more to do until six."

"Then," said Thorndyke, "we might have a cup of tea in the consulting-room and talk this affair over. I am rather taking possession of you, Jardine," he added, "but I think we ought to see where we are quite clearly, even if we decide finally to hand the case over to the police. Don't you agree with me?"

"Certainly," I agreed, highly flattered by the interest he was taking in my affairs; "naturally, I should like to get to the bottom of the mystery."

"So should I," said he, "and to that end, I propose that you give us a completely circumstantial account of the whole affair. I have had a talk with your very intelligent little maid, Maggie, and now I want to hear what happened after she left you."

"I don't think I have much to tell that you don't know," said I; "however, I will take up the story where Maggie left off," and I proceeded to describe the events in detail, much as I have related them to the reader.

Thorndyke listened to my story with profound attention, making an occasional memorandum but not uttering a word until I had finished. Then, after a rapid glance through his memoranda, he said: "You spoke of a note that was handed in to you. Have you got that note?"

"I left it on the writing-table, and it is probably there still. Yes, here it is."

I brought it over to the little table on which our tea was laid and handed it to him; and as he took it from me with the dainty carefulness of a photographer handling a wet plate, I noted mentally that the habit of delicate manipulation contracted in the laboratory makes itself evident in the most trifling of everyday actions.

"I see," he remarked, turning the envelope over and scrutinizing it minutely, "that this is addressed to 'Dr. H. Jardine.' It appears, then, that he knows your Christian name. Can you account for that?"

"No, I can't. The only letter I have had here was addressed 'Dr. Jardine', and I have signed no certificates or other documents."

He made a note of my answer, and, drawing the missive from its envelope, read it through. "The handwriting," he remarked, "looks disguised rather than illiterate, and the diction is inconsistent. The blatantly incorrect adverb at the end does not agree with the rest of the phraseology and the correct punctuation. As to the signature, we may neglect that, unless you are acquainted with anyone in these parts of the name of Parker."

"I am not," said I.

"Very well. Then if you will allow me to keep this note, I will file it for future reference. And now I will ask you a few questions about this adventure of yours, which is really a most astonishing and mysterious affair; even more mysterious, I may add, than it looks at the first glance. But we shall come to that presently. At the moment we are concerned with the crime itself-with a manifest attempt to murder you-and the circumstances that led up to it; and there are certain obvious questions that suggest themselves. The first is: Can you give any explanation of this attempt on your life?"

"No, I can't," I replied. "It is a complete mystery to me. I can only suppose that the fellow was a homicidal lunatic."

"A homicidal lunatic," said Thorndyke, "is the baffled investigator's last resource. But we had better not begin supposing at this stage. Let us keep strictly to facts. You do not know of anything that would explain this attack on you?"

"No."

"Then the next question is: Had you any property of value on your person?"

"No. Five pounds would cover the value of everything I had about me, including the instruments."

"Then that seems to exclude robbery as a motive. The next question is: Does any person stand to benefit considerably by your death? Have you any considerable expectations in the way of bequests, reversions or succession to landed property or titles?"

"No," I replied with a faint grin. "I shall come in for a thousand or two when my uncle dies, but I believe the

London Hospital is the alternative legatee, and I suppose we would hardly suspect the hospital governors of this little affair. Otherwise, the only person who would benefit by my death would be the undertaker who got the contract to plant me."

Thorndyke nodded and made a note of my answer. "That," said he "disposes of the principal motives for premeditated murder. There remains the question of personal enmity—not a common motive in this country. Have you, as far as you know, an enemy or enemies who might conceivably try to kill you?"

"As far as I know, I have not an enemy in the world, or anyone, even, who would wish to do me a bad turn."

"Then," said Thorndyke, "that seems to dispose of all the ordinary motives for murder; and I may say that I have only put these questions as a matter of routine precaution-ex abundantia cautelae, as Jervis says, when he is in a forensic mood—because certain other facts which I have learned seem to exclude any of these motives except, perhaps, robbery from the person."

"You haven't been long picking up those other facts," remarked Jervis. "Why the affair only happened last night."

"I have only made a few simple enquiries," replied Thorndyke. "This morning I called on Mr. Highfield, whose name, as solicitor and agent to the landlords, I copied from the notice on the gate at the works last night. He knows me slightly so I was able to get from him the information that I wanted. It amounts to this.

"About four months ago, a Mr. Gill wrote to him and offered a lump sum for the use of the mineral water works for six months. Highfield accepted the offer and drew up an agreement, as desired, granting Gill immediate possession of the premises and the small stock and plant, of which the residue was to be taken back at a valuation by the landlords at the expiration of the term.

"I noted Gill's address, as it appeared on the agreement, and sent my man, Polton, to make enquiries.

"The address is that of a West Kensington lodging house at which Gill was staying when he signed the agreement. He had been there only three weeks, he left two days after the date of the agreement and the landlady does not know where he went or anything about him."

"Sounds a bit fishy," Jervis remarked. "Did he tell Highfield what he wanted the premises for?"

"I understood that something was said about some assay work in connection with certain–or rather uncertain–mineral concessions. But of course that was no affair of Highfield's. His business was to get the rent, and, having got it, his interest in Mr. Gill lapsed. But you see the bearing of these facts. Gill's connection with these works does, as Jervis says, look a little queer, especially after what has happened. But, seeing that he made his arrangements four months ago, at a time when Jardine had no thought of coming into this neighbourhood, it is clear that those arrangements could have no connection with this particular attempt. Gill obviously did not take those works with the intention of murdering Jardine. He took them for some other purpose; quite possibly the purpose that he stated. And we must not assume that Gill was the perpetrator of this outrage at all. Could you identify the man who let you in?"

"No," I replied. "Certainly not. I hardly saw him at all. The place was pitch dark, and whenever he struck a match he was either behind me or in front with his back to me. The only thing I could make out about him was that he had some sort of coarse wash-leather gloves on."

"Ha!" exclaimed Thorndyke. "Then we were right, Jervis."

I looked in surprise from one to the other of my friends, and was on the point of asking Thorndyke what he meant, when he continued. "That closes another track. If you couldn't identify the man, a description of Gill, if we could obtain it, would not help us. We must begin at some other point."

"It seems to me," said Jervis, "that we haven't much to go upon at all."

"We haven't much," agreed Thorndyke, "but still we have something. We find that the motive of this attempt was apparently not robbery, nor the diversion of inheritable property, nor personal enmity. It must have been premeditated, but yet it could not have been planned more than a week in advance, for Jardine has only been in this neighbourhood for that time, and his coming was unexpected. The appearances very strongly suggest that the motive, whatever it was, has been generated recently and probably locally. So we had better make a start from that assumption."

"Is it possible," Jervis suggested, "that this man Gill may be some sort of anarchist crank? Or a sort of thug? It is actually conceivable that he may have taken these premises for the express purpose of having a secure place where he could perpetrate murders and conceal the bodies."

"It is quite conceivable," said Thorndyke, "and when we go and look over the works–which I propose we do presently–we may as well bear the possibility in mind. But it is merely a speculative suggestion. To return to your affairs, Jardine, has your stay here been quite uneventful?"

"Perfectly," I replied.

"No unusual or obscure cases? No injuries?"

"No, nothing out of the common," I replied.

"No deaths?"

"One. But the man died before I took over."

"Nothing unusual about that? Everything quite regular?"

"Oh, perfectly," I answered; and then with a sudden qualm, as I recalled Batson's uncertainty as to the actual cause of death, I added, "At least I hope so."

"You hope so?" queried Thorndyke. "Yes. Because it's too late to go into the question now. The man was cremated."

At this a singular silence fell. Both my friends seemed to stiffen in their chairs, and both looked at me silently but very attentively. Then Thorndyke asked, "Did you have anything to do with that case?"

"Yes," I replied. "I went with Batson to examine the body."

"And are you perfectly satisfied that everything was as it should be?"

I was on the point of saying "yes." And then suddenly there arose before my eyes the vision of Mrs. Samway looking at me over Batson's shoulder with that strange, inscrutable expression. And again, I recalled her unexplained anger and then her sudden change of mood. It had impressed me uncomfortably at the time, and it impressed me uncomfortably now.

"I don't know that I am, now that I come to think it over," I replied.

"Why not?" asked Thorndyke.

"Well," I said, a little hesitatingly, "to begin with, I don't think the cause of death was quite clear, Batson couldn't find anything definite when he attended the man, and I know that the patient's death came as quite a surprise."

"But surely," exclaimed Thorndyke, "he took some measures to find out the cause of death!"

"He didn't. He assumed that it was a case of fatty heart and certified it as 'Morbus cordis'; and a man named O'Connor confirmed his certificate after examining the body."

"After merely inspecting the exterior?"

"Yes."

My two friends looked at one another significantly, and Thorndyke remarked, with a disapproving shake of the head: "And this is what all the elaborate precautions amount to in practice. A case which might have been one of the crudest and baldest poisoning gets passed with hardly a pretence of scrutiny. And so it will always be. Routine precautions against the unsuspected are no precautions at all. That is the danger of cremation. It restores to the poisoner the security that he enjoyed in the old days when there were no such sciences as toxicology and organic chemistry, when it was impossible for him to be tripped up by an exhumation and an analysis."

"You don't think it likely that this was a case of poisoning, do you?" I asked.

"I know nothing about the case," he replied, "excepting that there was gross neglect in issuing the certificates. What do you think about it yourself? Looking back at the case, is there anything besides the uncertainty that strikes you as unsatisfactory?"

I hesitated, and again the figure of Mrs. Samway rose before me with that strange, baleful look in her eyes. Finally I described the incident to my colleagues. "Mrs. Samway!" exclaimed Jervis. "Is that the handsome Lucrezia Borgia lady with the mongoose eyes who called here this morning? By Jove! Jardine, you are giving me the creeps."

"I understand," said Thorndyke, "that you were making as if to feel the dead man's pulse?"

"Yes."

"There is no doubt, I suppose, that he really was dead?"

"None whatever. He was as cold as a fish, and, besides there was quite distinct rigor mortis."

"That seems conclusive enough," said Thorndyke, but he continued to gaze at his open note-book with a profoundly speculative and thoughtful expression.

"It certainly looks," said Jervis, "as if Jardine had either seen something or had been about to see something that he was not wanted to see; and the question is what that something could have been."

"Yes," I agreed, gloomily; "that is what I have just been asking myself. There might have been a wound or injury of some kind, or there might have been the marks of a hypodermic needle on the wrist. I wish I knew what she meant by looking at me in that way."

"Well," said Jervis, "we shall never know now. The grave gives up its secrets now and again, but the crematorium furnace never. Whether he died naturally or was murdered, Mr. Maddock is now a little heap of ashes with no message for anyone this side of the Day of Judgment."

Thorndyke looked up. "That seems to be so," said he, "and really, we have no substantial reasons for thinking that there was anything wrong. So we come back to your own affairs, Jardine, and the question is, what would you prefer to do?"

"In what respect?" I asked.

"In regard to this attempt on your life. You have told us that you have not an enemy in the world. But it appears as if you had; and a very dangerous one, too. Now would you like to put the case into the hands of the police, or would you rather that we kept our own counsel and looked into it ourselves?"

"I should like you to decide that," said I.

"The reason that I ask," said Thorndyke, "is this: the machinery of the police is adjusted to professional crime—burglary, coining, forgery, and so forth—and their methods are mostly based on 'information received.' The professional 'crook' is generally well known to the police, and, when wanted for any particular 'job,' can be found without much difficulty and the information necessary for his conviction obtained from the usual sources. But in cases of obscure, non-professional crime the police are at a disadvantage. The criminal is unknown to them; there are no confederates from whom to get information; consequently they have no starting-point for their enquiries. They can't create clues; and they, very naturally, will not devote time, labour and money to cases in which they have nothing to go on.

"Now this affair of yours does not look like a professional crime. No motive is evident and you can give no information that would help the police. I doubt if they would do much more than give you some rather disagreeable publicity, and they might even suspect you of some kind of imposture."

"Gad!" I exclaimed. "That's just what they would do. It's what they did last time, and this affair would write me down in their eyes a confirmed mystery-monger."

"Last time?" queried Thorndyke. "What last time is that? Have there been any other attempts?"

"Not on me," I replied. "But I had an adventure one night about six or seven weeks ago that has made the Hampstead police look on me, I think, with some suspicion"; and here I gave my two friends a description of my encounter with the dead (or insensible) cleric in Millfield Lane, and my discoveries on the following morning.

"But my dear Jardine!" Thorndyke exclaimed when I had finished, "what an extraordinary man you are! It seems as if you could hardly show your nose out of doors without becoming involved in some dark and dreadful mystery."

"Well," said I, "I hope I have now exhausted my gifts in that respect. I am not thirsting for more experiences. But what do you think about that Hampstead affair? Do you think I could possibly have been mistaken? Could the man have been merely insensible, after all, as the police suggested?"

Thorndyke shook his head. "I don't think," he replied, "that it is possible to take that view. You see the man had disappeared. Now he could not have got away unassisted, in fact he could not have walked at all. One would have to assume that some persons appeared directly after you left and carried him away; and that they appeared and retired so quickly as not to be overtaken by you on your return a few minutes later with the police. That is assuming too much. And then there are the traces which you discovered on the following day, which seem to suggest strongly that a body had been carried away to Ken Wood. It is a thousand pities that you encountered that keeper, if you could have followed the tracks while they were fresh you might have been able to ascertain whither it had been carried. But now, to return to your latest experience, what shall we do? Shall we communicate with the police, or shall we make a few investigations on our own account?"

"As far as I am concerned," I replied eagerly, "a private investigation would be greatly preferable. But wouldn't it take up rather a lot of your time?"

"Now, Jardine, you needn't apologize," said Jervis. "Unless I am much mistaken, my respected senior has 'struck soundings,' as the nautical phrase has it. He has a theory of your case, and he would like to see it through. Isn't that so, Thorndyke?"

"Well," Thorndyke admitted, "I will confess that the case piques my curiosity somewhat. It is an unusual affair and suggests some curious hypotheses which might be worth testing. So, if you agree, Jardine, that we make at least a few preliminary investigations, I suggest that, as soon as Batson returns, we three go over to the what the newspapers would call 'the scene of the tragedy' and reconstitute the affair on the spot."

"And what about Batson?" I asked. "Shall we tell him anything?"

"I think we must," said Thorndyke, "if only to put him on his guard; for your unknown enemy may be his enemy, too."

At this moment the street door banged loudly, a quick step danced along the hall, and Batson himself burst into the room.

"Good Lord!" he exclaimed, halting abruptly at the door and gazing in dismay at our little council. "What's the matter? Anything happened?"

Thorndyke laughed as he shook the hand of his quondam pupil. "Come, come, Batson, "said he, "don't make me out such a bird of ill-omen."

"I was afraid something awkward might have occurred, police job or inquest or something of that sort."

"You weren't so very far wrong," said Thorndyke. "When you are at liberty I'll tell you about it."

"I'm at liberty now," said Batson, dropping into a chair and glaring at Thorndyke through his spectacles. "No scandal, I hope."

Thorndyke reassured him on this point and gave him a brief account of my adventure and our proposed visit to the works; to which he listened with occasional ejaculations of astonishment and relief.

"By Gum!" he exclaimed, "what a mercy you got there in time. If you hadn't there'd have been an inquest and a devil of a fuss. I should never have heard the last of it. Ruined the practice and worried me into a lunatic asylum. Oh, and about those works. I wouldn't go there if I were you."

"Why not?" Thorndyke asked.

"Well, you may have to answer some awkward questions, and we don't want this affair to get about, you know. No use raising a dust. Rumpus of any kind plays the deuce with a medical practice."

Thorndyke smiled at my principal's frank egoism. "Jervis and I went over last night," said he, "and had a hasty look round and we found the place quite deserted. Probably it is so still."

"Then you won't be able to get in. How jer get in last night?"

"I happened to have a piece of stiff wire in my pocket," Thorndyke replied impassively.

"Ha!" said Batson. "Wire, eh? Picklock in fact. I wouldn't, if I were you. Devil of a bobbery if anyone sees you. Hallo! There goes the bell. Patient. Let him wait. 'Tisn't six yet, is it?"

"Two minutes past," replied Thorndyke, rising and looking at his watch. "Perhaps we had better be starting as it's now dark, and the business at the works, if there is any, is probably over for the day."

"Hang the works!" exclaimed Batson. "I wouldn't go nosing about there. What's the good? Jardine's alright and the chappie isn't likely to be on view. You'll only raise a stink for nothing and bring in a crowd of beastly reports humming about the place. There's that damn bell again. Well, if you won't stay, perhaps you'll look me up some other time. Always d'lighted to see you. Jervis too. You're not going, Jardine. I've got to settle up with you and bear your report."

"I'll look in later," said I; "when you've finished the evening's work."

"Right you are," said Batson, opening the door and adroitly edging us out. "Sorry you can't stay. Good-night! Good-night!"

He shepherded us persuasively and compellingly down the hall, with a skill born of long practice with garrulous patients, and, having exchanged us on the doorstep for a stout woman with two children, returned into the house with his prey and was lost to sight.

7
AN UNSEEN ENEMY

FROM my late principal's house we walked away quickly down the lamplit street, all, I think, dimly amused at the circumstances of our departure. "Is Batson always like that?" Thorndyke asked. "Always," I replied. "Hurry and bustle are his normal states."

"Dear, dear," commented Thorndyke, "what a terrible amount of time he must waste. Of course, one can understand now how that cremation muddle came about. Your incurable hustler is always thinking of the things he has got to do next instead of the thing that he is doing at the moment. By the way, Jardine, I am taking it for granted that you would like to inspect these premises. It is not essential. Jervis and I had a preliminary look round last night, and I daresay we picked up most of the facts that are likely to be of importance if we should be going farther into the matter."

"I think it would be as well for me to take a look at the place and show you exactly where and how the affair happened."

"I think so too," said Thorndyke. "It was all pretty evident, but you might be able to show us something that we had overlooked. Here we are. I wonder if Mr. Gill is on the premises–supposing him still to frequent them."

He looked up and down the street, and, taking a key from his pocket, inserted it into the lock. "Why, how on earth did you get the key?" I asked.

Thorndyke looked at me slyly. "We keep a tame mechanic," said he, as he turned the key and opened the wicket.

"Yes, but how did he get the pattern of the lock?" I asked.

Thorndyke laughed softly. "It is only a simple trade lock. The fact is, Jardine, that in our branch of practice we have occasionally to take some rather irregular proceedings. For instance, I usually carry a small set of picklocks–fortunately for you. That is how I got in last night. Then I never go abroad without a little box of moulding wax; a most invaluable material, Jardine, for collecting certain kinds of evidence. Well, with a slip of wood and a bit of wax I was able to furnish my man with the necessary data for filing up a blank key. One doesn't want to be seen using a picklock. Now, can you show us the way?"

He flashed a pocket electric lamp on the ground, and we advanced over the rough cobbles until we reached a door at the side. "This is where I went in," said I. "It opens into a sort of corridor, and at the end is a door opening on some steps that lead down to the passage below."

Thorndyke tried the handle of the door and pushed, but it was evidently locked or bolted. "I left this door unlocked last night," said he; "so it is clear that someone has been here since. I hardly expected that. I thought our friend would have cleared off for good. But it is possible that Gill had nothing to do with the attempt. The premises may have been used by someone who happened to know that they were unoccupied. It would have been quite easy for such a person to gain admittance; as you see."

While speaking, he had produced from his pocket a little bunch of skeleton keys, with one of which he now quietly unlocked the door. "These builders' locks," said he, "are merely symbolic of security. You are not expected to unfasten them without authority, but you can if you like and happen to have a bit of stiff wire."

We entered the corridor, and, as we proceeded, looked into the rooms that opened out of it. One of them was meagrely furnished as an office, but the thick layer of dust on the desk and stools showed clearly that it had been long disused; the other rooms were empty and desolate, and showed no trace of use or occupation.

"The worthy Gill," said Jervis, "seems to have been able, like Diogenes, to get on with a very modest outfit."

"Yes," agreed Thorndyke, "it is a little difficult to guess what his occupation is. The place looks as if it had never been used at all. Shall I go first?"

He halted for a moment, passing the light of his lamp over the massive door at the head of the steps, and then began to descend. It was certainly a horrible and repulsive place, especially to my eyes, with the recollection of my late experience fresh in my mind. The rough brick walls, covered with the crumbling remains of old white-wash, the black masses of cobwebs that drooped like funereal stalactites from the ceiling, the fungi that sprouted in corners, and the snail-tracks that glistened in the lamplight on the stone floor, all contributed to a vault-like sepulchral effect that was most unpleasantly suggestive of what might have been and very nearly had been.

My late prison was easily distinguished by the two holes in the door. We looked in; but that cellar was completely empty save for a few chips of wood and a pinch or two of sawdust; memorials of my sojourn in the lethal chamber at which I could hardly look without a shudder. Then we passed on to the next cellar-the one adjoining my prison-and this was an object of no little curiosity to me. Here, while I was securely bolted into my cell, that unknown villain had, deliberately and in cold blood, made all the arrangements for my murder; arrangements which he little suspected that I should survive to look upon.

Thorndyke, too, was interested. He stood at the open door, looking in as if considering the positions of various objects. As in fact he was.

"Someone has been here since last night, Jervis," said he.

"Yes," agreed Jervis.

"That gas bottle has been taken down from the opening. You see, Jardine," he continued, "he had stood that big packing-case up on end and laid the gas bottle along the top, with its nozzle just opposite the hole. Two other bottles were standing upright with their nozzles upwards."

"I understand," said Thorndyke, "that you heard three bottles only turned on?"

"Yes," I answered; "there was the one opposite the hole and two others."

"I ask," Thorndyke said, "because there are, as you see, seven other bottles, lying by the wall. Those are all empty. We tried them when we came here last night."

"I know nothing about those others," said I. "The three bottles that I have mentioned I heard distinctly, and after he had turned on the third, the man went out of the cellar and closed up the door."

"Then," said Thorndyke, "the other seven were presumably used for some other-and let us hope, more legitimate-purpose. I wonder why our friend has been at the trouble of moving the cylinders."

"Perhaps," suggested Jervis, "he thought that the arrangement might be a little too illuminating for the police, if they should happen to pay a visit to the place. He may not be aware that the apparatus had already been inspected in situ by us. Or, again, the cylinders may have been moved by someone else. We are assuming that he is a lawful occupant of the premises; but he may be a mere secret intruder like ourselves, who has discovered that the place is more or less unoccupied and has made use of the premises and plant for his own benevolent purposes."

"Yes," agreed Thorndyke, "that is perfectly true. But we can put the matter to the test, at least negatively. If the cylinders have been moved by an innocent stranger they will bear the prints of hands."

"But why shouldn't the man himself leave the prints of his hands on the cylinders?" I asked.

"Because, my dear Jardine, he is too knowing a bird. Jervis and I went carefully over the cylinders last night in the hope of getting a few finger-prints to submit to Scotland Yard; but not a vestige could we find. Our friend had seen to that. We assumed that he had operated in gloves and your description of him confirmed our assumption. Which, in its way, is an interesting fact, for a man who is knowing enough to take these precautions has probably had some previous experience of crime, or, at least, has some acquaintance with the ways of criminals. The suggestion, in fact, is that, although this is not an ordinary professional crime, the perpetrator may be a professional criminal. And the further suggestion is, of course, that of very deliberate premeditation."

While he had been speaking he had produced from his pocket a small, flattened bottle fitted with a metal cap and filled with a yellowish powder. Removing the cap and uncovering a perforated inner cap, like that of an iodoform dredger, he proceeded to shake a cloud of the light powder over the three upper cylinders, jarring them with his foot to make the powder spread. Then he blew sharply on them, one after the other, when the powder disappeared from their surfaces, leaving visible one or two shapeless whitened smears but never a trace of a finger-print or even the shape of a hand.

Thorndyke rose and slipped the bottle back in his pocket. "Apparently," said he, "the cylinders were moved by our unknown friend, with the same careful precautions as on the first occasion. A wary gentleman, this, Jervis. He'll give us a run for our money, at any rate."

"Yes," agreed Jervis; "he doesn't mean to give himself away. He preserves his incognito most punctiliously. I'll say that for him."

"And meanwhile," said Thorndyke, "we had better proceed with our measures for drawing him out of this modest retirement. I want you, Jardine, to look round this cellar and tell us if any of the things that you see in it reminds you of anything that has happened to you, or suggests any thought or reflection."

I looked round, I am afraid rather vacantly. A more unsuggestive collection of objects I have never looked upon. "There are the gas cylinders," I said, feebly; "but I have told you about them. I don't see anything else excepting a few oddments of rubbish."

"Then take a good look at the rubbish," said he. "Remember that it may be necessary at some future time for you to recall exactly what this cellar was like, and what it contained. You may even have to make a sworn statement. So cast your eye round and tell us what you see."

I did so, wondering inwardly what the deuce I was expected to see and what might be the importance of my seeing it. "I see," said I, "a mouldy-looking cellar about fifteen feet by twelve, with very bad brick walls, a plaster ceiling in an advanced stage of decay, and a concrete floor. In the left hand wall is a hole about six inches square opening into the adjoining cellar. The contents are ten gas cylinders, all apparently empty, a key or spanner which seems to have been used to turn the cocks, a large packing-case, which, to judge by its shape, seems to have contained gas cylinders–"

"The word 'large,'" interrupted Thorndyke, "is not a particularly exact one."

"Well, then, a packing-case about seven feet long by two and a half feet wide and deep."

"That's better," said Thorndyke. "Always give your dimensions in quantitative terms if possible. Go on."

"There are a couple of waterproof sheets," said I. "I don't see quite what they can have been used for."

"Never mind their use," said Thorndyke. "Note the fact that they are here."

"I have," said I; "and that seems to complete the list with the exception of the straw in which I suppose the gas cylinders were packed. There is a large quantity of that, but not more than would seem necessary for the purpose. And that seems to complete the inventory, and, I may say, that none of these things conveys any suggestion whatever to my mind."

"Probably not," said Thorndyke, "and it is quite possible that none of these things has any particular significance at all. But as they are the only facts offered us, we must make the best of them. There is one other cellar that we have not yet looked into, I think."

We came out, and, walking along the passage, came to another door which stood slightly ajar. Thorndyke opened it, and, throwing in the light of his lamp, revealed a considerable stack of long iron gas bottles, and one or two packing-cases similar to the one I had already seen.

"I presume," said he, "that these are full cylinders; the store from which our friend got his supply, but we may as well make sure."

He ran back into the adjoining cellar, and returned with the spanner, with which he proceeded to turn the cock of one of the topmost cylinders; upon which a loud hiss and a thin, snowy cloud showed that his surmise was correct.

He had just closed the cock and stepped out into the passage to take back the spanner, when I saw him stop suddenly as if listening. And then he sniffed once or twice.

"What is it?" asked Jervis; but Thorndyke, without replying, ran quickly along the passage and up the steps, and I heard him trying the door at the top.

"Bring up one of the empty cylinders," he said quietly. "They have bolted us in and apparently set fire to the place."

We did not require much urging to act quickly. Picking up one of the long, ponderous iron cylinders, we ran with it along the passage towards the light of Thorndyke's lamp. As we ascended the steps I became plainly aware of the smell of burning wood and of a crackling sound, faintly audible through the massive door.

"There is only one bolt," said Thorndyke; "I noticed it as we came in. I will throw my light on the part of the door where it is fixed, and you two must batter on that spot with the cylinder."

The door was, as I have said, a massive one, but it would have been a massive door indeed that could have withstood the blows of that ponderous iron cylinder, wielded by two strong men whose lives depended on their efforts. At the very first crash of the battering-ram, a tiny chink opened and at each thundering blow, the building shook. Furiously we pounded at the thick, plank-built door, and slowly the chink widened as the screws of the bolt tore out of the woodwork. And as the chink opened, a thin reek of pungent smoke filtered in, and the cold light of Thorndyke's lantern became contrasted with a red glare from without. And then suddenly, the door, under the heavy battering, burst from its fastenings and swung open. A blinding, choking cloud of smoke and sparks rolled in upon us, through which we could see in the corridor outside a pile of straw and crates and broken packing-cases, blazing and cracking furiously. It looked as if we were cut off beyond all hope.

Jervis and I had dropped the now useless cylinder and were gazing in horror at the blazing mass that filled the corridor and cut off our only means of escape, when we were recalled by the voice of Thorndyke, speaking in his usual quiet and precise manner.

"We must get the full cylinders up as quickly as possible," said he; and, running down the steps he made straight for the end cellar, whither we followed him. Picking up one of the cylinders, we carried it quickly to the top of the steps. "Lay it down," said Thorndyke, "and fetch another."

Jervis and I ran back to the cellar, and taking up another cylinder, brought it along the passage. As we were ascending the steps, there suddenly arose a loud, penetrating hiss, and as we reached the top, we saw Thorndyke disengaging the spanner from the cock of the cylinder out of which a jet of liquid was issuing, mingled with a dense, snowy cloud.

An instantaneous glance, as we laid down the fresh cylinder, reassured me very considerably. The icy, volatile liquid and the falling cloud of intensely cold carbonic acid snow had produced an immediate effect; as was evident in a blackened, smouldering patch in the midst of the blazing mass. With reviving hope I followed Jervis once more down the steps and along the passage to the end cellar, from which we brought forth a third cylinder.

By this time the passage was so filled with smoke that it was difficult either to see or to breathe, and the bright light that had at first poured in through the open doorway had already pulled down so far that Thorndyke's figure, framed in the opening, loomed dim and shadowy amidst the smoke and against the dusky red background. We found him, when we reached the top of the steps, holding the great gas bottle and directing the stream of snow and liquid on to those parts of the wood and straw from which flames still issued.

"It will be all right," he said in his calm, unemotional way; "the fire had not really got an effective start. The straw made a great show, but that is nearly all burnt now, and all this carbonic acid gas will soon smother the burning wood. But we must be careful that it doesn't smother us too. The steps will be the safest place for the present."

He opened the cock of the new cylinder and, having placed it so that it played on the most refractory part of the burning mass, backed to the steps where Jervis and I stood looking through the doorway. The fire was, as he has said, rapidly dying down. The volumes of gas produced by the evaporation of the liquid and the melting snow, cut off the supply of air so that, in place of the flames that had, at first, looked so alarming, only a dense reek of smoke arose.

"Now," said Thorndyke, after we had waited on the steps a couple of minutes more, "I think we might make a sortie and put an end to it. If we can get the smouldering stuff off that wooden floor down on to the stone, the danger will be over."

He led the way cautiously into the corridor, and, once more bringing his electric lamp into requisition, began to kick the smouldering cases and crates and the blackened masses of straw down the steps on to the stone floor of the passage, whither we followed them and scattered them with our feet until they were completely safe from any chance of re-ignition.

"There," said Jervis, giving a final kick at a small heap of smoking straw, "I should think that ought to do. There's no fear of that stuff lighting up again. And, if I may venture to make the remark, the sooner we are off these premises the happier I shall be. Our friend's methods of entertaining his visitors are a trine too strenuous for my taste. He might try dynamite next."

"Yes," I agreed; "or he might take pot shots at us with a revolver from some dark corner."

"It is much more likely," said Thorndyke, "that he has cleared off in anticipation of the alarm of fire. Still, it is undeniable that we shall be safer outside. Shall I go first and show you a light?"

He piloted us along the corridor and up the cobbled yard, putting away his lamp as he unlocked the wicket.

There was no sign of anyone about the premises nor, when we had passed out of the gate, was there anyone in sight in the street. I looked about, expecting to see some sign of the fire; but there was no smoke visible, and only a slight smell of burning wood. The smoke must have drifted out at the back.

"Well," Thorndyke remarked, "it has been quite an exciting little episode. And a highly satisfactory finish, as things turned out; though it might easily have been very much the reverse. But for the fortunate chance of those gas-bottles being available, I don't think we should be alive at this moment."

"No," agreed Jervis. "We should be in much the same condition by this time as Batson's late patient, Mr. Maddock, or at least, well on our way to that disembodied state. However, all's well that ends well. Are you coming our way, Jardine?"

"I will walk a little way with you," said I. "Then I must go back to Batson to settle up and fetch my traps."

I walked with them to Oxford Street and we discussed our late adventure as we went. "It was a pretty strong hint to clear out, wasn't it?" Jervis remarked.

"Yes," replied Thorndyke; "it didn't leave us much option. But the affair can't be left at this. I shall have a watch set on those premises, and I shall make some more particular enquiries about Mr. Gill. By the way, Jardine, I haven't your address. I'd better have it in case I want to communicate with you; and you'd better have my card in case anything turns up which you think I ought to know."

We accordingly exchanged cards, and, as we had now reached the corner of Oxford Street, I wished my friends adieu and thoughtfully retraced my steps to Jacob Street.

8
IT'S AN ILL WIND—

LONDON is a wonderful place. From the urban greyness of Jacob Street to the borders of Hampstead Heath was, even in those days of the slow horse tram, but a matter of minutes-a good many minutes, perhaps, but still, considerably under an hour. Yet, in that brief and leisurely journey, one exchanged the grim sordidness of a most unlovely street for the solitude and sweet rusticity of open and charming country.

A day or two after my second adventure in the mineral water works, I was leaning on the parapet of the viaduct–the handsome, red brick viaduct with which some builder, unknown to me, had spanned the pond beyond the Upper Heath, apparently with purely decorative motive, and in a spirit of sheer philanthropy. For no road seemed to lead anywhere in particular over it, and there was no reason why any wayfarer should wish to cross the pond rather than walk round it; indeed, in those days it was covered by a turfy expanse seldom trodden by any feet but those of the sheep that grazed in the meadows bordering the pond. I leaned on the parapet, smoking my pipe with deep contentment, and looking down into the placid water. Flags and rushes grew at its borders, water-lilies spread their flat leaves on its surface, and a small party of urchins angled from the margin, with the keen joy of the juvenile sportsman who suspects that his proceedings are unlawful.

I had lounged on the parapet for several minutes, when I became aware of a man, approaching along the indistinct track that crossed the viaduct, and, as he drew near, I recognized him as the keeper whom I had met in Ken Wood on the morning after my discovery of the body in Millfield Lane. I would have let him pass with a smile of recognition, but he had no intention of passing. Touching his hat politely, he halted, and, having wished me good-morning, remarked: "You didn't tell me, sir, what it was you were looking for that morning when I met you in the wood."

"No," I replied, "but apparently, someone else has."

"Well, sir, you see," he said, "the sergeant came up the next day with a plain-clothes man to have a look round, and, as the sergeant is an old acquaintance of mine, he gave me the tip as to what they were after. I am sorry, sir, you didn't tell me what you were looking for."

"Why?" I asked.

"Well," he replied, "we might have found something if we had looked while the tracks were fresh. Unfortunately there was a gale in the night that fetched down a lot of leaves, and blew up those that had already fallen, so that any foot-marks would have got hidden before the sergeant came."

"What did the police officers seem to think about it?" I asked.

"Why, to speak the truth," the keeper replied, "they seemed to think it was all bogey."

"Do you mean to say," I asked, "that they thought I had invented the whole story?"

"Oh, no, sir," he replied, "not that. They believed you had seen a man lying in the lane, but they didn't believe that he was a dead man and they thought your imagination had misled you about the tracks."

"Then, I suppose they didn't find anything?" said I.

"No, they didn't, and I haven't been able to find anything myself, though I've had a good look round."

And then, after a brief pause: "I wonder," he said, "if you would care to come up to the Wood and have a look at the place yourself."

I considered for a moment. I had nothing to do for I was taking a day off, and the man's proposal sounded rather attractive. Finally, I accepted his offer, and we turned back together towards the Wood.

Hampstead–the Hampstead of those days–was singularly rustic and remote. But, within the wood, it was incredible that the town of London actually lay within the sound of a church bell or the flight of a bullet. Along the shady paths, carpeted with moss and silvery lichen, overshadowed by the boughs of noble beeches; or in leafy hollows, with the humus of centuries under our feet, and the whispering silence of the woodland all around, we might have been treading the glades of some primeval forest. Nor was the effect of this strange remoteness less, when presently, emerging from the thicker portion of the wood, we came upon a moss-grown, half-ruinous boat-house on the sedgy margin of a lake, in which was drawn up a rustic-looking, and evidently, little-used punt.

"It's wonderful quiet about here, sir," the keeper remarked, as a water-hen stole out from behind a clump of high rushes and scrambled over the leaves of the water-lilies.

"And presumably," I remarked, "it's quieter still at night."

"You're right, sir," the keeper replied. "If that man had got as far as this, he'd have had mighty little trouble in putting the body where no one was ever likely to look for it."

"I suppose," said I, "that you had a good look at the edges of the lake?"

"Yes," he answered. "I went right round it, and so did the police, for that matter, and we had a good look at the punt, too. But, all the same, it wouldn't surprise me if, one fine day, that body came floating up among the lilies; always supposing, that is," he added, "that there really was a body."

"How far is it," I asked, "from the lake to the place where you met me that morning?"

"It's only a matter of two or three minutes," he answered, "we may as well walk that way and you can see for yourself."

Accordingly, we set forth together, and, coming presently upon one of the moss-grown paths, followed it past a large summerhouse until we came in sight of the beech beyond which I had encountered him while I was searching for the tracks. As we went, he plied me with questions as to what I had seen on the night in the lane, and I made no scruple of telling him all that I had told the police, seeing that they, on their side, had made no secret of the matter.

Of course, it was idle, after this long period-for it was now more than seven weeks since I had seen the body-to attempt anything in the nature of a search. It certainly did look as if the man who had stolen into that wood that night had been bound for the solitary lake. The punt, I had noticed, was only secured with a rope, so that the murderer—for such I assumed he must have been—could easily have carried his dreadful burden out into the middle, and there sunk it with weights, and so hidden it for ever. It was a quick, simple and easy method of hiding the traces of his crime, and, if the police had not thought it worth while to search the water with drags, there was no reason why the buried secret should not remain buried for all time.

After we had walked for some time about the pleasant, shady wood, less shady now that the yellowing leaves were beginning to fall with the passing of autumn, the keeper conducted me to the exit by which I had left on the previous occasion.

As I was passing out of the wicket, my eye fell once more on the cottage which I had then noticed, and, recalling the remark that my fair acquaintance had let fall concerning the artist to whom the derelict knife was supposed to belong, I said: "You mentioned, I think, that that house was let to an artist."

"It was," he replied; "but it's empty now, the artist has gone away."

"It must be a pleasant little house to live in," I said, "at any rate, in summer."

"Yes," he replied, "a country house within an hour's walk of the Bank of England. Would you like to have a look at it, sir? I've got the keys."

Now I certainly had no intention of offering myself as a tenant, but, yet, to an idle man, there is a certain attractiveness in an empty house of an eligible kind, a certain interest in roaming through the rooms and letting one's fancy furnish them with one's own household goods. I accepted the man's invitation, and, opening the wide gate that admitted to the garden from a byroad, we walked up to the door of the house.

"It's quite a nice little place," the keeper remarked. "There isn't much garden, you see, but then, you've got the Heath all around; and there's a small stable and coachhouse if you should be wanting to go into town."

"Did the last tenant keep any kind of carriage?" I asked.

"I don't think so," said the keeper, "but I fancy he used to hire a little cart sometimes when he had things to bring in from town; but I don't know very much about him or his habits."

We walked through the empty rooms together, looking out of the windows and commenting on the pleasant prospects that all of them commanded, and talking about the man who had last lived in the house.

"He was a queer sort of fellow," said the keeper. "He and his wife seem to have lived here all alone without any servant, and they seem often to have left the house to itself for a day or two at a time; but he could paint. I have stopped and had a look when he has been at work, and it was wonderful to see how he knocked off those pictures. He didn't seem to use brushes, but he had a lot of knives, like little trowels, and he used to shovel the paint on with them, and he always wore gloves when he was painting; didn't like to get the paint on his hands, I suppose."

"It sounds as if it would be very awkward," I said.

"Just what I should have thought," the keeper agreed. "But he didn't seem to find it so. This seems to be the place that he worked in."

Apparently the keeper was right. The room, which we had now entered, was evidently the late studio, and did not appear to have been cleaned up since the tenant left. The floor was littered with scraps of paper on which a palette-knife had been cleaned, with empty paint-tubes and one or two broken and worn-out brushes, and, in a packing-case, which seemed to have served as a receptacle for rubbish, were one or two canvasses that had been torn from their stretchers and thrown away. I picked them out and glanced at them with some interest, remembering what my fair friend had said. For the most part, they were mere experiments or failures, deliberately defaced with strokes or daubs of paint, but one of them was a quite spirited and attractive sketch, rough and unfinished, but skillfully executed and undefaced. I stretched out the crumpled canvas and looked at it with considerable interest, for it represented Millfield Lane, and showed the large elms and the posts and the high fence under which I had sheltered in the rain. In fact, it appeared to have been taken from the exact spot on which the body had been lying, and from which I had made my own drawing; not that there was anything in the latter coincidence, for it was the only sketchable spot in the lane.

"It's really quite a nice sketch," I said; "it seems a pity to leave it here among the rubbish."

"It does, sir," the keeper agreed. "If you like it, you had better roll it up and put it in your pocket. You won't be robbing anyone."

As it seemed that I was but rescuing it from a rubbish-heap, I ventured to follow the keeper's advice, and, rolling the canvas up, carefully stowed it in my pocket. And shortly after as I had now seen all that there was to see, which was mighty little, we left the house, and, at the gate, the keeper took leave of me with a touch of his hat.

I made my way slowly back towards my lodgings by way of the Spaniard's Road and Hampstead Lane, turning over in my mind as I went, the speculation suggested by my visit to the wood. Of the existence of the lake I had not been previously aware. Now that I had seen it, I felt very little doubt that it was known to the mysterious murderer–for such I felt convinced he was–who must have been lurking in the lane that night when I was sheltering under the lee of the fence. The route that he had then taken appeared to be the direct route to the lake. That he was carrying the body, I had no doubt whatever; and, seeing that he had carried it so far, it appeared probable that he had some definite hiding-place in view. And what hiding-place could be so suitable as this remote piece of still water? No digging, no troublesome and dangerous preparation would be necessary. There was the punt in readiness to bear him to the deep water in the middle; a silent, easily-handled conveyance. A few stones, or some heavy object from the boat-house, would be all that was needful; and in a moment he would be rid forever of the dreadful witness of his crime.

Thus reflecting–not without dissatisfaction at the passive part that I had played in this sinister affair–I passed through the turnstile, or "kissing-gate," at the entrance to Millfield Lane. Almost certainly, the murderer or the victim or both, had passed through that very gate on the night of the tragedy. The thought came to me with added solemnity with the recollection of the silent wood and the dark, still water fresh in my mind, and caused me unconsciously to tread more softly and walk more sedately than usual.

The lane was little frequented at any time and now, at mid-day, was almost as deserted as at midnight. Very remote it seemed, too, and very quiet, with a silence that recalled the hush of the wood. And yet the silence was not quite unbroken. From somewhere ahead, from one of the many windings of the tortuous lane, came the sound of hurried footsteps. I stopped to listen. There were two persons, one treading lightly, the other more heavily, apparently a man and a woman. And both were running— running fast.

There was nothing remarkable in this, perhaps; but yet the sound smote on my ear with a certain note of alarm that made me quicken my pace and listen yet more intently. And suddenly there came another sound; a muffled, whimpering cry like that of a frightened woman. Instantly I gave an answering shout and sprang forward at a swift run.

I had turned one of the numerous corners and was racing down a straight stretch of the lane when a woman darted round the corner ahead, and ran towards me, holding out her hands. I recognised her at a glance, though now she was dishevelled, pale, wild-eyed, breathless and nearly frantic with terror, and rage against her assailant spurred me on to greater speed. But when I would have passed her to give chase to the wretch, she clutched my arm frantically with both hands and detained me.

"Let me go and catch the scoundrel!" I exclaimed; but she only clung the tighter.

"No," she panted, "don't leave me! I am terrified! Don't go away!"

I ground my teeth. Even as we stood, I could hear the ruffian's footsteps receding as rapidly as they had advanced. In a few moments he would be beyond pursuit.

"Do let me go and stop that villain!" I implored. "You're quite safe now, and you can follow me and keep me in sight."

But she shook her head passionately, and, still clutching my sleeve with one hand, pressed the other to her heart.

"No, no, no!" she gasped, with a catch in her voice that was almost a sob, "I can't be alone! I am frightened. Oh! Please don't go away from me!"

What could I do? The poor girl was evidently beside herself with terror, and exhausted by her frantic flight. It would have been cruel to leave her in that state. But all the same, it was infuriating. I had no idea what the man had done to terrify her in this way. But that was of no consequence. The natural impulse of a healthy young man when he learns that a woman has been ill-used is to hammer the offender effectively in the first place, and then to inquire into the affair. That was what I wanted to do; but it was not to be.

"Well," I said, by way of compromise, "let us walk back together. Perhaps we may be able to find out which way the man went."

To this she agreed. I drew her arm through mine–for she was still trembling and looked faint and weak–and we began to retrace her steps towards Highgate. Of course the man was nowhere to be seen, and by the time that we had turned the sharp corner where I had found the body of the priest, the man was not only out of sight, but his footsteps were no longer audible.

Still we went on for some distance in the hopes of meeting someone who could tell us which way the miscreant had gone. But we met nobody. Only, some distance past the posts, we came in sight of a sketching box and a camp-stool, lying by the side of the path.

"Surely those are your things?" I said.

"Yes," she answered. "I had forgotten all about them. I dropped them when I began to run."

I picked up the box and the stool, and debated with myself whether it was worthwhile to go on any farther. From where we stood, nothing was to be seen, for the lane was still enclosed on both sides by a seven foot fence of oak boards. But the chance of overtaking the fugitive was not to be considered; by this time he was probably out of the lane on the Heath or in the surrounding meadows; and meanwhile, my companion, though calmer and less breathless, looked very pale and shaken.

"I don't know that it's any use," I said, "to tire you by going any farther. The man is evidently gone."

She seemed relieved at my decision, and it then occurred to me to suggest that she should sit down awhile on the bank under the high fence to recover herself, and to this, too, she assented gladly.

"If it wouldn't distress you," I said, "would you mind telling me what had happened?"

She pondered for a few seconds and then answered: "It doesn't sound much in the telling and I expect you will think me very silly to be so much upset."

"I'm sure I shan't," I said, with perfect confidence in the correctness of my statement.

"Well," she said, "what happened was this as nearly as I can remember: I was coming up the path from the ponds and I had to pass a man who was leaning against the fence by the stile. As I came near to him, he looked at me, at first, in quite an ordinary way, and then, he suddenly began to stare in a most singular and disturbing fashion, not at me, so much, as at this little crucifix which I wear hung from my neck. As I passed through the turnstile, he spoke to me: 'Would you mind letting me look at that crucifix?' he asked. It was a most astonishing piece of impertinence, and I was so taken aback that I hardly had the presence of mind to refuse. However, I did, and very decidedly, too. Then he came up to me, and, in a most threatening and alarming manner, said: 'You found that crucifix. You picked it up somewhere near here. It's mine, and I'll ask you to let me have it, if you please.'

"Now this was perfectly untrue. The crucifix was given to me by my father when I was quite a little child, and I have worn it ever since I have been grown up–ever since he died, in fact, six years ago. I told the man this, but he made no pretence of believing me, and was evidently about to renew his demand, when two labourers appeared, coming down the lane. I thought this a good opportunity to escape, and walked away quickly up the lane; it was very silly of me; I ought to have gone the other way."

"Of course you ought," I agreed, "you ought to have got out into a public road at once."

"Yes, I see that now," she said. "It was very foolish of me. However, I walked on pretty quickly, for there was something in the man's face that had frightened me, and I was anxious to get home. I looked back, from time to time, and, when I saw no sign of the man, I began to recover myself; but just as I had got to the most solitary part of the lane, just about where we are now, shut in by these high fences, I heard quick footsteps behind me. I looked back and saw the man coming after me. Then, I suppose, I got in a sudden panic, for I dropped my sketching things and began to run. But as soon as I began to run, the man broke into a run too. I raced for my life, and when I heard the man gaining on me, I suppose I must have called out. Then I heard your shout from the upper part of the lane and ran on faster than ever to gain your protection. That's all, and I suppose you think that I have been making a great fuss about nothing."

"I don't think anything of the kind," I said, "and neither would our absent friend if I could get hold of him. By the way, what sort of person was he?-a tramp?"

"Oh, no, quite a respectable looking person; in fact, he would have passed for a gentleman."

"Can you give any sort of description of him, not that verbal descriptions are of much use except in the case of a hunchback or a Chinaman or some other easily identifiable creature."

"No, they are not," she agreed, "and I don't think that I can tell you much about this man excepting that he was clean-shaved, of medium height, quite well dressed, and wore a round hat and slate-coloured suede gloves."

"I'm afraid we shan't get hold of him from that description," I said. "The only thing that you can do is to avoid solitary places for the present and not to come through this lane again alone."

"Yes," she said. "I suppose I must, but it's very unfortunate. One cannot always take a companion when one goes sketching even if it were desirable, which it is not."

As to the desirability, in the case of a good-looking girl, of wandering about alone in solitary places, I had my own opinions; and very definite opinions they were. But I kept them to myself. And so we sat silent for awhile. She was still pale and agitated, and perhaps her recital of her misadventure had not been wholly beneficial. At the moment that this idea occurred to me, a crackling in my breast-pocket reminded me of the forgotten canvas, and I bethought me that perhaps a change of subject might divert her mind from her very disagreeable experience. Accordingly, I drew the canvas out of my pocket, and, unrolling it, asked her what she thought of the sketch. In a moment she became quite animated.

"Why," she exclaimed, "this looks exactly like the work of that artist who was working on the Heath a little while ago."

"It is his," I replied, considerably impressed and rather astonished at her instantaneous recognition; "but I didn't know you were so familiar with his work."

"I'm not very familiar with it," she replied; "but, as I told you, I sometimes managed to steal a glance or two when I passed him. You see, his technique is so peculiar that it's easily recognised, and it interested me very much. I should have liked to stop and watch him and get a lesson."

"It is rather peculiar work," I said, looking at the canvas with new interest. "Very solid and yet very smooth."

"Yes. It is typical knife-work, almost untouched with the brush. That was what interested me. The knife is a dangerous tool for a comparative tyro like myself, but yet one would like to learn how to use it. Did he give you this sketch?"

I smiled guiltily. "The truth is," I admitted, "I stole it."

"How dreadful of you!" she said, "I suppose that you could not be bribed to steal another?"

"I would steal it for nothing if you asked me," I answered, "and meanwhile, you had better take possession of this one. It will be of more use to you than to me."

She shook her head: "No, I won't do that," she said, "though it is most kind of you. You paint, I think, don't you?"

"I'm only the merest amateur," I replied. "I annexed the sketch for the sake of the subject. I have rather an affection for this lane."

"So had I," said she, "until today. Now, I hate it, but, might I ask how you managed your theft?"

I told her about the empty cottage and the rejected canvasses in the rubbish box. "I'm afraid none of the others would be of any use to you because he had drawn a brushful of paint across each of them."

"Oh, that wouldn't matter," she said. "The brush-strokes would be on dry paint and could easily be scraped off. Besides, it is not the subject but the technique that interests me."

"Then I will get into the cottage somehow and purloin the remaining canvasses for you."

"Oh, but I mustn't give you all this trouble," she protested.

"It won't be any trouble," I said. "I shall quite enjoy a deliberate and determined robbery. But where shall I send the spoil?"

She produced her card-case, and, selecting a card, handed it to me, with a smile: "It seems to me," she said, "that I am inciting you to robbery and acting as a receiver of stolen goods, but I suppose there's no harm in it, though I feel that I ought not to give you all this trouble."

I made the usual polite rejoinder as I took from her the little magical slip of pasteboard that, in a moment, transformed her from a stranger to an acquaintance, and gave her a local habitation and a name. Before bestowing it in my pocket-book, I glanced at the neat copper-plate and read the inscription: "*Miss Sylvia Vyne. The Hawthorns. North End.*"

The effect of our conversation had answered my expectations. Her agitation had passed off, the colour had come back to her cheeks, and, in fact, she seemed quite recovered. Apparently she thought so herself, for she rose, saying that she now felt well enough to walk home, and held out her hand for the colour-box and stool.

"I think," said I, "that if you won't consider me intrusive, I should like to see you safely out on to an inhabited road at least."

"I shall accept your escort gratefully," she replied, "as far as the end of the lane, or farther if it is not taking you too much out of your way."

Needless to say, I would gladly have escorted so agreeable and winsome a protégée from John o' Groats to Land's End and found it not out of my way at all; and when she passed out of the gate into Hampstead Lane, I clung tenaciously to the box and stool and turned towards "The Spaniards" as though no such thing as a dismissal had ever been contemplated. In fact, with the reasonable excuse of carrying the impedimenta, I maintained my place by her side in the absence of a definite conge; and so we walked together, talking quite easily, principally about pictures and painting, until, in the pleasant little hamlet, she halted by a garden gate, and, taking her possessions from me, held out a friendly hand.

"Good-bye," she said. "I can't thank you enough for all your help and kindness. I hope I have not been very troublesome to you."

I assured her that she had been most amenable, and, when I had once more cautioned her to avoid solitary places, we exchanged a cordial hand-shake and parted, she to enter the pleasant, rustic-looking house, and I to betake myself back to my lodgings, lightening the way with much agreeable and self-congratulatory reflection.

9
THORNDYKE TAKES UP THE SCENT

AT my lodgings, which I reached at an unconscionably late hour for lunch, I found a little surprise awaiting me; a short note from Dr. Thorndyke asking me if I should be at liberty early on the following afternoon to show him the spot on which I had found the mysterious body. Of course, I answered by return, begging him to come straight on from the hospital to an early lunch, over which we could discuss the facts of the case before setting out. Having dispatched my letter, I called at the offices of the house agent who had the letting of the cottage on the Heath, to see if he had duplicate keys. Fortunately he had, and was willing to entrust them to me on the understanding that they should be returned some time during the next day. I did not, however, go on to the cottage, for it occurred to me that Thorndyke would probably wish to visit the wood, and I could make my visit and purloin the canvasses then.

A telegram on the following morning informed me that Thorndyke would be with me at twelve o'clock, and, punctually to the minute, he arrived. "I hope you don't mind me swooping down on you in this fashion," he said, as the servant showed him into the room.

I assured him, very truthfully, that I was delighted to be honoured by a visit from him, and he then proceeded to explain. "You may wonder, Jardine, why I am busying myself about this case, which is really no business of mine, or, at least, appears to be none; but the fact is, that as a teacher and a practitioner of Medical Jurisprudence, I find it advisable to look into any unusual cases. Of course, there is always a considerable probability that I may be consulted concerning any out of the way case; but, apart from that, I have the ordinary specialist's interest in anything remarkable in my own speciality."

"I should think," said I, "that it would be well for me to give you all the facts before we start."

"Exactly, Jardine," he replied, "that is what I want. Tell me all you know about the affair and then we shall be able to test our conclusions on the spot."

He produced a large scale ordnance map, and, folding it under my direction, so that it showed only the region in which we were interested, he stood it up on the table against the water bottle, where we could both see it, and marked on it with a pencil each spot as I described it.

It is not necessary for me to record our conversation. I told him the whole story as I have already told it to the reader, pointing out on the map the exact locality where each event occurred.

"It's a most remarkable case, Jardine," was his thoughtful comment when I had finished, "most remarkable; curiously puzzling and inconsistent too. For you see that on the one hand, it looks like a casual or accidental crime, and yet, on the other, strongly suggests premeditation. No man, one would think, could have planned to commit a murder in what is, after all, a public thoroughfare; and yet, the long distance which the body seems to have been carried, and the apparently selected hiding-place, seem to suggest a previously considered plan."

"You think that there is no doubt that the man was really dead?" I asked.

"Had you any doubt at the time yourself?"

"None at all," I replied, "it was only the disappearance of the body, and, perhaps, the sergeant's suggestion, that made me think it possible that I might have been mistaken."

Thorndyke shook his head. "No, Jardine," said he, "the man was dead. We are safe in assuming that; and on that assumption our investigations must be based. The next question is, how was the body taken away? Did you measure the fence?"

"No, but I should say it is about seven feet high."

"And what kind of fence is it? Are there any footholds?"

"I can show you exactly what the fence is like," I answered. "That sketch, which I have pinned up on the wall, was apparently painted from the exact spot on which the body lay. That fence on the right-hand side is the one under which I sheltered and is exactly like the one over which the body seems to have been lifted."

Thorndyke rose and walked over to the sketch, which I had fixed to the wall with drawing-pins. "Not a bad sketch, this, Jardine," he remarked; "very smartly put in, apparently mostly with the knife. Where did you get it?"

I had to confess that the canvas was unlawfully come by, and told him how I had obtained it.

"You don't know the artist's name?" said Thorndyke, looking closely at the sketch.

"No. In fact, I know nothing about him, excepting that he worked mostly with a small painting-knife, and usually wore kid gloves."

"You don't mean that he worked in gloves?" said Thorndyke.

"So I am told," said I. "I never saw him."

"It's very odd," said Thorndyke. "I have heard of men wearing a glove on the palette-hand to keep off the midges, and many men paint in gloves in exceptionally cold weather. But this sketch seems to have been painted in the summer."

"I suppose," said I, "the midges don't confine their attentions to the palette-hand. And after all, to a man who worked entirely with the knife, a glove wouldn't be really in the way."

"No," Thorndyke agreed, "that is true."

He looked closely at the sketch, and even took out his pocket lens to help his vision, which seemed almost unnecessary. It appeared that he was as much interested in the unknown artist's peculiar technique as was my friend, Miss Sylvia Vyne.

"By the way," said he, when he had resumed his seat at the table," you were telling me about some kind of gold trinket that you had picked up at the foot of the fence. Shall we have a look at it?"

I fetched the little gold object from the dispatch box in which I had locked it up, and handed it to him. He turned it over in his fingers, read the letters that were engraved on it, and examined the little piece of silk cord that was attached to one ring.

"There is no doubt," said he, "as to the nature of this object, nor of its connection with the dead man. This is evidently a reliquary, and these initials engraved upon it bear out exactly your description of the body. S.V.D.P evidently means St. Vincent de Paul, who, as you probably know, was a saint who was distinguished for his works of charity. You have mentioned that the dead man wore a Roman collar, with a narrow, dark stripe up the front. That means that he was the lay-brother of some religious order, probably some philanthropic order, to whom St. Vincent de Paul would be an object of special devotion. The other letters, A.M.D.G., are the initials of the words *Ad Majorem Dei Gloriam*—the motto of the Society of Jesus. But as St. Vincent de Paul was not a Jesuit saint, the motto probably refers to the owner of the reliquary, who may have been a Jesuit or a friend of the Society. It was apparently attached—perhaps to the neck— by this silk cord, which seems to have been frayed nearly through, and probably broke when the body was drawn over the top of the fence."

"I suppose I ought to have shown it to the police," I said.

"I suppose you ought," he replied, "but, as you haven't, I think we had better say nothing about it now."

He handed it back to me, and I dropped it into my pocket, intending to return it presently to the dispatch box. A few minutes later, we sallied forth on our journey of exploration.

It is not necessary to describe this journey in detail since I have already taken the reader over the ground more than once. We went, of course, to the place where I had found the body and walked right through to Hampstead Lane. Then we returned, and reconstituted the circumstances of that eventful night, after which, I conducted Thorndyke to the place where I assumed that the body had been lifted over the fence.

"I suppose," I said, "we must go round and pick up the track from the other side."

He looked up and down the lane and smiled. "Would your quondam professor lose your respect for ever, Jardine, if you saw him climb over a fence in a frock coat and a topper?"

"No," I answered, "but it might look a little quaint if anyone else saw you."

"I think we will risk that," he said. "There is no one about, and I should rather like to try a little experiment. Would you mind if I hoisted you over the fence? You are something of an out-size, but then, so am I, too, which balances the conditions."

Of course I had no objection, and, when we had looked up and down the lane and listened to make sure that we had no observers, Thorndyke picked me up, with an ease that rather surprised me, and hoisted me above the level of the fence.

"Is it all clear on the other side?" he asked.

"Yes," I answered, "there's no one in sight."

"Then I want you to be quite passive," he said, and with this, he hoisted me up further until I hung with my own weight across the top of the fence. Leaving me hanging thus, he sprang up lightly, and, having got astride at the top, dropped down on the other side, when he once more took hold of me and drew me over. "It wasn't so very difficult," he said. "Of course, it would have been more so to a shorter man, but, on the other hand, it is extremely unlikely that the body was anything like your size and weight."

We now followed the track up to the wood, which we entered by an opening in the fence, through which I assumed that the murderer had probably passed. I conducted Thorndyke by the nearest route to the boat-house, and, when he had thoroughly examined the place and made notes of the points that appeared to interest him, I showed him the way out by the turnstile.

It was here when we came in sight of the cottage that I bethought me of my promise to Miss Vyne, and somewhat sheepishly explained the matter to Thorndyke.

"It won't take me a minute to go in and sneak the things," I said apologetically, and was proposing that he should walk on slowly, when he interrupted me.

"I'll come in with you," said he. "There may be something else to filch. Besides, I am rather partial to empty houses. There is something quite interesting, I think, in looking over the traces of recent occupation, and speculating on the personality and habits of the late occupiers. Don't you find it so?"

I said "Yes," truthfully enough, for it was a feeling of this kind that had first led me to look over the cottage. But my interest was nothing to Thorndyke's; for no sooner had I let him in at the front door, than he began to browse about through the empty rooms and passages, for all the world like a cat that has just been taken to a new house.

"This was evidently the studio," he remarked, as we entered the room from which I had taken the canvas, "he doesn't seem to have had much of an outfit, as he appears to have worked on his sketching-easel; you can see the indentations made by the toe-points, and there are no marks of the castors of a studio easel. You notice, too, that he sat on a camp-stool to work."

It did not appear to me to matter very much what he had sat on, but I kept this opinion to myself and watched

Thorndyke curiously as he picked up the empty paint tubes and scrutinized them one after the other. His inquisitiveness filled me with amused astonishment. He turned out the rubbish box completely, and having looked over every inch of the discarded canvasses, he began systematically to examine, one by one, the pieces of paper on which the late resident had wiped his palette-knife.

Having rolled up and pocketed the waste canvasses, I expressed myself as ready to depart.

"If you're not in a hurry," said Thorndyke, "I should like to look over the rest of the premises."

He spoke as though we were inspecting some museum or exhibition, and, indeed, his interest and attention, as he wandered from room to room, were greater than that of the majority of visitors to a public gallery. He even insisted on visiting the little stable and coachhouse, and when he had explored them both, ascended the ricketty steps to the loft over the latter.

"I suppose," said I, "this was the lumber room or store. Judging by the quantity of straw it would seem as if some cases had been unpacked here."

"Probably," agreed Thorndyke. "In fact, you can see where the cases have been dragged along, and also, by that smooth indented line, where some heavy metallic object has been slid along the floor. Perhaps if we look over the straw, we may be able to judge what those cases contained."

It didn't seem to me to matter a brass farthing what they contained, but again I made no remark; and together we moved the great mass of straw, almost handful by handful, from one end of the loft to the other, while Thorndyke, not only examined the straw but even closely scrutinized the floor on which it lay.

As far as I could see, all this minute and apparently purposeless searching was entirely without result, until we were in the act of removing the last armful of straw from the corner; and even then the object that came to light did not appear a very remarkable one under the circumstances, though Thorndyke seemed to find what appeared to me a most unreasonable interest in it. The object was a pair of canvas-pliers, which Thorndyke picked up almost eagerly and examined with profound attention.

"What do you make of that, Jardine?" he asked, at length, handing the implement to me.

"It's a pair of canvas-pliers," I replied.

"Obviously," he rejoined," but what do you suppose they have been used for?"

I opined that they had been used for straining canvasses, that being their manifest function.

"But," objected Thorndyke, "he would hardly have strained his canvasses up here. Besides, you will notice that they have, in fact, been used for something else. You observe that the handles are slightly bent, as if something had been held with great force, and if you look at the jaws, you will see that that something was a metallic object about three quarters of an inch wide with sharp corners. Now, what do you make of that?"

I looked at the pliers, inwardly reflecting that I didn't care twopence what the object was, and finally said that I would give it up.

"The problem does not interest you keenly," Thorndyke remarked with a smile; "and yet it ought to, you know. However, we may consider the matter on some future occasion. Meanwhile, I shall follow your pernicious example and purloin the pliers."

His interest in this complete stranger appeared to me very singular, and it seemed for the moment to have displaced that in the mysterious case which was the object of his visit to me.

"A strange, vagabond sort of man that artist must have been," he remarked, as we walked home across the Heath, "but I suppose one picks up vagabond habits in travelling about the world."

"Do you gather that he had travelled much, then?" I asked.

"He appears to have visited New York, Brussels and Florence, which is a selection suggesting other travels."

I was wondering vaguely how Thorndyke had arrived at these facts, and was indeed about to ask him, when he suddenly changed the subject by saying: "I suppose, Jardine, you don't wander about this place alone at night?"

"I do sometimes," I replied.

"Then I shouldn't," he said; "you must remember that a very determined attempt has been made on your life, and it would be unreasonable to suppose that it was made without some purpose. But that purpose is still unaccomplished. You don't know who your enemy is, and, consequently, can take no precautions against him excepting by keeping away from solitary places. It is an uncomfortable thought, but at present, you have to remember that any chance stranger may be an intending murderer. So be on your guard."

I promised to bear his warning in mind, though I must confess his language seemed to me rather exaggerated; and so we walked on, chatting about various matters until we arrived at my lodgings.

Thorndyke was easily persuaded to come in and have tea with me, and while we were waiting for its arrival, he renewed his examination of the sketch upon the wall.

"Aren't you going to have this strained on a stretcher?" he asked.

I replied "Yes," and that I intended to take it with me the next time I went into town.

"Let me take it for you," said Thorndyke. "I should like to show it to Jervis to illustrate the route that we have marked on the map. Then I can have it left at any place that you like."

I mentioned the name of an artist's-colourman in the Hampstead Road, and, unpinning the canvas, rolled it up and handed it to him.

He took it from me and, rolling it up methodically and carefully, bestowed it in his breast pocket. Then he brought forth the map, and, as we drank our tea and talked over our investigations, he checked our route on it and marked the position of the cottage. Shortly after tea he took his leave, and I then occupied an agreeable half-hour in composing a letter to Miss Vyne to accompany the loot from the deserted house.

10
THE UNHEEDED WARNING

THOBNDYKE'S warning, so emphatically expressed, ought to have been alike unnecessary and effective. As a matter of fact, it was neither. I suppose that to a young man, not naturally timorous, the idea of a constantly lurking danger amidst the prosaic conditions of modern civilization is one that is not readily accepted. At any rate, the fact is that I continued to walk abroad by day and by night with as much unconcern as if nothing unusual had ever befallen me. It was not that the recollection of those horrible hours in the poisoned cellar had in any way faded. That incident I could never forget. But I think, that in the back of my mind, there still lingered the idea of a homicidal lunatic; though that idea had been so scornfully rejected by Thorndyke.

But before I describe the amazing experience by which I once more came within a hair's breadth of sudden and violent death, I must refer to another incident; not because it seemed to be connected with that alarming occurrence, but because it came first in the order of time, and had its own significance later.

It was a couple of days after Thorndyke's visit that I walked down the Hampstead Road with the intention of fetching the sketch from the artist's-colourman's. The shop was within a few hundred yards of Jacob Street, and as I crossed the end of that street, I was just considering whether I ought to look in on Batson, when a lady bowed to me and made as if she would stop. It was Mrs. Samway. Of course, I stopped and shook hands, and while I was making the usual polite enquiries, I felt myself once more impressed with the unusualness of the woman. Even in her dress she was unlike other women, though not in the least eccentric or bizarre. At present, she was clothed from head to foot in black; but a scarlet bird's wing in the coquettish little velvet toque, and a scarlet bow at her throat, gave an effect of colour that, unusual as it was, harmonized completely and naturally with her jet-black hair and her strange, un-English beauty.

"So you haven't started for Paris yet," I remarked.

"No," she replied; "my husband has gone and may, perhaps, come back. At any rate, I am staying in England for the present."

"Then I may possibly have the pleasure of seeing you again," I said, and she graciously replied that she hoped it might be so, as we shook hands and parted. A few minutes later, in the artist's-colourman's shop, I had another chance meeting and a more agreeable one. The proprietor had just produced the sketch, now greatly improved in appearance by being strained on a stretcher, when the glass door opened and a young lady entered the shop. Imagine my surprise when that young lady turned out to be none other than Miss Vyne.

"Well," I exclaimed, as we mutually recognized each other, "what an extraordinary coincidence!"

"I don't see that it is very extraordinary," she replied. "Most of the Hampstead people come here because it's the nearest place where you can get proper artist's materials. Is that the sketch you were telling me about?"

"Yes," I answered; "and it's the pick of the loot. But it isn't too late to alter your mind. Say the word and it's yours."

"Well," she replied, with a smile, "I am not going to say the word, but I want to thank you for rescuing those other treasures for me."

She had, as a matter of fact, already thanked me in a very pretty little note, but I was not averse to her mentioning the subject again. We stepped back to the door, and in the brighter light, looked at the sketch together.

"It's a pity," she remarked, "that he handled it so carelessly before the paint was hard. Those fingermarks wouldn't matter a bit on a brush-painted surface; but on the smooth knife-surface they are rather a disfigurement."

She placed the sketch in my hand, and I backed nearer to the glass door to get a better light. Happening to glance up, I noticed that a sudden and very curious change had come over her; a look of haughty displeasure and even anger, apparently directed at somebody or something outside the shop.

For a few moments I took no notice; then, half-unconsciously, I looked round just as some person moved away from the door. I looked once more at Miss Vyne. She was quite unmistakably angry. Her cheeks were flushed and there was a resentful light in her eyes that gave her an expression quite new to me.

I suppose she caught my enquiring glance for she exclaimed: "Did you see that woman? I never heard of such impertinence in my life."

"What did she do?" I asked.

"She came right up to the doorway and looked over your shoulder; and then stared at me in the most singular and insolent manner. I could have slapped her face."

"Not through the glass door," I suggested; on which her anger subsided in a ripple of laughter as quickly as it had arisen. "What was this objectionable person like?" I asked. "Was she a charwoman or a slavey?"

"Oh, not at all," replied Miss Vyne. "Quite a ladylike looking person, except for her manners. Rather tastefully dressed, too; a black and vermilion scheme of colour."

The reply startled me a little. "Had she a scarlet bird's wing in her hat?" I asked.

"Yes, and a scarlet bow at her throat. I hope you are not going to say that you know her."

It was a rather delicate situation. I could not actually disavow the acquaintance, but I did not feel inclined to have a black and scarlet fly introduced into the sweet-smelling ointment of my intercourse with the fair Sylvia; so I explained with great care the exact scope of the acquaintance; on which Miss Vyne remarked that "she supposed that doctors could not be held responsible for the people they knew"; and proceeded to make her purchases.

I did not take the sketch away with me after all, for it occurred to me that I might as well leave it to be framed; but instead, I carried forth with me the parcel containing Miss Vyne's purchases. I had not far to carry it, for she was returning at once to Hampstead. I was tempted to return, for the sake of enjoying a chat with her, too, but discreetly withstood the temptation, and, having escorted her to a tram, I turned my face south and walked away at a leisurely pace into the jaws of an all-unsuspected danger.

It was some hours, however, before anything remarkable happened.

My immediate objective was Lincoln's Inn Fields, where, at the College of Surgeons, a lecture on Epidermic Appendages was to be delivered by the Hunterian Professor; and there, in the college theatre, I spent a delightful hour while the genial professor took his hearers with him on a personally-conducted tour among structures that ranged from the plumage of the sun-bird to the dermal plates of the crocodile, from the silken locks of beauty to the quills of the porcupine or the mail of the armadillo.

When I came out, the dusk was just closing in. It was a slightly foggy evening. The last glow of the sunset in the western sky lighted up the haze into a rosy background, against which the shadowy buildings were relieved in shapes of cloudy grey. It was a lovely effect; an effect such as London alone can show, and fugitive as a breath on a mirror. As I sauntered westward up the Strand I presently bethought me that, before the light should have faded completely, I would see how the effect looked by the riverside. Walking quickly down Buckingham Street, I came out on to the Embankment and looked into the west. But the light was nearly gone, the shadows of evening were closing in fast, and the fog, creeping up the river, ushered in the night.

I leaned on the parapet and watched the last glimmer die away; watched the darkness deepen on the river and the faint lights on the barges moored on the southern shore at first twinkle pallidly and then fade out as the fog thickened. I lit my pipe and looked down at the dark water swirling past, and gradually fell into a train of half-dreamy meditation.

Not for the first time since the occurrence, my thoughts turned to Mrs. Samway. Why had she stared at Miss Vyne in that singular manner–if indeed it was really Mrs. Samway, and if she really had stared in the manner alleged? It was an odd affair; but, after all, it did not very much matter. And with this, my thoughts rambled off in a new direction.

It was to the cottage on the Heath that they wandered this time, and the picture of Thorndyke's cat-like prowlings and pryings arose before me. That was very queer, too. Was it possible that this learned and astute man habitually went about eagerly probing into the personal habits and trivial actions of chance strangers? The apparently puerile inquisitiveness that he had displayed seemed totally out of character with all that I knew about the man; but then it often happens that the private life of public men develops personal traits that are surprising and disappointing to those who have only known them in connection with their public activities.

I had become so completely immersed in my thoughts as to be almost oblivious of what was happening around. Indeed, there was mighty little happening. The gathering darkness and the thin fog limited my view to a few square yards. Now and again, a muffled hoot from the lower river spoke of life and movement on the water, and at long intervals an occasional wayfarer would pass along the pavement behind me.

My reflections had reached the point recorded above, when a person emerged from the obscurity near to the parapet and approached as if to pass close behind me. I only caught the dusky shape indistinctly with the tail of my eye; so indistinctly that I could not say certainly whether it was that of a man or a woman, for I was still gazing down at the dark water. He or she approached quietly, swerving towards me across the wide pavement, and was in the act of passing quite close to me when the thing happened. Of a sudden, I felt my knees clasped in a powerful grip, and at the same moment I was lifted off my feet and thrust forward over the parapet. Instinctively, I clutched at the stonework, but its flat surface offered nothing for my fingers to grasp. Then my assailant let go, and the next instant I plunged head-first into the icy water.

It was fortunate for me that the tide was nearly full, else must I, almost certainly, have broken my neck. As it was, my head struck on the firm mud at the bottom with such force, that for some moments I was half-stunned. Nevertheless, I must have struck out automatically, for when I began to recover my wits my head was above water, and I was swimming as actively as my clinging garments would let me. But, apparently, in those moments of dazed semi-consciousness, I must have struck out towards the middle of the river, for now I was encompassed by a murky void in which nothing was visible save one or two reddish, luminous patches- presumably, the lamps on the Embankment.

Towards one of these I turned and struck out vigorously. The water was desperately cold, and hampered as I was with my clothing, I felt that I should not be able to keep myself afloat very long, strong swimmer as I was. The dim, red nebula of the unseen lamps moved past slowly, showing me that I was drifting down on the ebb-tide. Before me, I knew, was the long, inhospitable wall of the Embankment. True, there were some steps, if I was not mistaken, by Cleopatra's Needle, but the question was whether I had not drifted past them already. I had given one or two lusty shouts as soon as I had cleared my chest of the mouthful of water that I got in my first plunge, and I was now letting off another yell, when, out of the darkness behind me, came a prolonged hoot.

I looked round quickly in the direction whence the sound had come, and then became aware of the churning of a propeller. Almost at the same moment, a dim, ruddy smudge of light broke through the darkness over the river, and began rapidly to brighten until it took the form of the twin mast-head lights of a tug with a vessel in tow.

For a moment I hesitated. My first impulse was to avoid the danger of being run down; but suddenly I altered my mind. For, as the tug bore down on me, with a roaring of water and a loud clank of machinery, I saw that she was not absolutely end-on, for her green starboard light, which had been for a moment visible, suddenly disappeared. Of what happened during the next few moments, I have but a confused recollection.

A splashing and churning, with the loud wash of water, the throb of the engines and a glare of light which blazed before my eyes for a moment, to vanish in an instant into pitchy darkness; a huge, black object, felt rather than seen to sweep past before me; and then my hand clutched a wooden projection, and I felt myself dragged violently through the water. The projection that I had laid hold of was the lee-board of a sailing barge, as I discovered when the rush of the water banged me against it; and much ado I had to hold on, with the water dragging at me and spouting up over my head. But, with what strength was left to me, I reached out with the other hand and clawed hold of the dwarf bulwark over which the water was lapping; and so, with a last violent effort, contrived to drag myself up on to the deck.

I essayed to stand up, and did, in fact, succeed, but as my sensations suggested those of a leaden statue with india-rubber legs, I sat down hastily on the hatch-cover to avoid going overboard. And there I sat for a minute or two leaning against the lowered mast with my teeth chattering, and seeming to grow more and more chilled and exhausted every moment.

Numb as my mind was by this time, my medical instincts told me that this would not do. Somehow I must get warmth and shelter, for I might as well have been drowned at once as die of exposure and cold. I looked round lethargically. There was no sign of any-one on board. Another barge was towing alongside, and the bows of two others were dimly visible astern. On those rear-most barges there must certainly have been someone steering. But they were inaccessible to me, and I had not the energy to shout; nor could anyone have got across to me if I had.

Suddenly my eye fell on the little chimney that rose by the cabin scuttle. A thin stream of smoke issued from it and blew away astern. Perhaps, then, the crew were below, or, if not, at least there was a fire. I crawled aft, holding on with my hands, and, pushing back the scuttle, backed cautiously down the ladder closing the scuttle after me.

There seemed to be nobody below, and the cabin was in darkness, save for the glow of the fire that burned in the little grate. The air was probably warm, though to me it felt icy; but, at least, there was no wind to play on my wet clothes.

I sat down on the locker as near to the fire as I could, and rested my elbows on the little triangular table. Chilled to the marrow and utterly exhausted, I was sensible of a growing desire to sleep; a desire which I repressed, as I believed, with noble resolution. But apparently my efforts in this respect were not so successful as I had supposed, for the next incident opened with suspicious suddenness.

A vigorous shake, which dislodged one of my elbows, introduced the episode.

I looked up, blinking sulkily, at a bright and most objectionably dazzling light, which further inspection showed to proceed from a hurricane lamp held by a rather dirty hand.

"Here, wake up, mister," said a hoarse voice, "this here ain't the Hotel Cecil, you know."

I sat up and stared vaguely at the speaker, or at least, the holder of the lamp, but could not think of anything appropriate to say. Then another voice emerged from nowhere in particular.

"'E's been overboard, that's what 'e's been."

"Any fool can see that," said the first man;" but the question is, who is he and what's he a-doin' in my cabin? Who are yer, mister?"

Now, that would seem to be a perfectly simple and straightforward question. But it is not so simple as it seems. To a complete stranger, the bare mention of a name is unilluminating. Further explanations are needed. And at that moment I did not feel equal to explanations. Besides, I was not so very clear on the subject myself. Consequently, I preserved a silence which, perhaps, was wooden rather than golden.

"D'ye 'ear?" persisted the first man. "I'm a-arskin' you a question."

"What'a the good of arskin' questions of a man what's been a-rammin' 'is crumpet aginst the bottom of the river?" protested the other man.

"What d'ye mean?" demanded the first mariner.

"Can't you see?" retorted the other," as 'e's took the ground 'ard? Look at 'is 'ed."

Here the first mariner–Lucifer, or lamp-bearer–wiped his hand over the top of my head and then examined the tip of his forefinger critically as though it were the arming of a deep-sea lead.

"You're right, Abel," said he. "That's mud off the bottom, that is. He must have took a regular header. Sooicide perhaps, and altered his mind. Found it a bit damper'n what he expected. Put the kittle on, Abe."

From this moment, the two mariners treated me as if I had been a lay-figure. Silently, they peeled off my wet clothes, and dried my skin with vigorous friction as if it had been a wet deck. They not only asked no further questions, but when I would have spoken they urged me to economize my wind. They inducted me into stiff and hairy garments of uncouth aspect, and filially, Abe set before me on the table a large earthenware mug, the contents of which steamed and diffused through the cabin a strong odour of Dutch gin.

"You git outside that, mister," said the luminiferous mariner (who turned out subsequently to be the skipper), "and then you'd best turn in."

The treatment was not strictly orthodox, but I obeyed without demur. Most people would have done the same under the circumstances. But the process of "getting outside" it took time, for the grog was boiling hot and had been brewed with a flexible wrist. By the time that I had emptied the mug I was not only revived, but (so far as my memory serves) rather disposed to be garrulously explanatory and facetious. I even felt a slight inclination to sing. But my friends would stand no nonsense. As soon as the mug was fairly empty, they bundled me, neck and crop, into a sort of elongated cupboard and proceeded to pile on me untold quantities of textile fabrics, including a complete suit of oilskins. Then they commanded me to go to sleep; which I believe I must have done almost instantly.

11
A CHAPTER OF ACCIDENTS

AWAKENING in a strange place is always a memorable experience; especially to the young, in whom the capacity for novel sensations has not yet been exhausted by repetition. When I emerged, somewhat gradually, from the unconsciousness of sleep, my first impressions concerned themselves with the unusual appearance of the bedroom wall and its remarkable proximity to my nose. I further noticed that the bedstead had become inexplicably tilted and that the house appeared to be swaying; and as I mused on these phenomena with the vagueness of the half-awake, a loud voice, proceeding apparently from the floor above, roared out the mystic words, "Lee-O!" whereupon there ensued a sound like the shaking of colossal table cloths and the loud clanking of chains, and my bedstead took a sharp tilt to the opposite side. This roused me pretty completely, and turning over in the bunk, I looked out into the barge's cabin.

It was broad daylight and evidently not early, for a square patch of sunlight crept to and fro on the little table, whence presently it slipped down to the floor and slithered about unsteadily, as if Phoebus had overdone his morning dram and could not drive his chariot straight. I watched it lazily for some time and then, becoming conscious of a vacancy within, crept out from under the mountain of bedclothes and made my way to the ladder.

As I put my head through the companion hatch, a man who stood at the wheel regarded me stolidly.

"So you've woke up, have yer?" said he. "Thought you was going right round the clock. Abel! He's woke up. Tell young Ted to stand by with them heggs and that there 'addick."

Here Abel looked round from behind the luff of the mainsail, and having verified the statement, conveyed the order to some invisible person in the fore-peak. Then he came aft with an obvious air of business. The time for explanations had arrived.

Accordingly I proceeded to "pitch them my yarn," as they expressed it; to which they listened with polite attention and manifest disappointment, clearly regarding the story as a fabrication from beginning to end. And no wonder. The whole affair was utterly incredible even to me; to them it must have seemed sheer nonsense. Their own verdict of "sooicide" during very temporary insanity with sudden mental recovery, under the influence of cold water, was so much more rational. Not that they obtruded their views. They listened patiently and said nothing; and nothing that they could have said could have been more expressive.

Meanwhile I looked about me with no little surprise. Some miles away to the south lay a stretch of low land, faint and grey, with a single salient object, apparently a church with two spires. In every other direction was the unbroken sea horizon.

"You seem to have made a pretty good passage," I remarked.

"We've had sixteen hours to do it in," replied the skipper," and spring tides and a nice bit of breeze. If it 'ud only hold-which I'm afraid it won't-we'd be in Folkestone Harbour this time to-morrow, or even sooner. Folkestone be much out of your way?"

I smiled at the artlessness of the question. It was undeniable that the route from Charing Cross to Hampstead by way of Folkestone was slightly indirect. But there was no need to insist on the fact. My hospitable friends had acted for the best and their prudence was justified by the result; for here I was, not a whit the worse for my ducking save that I badly wanted a bath.

"Folkestone will suit me quite well," I replied, "if there is enough money left in my pockets to pay my fare home." "That's all right," said the skipper. "I cleared out your pockets myself. You'll find the things in a mug in the starboard locker. Better overhaul 'em when you go below and see if you've dropped anything. Here comes young Ted with your grub."

As he spoke the apprentice rose through the fore-hatch like a stage apparition–if one can imagine an apparition burdened with a tin tea-pot, two "heggs" and an "'addick"–and came grinning along the weather side-deck, to vanish through the cabin hatchway. I followed gleefully, and, almost before young Ted had finished the somewhat informal table arrangements, fell to on the food with voracious joy.

"If you want any more eggs or anythink," said the apprentice, "all you've got to do is just to touch the electric bell and the waiter'll come and take your orders," and having delivered this delicate shaft of irony he presented me with an excellent back view of a pair of brown dreadnoughts as he retired up the ladder.

As I consumed the rough but excellent breakfast I reflected on the strange events that had placed me in my present odd situation. For the first time, I began fairly to realize that I was in some way involved in a nexus of circumstances that I did not in the least understand. I had an enemy; a vindictive enemy, too, in whose eyes mere human life was a thing of no account. But who could he be? I knew of no one on whom I had ever inflicted the smallest injury. I bore no man any grudge and had never to my knowledge had unfriendly dealings with any human creature. Was this inveterate enemy of mine anyone whom I knew? Or was he some stranger whose path I had crossed without knowing it, and whom I should not recognize even if I saw him?

This last supposition was highly disquieting, especially as it seemed rather probable; for if my enemy was unknown to me, what precautions could I take? Then, again, there was the question! What was the occasion of this extraordinary vendetta? What had I done to this man that he should pursue me with such deadly purpose? As to Jervis's suggestion, that I had seen something at the Samways' house that I was not wanted to see, there was nothing in it; for, as a matter of fact, I had seen nothing. There was nothing to see. The man Maddock was certainly dead. As to what he died of, that was Batson's affair; but even in that there was no sign of anything suspicious. The man himself had consulted Batson, and had thought so badly of himself that he had made his will in Batson's presence. The patient himself was fully aware of his serious condition; it was only Batson, with his eternal hurry and bustle and his defective eyesight, who had missed observing it. The only circumstance that supported Jervis's view was that the acts of violence seemed to be connected with the locality of Batson's house.

Of course there remained the mystery of the dead priest or lay-brother. But with that these attempts seemed to have no connection. Nor was there any reason why the murderer should pursue me. I had seen the body, it is true; but nobody believed me and no proceedings were being taken. Nor could I have identified the murderer if I had been confronted with him. Clearly, he had nothing to fear from me.

From the causes of my present predicament I passed to the immediate future. I should have to get back from Folkestone, and I ought to send a telegram to my landlady, Mrs. Blunt, who would probably be in a deuce of a twitter about me. I raised the lid of the locker, and, reaching out the big earthenware mug, emptied its contents on the table. All my portable property seemed to be there, including the little gold reliquary, which I had carelessly carried in my pocket ever since I had shown it to Thorndyke. My available funds were some four or five pounds; amply sufficient to get me home and to discharge my liability to the skipper as well. I swept the things back into the mug, which I returned to the locker, and having cut myself another thick slice of bread, proceeded with the largest breakfast that I have ever eaten.

The skipper's forebodings were justified by the course of events. When I came on deck the breeze had died down to a mere faint breath, hardly sufficient to keep the big red main-sail asleep—as the pretty old nautical phrase has it. The skipper was still at the wheel and Abel was anxiously taking soundings with a hand-lead.

"You won't do it, Bill," said the latter, coiling up the lead-line with an air of finality, "this 'ere breeze is a-petering right out."

The skipper said nothing, but stared gloomily at the land which was now right ahead and much nearer than when I had last looked; and from the land his eye travelled to a sand-bank from which rose a tall post at the top of which was an inverted cone.

"Ought to a-gone about a bit sooner, Bill," pursued Abel; whereupon the skipper turned on him fiercely.

"What's the good o' saying that now!" he demanded. "If you'd a-told me the wind was going to drop, I a-gone about sooner. What water is there?"

"Five fathom here," replied Abel; "that means one and a quarter on the Woolpack. You'd best shove her nose round now, Bill."

"Oh, all right!" retorted the skipper, "Lee-O! This is going to be an all-night job, this is," and with this gloomy prediction, he spun the wheel round viciously, and once more headed away from the land.

Prophecy appeared to be the skipper's speciality and, like most prophets, he tended to view the future with an unfavourable eye. Gradually the breeze died away into a dead calm, so that we had presently to let go the anchor to avoid drifting on to a great sand-bank which now lay between us and the land. And here we remained not only for the rest of the day and the succeeding night, as the skipper had promised, but throughout the whole of the next day and following night. I have already remarked on the incalculable chances by which the course of a man's life is determined. Looking back now, I see that the skipper's little miscalculation and his failure to cross the Woolpack Shoal into the inshore channel, was an antecedent determining the most momentous consequences for me. For had the barge been becalmed in the inshore channel, I could, and should, have landed in the boat and returned home forthwith; and if I had, certain events would not have happened and my life might have run a very different course. As it was miles of sea and the great bank known as the Margate Sand, lay between me and the-shore; whence I was committed to the wanderings and dallyings of the barge as irrevocably as if we were crossing the Pacific.

We lay, then, in the Queen's Channel, outside Margate Sand, for two whole days and nights; during which time the skipper and Abel slept much and smoked more, and young Ted, having cleaned and dried my clothes, inducted me into the art of bottom-fishing. On the third day, a faint breath of breeze enabled us to crawl round the North Foreland, and the skipper having elected to pass outside the Goodwin, managed to get becalmed again in the neighbourhood of the East Goodwin Lightship. A little breeze at night enabled us to move on a few miles farther; and so we continued to crawl along at intervals, mainly on the tide, until nine o'clock in the morning of the fifth day, when we finally crawled into Folkestone Harbour.

As soon as the barge was brought up to a buoy, young Ted was detailed to put me ashore in the boat. The skipper and Abel had insisted on treating me as a guest, and I had perforce to accept the position. But young Ted had no such pride; and when I ran up the wooden steps by the old fish-market, I left him on the stage below, staring with an incredulous grin at a gold coin in his none-too-delicate palm.

I was not sorry to be landed in this unfashionable quarter of the town, for in spite of young Ted's efforts, my turn-out left much to be desired, especially in the matter of shirt-cuffs and collar, and I was, moreover, hatless and somewhat imperfectly shaved. Accordingly, I slunk inconspicuously past the market and the groups of lounging fishermen, and when I saw a well-dressed, lady-like woman preceding me into the little narrow street, known as the Stade, I slackened my pace so as not to overtake her. She sauntered along with a leisurely air as if she were waiting for something or somebody, and this and the fact that she carried a light canvas portmanteau and a rug, suggested to me that she was probably travelling by the cross-channel boat which was due to start presently.

Suddenly my attention was diverted from her by a loud chattering and a series of shouts. A small crowd of men and women ran excitedly past the end of the little street. The clattering rapidly drew nearer; and then a horse, with a light van, swept round the corner and passing under an archway, advanced at a furious gallop. Evidently the horse had bolted and now, mad with terror, dashed forward with trailing reins, zigzagging erratically and making the van sway to and fro, so that it took up the whole of the narrow street. The few wayfarers darted into doorways and sheltered corners, and I was about to secure my own safety in a similar manner, when I noticed that the woman in front of me had apparently become petrified with terror, for she stood stock still, gazing helplessly at the approaching horse. It was no time for ceremony. The infuriated animal and the swaying van were thundering up the street like an insane Juggernaut, With a hasty apology, I seized the woman from behind and half-dragged, half-carried her to the opening of a little yard beside a sail-loft. And even then, I was hardly quick enough, for as the van roared past, some projecting object struck me between the shoulders and sent me flying, face downwards, on to a pile of tarred drift-net.

I had had the presence of mind to let go, as I was struck, so that my fair protégée was not involved in my downfall; but in a moment, she was stooping over me, and with many expressions of concern, endeavouring to help me to rise. Beyond a thump in the back, however, I was not hurt in the least, but picked myself up, grinning and turned to reassure her. And then I really did get a shock; for as I turned, the woman gave a shriek and fell back on the steps of the sail-loft, gasping, and staring at me with an expression of the utmost astonishment and terror. I supposed the accident had upset her nerves; but to be sure, my own received, as I have said, a pretty severe shock. For the woman was Mrs. Samway.

We remained for a moment or two gazing at one another in mute astonishment. Then I recollected myself, and advanced to shake hands; but to my discomfiture, she shrank away from me and began to sob and laugh in an unmistakably hysterical fashion. I must confess that I was somewhat surprised at these manifestations in so robust a woman as Mrs. Samway. Unreasonably so, indeed, for all women-kind are more or less prone to hysteria; but whereas the normal woman tends to laugh and cry, the weaker vessels develop inexplicable diseases, with a tendency to social reform and emancipation.

I put on my best bedside manner, at once matter-of-fact and persuasive.

"You seem quite upset," I said, "and all about nothing, for the poor beggar of a horse must be half a mile away by now."

"Yes," she answered shakily, "it's ridiculous of me, but it was so sudden and so—" here she laughed noisily, and as the laugh ended in a portentous sniff, I hastened to continue the conversation.

"Yes, it was a bit of a facer to see that beast coming up the street as if it was Tottenham Corner. Why on earth didn't you get out of the way?"

"I am sure I don't know." she answered. "I seemed to be paralyzed and idiotic and–" here the laughter began again.

"Well," I interrupted cheerfully," you didn't get rolled on those tarred nets, so that's something to be thankful for."

This was a rather unlucky shot, for the semblance of facetiousness started a most alarming train of giggles, interrupted by rather loud sobs; but at this point, a new curative influence made itself manifest. Two smack boys halted outside the opening and surveyed her with frank interest and pleased surprise. Simultaneously, an elderly mariner appeared at the door of the sail-loft, grasping a black bottle and a tea-cup, and rather shyly descending the steps, suggested that "perhaps a drop o' sperits might do the lady good."

Mrs. Samway bounced off the steps, her hitherto pale cheeks aflame with anger. "I am making a fool of myself," she exclaimed. "Let us go away from here."

She walked out into the street, and I, having thanked the old gentleman for his most efficacious remedy, followed. As soon as I caught her up, she turned on me quickly and held out her hand.

"Good-bye, Dr. Jardine," she said, "and thank you so very much for risking your life for a–for a wretched giggling woman."

"Oh, you're not going to send me packing like this," I protested, 'when we've hardly said good morning. Besides, you're not fit to be left. But you're not to begin laughing again," I added, threateningly, for an ominous twitching of her mouth seemed to herald a relapse, "or I shall go back and get that black bottle."

She shook her head impatiently, but without looking at me. "I would rather you went away, Dr. Jardine," she said in an agitated voice. "I would, really. I wish to be alone. Don't think me ungracious. I am really most grateful to you, but I would rather you left me now."

Of course there was nothing more to be said. She was not really ill or in need of assistance, and probably her instinct was right. Hysteria is not one of those affections which waste their sweetness on the desert air, I shook her hand cordially and, advising her to keep out of the way of stray vans and horses, once more pursued my way towards the town, meditating as I went, on the oddity of the whole affair. It was an astonishing coincidence that I should have run against this woman in this out of the way place. I had left her but a few days since apparently firmly rooted in the Hampstead Road, and now, behold, as I step ashore from the barge, she is almost the first person that I meet. And yet the coincidence, which had evidently hit her as hard as it had me, like most coincidences, tended to disappear on closer inspection. The only really odd feature was my own presence in Folkestone. As to Mrs. Samway, she had probably been sent for by her husband, and was crossing by the boat that was now due to start.

Her anxiety to get rid of me was more puzzling, until I suddenly remembered my bare head, my crumpled collar and generally raffish and disreputable appearance. The latter was, in fact, at this moment brought to my notice by a man, with whom, in my preoccupation, I collided; who first uttered an impatient exclamation and then, bestowing on me a quick stare of astonishment, muttered a hasty apology and hurried past. The incident emphasized the necessity for some reform, and I mended my pace towards the region of shops in a very ferment of uncomfortable self-consciousness.

With the purchase of a new hat, a collar, a pair of cuffs, a neck-tie, a pair of gloves and a stick, some faint glimmer of self-respect revived in me. I was even conscious of a temptation to linger in Folkestone and spend a few hours by the sea; but a sense of duty, aided by a large, muddy stain on my coat, finally decided me to return to town at once. Accordingly, having sent off a telegram to my landlady and ascertained that a train left for London in about twenty minutes, I betook myself to the station.

There were comparatively few people travelling by this particular train; in fact, when I had established myself with the morning paper in the off-side corner seat of a smoking compartment, I began, with an Englishman's proverbial unsociability, to congratulate myself on the prospect of having the compartment to myself, when my hopes were dashed by the entrance of an elderly clergyman; who not only broke up my solitude, but aggravated the offence by quite unnecessarily seating himself opposite to me. I was almost tempted to move to another corner, for my length of leg gives an added value to space; but it seemed a rude thing to do; and as the train moved off at this moment, I resigned myself to the trifling discomfort.

My clerical friend was a somewhat uncommon-looking man, with a countenance at once strong and secretive; a rectangular, masterful face, with a bull-like dew-lap and a small, and very sharp, Roman nose. On further inspection, I decided that he was either a High-Church parson or a Roman Catholic priest. His proceedings seemed to favour the latter hypothesis, for the train was barely out of the station before he had whisked out of his pocket an ecclesiastical-looking volume, which he opened at a marked place, and instantly began to read. I watched him with inquisitive interest, for his manner of reading was very singular. There was something habitual, almost mechanical, about it, suggesting an allotted and familiar task, and a lack of concentration that suggested a corresponding lack of novelty in the matter. As he read, his lips moved, and now and again I caught a faint whisper, by which I gathered that he was reading rapidly; but the most singular phenomenon was, that when his eyes strayed out of the carriage window, as they did at frequent intervals, his lips went on sputtering with unabated rapidity. Quite suddenly he appeared to come to the end of a sort of literary measured mile, for even as his lips were still moving, he clapped in the book-mark, shut the volume, and returned it to his pocket with a curious air of businesslike finality.

As his eyes were no longer occupied with the book, my observations had to be suspended, and my attention was now turned to my own affairs. Putting my hand in my coat pocket for my pipe and pouch, I became aware of a state of confusion in the said pocket which I had already noticed when making my purchases. The fact is, that I had nearly come away from the barge without my portable property. It was only at the last moment that the skipper, remembering the mug, had fetched it hurriedly from the locker and shot its contents bodily into my coat pocket. The present seemed a good opportunity for distributing the various articles among their proper receptacles. Accordingly I turned out the whole pocketful on the seat by my side, and a remarkably miscellaneous collection they formed; comprising knives, pencils, match-box, keys, the minor implements of my craft, and various other objects, useful and useless, including the little gold reliquary.

My neighbour opposite was, I think, quite interested in my proceedings, though he kept up a dignified pretence of being entirely unaware of my existence. Only for a while, however. Suddenly he sat up, very wide awake, and slewing his head round, stared with undisguised intentness at my little collection. I guessed at once what it was that had attracted his attention. A cleric would not be thrilled by the sight of a clinical thermometer or an ophthalmoscope. It was the reliquary that had caught his eye. That was an article in his own line of business.

With deliberate mischief, I left the little bauble exposed to view as I very slowly and methodically conveyed the other things one by one, each to its established pocket. Last of all, I picked up the reliquary and held it irresolutely as if debating where I should stow it. And at this point His Reverence intervened, unable any longer to contain his curiosity. "Zat is a very remargable liddle opchect, sir," he said in excellent Anglo-German. "Might one bresume to ask vat it's use is?"

I handed the reliquary to him and he took it from me with ill-disguised eagerness. "I understand," said I, "that it is a reliquary. But you probably know more about such things than I do. I haven't opened it so I can't say what is inside."

He nodded gravely. "Zo! I am glad to hear you zay zat. Brobably zere is inside some holy relic vich ought not to be touched egzepting by bious handts."

He turned the case over, and, putting on a pair of spectacles–which he had not appeared to require for reading–closely scrutinized the inscriptions, and even the wisp of cord that remained attached to one of the rings.

"You zay," he resumed without raising his eyes, " zat you understandt zat zis is a reliquary. Do you not zen know? Ze berson who gafe it to you, did he not tell you vat it gondained?"

"It wasn't given to me at all," I replied. "In fact, it isn't properly mine. I picked it up and am merely keeping it until I find the owner."

He pondered this statement with a degree of profundity that seemed rather out of proportion to its matter; and he continued to gaze at the reliquary, never once raising his eyes to mine. At length, after a considerable pause and a most unnecessary amount of reflection, he asked: "Might one ask, if you shall bardon my guriosity, vere you found zis liddle opchect?"

I hesitated before replying. My first, and natural, impulse was to tell him exactly where and under what circumstances I had found the "opchect." But the way in which my information had been received by the police had made me rather chary of offering confidences; besides which, I had half promised them not to talk about the affair. And, after all, it was no business of this good gentleman's where I found it. My answer was, therefore, not very explicit.

"I picked it up in a lane at Hampstead, near London."

"At Hampstead!" he repeated. "Zo! Zat would be-a very good blace to find such sings. I mean," he added, hastily, "zere are many beople in zat blace and some of zem will be of ze old religion."

Now, this last remark was such palpable nonsense that it set me speculating on what he had intended to say, for it was obvious that he had altered his mind in the middle of the sentence and completed it with the first words that came to hand. However, as I could read no sense into it at all, I said that "perhaps he was right," which seemed an eminently safe rejoinder to an unintelligible statement.

When he had finished his minute examination of the reliquary, he handed it back to me with such evident reluctance that, if it had been mine, I should have been tempted to ask him to accept it. But it was not mine. I was only a trustee. So I made no remark, but watched him as he, very deliberately, took off his spectacles and returned them to their case, looking meanwhile, at the floor with an air of deep abstraction. He appeared to be thinking hard, and I was quite curious as to what his next remark would be. A considerable interval elapsed before he spoke again; but at last the remark came, in the form of a question, and very disappointing it was.

"You are not berhaps very much interested in relics and reliquaries?"

As a matter of fact, I didn't care two straws for either the one or the other; but there was no need to put it as strongly as that.

"We are apt," I replied, "to find a lack of interest in subjects of which we are ignorant." (That was a fine sentence. It might have come straight out of Sandford and Merton.

"Zat is vat I sink, too," he rejoined. "Ve do not know; ve do not care. But zere is a very eggeilent liddle book vich egsplains all ze gustoms and zeremonies gonnected vid relics of ze zainte. I should like you to read zat book. Vill you bermit me to send you a gobby vich I haf?"

Of course I said I should be delighted. It was an outrageous falsehood, but what else could I say?

"Zen," said he, "I shall haf great pleasure in zending it to you if you vill kindly tell me how I shall address it."

I presented him with my card, which he read very attentively before bestowing it in his pocket-book.

"I see," he remarked, "zat you are a doctor of medicine. It is a fine brofession, if one does not too much vorget ze spiritual life in garing for zat of ze body."

In this I acquiesced vaguely, and the conversation drifted into detached commonplaces, finally petering out as we approached Paddock Wood; where my reverend acquaintance bought a newspaper and underwent a total eclipse behind it.

As soon as the train started again, I took up my own paper; and the very first glance at it gave me a shock of surprise that sent all other matters clean out of my mind. It was an advertisement in the column headed "Personal" that attracted my attention, an advertisement that commenced with the word "Missing," in large type, and went on to offer Two Hundred Pounds Reward: thus: –

"MISSING. TWO HUNDRED POUNDS REWARD.

Whereas, on the 14th inst., Dr. Humphrey Jardine disappeared from his home and his usual places of resort; the above reward will be paid to any person who shall give information as to his whereabouts, if alive, or the whereabouts of his body if he is dead. He was last seen at 12.20 pm on the above date in the Hampstead Road, and was then walking towards Euston Road. The missing man is about twenty-six years of age; is somewhat over six feet in height; of medium complexion; has brown hair, grey eyes, straight nose and a rather thin face, which is clean-shaved. He was wearing a dark tweed suit, and soft felt hat.

"Information should be given to Hector Brodribb, Esquire, 65, New Square, Lincoln's Inn, by whom the above reward will be paid."

Here was a pretty state of affairs: It seemed that while I was placidly taking events as they came; smoking the skipper's tobacco and bottom-fishing with young Ted; my escapade had been producing somewhere a most almighty splash. I read the advertisement again, with a self-conscious grin, and out of it there arose one or two rather curious questions. In the first place, who the deuce was Hector Brodribb? And what concern was I of his? And how came he to know that I was walking down Hampstead Road at 12.20 on the 14th inst.?

I felt very little doubt it was actually Thorndyke who was tweaking the strings of the Brodribbian puppet. But even this left the mystery unsolved. For how did Thorndyke know? This was only the fifth day after my disappearance, and it would seem that there had hardly been time for exhaustive enquiries.

Then another highly interesting fact emerged. The only person who had seen me walk away down Hampstead Road was Sylvia Vyne; whence it followed that Thorndyke, or the mysterious Brodribb, had in some way got into touch with her. And reflecting on this, the mechanism of the enquiry came into view. The connecting-link was, of course, the sketch. Thorndyke had, himself, left the canvas with Mr. Robinson, the artist's-colourman, and he must have called to enquire if I had collected it. Then, he would have been told of my meeting with Miss Vyne, and as she was a regular customer, Mr. Robinson would have been able to give him her address. It was all perfectly simple, the only remarkable feature being the extraordinary promptitude with which the inquiry had been carried out. Which went to show how much more clearly Thorndyke had realized the danger that surrounded me than I had myself.

These various reflections gave me full occupation during the remainder of the journey, extending themselves into consideration of how I should act in the immediate future. My first duty was obviously to report myself to Thorndyke without delay; after which, I persuaded myself, it would be highly necessary for me personally to re-assure the fair, and, perhaps, anxious Sylvia. As to how this was to be managed, I was not quite clear, and in spite of the most profound cogitation, I had reached no conclusion when the train rumbled into Charing Cross Station.

12
MISS VYNE

As I stepped out on to the platform with a valedictory bow to my reverend fellow-passenger, my irresolution came to an end and my duty became clear. I must, in common decency, report myself at once to Thorndyke, seeing that he had been at so much trouble on my account. His card, which he had given me, I had unfortunately—or perhaps fortunately, as it turned out—left on the mantelpiece at my lodgings; but I remembered that the address was King's Bench Walk and assumed that I should have no difficulty in finding the house. Nor had I, for, as I entered the Temple by the Tudor Street gate—having overshot my mark on the Embankment—I was almost immediately confronted by a fine brick doorway surmounted by a handsome pediment and bearing legibly painted on its jamb, "First pair, Dr. Thorndyke."

I ascended the "first pair" of stairs, which brought me to an open oak door, massive and iron-bound, and a closed inner door, on the brass knocker of which I executed a flourish that would have done credit to a Belgravian footman; whereupon the door opened and a small man of sedate and clerical aspect regarded me with an air of mild enquiry.

"Is Dr. Thorndyke at home?" I asked.

"No, sir. He is at the hospital."

"Dr. Jervis?"

"Is watching a case in the Probate Court. Perhaps you would like to leave a message or write a note. A message in writing would be preferable."

"I don't know that it's necessary," said I. "My name is Jardine, and if you tell him that I called that will probably be enough."

The little man gave me a quick, bird-like glance of obviously heightened interest. "If you are Dr. Humphrey Jardine," said he, "I think a few explanatory words would be acceptable. The Doctor has been extremely uneasy about you. A short note and an appointment, either here or at the hospital, would be desirable."

With this he stepped back, holding the door invitingly open, and I entered, wondering who the deuce this prim little cathedral dean might be, with his persuasive manners and his quaintly precise forms of speech. He placed a chair for me at the table, and, having furnished me with writing materials, stood a little way off, unobtrusively examining me as I wrote. I had finished the short letter, closed it up and addressed it, and was rising to go, when, almost automatically, I took out my watch and glanced at it. Of course it had stopped.

"Can you tell me the time?" I asked.

My acquaintance drew out his own watch and replied deliberately: "Seventeen minutes and forty seconds past one." He paused for a moment and then added: "I hope, sir, you have not got any water into your watch."

"I'm afraid I have," I replied, rather taken aback by the rapidity of his diagnosis. "But I'll just wind it up to make sure."

"Oh, don't do that, sir!" he exclaimed. "Allow me to examine it before you disturb the movement."

He whipped out of his pocket a watchmaker's eyeglass, which miraculously glued itself to his eye, and, having taken a brief glance at the opened watch, produced a minute pocket screw-driver and a sheet of paper; and, in the twinkling of an eye, as it seemed to me, the paper was covered with the dismembered structures which had in their totality formed my timepiece.

"It's quite a small matter, sir," was his report, as he rose from his inspection and pocketed his eye-glass. "Just a speck or two of rust. If you will take my watch for the present, I will have your own in going order by the next time you call."

It seemed an odd transaction; but the little man's manner, though quiet, was so decisive that I took his proffered watch, and, affixing it to my chain, thanked him for his kindness and departed, wondering if it was possible that this prim clerical little person could possibly be the "tame mechanic" of whom Thorndyke had spoken.

Travelling in London was comparatively slow in those days—which, perhaps, was none the worse for a near and pleasant suburb like Hampstead; it had turned half-past two when I let myself into my lodgings with a rather rusty key and almost literally, fell into the arms of Mrs. Blunt. I feared, for a moment, that she was going to kiss me. But that was a false alarm. What she actually did was to seize both my hands and burst into tears with such violence as to cover me with confusion and cause the servant maid to rise like a domestic, and highly inquisitive, apparition from the kitchen stairs. I pacified Mrs. Blunt as well as I could and shook hands heartily with the maid, who thereupon retired, much gratified, to the underworld, whence presently issued an odour suggestive of sacrificial rites, not entirely unconnected with fried onions, and accompanied by an agreeable hissing sound.

"But wherever have you been all this time?" Mrs. Blunt asked, as she preceded me up the stairs wiping her eyes," and why didn't you send us a line just to say that you were all right?"

To this question I made a somewhat guarded answer in so far as the cause of my immersion in the river was concerned; otherwise I gave her a fairly correct account of my adventures.

"Well, well," was her comment, "I suppose it was all for the best, but I do think those sailors might have put you on shore somewhere. Dear me, what a time it has

been. I couldn't sleep at night for thinking of you, and
what Susan and I have eaten between us wouldn't have
kept a sparrow alive. And Dr. Thorndyke, too, I'm sure he
was very anxious and worried about you, though he is
such a quiet, self-contained man that you can't tell what
he is thinking of. And Lord; what a lot of questions he do
ask, to be sure!"

"By the way, how did he come to know that I was
missing?"

"Why I told him, of course. When you didn't come
home that night–which Susan and me sat up for you until
three in the morning–I thought there must be something
wrong, you being so regular in your habits; so next day,
the very first thing, I took his card from your mantelpiece
and down I went to his office and told him what had
happened. He came up here that evening to see if you had
come home, and he's been here every day since to
enquire."

"Has he really?"

"Yes. In a hansom cab. Every single day. And so has
the young lady."

"The young lady!" I exclaimed. "What young lady?"

Mrs. Blunt regarded me with something as nearly
approaching a wink as can be imagined in association
with an elderly female of sedate aspect.

"Now," she protested slyly, "as if you didn't know!
What young lady indeed! Why, Miss Vyne, to be sure; and
a very sweet young lady she is, and talked to me just as
simple and friendly as if she'd been an ordinary young
woman."

"How do you know that she isn't an ordinary young
woman?" I asked.

Mrs. Blunt was shocked. "Do you suppose, Mr.
Jardine, sir," she demanded severely, "that I who have
been a head parlour-maid in a county family where my
poor husband was coachman, don't know a real
gentlewoman when I meet one? You surprise me, sir."

I apologized hastily and suggested that, as so many kind enquiries had been made, the least I could do was to call and return thanks without delay.

"Certainly, sir," Mrs. Blunt agreed; "but not until you have had your lunch. It's a small porterhouse steak," she added alluringly, being evidently suspicious of my intentions.

The announcement, seconded by an appetizing whiff from below, reminded me that I was prodigiously sharp set, having tasted no food since I had come ashore at Folkestone, and put the grosser physiological needs of the body, for the moment, in the ascendant. But even as I was devouring the steak with voracious gusto, my mind occupied itself with plans for a strategic descent on the abode of the fair Sylvia and with speculations on the reception I should get; and the noise of water running into the bath formed a pleasing accompaniment to the final mouthfuls.

When I had bathed, shaved and attired myself in carefully selected garments, I set forth, as smart and spruce as the frog that would a-wooing go–saving the opera hat, which would have been inappropriate to the occasion. The distance to Sylvia's house was not great, and a pair of long and rapidly-moving legs consumed it to such purpose that it was still quite reasonable calling time when I opened the gate of "The Hawthorns" and gave a modest pull at the bell. My summons was answered by a rather foolish-looking maid, by whom I was informed that Miss Vyne was at home, and when I had given her my name-which she seemed disposed to confuse with that of a well-known edible fish–she ushered me down a passage to a room at the back of the house, and, opening the door, announced me–correctly, I was glad to note; whereupon I assumed an ingratiating smile and entered.

Now there is nothing more disconcerting than a total failure of agreement between anticipation and realization. Unconsciously, I had pictured to myself the easy-mannered, genial Sylvia, seated, perhaps, at an easel or table, working on one of her pictures, and had prepared myself for a reception quite simple, friendly and unembarrassing. Confidently and entirely at my ease, I walked in through the doorway; and there the pleasant vision faded, leaving me with the smile frozen on my face, staring in consternation at one of the most appalling old women that it has ever been my misfortune to encounter.

I am, in general, rather afraid of old women. They are, to my mind, a rather alarming class of creature; but the present specimen exceeded my wildest nightmares. It was not merely that she was seated unnaturally in the exact centre of the room and that she sat with unhuman immobility, moving no muscle and uttering no sound as I entered, though that was somewhat embarrassing. It was her strange, forbidding appearance that utterly shattered my self-possession and seemed to disturb the very marrow in my bones.

She was a most remarkable-looking person. An immense Roman nose, a mop of frizzy grey fringe and a lofty surmounting cap or head-dress of some kind, suggested that monstrous and unreal bird, the helmeted hornbill; and the bird-like character was heightened by her eyes, which were small and glittering and set in the midst of a multitude of radiating wrinkles.

To this most alarming person I made a low bow—and dropped my stick, of which the maid had neglected to relieve me and for which I had found no appointed receptacle. As I stooped hastily to pick it up, my hat slipped from my grasp, and, urged by the devil that possess disengaged hats, instantly rolled under a deep ottoman, whence I had to hook it out with the handle of my stick. I rose, perspiring with embarrassment, to confront that immovable figure, and found the glittering eyes fixed on me attentively but without any sign of expression of human emotion. Haltingly I essayed to stammer out an explanation of my visit.

"Er-I have-er-called-"

Here I paused to collect my ideas and the old lady watched me stonily without offering any remark; indeed no comment was needed on a statement so self-evidently true. After a brief and hideous silence I began again.

"I-er-thought it desirable-er-and in fact necessary and-er-proper to call-er and -"

Here my ideas again petered out and a horrid silence ensued, amidst which I heard a still, emotionless voice murmur: "Yes. And you have accordingly called."

"Exactly," I agreed, grasping eagerly at the slenderest straw of suggestion. "I have called to-er-well, the fact is that my-er-very remarkable absence seemed to call for some explanation, especially as certain enquiries-er -"

At this point I stopped suddenly with a horrible doubt as to whether I was not saying more than was discreet; and the misgiving was intensified by that chilly, calm voice, framing the question: "Enquiries made personally?"

Now this was a facer. I seemed to have put my foot in it at the first lead off. Supposing Sylvia had said nothing about her little visits to Mrs. Blunt? It would never do to give her away to this inquisitorial old waxwork. I endeavoured to temporize.

"Well," I stammered, "not exactly made personally to me."

"By letter, perhaps?" the voice suggested in the same even, impassive tone.

"Er-no. Not by letter."

There was a short embarrassing pause, and then the old lady, as if summing up the case, said frigidly: "Not exactly personally and not by letter."

I was so utterly confounded by her judicial manner, her immovable, expressionless face and the hypnotic quality of those glittering eyes, that for the moment I could think of nothing to say.

"Don't let me interrupt you," said she after some seconds of agonized silence on my part; whereupon I pulled myself together and made a fresh start.

"I should, perhaps, have explained that I have been unavoidably absent from home for some time, and, as I was unable to communicate with my friends, I have, I am afraid, caused them some anxiety. It was this that seemed to make it necessary for me to call and give an account of myself."

She pondered awhile on this statement–if a graven image can be said to ponder–and at length enquired: "You spoke of your friends. Are any of them known to me?"

"Well," I replied, "I was referring more particularly to your daughter."

She continued to regard me fixedly, and, after a brief interval, rejoined: "You are referring to my daughter. But I do not recall the existence of any such person. I think you must be mistaken."

It seemed extremely probable, and I hastened to amend the description. "I beg your pardon. I should have said Miss Vyne. But perhaps she is not at home."

"You are evidently mistaken," was the paralyzing reply. "I am Miss Vyne; and I need not add that I am at home."

"But," I demanded despairingly, "is there not another Miss Vyne?"

"There is not," she answered. "But it is possible that you are referring to Miss Sylvia Vyne. Is that so?"

I replied sulkily that it was; and being somewhat nettled by this unnecessary and rather offensive hairsplitting, offered no further remark. How the conversation would have proceeded after this, I cannot even surmise. But it did not proceed at all, for the embarrassing silence was brought to an end by a very agreeable interruption. The door opened softly and for one moment Sylvia herself stood framed in the portal; then, with a little cry, she ran towards me with her hands held out impulsively and the prettiest smile of welcome.

"So it is really you!" she exclaimed. "That silly little goose of a maid has only just told me you were here. I am glad to see you. When did you graciously please to descend from the clouds?"

"I arrived home this afternoon, and as soon as I had changed and had lunch I came here to report myself."

"How nice of you," said Sylvia. "I suppose you guessed how anxious we should be?"

"I didn't presume to think that you would actually be anxious about me," I replied, with a furtive eye on the waxwork," though I knew that you had been kind enough to express an interest in my fate."

"What a cold-bloodedly polite way to put it!" laughed Sylvia. "'Express an interest,' indeed! We were most dreadfully worried about you."

To a somewhat friendless man like myself this sympathetic warmth was very delightful, and my pleasure was not appreciably damped when a chill, emotionless voice affirmed: "The use of the first person singular would, I think, be preferable."

Sylvia turned on her aunt with mock ferocity. "Well, really!" she exclaimed. "You are a dreadful impostor, Mopsy, dear! Just listen to her, Dr. Jardine. And if you had only seen what a twitter she was in as the time went on and no news came!"

I gasped, and the hair seemed to stir on my scalp. Mopsy! The name was obviously not applied to me. But could it be-was it possible that such a name could be associated with that terrific old lady? It was inconceivable. It was positively profane! It was almost as if one should presume to address the Deity as "old chap." I could hardly believe my ears.

I glanced at her nervously and caught her glittering eye; but the grotesque face was as immovable as everlasting granite, though, indeed, by some ventriloquial magic, the word "Rubbish." managed to disengage itself from her person.

"It isn't rubbish," retorted Sylvia. "It's the plain truth.
We were both worried to death about you. And no
wonder. Dr. Thorndyke was very quiet and matter-of-fact,
but there was no disguising his fear that something
dreadful had happened to you. And then there was the
advertisement in the papers. Did you see that? Oh, it's
nothing to grin about. You've given us all a nice fright;
and me especially, because, of course, I naturally thought
of that ruffian from whom you rescued me in the lane."

"But he never saw me."

"You don't know. He may have done. At any rate, you
owe us an explanation; so, when the tea comes in you
shall give us the true story of your adventures. I hope
you've let Dr. Thorndyke know about your resurrection."

I reassured her on this point, and as the "goose of a
maid" now brought in the tea, I proceeded to "pitch my
yarn," as the skipper had expressed it, without those
reservations that I had considered necessary in the case
of Mrs. Blunt.

The old lady, having been unmasked by Sylvia,
developed a slight tendency to thaw. She even
condescended, in a rigid and effigean fashion, to consume
bread and butter; a proceeding that seemed to me weirdly
incongruous, as though one should steal into the British
Museum in off hours and find the seated statue of
Amenhotep the Third in the act of refreshing itself with a
sandwich and a glass of beer. But I was less terrified of
her now since I had gathered that a core of warm
humanity was somewhere concealed within that grim
exterior; and even though her little sparkling eyes were
fixed on me immovably, I told my story to the end without
flinching.

Sylvia listened to my narration with a rapt attention
that greatly flattered my vanity and made me feel like a
very Othello, and when I had finished, she regarded me
for a while silently and with an air of speculation.

"It's a queer affair," she said at length, "and there is a
smack of mystery and romance about it that is rather

refreshing in these commonplace days. But I don't like it. Adventure is all very well, but there seems to have been a deliberate attempt to make away with you; unless you think it may have been a piece of silly horse-play that went farther than it was meant to."

"That is quite possible," I replied untruthfully–for I didn't think anything of the sort, and only made this evasive answer to avoid raising other and more delicate issues.

"I hope that is the explanation," said Sylvia, "though it sounds rather a lame one. You would know if you had an enemy who might wish to get rid of you. I suppose you don't know of any such person?"

It was a rather awkward question, I didn't want to tell an untruth, but, on the other hand, I knew that Thorndyke would not wish to have my affairs discussed while his investigations were in progress; so I "hedged" once more, replying, quite truthfully, that I was not acquainted with anyone who bore me the slightest ill-will.

My adventures done with, the talk drifted into other channels and presently came round to the little crucifix that had been the occasion of Sylvia's disagreeable experience in the lane. In spite of my confusion, I had noticed, on first entering the room, that the old lady was wearing suspended from her neck, a small enamelled crucifix, and had instantly identified it and wondered not a little that she should be thus disporting herself in borrowed ornaments; but when Sylvia had arrived, behold, the original crucifix was hanging on its chain from her neck. From time to time during my recital my eyes had wandered from one to the other seeking some difference or variation but finding none, and at length my inquisitive glances caught the younger lady's attention.

"I can see. Dr. Jardine," said she, "that you are eaten up with curiosity about the crucifix that my Aunt is wearing. Now confess. Aren't you?"

"I am," I admitted. "When I first came in I naturally thought it was yours. Is it a copy?"

"Certainly not," said Miss Vyne, the elder. "They are duplicates."

Sylvia laughed. "You'd better not talk about copies," said she. "My aunt has only acquired her treasure lately, and she is as proud of it as a peacock; aren't you, dear?"

"The sensations of a peacock," replied Miss Vyne," are unknown to me. I am very gratified at possessing the ornament."

"Gratified indeed!" said Sylvia. "I consider such vanity most unsuitable to a person of your age. But they are very charming, and there is quite a little story attached to them. My father and a cousin of his–"

"By marriage," interposed Miss Vyne.

"You needn't insist on that," said Sylvia, "as if poor old Vitalia were a person to be ashamed of. Well, my father and this cousin were at a Jesuit school in Belgium–at Louvain, in fact–and among the teachers in the school was an Italian Jesuit named Giglioli. Now the respected Giggley–"

"– oli," interposed Miss Vyne in a severe voice.

"–oli," continued Sylvia, "had formerly been a goldsmith; and the Father Superior, with that keen eye to the main chance which you may have noticed among professed religious, furnished him with a little workshop and employed him in making monstrances, thuribles and church plate in general. It was he who made these two crucifixes; and, with the Father Superior's consent, he gave one to my father and the other to the cousin as parting gifts on their leaving school. As the boys were inseparable friends, the two crucifixes were made absolute duplicates of one another, with the single exception that each had the owner's name engraved on the back. When my poor father died his crucifix became mine, and a short time ago, his cousin–who is now getting an old man–took a fancy that he would like the two crucifixes to be together once more and gave his to my aunt. So here they are, after all these years, under one roof again."

As she finished speaking, she detached the crucifix from her neck and, having given it to me to examine, proceeded to remove its fellow from the neck of the elder lady–who not only submitted quite passively but seemed to be unaware of the transaction–and handed that to me also.

I laid them side by side in my palm and compared them, but could not detect the slightest difference between them. They were complete duplicates. Each was a Latin cross with trefoiled extremities, wrought from a single piece of gold and enriched with champlevé enamel. The body of the cross was filled with a ground of deep, translucent blue, from which the figure stood out in rather low relief, and the space between each of the trefoils was occupied by a single Greek letter-Iota and Chi at the top and bottom respectively, and at the ends of the horizontal arm Alpha and Omega. On turning them over, I saw that the back of each bore an engraved inscription carried across the horizontal arm, that on Sylvia's reading: "A. M. ROBERTUS, D.G.," while that on the other read: "A. M. VITALIS, D.G."

"They are very charming little things," I said, as I returned them to Sylvia; "and it was a pretty idea of the old Jesuit to make them both alike for the two friends. I suppose he didn't make any more of them for his other pupils?"

"What makes you ask that?" demanded Sylvia.

"I am thinking of that man in the lane. He must have had some reason for claiming the crucifix as his, one would think; and as these are quite unlike any ordinary commercial jewellery, the suggestion is that the worthy Giglioli was tempted to repeat his successes. What do you think?"

"I think," said Miss Vyne, "that the suggestion is inadmissable. Father Giglioli was an artist, and an artist does not repeat himself."

"I am inclined to agree with my aunt," said Sylvia. "An artist does not care to repeat a design, excepting for a definite purpose, as in the case of these duplicates; especially when the thing designed is intended as a gift."

To this I gave a somewhat qualified assent, though I found the argument far from convincing; and, as I had made a very long visitation, especially for a first call, I now rose to depart.

"I hope I may be allowed to come and see you again," I ventured to say as Miss Vyne raised a sort of semaphore arm to my extended hand.

"I see no reason why you should not," she replied judicially. "You seem to be a well-disposed young man, though indiscreet. Good-afternoon."

I bowed deferentially and then, to my gratification, was escorted as far as the garden gate by Sylvia; who evidently wished to gather my impressions of her relative, for, as she let me out, she asked with a mischievous smile: "What do you think of my aunt, Dr. Jardine?"

"She is rather a terrifying old lady," I replied.

Sylvia giggled delightedly. "She does look an awful old griffin, doesn't she? But it's all nonsense, you know. She is really a dear old thing, and as soft as butter."

"Well," I said," she conceals the fact most perfectly."

"She does. She is a most complete impostor. I'll tell you a secret, Dr. Jardine," Sylvia added in a mysterious whisper, as we shook hands over the gate; "she trades on her nose. I've told her so. Her nose is her fortune, and she plays it for all it's worth. Goodbye-or rather, au revoir! For you've promised to come and see us again."

With a bright little nod she turned and ran up the garden path, still chuckling softly at her joke; and I wended homewards, very well pleased with the circumstances of my visit, despite the soul-shaking incidents with which it had opened.

13
A MYSTERIOUS STRANGER

ON the following morning I betook myself to the hospital intending to call later in the day at Dr. Thorndyke's chambers; but that visit turned out to be unnecessary, for, as I ran my eye over the names on the attendance board in the entrance hall, I saw that Thorndyke was in the building, although it was not the day on which he lectured. I found him, as I had expected, in the museum and was greeted with a hearty grip of the hand and a welcome, the warmth of which gratified me exceedingly.

"Well, Jardine," he said, "you've given us all a pretty fine shake up. I have never been more relieved in my life than I was when my man Polton gave me your note. But you seem to have had another fairly close shave. What a fellow you are, to be sure! You seem to be as tenacious of life as the proverbial cat."

"So that little archbishop is your man Polton, is he?"

"Yes; and a most remarkable man, Jardine, and simply invaluable to me, though he ought to be in a very different position. But I think he is quite happy with me—especially now that he has got your watch to experiment on. You will see that watch again some day, when he has rated it to half a second. And meanwhile let us go into the curator's room and reconstitute your adventures."

The curator's room was empty at the moment; empty, that is to say, so far as human denizens were concerned. Otherwise it was decidedly full; the usual wilderness of glass jars, sepulchral slate tanks, bones in all stages of preparation and unfinished specimens, being supplemented by that all-pervading, unforgettable odour peculiar to curator's rooms, compounded of alcohol and mortality, and suggesting a necropolis for deceased dipsomaniacs. Thorndyke seated himself on a well-polished stool by the work-bench, and, motioning me to another, bade me speak on. Which I did in exhaustive detail; giving him a minute history of my experiences from the time of my parting from Sylvia to the present moment, not omitting my encounter with Mrs. Samway and the clerical gentleman in the train.

He listened to my narrative in his usual silent, attentive fashion, making no comments and asking no questions until I had finished; when he cross-examined me on one or two points of detail.

"With regard to Mrs. Samway," he asked; "did you gather that she was crossing by the Boulogne boat?"

"I inferred that she was, but she said nothing on the subject."

He nodded and then asked; "Do I understand that you never saw your assailant at all?"

"I never got the slightest glimpse of him; in fact I could not say whether the person who attacked me was a man or a woman excepting that the obvious strength and the method of attack suggest a man."

To this he made no reply, but sat a while absorbed in thought. It was evident that he was deeply interested in the affair, not only on my account but by reason of the curious problems that it offered for solution. Indeed, his next remark was to this effect.

"It is a most singular case, Jardine," he said. "So much of it is perfectly clear, and yet so much more is unfathomable mystery. But just now, the speculative interest is overshadowed by the personal. I am rather doubtful as to what we ought to do. It almost looks as if you ought not to be at large."

"I hope, sir, you don't suggest shutting me up," I exclaimed with a grin.

"That was in my mind," he answered. "You are evidently in considerable danger, and you are not as cautious as you ought to be."

"I shall be mighty cautious after this experience," I rejoined; "and you have yourself implied that I have nine lives."

"Even so," he retorted, "you have played away a third of them pretty rapidly. If you are not more careful of the other six, I shall have to put you somewhere out of harm's way. Do, for goodness sake, Jardine, keep away from unpopulated places and see that no stranger gets near enough to have you at a disadvantage."

I promised him to keep a constant watch for suspicious strangers and to avoid all solitary neighbourhoods and ill-lighted thoroughfares, and shortly after this we separated to go our respective ways, he back to the museum and I to the surgical wards.

For some time after this, the record of my daily life furnishes nothing but a chronicle of small beer. I had resumed pretty regular attendance at the hospital, setting forth from my lodgings in the morning and returning thither as the late afternoon merged into evening; taking the necessary exercise in the form of the long walk to and from the hospital, and keeping close indoors at night. It began to look as though my adventures were at an end and life were settling down to the old familiar jog trot.

And yet the beer was not quite so small as it looked. Coming events cast their shadows before them, but often enough those shadows wear a shape ill-defined and vague, and so creep on unnoticed. Thus it was in these days of apparent inaction, though even then there were certain little happenings at which I looked askance. Such an episode occurred within a few days of my return, and gave me considerable food for thought. I had climbed on to the yellow 'bus in tho Tottenham Court Road and was seated on the top, smoking my pipe, when, as we passed up the Hampstead Road, I noticed a woman looking into the window of Mr. Robinson, the artist's-colourman. Something familiar or distinctive in the pose of the figure made me glance a second time; and then I think my eyes must have grown more and more round with astonishment as the 'bus gradually drew me out of range. For the woman was undoubtedly Mrs. Samway.

It was really a most surprising affair. This good lady seemed to be ubiquitous; to fly hither and thither and drop from the clouds as if she were the possessor of a magic carpet. Apparently she had not gone to Boulogne after all; or if she had, her stay on the Continent must have been uncommonly short. But if she had not crossed on the boat, what was she doing in Folkestone? It was all very well to say that she had as much right to be in Folkestone as I had. That was true enough, but it was a lame conclusion and no explanation at all.

It was my custom, as I have said, to walk from my lodgings to the hospital, a distance of some five miles; but this was practicable only in fine weather. On wet days I took the tram from the "Duke of St. Alban's"; and beguiled the slow journey by reading one of my text-books and observing the manners and customs of my fellow-passengers. Such a day was the one that followed the re-appearance of Mrs. Samway. A persistent drizzle put my morning walk out of the question and sent me reluctant but resigned to seek the shelter of the tram, where having settled myself with a volume of Gould's "Surgical Diagnosis," I began to read to the accompaniment of the monotonous rhythm of the horses' hoofs and the sleepy jingle of their bells. From time to time I looked up from my book to take a glance at the other occupants of the steamy interior, and on each occasion that I did so, I caught the eye of my opposite neighbour roving over my person as it taking an inventory of my apparel. Whenever he caught my eye, he immediately looked away; but the next time I glanced up I was sure to find him once more engaged in a leisurely examination of me.

There was nothing remarkable in this. People who sit opposite in a public vehicle unconsciously regard one another, as I was doing myself; but when I had met my neighbour's eye a dozen times or more, I began to grow annoyed at his persistent inspection; and finally, shutting up my book, proceeded to retaliate in kind.

This seemed to embarrass him considerably. Avoiding my steady gaze, his eyes flitted to and fro, passing restlessly from one part of the vehicle to another; and then it was that my medical eye noted a fact that gave an intrinsic interest to the inspection. The man had what is called a nystagmus; that is, a peculiar oscillatory movement of the eyeball. As his eyes passed quickly from object to object, they did not both come to rest instantaneously, but the right eye stopped with a sort of vertical stagger as if the bearings were loose. The condition is not a very common one, and the one-sided variety is decidedly rare. It is usually associated with some defect of vision or habitual strain of the eye-muscles, as in miners' nystagmus; whence my discovery naturally led to a further survey and speculation as to the cause of the condition in the present case.

The man was obviously not a miner. His hands–with a cigarette stain, as I noticed, on the left middle finger–were much too delicate, and he had not in any way the appearance of a labourer. Then the spasm must be due to some defect of eyesight. Yet he was not near-sighted, for, as we passed a church at some distance, I saw him glance out through the doorway at the clock and compare it with his watch; and again, I noticed that he took out his watch with his left hand. Then perhaps he had a blind eye or unequal vision in the two eyes; this seemed the most likely explanation; and I had hardly proposed it to myself when the chance was given to me to verify it. Confused by my persistent examination of him, my unwilling patient suddenly produced a newspaper from his pocket and, clapping a pair of pince-nez on his nose, began to read. Those pince-nez gave me the required information, for I could see that one glass was strongly convex while the other was nearly plane.

The question of my friend's eyesight being disposed of, I began to debate the significance of that stain of the left middle finger. Was he left-handed? It did not follow, though it seemed likely; and then I found myself noting the manner in which he hold his paper, until, becoming suddenly conscious of the absurdity of the whole affair, I impatiently picked up my book and reverted to the diagnosis of renal calculus. I was becoming, I reflected disparagingly, as inquisitive as Thorndyke himself; from whom I seemed to have caught some infection that impelled me thus to concern myself with the trifling peculiarities of total strangers.

The trivial incident would probably have faded from my recollection but for another, equally trivial, which occurred a day or two later. I was returning home by way of Tottenham Court Road and had nearly reached the crossing at the north end when I suddenly remembered that I had come to the last of my note-books. The shop at which I obtained them was in Gower Street, hard by, and as the thought of the books occurred to me, I turned abruptly and, running across the road, strode quickly down a by-street that led to the shop.

As I came out into Gower Street I noticed a small, but rapidly augmenting crowd on the pavement, and, elbowing my way through, found at its centre a man lying on the ground, writhing in the convulsions of an epileptic fit. I proceeded to ward off the well-meant attentions of the usual excited bystanders, who were pulling open his hands and trying to sit him up, and had thrust the corner of a folded newspaper between his teeth to prevent him from biting his tongue when a constable arrived on the scene; upon which, as the officer bore on his sleeve the badge of the St. John's Ambulance Society, I gave him a few directions and began to back out of the crowd.

At this moment, I became aware of a pressure behind me and a suspicious fumbling, strongly suggestive of the presence of a pick-pocket. Instantly, I turned to the right about and directed a searching look at the people behind me, and especially at a bearded, nondescript person who seemed also to be backing out of the crowd. He gave me a single, quick glance as I followed him through the press and then averted his eyes; and as he did so, I noticed, with something of a start, that his right eye came to rest with a peculiar, rapid up-and-down shake. He had, in fact, a right-sided nystagmus.

The coincidence naturally struck me with some force. A nystagmus is not, as I have said, a very common condition; one-sided nystagmus is actually a rare one; and, of the one-sided instances, only some fifty per cent will affect the right eye. The coincidence was therefore quite a notable one; but had it any particular bearing? I had a half-formed inclination to follow the man; but he had not actually picked my pocket or done any other overt act, and one could hardly follow a person merely because he happened to suffer from an uncommon nervous affection.

The man was now walking up the street, briskly, but without manifest hurry; looking straight before him and swinging his stick with something of a flourish. I watched him speculatively, as I walked in the same direction, and then suddenly realized that he was carrying his stick in his left hand, and carrying it, too, with the unmistakable ease born of habit. Then he was left-handed! And here was another coincidence; not a remarkable one in itself, but, when added to the other, so singular and striking that I insensibly quickened my pace.

As my acquaintance reached the corner of the Euston Road, an omnibus stopped to put down a passenger. It was about to move on when he raised his stick, and, following it, stepped on the footboard and mounted to the roof. I was undecided what to do. Should I follow him? And, if so, to what purpose? He would certainly notice me if I did and be on his guard, so that I should probably have my trouble for nothing and possibly look like a fool into the bargain. And while I was thus standing irresolute at the corner, the omnibus rumbled away westward and decided the question for me.

I am not, as the reader may have gathered, a particularly cautious man or much given to suspicion. But recent events had made me a good deal more wary and had taught me to look with less charity on chance fellow creatures; and this left-handed person with the nystagmus occupied my thoughts to no small extent during the next day or two. Was he the man whom I had seen in the tram? Apparently not. The latter had been clean shaven and dressed neatly in the style of a clerk or ordinary City man, whereas the former wore a full beard and was shabby, almost beyond the verge of respectability. As to their respective statures, I could not judge, as I had seen the one man seated and the other standing; but, superficially, they were not at all alike, and, in all probability they were different persons.

But this conclusion was not at all inevitable. When I reflected on the matter, I saw that the resemblances and differences did not balance. The two men resembled one another in qualities that were inherent and unalterable, but they differed in qualities that were superficial and subject to change. A man cannot assume or cast off a nystagmus, but he can put on a false beard. A left-handed man may endeavour to conceal his peculiarity, but the superior deftness of the habitually used hand will make itself apparent in spite of his efforts; whereas he can make any alterations in his clothing that he pleases. And thus reflecting, the suspicion grew more and more strong that the two men might very well have been one and the same person, and that it would be discreet to keep a bright look-out for a left-handed man with a right-sided nystagmus.

During all this time I had seen nothing of my new friend Miss Sylvia. But I had by no means forgotten her. Without wishing to exaggerate my feelings, I may say that I had taken a strong liking to that very engaging young lady. She was a pleasant, easy-mannered girl, evidently good-tempered, and very frank and simple; a girl–as Mr. Sparkler would have said–"with no bigod nonsense about her." Her tastes ran along very similar lines to my own, and she was clever enough to be a quite interesting companion. Then it was evident that she liked me–which was in itself an attraction, to say nothing of the credit that it reflected on her taste–and, in a perfectly modest way, she had made no secret of the fact. And finally, she was exceptionally good-looking. Now people may say, as they do, that beauty is only skin deep–which is perfectly untrue, by the way; but even so, one is more concerned with the skins of one's fellow creatures than with their livers or vermiform appendices. The contact of persons, as of things, occurs at their respective surfaces.

From which it will be gathered that I was only allowing a decent interval to elapse before repeating my visit to "The Hawthorns"; indeed, I was beginning to think that a sufficient interval had already passed and to contemplate seriously my second call, when my intentions were forestalled by Sylvia herself. Returning home one Friday evening, I found on my mantelpiece a short letter from her, enclosing a ticket for an exhibition of paintings and sculpture at a gallery in Leicester Square, and mentioning–incidentally–that she proposed to visit the show on the following morning in order to see the works by a good light; which seemed such an eminently rational proceeding in these short winter days, that I determined instantly to follow her example and get the advantage of the morning light myself.

I acted on this decision with such thoroughness that, when I arrived at the gallery, I found the attendant in the act of opening the doors, and, for nearly half an hour I was in sole possession of the premises. Then, by twos and threes, other visitors began to straggle in, and among them Sylvia, looking very fresh and dainty and obviously pleased to see me.

"I am glad you were able to come," she said, as we shook hands. "I thought you would, somehow. It is so much nicer to have someone to talk over the pictures with, isn't it?"

"Much more interesting," I agreed. "I have been taking a preliminary look round and have already accumulated quite a lot of profound observations to discharge at you as occasion offers. Shall we begin at number one?"

We began at number one and worked our way methodically picture by picture, round the room, considering each work attentively with earnest discussion and a wealth of comment. As the morning wore on, visitors arrived in increasing numbers, until the two large rooms began to be somewhat inconveniently crowded. We had made a complete circuit of the pictures and were about to turn to the sculpture, which occupied the central floor space, when Sylvia touched me on the arm.

"Let us sit down for a minute," said she. "I want to speak to you."

I led her to one of the large settees that disputed the floor-space with the busts and statuettes, and, somewhat mystified by her serious tone and by the rather agitated manner, which I now noticed for the first time, seated myself by her side.

"What is it?" I asked.

She looked anxiously round the room, and, leaning towards me, said in a low tone: "Have you noticed a man who has been keeping near us and listening to our conversation?"

"No, I haven't," I replied. "If I had I would have given him a hint to keep farther off. But there's nothing in it, you know. In picture galleries it is very usual for people to hang about and try to overhear criticisms. This man may be interested in the exhibits."

"Yes, I know. But I don't think this person was so much interested in the exhibits. He didn't look at the pictures, he looked at us. I caught his eye several times reflected in the picture-glasses, and once or twice I saw him looking most attentively at this crucifix of mine. That was what really disturbed me. I wish, now, that I hadn't unbuttoned my coat."

"So do I. You will have to leave that crucifix at home if it attracts so much undesirable attention. Which is the man? Is he in this room?"

"No, I don't see him now. I expect he has gone into the next room."

"Then let us go there, too; and if you will point him out to me, I will pay him back in his own coin."

We rose and made our way to the door of communication, and, as we passed into the second room, Sylvia grasped my arm nervously.

"There he is–don't let him see us looking at him–he is sitting on the settee at the farther end of the room."

It was impossible to make a mistake since the settee held only a single person; a fairly well-dressed, ordinary-looking man, rather swarthy and foreign in appearance, with a small waxed moustache. He was sitting nearly opposite the entrance door and seemed, at the moment to be reading over the catalogue, which he held open on his knee; but, as he looked up almost at the moment when we entered, I turned my back to him and continued my inspection with the aid of the reflection in a picture-glass.

"He is probably a journalist," I said. "You see he is scribbling some notes on the blank leaves of his catalogue; probably some of your profound criticisms, which will appear, perhaps to-morrow morning, clothed in super-technical jargon, in a daily paper."

Here I paused suddenly, for I had made a rather curious observation. The reflection in a mirror is, as everybody knows, reversed laterally; so that the right hand of a person appears to be the left, and vice versa. But in the present case, no reversal seemed to have taken place. The figure in the reflection was writing with his

right hand. Obviously, then, the real person was writing
with his left.

This put a rather different aspect on the affair. Up to
the present, I had been disposed to think that Sylvia had
been unduly disturbed; for there are plenty of ill-bred
bounders to be met in any public place who will stare a
good-looking girl out of countenance. But now my
suspicions were all awake. It is true that left-handed men
are as common as blackberries; but still—

"Can you tell me, Miss Vyne," I asked, as we worked
our way towards the other end of the room, "if this man is
at all like the one who frightened you so in Millfield
Lane?"

"No, he is not. I am sure of that. The man in the lane
was a good deal taller and thinner."

"Well, said I, "whoever he is, I want to have a good
look at him, and the best plan will be to turn our
attention to the sculpture. Shall we go and look at that
rather remarkable pink bust? That will give our friend a
chance of another stare at you, and, if he doesn't take it, I
will go and inspect him where he sits."

The bust to which I had referred was executed in a
curious, rose-tinted marble, very crystalline and
translucent, a material that suited the soft, girlish
features of its subject admirably. It stood on an isolated
pedestal quite near the settee on which the suspicious
stranger was sitting, and I hoped that our presence might
lure him from his retreat.

"I don't think," I said, taking up a position with my
back to the settee," that I have ever seen any marble
quite like this. Have you?"

"No," replied Sylvia. "It looks like coarse lump sugar
stained pink. And how very transparent it is; too
transparent for most subjects."

Here she gave a quick, nervous glance at me, and I
was aware of a shadow thrown by some person standing
behind me. Had our friend risen to the bait already?

I continued the conversation in good audible tones. "Very awkward these isolated pedestals would be for slovenly artists who scamp the back of their work." With this remark I moved round the pedestal as if to examine the back of the bust, and Sylvia followed. The move brought us opposite the person who had been standing behind me; and, sure enough, it was the gentleman from the settee. I continued to talk–rather blatantly, I fear–commenting on the careful treatment of the hair and the backs of the ears; and meanwhile took an occasional swift glance at the man opposite. He appeared to be gazing in wrapt admiration at the bust, but his glance, too, occasionally wandered; and when it did, the "point of fixation," as the oculists would express it, was Sylvia's crucifix, which was still uncovered.

Presently I ventured to take a good, steady look at him and was for a few moments unobserved. His left eye moved, as I could see, quite smoothly and evenly from point to point; but the right, at each change of position, gave a little, rapid, vertical oscillation. Suddenly he became aware of my, now undisguised, inspection of him, and, immediately, the oscillation became much more marked, as is often the case with these spasmodic movements. Perhaps he was conscious of the fact; at any rate, he turned his head away and then moved off to examine a statuette that stood near the middle of the room.

I looked after him, wondering what I ought to do. That he was the man whom I had seen on the two previous occasions I had not the slightest doubt, although I was still unable to identify his features or anything about him excepting the nystagmus and the left-handed condition. But there could be no question that he was the same man; and this very variability in his appearance only gave a more sinister significance to the affair, pointing clearly, as it did, to careful and efficient disguise. Evidently he had been, and still was, shadowing me, and, what was still worse, he seemed to be taking a most undesirable interest in Sylvia. And yet what could I do? My small knowledge of the law suggested that shadowing was not a criminal act unless some unlawful intent could be proved. As to punching the fellow's head—which was what I felt most inclined to do—that would merely give rise to disagreeable, and perhaps dangerous, publicity.

"My lord is pleased to meditate," Sylvia remarked at length, breaking in upon my brown study.

"I beg your pardon," I exclaimed. "The fact is I was wondering what we had better do next. Do you want to see anything else?"

"I should rather like to see the outside of the building," she answered. "That man has made me quite nervous."

"Then we will go at once, and we won't sign the visitor's book."

I led her to the door, and, as we rapidly descended the carpeted stairs, I considered once more what it were best to do. Had I been alone I would have kept our watcher in view and done a little shadowing on my own account; but Sylvia's presence made me uneasy. It was of the first importance that this sinister stranger should not learn where she lived. The only reasonable course seemed to be to give him the slip if possible.

"What did you make of that man?" Sylvia asked when we were outside in the square. "Don't you think he was watching us?"

"Yes, I do. And I may say that I have seen him before."

She turned a terrified face to me and asked: "You don't think he is the wretch who pushed you into the river?"

Now this was exactly what I did think, but it was not worthwhile to say so. Accordingly I temporized. "It is impossible to say. I never saw that man, you know. But I have reason for thinking that this fellow is keeping a watch on me, and it occurs to me that, if he appears still to be following us, I had better put you into a hansom and keep my eye on him until you are out of sight."

"Oh, I'm not going to agree to that," she replied with great decision. "I don't suppose that my presence is much protection to you, but still, you are safer while we are together, and I'm not going to leave you."

This settled the matter. Of course she was quite right. I was much safer while she was with me, and if she refused to go off alone, we must make our escape together. I looked up the square as we turned out of it towards the Charing Cross Road, but could see no sign of our follower, and, as we walked on at a good pace, I hoped that we might get clear away. But I was not going to take any chances. Before turning homewards, I decided to walk sharply some distance in an easterly direction and then see if there was any sign of pursuit; for my previous experiences of this good gentleman led me to suspect that he was by no means without skill and experience in the shadowing art.

We walked down to Charing Cross and turned eastward along the north side of the Strand. I had chosen this thoroughfare as offering a good cover to a pursuer, who could easily keep out of sight among the crowd of way-farers who thronged the pavement for the first question to be settled was whether we were or were not being shadowed.

"Where are we going now?" Sylvia asked.

"We are going up Bedford Street," I answered. "There is a book shop on the right-hand side where we can loiter unobtrusively and keep a look-out. If we see nobody, we will try one of the courts off Maiden Lane where we should be certain to catch anyone who was following. But we will try the bookstall first because, if our friend is in attendance, I have a rather neat plan for getting rid of him."

We accordingly made our way to the bookstall in Bedford Street and began systematically to look through the second-hand volumes; and as we pored over an open book, we were able to keep an effective watch on the end of the street and the Strand beyond. Our vigil was not a long one. We had been at the stall less than a minute when Sylvia whispered to me: "Do you see that man looking in the shop on the farther side of the Strand?"

"Yes," I replied, "I have noticed him. He has only just arrived, and I fancy he is our man. If he is, he will probably go into the doorway so as not to have to keep his back to us."

Almost as I spoke, the man moved into the deep doorway as if to inspect the end of the shop window, and Sylvia exclaimed: "I'm sure that is the man. I can see his profile now."

There could be no doubt of the man's identity; and, at this moment, as if to clinch the matter, he took out a cigarette and lighted it, striking the match with his left hand.

"Come along," said I. "We will now try my little plan for getting rid of him. We mustn't seem to hurry."

We sauntered up to the corner of Maiden Lane and there stood for a few moments looking about us. Then we strolled across to the farther side of Chandos Street, and, as soon as we were out of sight of our follower, crossed the road and slipped in at the entrance to the Civil Service Stores. Passing quickly through the provision department, we halted at the glazed doors, from which we could look out through the Bedford Street entrance.

"There he is!" exclaimed Sylvia. And there he was, sure enough, walking rather quickly up the east side of Bedford Street. "Now," said I, "let us make a bolt for it. This way."

We darted out through the china, furniture and ironmongery departments, across the whole width of the building and out of the Agar Street entrance, where we immediately crossed into King William Street, turned down Adelaide Street, shot through the alley by St. Martin's Church, and came out opposite the National

Portrait Gallery just as a yellow omnibus was about to start. We sprang into the moving vehicle, and, as it rumbled away into the Charing Cross Road, we kept a sharp watch on the end of King William Street. But there was no sign of our pursuer. We had got rid of him for the present, at any rate.

"Don't you think," said Sylvia, "that he will suspect that we went into the Stores?"

"I have no doubt he will, and that is where we have him. He can't come away and leave the building unsearched. Most probably he is, at this very moment, racing madly up and down the stairs and trying to watch the three entrances at the same time."

Sylvia chuckled gleefully. "It has been quite good fun," she said, "but I am glad we have shaken him off. I think I shall stay indoors for a day or two and paint, and I hope you'll stay indoors, too. And that reminds me that I am out of Heyl's white. I must call in at Robinson's and get a pound tube. Do you mind? It won't delay us more than a few minutes."

Now I would much rather have gone straight on to Hampstead, for our unknown attendant certainly knew the whereabouts of my lodgings and might follow us when he failed to find us in the stores. Moreover, I had, of late, given the neighbourhood of the artist's-colourman's shop a rather wide berth, having seen Mrs. Samway from afar once or twice, thereabouts, and having surmised that she tended to haunt, that particular part of the Hampstead Road. But the fresh supply of flake white seemed to be a necessity, so I made no objection, and we accordingly alighted opposite the shop and entered. Nevertheless, while Sylvia was making her purchase, I stood near the glass door and kept a watchful eye on the street. When a tram stopped a short distance away, I glanced quickly over its passengers, as well as I could, though without observing anyone who might have been our absent friend. But just as it was about to move on, I saw a woman run out from the pavement and enter; and though I got but an indifferent view of her, I felt an uncomfortable suspicion that the woman was Mrs. Samway.

Looking back, I do not quite understand why I had avoided this woman or why I now looked with distaste on the fact that she was travelling in our direction. She was a pleasant-spoken, intelligent person, and I had no dislike of her, nor any cause for dislike. Perhaps it was the recollection of the offence that she had given Sylvia in this very shop, but a short time since, that made me unwilling to encounter her now in Sylvia's company. At any rate, whatever the cause may have been, throughout the otherwise, pleasant journey, and in spite of an animated and interesting conversation, the thought of Mrs. Samway continually recurred, and this notwithstanding that I kept a constant, unobtrusive look-out for the mysterious spy who might, even now, be hovering in our rear.

We alighted from the tram at the "Duke of St. Alban's" and made our way to North End by way of the Highgate Ponds. As we crossed the open fields and the Heath, I turned at intervals to see if there was any sign of our being followed; but no suspicious-looking person appeared in sight, though on two separate occasions, I noticed a woman ahead of us, and walking in much the same direction, turn round and look our way. There was no reason, however, to suppose that she was looking at us, and, in any case, she was too far ahead to be recognizable. At last, somewhere in the neighbourhood of the Spaniard's Road, she finally disappeared, possibly into the hollow beyond, and I saw no more of her.

At the gate of "The Hawthorns" I delivered up the heavy tube of paint, and thus, as it were, formally brought our little outing to an end; and as we shook hands Sylvia treated me to a parting exhortation.

"Now do take care of yourself and keep out of harm's way," she urged. "You are so large, you see," she added with a smile," and such a very conspicuous object that you ought to take special precautions. And you must come and see us again quite soon. I assure you my aunt is positively pining for another conversation with you. Why shouldn't you drop in to-morrow and have tea with us?"

Now this very idea had already occurred to me, so I hastened to close with the invitation; and then, as she retired up the path with another "good-bye" and a wave of the hand, I turned away and walked back towards the Heath.

For some minutes I strode on, across furzy hollows or over little hills, traversed by sunken, sandy paths, occupying myself with thoughts of the pleasant, friendly girl whom I had just left and reflections on the strange events of the morning. Presently I mounted a larger hill, on which was perched a little, old-fashioned house. Skirting the wooden fence that enclosed it, I turned the corner and saw before me, at a distance of some forty yards, a rough, rustic seat. On that seat a woman was sitting; and somehow, when I looked at her and noted the graceful droop of the figure, it was without any feeling of surprise-almost that of realized expectation-that I recognized Mrs. Samway.

14
A LONELY WOMAN

IF I had had any intention of avoiding Mrs. Samway, that intention must inevitably have been frustrated, for her recognition was as instantaneous as my own. Almost as I turned the corner, she looked up and saw me; and a few moments later, she rose and advanced in my direction, so that, to an onlooker it would have appeared as if we had met by appointment. There was obviously nothing for it but to look as pleased as I could manage at such short notice; which I did, shaking her hand with hypocritical warmth.

"And I suppose. Dr. Jardine," said she, "you are thinking what a very odd coincidence it is that we should happen to meet here?"

"Oh, I don't know that it is so very odd. I live about here and I understood you to say that you often come up to the Heath. At any rate, our last meeting was a good deal more odd."

"Yes, indeed. But the truth is that this is not a coincidence at all. I may as well confess that I came here deliberately with the intention of waylaying you."

This very frank statement took me aback considerably; so much so that I could think of no appropriate remark beyond mumbling something to the effect that "it was very flattering of her."

"I have been trying," she continued, "to get a few words with you for some time past; but, although I have lurked in your line of march in the most shameless manner, I have always managed to miss you. I thought, from what you told me, that you passed Robinson's shop on your way to the hospital."

"So I do," I replied mendaciously; for I could hardly tell her that I had lately taken to shooting up bystreets with the express purpose of avoiding that particular stretch of pavement.

"It's rather curious that I never happened to meet you there. However, I didn't, so, today, I determined to take the bull by the horns and catch you here."

This last statement, like the former ones, gave me abundant matter for reflection. How the deuce had she managed to "catch me here?" I supposed that she had seen Sylvia and me in the Hampstead Road and had guessed that we were coming on to this neighbourhood. That was a case of feminine intuition; which, like the bone-setter's skill, is a wonderful thing—when it comes off (and when it doesn't one isn't expected to notice the fact). Then she had gone on ahead—still guessing at our final destination—and kept us in sight while keeping out of view herself. It was not so very easy to understand and not at all comfortable to think of, for there was a disagreeable suggestion that she had somehow ascertained Sylvia's place of abode beforehand. And yet—well, the whole affair was rather mysterious.

"You don't ask why it was that I wanted to waylay you," she said, at length, as I made no comment on her last statement.

"There is an old saying," I replied, "that one shouldn't look a gift-horse in the mouth."

"That is very diplomatic," she retorted with a laugh. "But I daresay your knowledge of women makes the question unnecessary."

"My knowledge of women," said I, "might be put into a nutshell and still leave plenty of room for the nut and a good, fat maggot besides."

"Then I must beware of you. The man who professes to know nothing of women is the most deep and dangerous class of person. But there is one item of knowledge that you seem to have acquired. You seem to know that women like to have pretty things said to them."

"If you call that knowledge," said I, "you must apply the same name to the mere blind impulse that leads a spider to spin a nice, symmetrical web."

She laughed softly and looked up at me with an expression of amused reflection. "I am thinking," she said, "what a very fine symmetrical web you would spin if you were a spider."

"Possibly," I replied. "But it looks as if the role of bluebottle were the one that is being marked out for me."

"Oh! Not a bluebottle. Dr. Jardine. It doesn't suit you at all. If you must make a comparison, why not say a Goliath beetle, and have something really dignified–and not so very inappropriate."

"Well, then, a Goliath beetle, if you prefer it; not that he would look very dignified, kicking his heels in the elegant web of the superlatively elegant feminine spider."

"Oh, but that isn't pretty of you at all, Dr. Jardine. In fact it is quite horrid; and unfair, too; because you are trying to get the information without asking a direct question."

"What question am I supposed to ask?"

"You needn't ask any. I will take pity on your masculine pride and tell you why I have been lying in wait for you, although I daresay you have guessed. The truth is, I am simply devoured by curiosity."

"Concerning what?"

"Now, how can you ask? Just think! One day I meet you in the Hampstead Road, going about your ordinary business, apparently a fixture, at least for months. A few days later, a hundred miles from London, I feel myself suddenly seized from behind; I turn round and there are you with tragedy and adventure written large all over you."

"I thought the tragedy was rather on your side; and so did the ancient mariner with the black bottle and the tea cup. But–"

"I don't wish to discuss the views of that well-meaning old brute. I want an explanation. I want to know how you came to be in Folkestone and in that extraordinary condition. I am sure something strange must have happened to you."

"Why? Haven't I as much right to be in Folkestone as you have?"

"That is mere evasion. When I see a man who is usually rather carefully and very neatly dressed, walking in the streets of a seaport town without hat or a stick and with a collar that looks as if it had been used to clean out a saucepan, and great stains on his clothes, I am justified in inferring that something unusual has happened to him."

"I didn't think you had noticed my neglige get-up."

"At the time I did not. I was very upset and agitated, I had just had a lot of worry and was compelled to cross to France at a moment's notice; and then there was that horrible horse, and the sudden way that you seized me and then got knocked down; and the– -"

"The ancient mariner."

"Yes, the ancient mariner; and the knowledge that I was behaving like an idiot and couldn't help it–though you were so nice and kind to me. So you see, I was hardly conscious of what was happening at the time. But afterwards, when I had recovered my wits a little, I recalled the astonishing figure that you made, and I have been wondering ever since what had happened to you. I assure you. Dr. Jardine, you looked as if you might have swum to Folkestone."

"Did I, by Jove!" I exclaimed with a laugh. "Well, appearances weren't so very deceptive. The fact is that I had swum part of the way."

She looked at me incredulously. "Whatever do you mean?" she asked.

"I mean that you are now looking on a modern and strictly up-to-date edition of Sinbad the Sailor."

"That isn't very explanatory. But I suppose it isn't meant to be. It is just a preliminary stimulant to whet my appetite for marvels, and a most unnecessary one, I can assure you, for I am absolutely agape with curiosity. Do go on. Tell me exactly what had happened to you."

Now the truth is that I had already said rather more than was strictly discreet and would gladly have drawn in my horns. But I had evidently let myself in for some sort of plausible explanation, and a lack of that enviable faculty that enables its possessor to tell a really convincing and workmanlike lie, condemned me to a mere unimaginative adherence to the bald facts, though I did make one slight and amateurish effort at prevarication.

"You want a detailed log of Sinbad's voyages, do you?" said I. "Then you shall have it. We will begin at the beginning. The port of departure was the Embankment somewhere near Cleopatra's Needle. I was leaning over the parapet, staring down at the water like a fool, when some practical joker came along, and, apparently thinking it would be rather funny to give me a fright, suddenly lifted me off my feet. But my jocose friend hadn't allowed for the top-heaviness of a person of my height, and, before you could say ' knife,' I had slipped from his hold and taken a most stylish header into the water. Fortunately for me, a barge happened at the moment to be towing past, and, when I had managed to haul myself on board, I fell into the arms of a marine species of Good Samaritan, who, not having a supply of the orthodox oil and wine, proceeded to fill me up with hot gin and water, which is distinctly preferable for internal application. Then the Samaritan aforesaid clothed me in gorgeous marine raiment and stowed me in a cupboard to sleep off the oil and wine, which I did after some sixteen hours, and then awoke to find our good ship on the broad bosom of the ocean. And so—not to weary you with the incidents of the voyage–I came to Folkestone, where I found a beautiful lady endeavouring, very unsuccessfully, to hypnotize a run-away horse; and so to the adventure of the tarred nets and the ancient mariner with the black bottle."

Mrs. Samway smiled a little consciously as I mentioned the last incidents, but the smile quickly faded and left a deeply thoughtful expression on her face.

"You take it all very calmly," said she, "but it seems to me to have been a rather terrible experience. You really had a very narrow escape from death."

"Yes; quite near enough. I'm far from wanting any more from the same tap."

"And I don't quite see why you assume that it was a mere clumsy joke that sent you into the river by accident."

"Why, what else could it have been?"

"It looks more like a deliberate attempt to drown you. Perhaps you have some enemy who might want to make away with you."

"I haven't. There isn't a soul in the world who owes me the slightest grudge."

"That seems rather a bold thing to say, but I suppose you know. Still, I should think you ought to bear this strange affair in mind, and be a little careful when you go out at night; to avoid the riverside, for instance. Have you–did you give any information to the police about this accident, as you call it?"

"Good Lord! No! What would have been the use?"

"I thought you might have given them some description of the man who pushed you over."

"But I never saw him. I don't even know for certain that it was a man. It might have been a woman for all that I can tell."

Mrs. Samway looked, up at me with that strangely penetrating expression that I had seen before in those singular, pale eyes of hers.

"You don't mean that?" she said. "You don't really think that it could have been a woman?"

"I don't think very much about it; but as I never saw the person who did me the honour of hoisting me overboard, I am clearly not in a position to depose as to the sex of that person. But if it was a woman, she must have been an uncommonly strong one."

Mrs. Samway continued to look at me questioningly. "I thought you seemed to hint at a suspicion that it actually was a woman. You would surely be able to tell."

"I suppose I should if there were time to think about the matter; but, you see, before I was fairly aware that anyone had hold of me, I was sticking my head into the mud at the bottom of the river, which is a process that does not tend very much to clarify one's thoughts."

"No, I suppose not," she agreed. "But it is a most mysterious and dreadful affair. I can't think how you can take it so calmly. You don't seem to be in the least concerned by the fact that you have been within a hairsbreadth of being murdered. What do your friends think about it?"

"Well, you see, Mrs. Samway," I replied evasively, "one doesn't talk much about incidents of this kind. It doesn't sound very credible, and one doesn't want to gain a reputation as a sort of modern Munchausen. I shouldn't have told you but that you were already partly in the secret and that you cross-examined me in such a determined fashion."

"But," she exclaimed, "do you mean to tell me that you have said nothing to anyone about this extraordinary adventure of yours?"

"No, I don't say that. Of course, I had to give some sort of explanation to my landlady, for instance, but I didn't tell her all that I have told you; and I would rather, if you don't mind, that you didn't mention the affair to anyone. I should hate to be suspected of romancing."

"You shan't be through anything that I may say," she replied, "though I should hardly think that anyone who knew you would be likely to suspect you of inventing imaginary adventures." For some minutes after this we walked on without speaking, and, from time to time, I stole a glance at my companion. And, once again, I found myself impressed by something distinctive and unusual in her appearance. Her unquestionable beauty was not like that of most pretty women, localized and unequal, having features of striking attractiveness set in an indifferent or even defective matrix. It was diffused and all pervading, the product of sheer physical excellence. With most women one feels that the more attractive wares are judiciously pushed to the front of the window while a discreet reticence is maintained respecting the unpresentable residue. Not so with Mrs. Samway. Her small, shapely head, her symmetrical face, her fine supple figure, and her easy movements, all spoke of a splendid physique. She was not merely a pretty woman, she was that infinitely rarer creature, a physically perfect human being; comely with the comeliness of faultless proportion, graceful with the grace of symmetry and strength.

Suddenly she looked up at me with just a hint of shyness and a little heightening of the colour in her cheek.

"Are you going to tell me again, Dr. Jardine, that a cat may look at a king? Or was it that a king may look at a cat?"

"Whichever you please," I replied. "We will put them on a footing of equality, excepting that the king might have the better claim if the cat happened to be an exceptionally good-looking cat. But I wasn't really staring at you this time, I was only giving you a sort of friendly look over. You weren't quite yourself, I think, when we met last."

"No, I certainly was not. So you are now making an inspection. May I ask if I am to be informed of the diagnosis, as I think you call it?"

Now, to tell the truth, I had thought her looking rather haggard and worn and decidedly thinner; and when her sprightliness subsided in the intervals of our somewhat flippant talk, it had seemed to me that her face took on an expression that was weary and even and. But it would hardly do to say as much.

"It is quite irregular," I replied. "The diagnosis is for the doctor; the patient is only concerned with the treatment. But I'll make an exception in your case, especially as my report is quite unsensational. I thought you looked as if you had been doing rather too much and not greatly enjoying the occupation. Am I right?"

"Yes. Quite right. I've had a lot of worry and bother lately, and not enough rest and peace."

"I hope all that is at an end now?"

"I don't know that it is," she replied, wearily, "or, for that matter, that it will ever be. Fate or destiny, or whatever we may call it, starts us upon a certain road, and along that road we must needs trudge, wherever it may lead."

I was rather startled at the sudden despondency of her tone. Apparently the road that Mrs. Samway trod was not strewn with roses.

"Still," I said," it is a long road that has no turning."

"It is," she agreed, bitterly, "but many have to travel such a road, to find the turning at last barred by the churchyard gate."

"Oh, come!" I protested, "we don't talk of churchyards at your time of life. We think of the jolly wayside inns and the buttercups and daisies and the may-blossom in the hedgerows. Churchyard indeed! We will leave that to the old folk and the village donkey, if you please."

She smiled rather wanly. Her gaiety seemed to have deserted her for good.

"The wayside inns and the wayside flowers," said she, "are your portion—at least, I hope so. They are not for me. And, after all, there are worse things to think of than a nice quiet churchyard, with the village donkey browsing among the graves, as you say."

"I quite agree with you. From the standpoint of the disinterested spectator, not contemplating freehold investments, nothing can be more delightfully rustic and peaceful. It is the personal application that I object to."

Again she smiled, but very pensively, and for a while we walked on in silence. Presently she resumed. "I used to think that the shortness of life was quite a tragedy. That was when I was young. But now —"

"When you were young!" I interrupted. "Why, what are you now? I can tell you, Mrs. Samway, that there is many a girl of twenty who would be only too delighted to exchange personalities with you, and who would stand to make a mighty fine bargain if she could do it. If you talk like this, I shall have to refer you to the great Leonardo's advice to painters."

"What is that?" she asked.

"He recommends the frequent use of a looking-glass." She gave me a quick glance and then blushed so very deeply that I was quite alarmed lest I should have given offence. But her next words reassured me.

"It was nice of you to say that, and most kindly meant. I won't say that I don't care very much how I look, because that would be an ungracious return for your compliment and it wouldn't be quite true. There are times when one is quite glad to feel that one looks presentable; the present moment, for instance."

I acknowledged the compliment, with a bow. "Thank you." I said. "That was more than I deserved. I only wish that your fortune was equal to your looks, but I am afraid it isn't. I have an uncomfortable feeling that you are not very happy."

"I'm afraid I'm not," she replied. "Life is rather a lottery, you know, and the worst of it is that you can only take a single ticket. So, when you find that you've drawn the wrong number and you realize that there is no second chance–well, it isn't very inspiriting, is it?"

I had to admit that it was not; and, after a short pause, she continued: "Women are poor dependent creatures, Dr. Jardine; dependent, I mean, for their happiness on the people who surround them."

"But that is true of us all."

"Not quite. A man–like yourself, for instance–has his work and his ambitions that make him independent of others. But, for a woman, whatever pretences she may make as to larger interests in life, a husband, a home and one or two nice children form the real goal of her ambition."

"But you are not a lone spinster, Mrs. Samway," I reminded her.

"No, I am not. But I have no children, no proper home, and not a real friend in the world–unless I may think of you as one."

"I hope you always will," I exclaimed impulsively; for there was, to me, something very pathetic in the evident loneliness of this woman. She must, I felt, be friendless indeed if she must needs appeal for friendship to a comparative stranger like myself.

"I am glad to hear you say that," she replied, "for I am making you bear a friend's burden. I hope you will forgive me for pouring out my complaints to you in this way."

"It isn't difficult," said I, "to bear other people's troubles with fortitude. But if sympathy is any good, believe me, Mrs. Samway, when I tell you that I am really deeply grieved to think that you are getting so much less out of life than you ought. I only wish that I could do something more than sympathize."

"I believe you do," she said. "I felt, at Folkestone, how kind you were–as a good man is to a woman in her moments of weakness. That is why, I suppose, I was impelled to talk to you like this. And that is why," she added, after a little pause, "I felt a pang of envy when I saw you pass with your pretty companion."

I started somewhat at this. Where the deuce could she have seen us near enough to tell whether my companion was pretty or not? I turned the matter over rapidly in my mind, and meanwhile, I said: "I don't quite see why you envied me, Mrs. Samway."

"I didn't say that I envied you," she replied, with a faint smile and the suspicion of a blush.

"Or her either," I retorted. "We are only the merest acquaintances."

My conscience smote me somewhat as I made this outrageous statement, but Mrs. Samway took me up instantly. "Then you've only known her quite a short time?"

The rapidity with which she had jumped to this conclusion fairly took my breath away, and I had answered her question before I was aware of it.

"But," I added, "I don't quite see how you arrived at your conclusion."

"I thought," she replied, "that you seemed to like one another very well."

"So we do, I think. But can't acquaintances like one another?"

"Oh, certainly; but if they are a young man and a maiden they are not likely to remain mere acquaintances very long. That was how I argued."

"I see. Very acute of you. By the way, where did you see us? I didn't see you."

"Of course you didn't. Yet you passed quite close to me on the Spaniard's Road, immersed in conversation, and little suspecting that the green eyes of envy were fixed on you."

"Oh, now, Mrs. Samway, I can't have that. They're not green, you know, although what their exact colour is I shouldn't like to say offhand."

"What! Not after that careful inspection?"

"That didn't include the eyes. Perhaps you wouldn't mind if I made another, just to satisfy my curiosity and settle the question for good."

"Oh, do, by all means, if it is such a weighty question."

We both halted and I stared into the clear depths of her singular, pale hazel eyes with an impertinent affectation of profound scrutiny, while she looked up smilingly into mine. Suddenly, to my utter confusion, her eyes filled and she turned away her head.

"Oh! Please forgive me!" she exclaimed. "I beg your pardon–I do beg your pardon most earnestly for being such a wretched bundle of emotions. You would forgive me if you knew–what I can't tell you."

"There is no need, dear Mrs. Samway," I said very gently, laying my hand on her arm. "Are we not friends? And may I not give you my warmest sympathy without asking too curiously what brings the tears to your eyes?"

I was, in truth, deeply moved, as a young man is apt to be by a pretty woman's tears. But more than this, something whispered to me that my playful impertinence had suddenly brought home to her the void that was in her life; the lack of intimate affection at which she had seemed to hint. And, instantly, all that was masculine in me had risen up with the immemorial instinct of the male in defence of the female; for, whatever her faults may have been, Mrs. Samway was feminine to the finger-tips.

She pressed my hand for a moment and impatiently brushed the tears from her eyes.

"I do hope, Dr. Jardine." she said, looking up at me with a smile, "that your wife will be a good woman. You'll be a dreadful victim if she isn't, with your quick sympathy and your endless patience with feminine silliness. And now I won't plague you any more with my tantrums. I hope I am not bringing you a great deal out of your way. You do live in this direction, don't you?"

"Yes; and I have been assuming that my direction was yours, too. Is that right? Are you going back to Hampstead Road?"

"Not at once. I'm going to make a call at Highgate first."

"Then you'll want to go up Highgate Rise or Swain's Lane; and I will walk up with you if you'll let me."

"I think my nearest way will be up the little path that leads out of Swain's Lane. You know it, I expect?"

"Yes. It is locally known as Love Lane: it leads to the crest of the hill."

"That is right. You shall see me to the top of it and then I'll take myself off and leave you in peace."

We had by this time crossed Parliament Hill Fields and passed the end of the Highgate Ponds. A few paces more brought us out at the top of the Grove and a few more to the entrance of the rather steep and very narrow lane. For some time Mrs. Samway walked by my side in silence, and, by the reflective way in which she looked at the ground before her, seemed to be wrapped in meditation, which I did not disturb. As we entered the lane, however, she looked up at me thoughtfully and said: "I wonder what you think of me, Dr. Jardine."

It was a fine opening for a compliment, but somehow, compliments seemed out of place, after what had passed between us. I accordingly evaded the question with another.

"What do you suppose I think of you?"

"I don't know. I hardly know what I think of myself. You would be quite justified in thinking me rather forward, to waylay you in this deliberate fashion."

"Well, I don't. Your curiosity about that Folkestone affair seems most natural and reasonable."

"I'm glad you don't think me forward," she said; "but, as to my curiosity, I am beginning to doubt whether it was that alone that determined me of a sudden to come here and talk to you. I half suspect that I was feeling a little more solitary than usual, and that some instinct told me that you would be kind to me and say nice things and pet me just a little–as you have done."

I was deeply touched by her pathetic little confession; so deeply that I could find nothing to say in return.

"You don't think any the worse of me," she continued, "for coming to you and begging a little sympathy and friendship?"

As she spoke, she looked up very wistfully and earnestly in my face, and rested her hand for a moment on my arm. I took it in mine and drew her arm under my own as I replied: "Of course I don't. Only I think it a wonder and a shame that my poor friendship and sympathy should be worth the consideration of a woman like you."

She pressed my arm slightly, and, after a little interval, said in a low voice with just the suspicion of a tremor in it: "You have been very kind to me, Dr. Jardine; more kind than you know. I am very, very grateful to you for taking what was really an intrusion so nicely."

"It was not in the least an intrusion," I protested; "and as to gratitude, a good many men would be very delighted to earn it on the same terms. You don't seem to set much value on your own exceedingly agreeable society."

She smiled very prettily at this, and again we walked on for a while up the slope without speaking. Once she turned her head as if listening for some sound from behind us, but our feet were making so much noise on the loose gravel, and the sound reverberated so much in the narrow space between the wooden fences that I, at least, heard nothing. Presently we turned a slight bend and came in sight of the opening at the top of the hill, guarded by a couple of posts. Within a few yards of the latter she halted, and withdrawing her hand from my arm, turned round and faced me.

"We must say 'Good-bye' here," said she. "I wonder if I shall ever see you again."

For a moment I felt a strong impulse to propose some future meeting at a definite date, but fortunately some glimmering of discretion–and perhaps some thought of Sylvia–restrained me.

"Why shouldn't you?" I asked.

"I don't know. But mine is rather a vagabond existence, and I suppose you will be travelling about I hope we shall meet again soon; but if we do not, I shall always think of you as my friend, and you will have a kind thought for me sometimes, won't you?"

"I shall indeed. I shall think of you very often and hope that your life is brighter than it seems to be now."

"Thank you," she said earnestly; "and now 'Good-bye!'"

She held out her hand, and, as I grasped it, she looked in my face with the wistful, yearning expression that I had noticed before, and which so touched me to the heart that, yielding to a sudden impulse, I drew her to me and kissed her. Dim as was the light of the fading winter's day, I could see that she had, in an instant, turned scarlet. But she was not angry; for, as she drew away from me, shyly and almost reluctantly, she gave me one of her prettiest smiles and whispered "Good-bye" again. Then she ran out between the posts, and, turning once again–and still as red as a peony–waved me a last farewell.

I stood in the narrow entrance looking out after her with a strange mixture of emotions; pity, wonder and admiration and a little doubt as to my own part in the late transaction. For I had never before kissed a married woman, and cooling judgment did not altogether approve the new departure; for if Mr. Samway was not all that he might be, still he was Mr. Samway and I wasn't. Nevertheless, I stood and watched my late companion with very warm interest until she faded into the dusk; and even then I continued to stand by the posts, gazing out into the waning twilight and cogitating on our rather strange interview.

Suddenly my ear caught a sound from behind me, down the lane; a sound which, while it set my suspicion on the alert, brought a broad grin to my face. It was what I suppose I must call a stealthy footstep, but the stealthiness might have stood for the very type and essence of futility, for, as I have said, the ground sloped pretty steeply and was covered with loose pebbles, whereby every movement of the foot was rendered as audible as a thunderclap. However, absurd as the situation seemed–if the unseen person was really trying to approach by stealth–it was necessary to be on my guard. Moreover, if this should chance to be the person with the nystagmus, the present seemed to be an excellent opportunity for coming to some sort of understanding with him.

Accordingly I wheeled about and began to walk back down the lane. Instantly, the steps–no longer stealthy– began to retire. I quickened my pace; the unknown and invisible eavesdropper quickened his. Then I broke into a run, and so did he, notwithstanding which, I think I should have had him but for an untoward accident. The ground was not only sloping, but, under the loose gravel, was as hard as stone.

Consequently, the foothold was none of the best, as I presently discovered, for, as I raced down one of the steepest slopes, the pebbles suddenly rolled away under my foot and I lost my balance. But I did not fall instantly. Half recovering, I flew forward, clawing the air, stamping, staggering, kicking up the gravel, and making the most infernal hubbub and clatter, before I finally subsided into a sitting posture on the pebbles. When I rose, the footsteps were no longer audible, though the lower end of the lane was still some distance away.

I resumed my progress at a more sedate pace and kept a sharp look-out for a possible ambush, though the lane was too narrow, even in the darkness that now pervaded it, to furnish much cover to an enemy. Some distance down, I came to an opening in the fence, where one or two boards had become loose, and was half disposed to squeeze through and explore. But I did not, for, on reflection, it occurred to me that if the man was not there it would be useless for me to go, while if he should be hiding behind the fence it would be simply insane of me to put my head through the hole.

When I emerged into the road at the bottom, I looked about vaguely, but, of course there was no sign of the fugitive—nor, indeed, could I have identified him if I had met him. I loitered about undecidedly for a minute or two, and then, realizing the futility of keeping a watch on the entrance of the lane for a man whom I could not recognize, and becoming conscious of a ravenous desire for food I made my way down the Grove in the direction of my lodgings.

15
EXIT DR. JARDINE

MY second visit to "The Hawthorns," to which I had looked forward with some eagerness, had, after all, to be postponed indefinitely. I say "had," since, under the circumstances, it appeared to be so unsafe that I could not fairly take the risk that it involved. I had made the engagement thoughtlessly, and, in my preoccupation with Mrs. Samway, had not realized the indiscretion to which I had committed myself until I was brought back sharply to the actual conditions by the incident in Love Lane which I have mentioned. But, after that, I saw that it would be the wildest folly to show myself in the vicinity of Sylvia's house. Evidently the spy, after we had given him the slip so neatly, had made direct for my lodgings and lurked in the neighbourhood, and there it must have been that he had picked me up again as I passed with Mrs. Samway. Of course it was possible that the unseen person in the lane was not really shadowing me at all; but his stealthy approach, his hasty retreat and his mysterious disappearance, left me in very little doubt on the subject.

I was not very nervous about this enigmatical person on my own account. In spite of my alarming experiences, I found it difficult to take him as seriously as I should have done, and still felt a quite unjustifiable confidence in my capability of taking care of myself. But on Sylvia's account I was exceedingly uneasy. The interest that this man had shown in the unlucky little ornament that she wore, associated itself in my mind most disagreeably with her mysterious and terrifying adventure in Millfield Lane, and made me feel that it would be sheer insanity for me to go from my house to hers and so possibly give this unknown villain the clue to her whereabouts.

This conclusion, at which I had arrived overnight, was confirmed on the following morning, for, having taken a brisk walk out in the direction of Harrow, and having kept a very sharp look-out, I was distinctly conscious of the fact that there always appeared to be a man in sight. I never got near him and was not able to recognize him, but at intervals throughout the morning he continually reappeared in the distance, even on the comparatively solitary country roads and the hedge-divided meadows. It was excessively irritating. Yet what could I do? Even if I could have identified him with the man who had apparently shadowed me before, I really had nothing against him. And cogitating on the matter, with no little annoyance, I determined to take counsel with Thorndyke, and meanwhile to avoid the neighbourhood of "The Hawthorns."

After lunch, I wrote a letter to Sylvia, briefly explaining the state of affairs, and, having given it to our maid to deliver, I took the precaution to go out and saunter towards Kentish Town with the object of engaging the spy's attention and preventing him from following my messenger to North End. The rest of the day I spent at home and occupied my time in writing a long letter to Thorndyke in which I gave a pretty detailed account of my recent experiences; which letter was duly posted by Mrs. Blunt herself in time for the evening collection.

I had barely seated myself at the breakfast table on the following morning when a telegram was brought to me. On opening it I found that it was from Thorndyke, advising me that a letter had been dispatched by hand and asking me to stay at home until I had received it; which I did; and within an hour it arrived and was delivered into my own hands by a messenger boy.

It was curt and rather peremptory in tone, desiring me to meet him at one o'clock at Salter's Club in a turning off St. James's Street and concluding with these somewhat remarkable instructions: "I want you to wear an overcoat and hat of a distinctive and easily recognizable character and to take every means that you can of being seen and, if possible, followed to the club. You had better put a few necessaries in a bag or suit-case and tell your landlady that you may not be home tonight. Follow these instructions to the letter and bring this note with you."

At the latter part of these directions I was somewhat disposed to boggle, remembering my worthy teacher's threat to put me somewhere out of harm's way. But Thorndyke was a difficult man to disobey. Suave and persuasive as his manners were, he had a certain final and compelling way with him that silenced objections and produced a sort of frictionless obedience without any sense of compulsion. Hence, notwithstanding a slight tendency to bluster and tell myself that I would see him hanged before I would submit to being mollycoddled like an idiot, I found myself, presently, walking down the Grove in a buff overcoat and a grey felt hat, carrying a green canvas suit-case in which were packed the necessaries for a brief stay away from home, and bearing in my pocket the incriminating letter.

I walked slowly as far as the Junction Road in order to give any pursuer a fair opportunity to take up the chase and to make the necessary observations on my tasteful turn-out. At the Junction I waited for a tram and carefully abstained from staring about in a manner which would have embarrassed any person who might wish unobserved to share the conveyance with me; and from the terminus at Euston Road I proceeded in leisurely fashion on foot, still resisting the temptation to look about and see if I had picked up a companion by the way.

Salter's Club was domiciled in a typical West End house situated in a quiet street of similar houses, graced at one end by a cabstand. I timed my arrival with such accuracy that a neighbouring church-clock struck one as I ascended the steps; and on my entering the hall, I was met by an elderly man in a quiet livery who seemed to expect me, for, when I mentioned Thorndyke's name, he asked,

"Dr. Jardine, sir?" and, hardly waiting for my reply, showed me to the cloak-room. "Dr. Thorndyke," said he, "will be with you in a few minutes. When you have washed, I will show you to the dining room where he wished you to wait for him."

I was just a little surprised at even this short delay, for Thorndyke was the soul of punctuality. However, I had not to wait long. I had been sitting less than three minutes at a small table laid for two in the deep bay window, scanning the street through the wire-gauze blinds, when he arrived.

"I needn't apologize, I suppose, Jardine," he said, shaking my hand heartily. "You will have guessed why I have kept you waiting."

"You flatter me, sir," I replied with a slight grin. "I haven't your powers of instantaneous deduction."

"You hardly needed them," he retorted. "Of course I was watching your approach and observing the corner by which you entered the street to see who came after you."

"Did anyone come after me?"

"Several persons. I examined them all very carefully with a prism binocular that magnifies twelve times linear, and an assistant is now at the same window—the one over this—following the fortunes of those persons with the same excellent glass."

"Did you spot anyone in particular as looking a likely person?"

"Yes. The second man who came after you seemed to be sauntering in a rather unpurposive fashion and looking a little obtrusively unconcerned. I noticed, too, that he was carrying an umbrella in his left hand. But we needn't concern ourselves. If anyone is shadowing you we are certain to see him. He must expose himself to view from time to time, for he can't afford to lose sight of our doorway for more than a few seconds, and there is practically no cover in this street."

"He might hide in a doorway," I suggested.

"Oh, might he! These are all clubs in this street. He'd very soon have the servants out wanting to know his business. No; he'll have to keep on the move and he'll have to keep mostly in sight of this house. And meanwhile we are going to take our lunch at our leisure and have a little talk to while away the time."

The lunch was on a scale that my youthful appetite approved strongly, though the number of courses and irrelevant, time-consuming kickshaws struck me as rather unusual. And I never saw a man eat so slowly and delay a meal so much as Thorndyke did on that occasion. I believe that it took him fully twenty minutes to consume a fried sole; and even then he created a further delay by drawing my attention to the skeleton on his plate as an illustration of inherited deformity adjusted to special environmental conditions. But all the time, whether eating or talking, I noticed that his eye continually travelled up and down the stretch of street that was visible through the wire blinds.

"You haven't told me why you sent for me, sir," I said, after waiting patiently for him to open the subject.

"I dare say you have guessed," he replied; "but we may as well thrash the matter out now. You realize that you are running an enormous and unnecessary risk by going abroad with this man at your heels?"

"Well, I don't suppose he is following me about from sheer affection."

"No. I thought it possible that he might be a plain-clothes policeman, but I have ascertained that he is not. Who he is we don't know, but we have the strongest reasons for suspecting his intentions. There have been three very determined attempts on your life. They were all made with such remarkable caution and foresight that, though they failed, practically no traces have been left. Those attempts imply a strong motive, though to us, an unknown one; and that motive, presumably, still exists. Your enemy may well be getting desperate, and may be prepared to take greater risks to get rid of you; and if he is, the chances are that he will succeed sooner or later. Murder isn't very difficult to a cool-headed man who means business."

"Then what do you propose, sir?"

"I propose that you disappear from your ordinary surroundings and come and stay, for a time, at my chambers in the Temple."

This was no more than I had expected, but my jaw dropped considerably, notwithstanding. "It's awfully good of you, sir," I stammered—and so, to be sure, it was—"but don't you think it would be simpler to turn the tables on this Johnnie and shadow him?"

"An excellent idea, Jardine, and one, I may say, that I am acting on at this moment. But there isn't so much in it as you seem to think. Supposing we identify this man and even run him to earth? What then? We have nothing against him. We know of no crime that has been committed. We may suspect that the man whom you saw at Hampstead had been murdered. But we can't prove it. We can't produce the body or even prove that the man was dead. And we couldn't connect this person with the affair because nobody was known to be connected with it. I should like to know who this man is, but I don't want to put him on his guard; and above all, I can't agree to your going about as a sort of live-bait to enable us to locate him. By the way, that man on the opposite side of the street is the one whom I selected as being probably your attendant. Apparently I was right, as this is the third time he has passed. Do you recognize him?"

I looked attentively at the uncharacteristic figure on the farther side of the street, but could find nothing familiar in his appearance.

"No," I replied; "he doesn't look to me like the same man. He is dressed differently—but that's nothing, as he has been dressed differently on each occasion–and that torpedo beard and full moustache are quite unlike, though there's nothing in that either; but the man looks different altogether–distinctly taller, for instance."

Thorndyke chuckled. "Good," said he. "Now look at his feet, as he passes opposite. Did you ever see an instep set at that angle to the sole? And does not your anatomical conscience cry out at a foot of that thickness?"

"Yes, by Jove!" I exclaimed; "there's room for a double row of metatarsals. It is a fake of some kind, I suppose?"

"Cork 'raisers' inside high-heeled boots. Through the glasses I could see that the boots gaped considerably at the instep, as they will when there is a pad inside as well as a foot. But you notice, also, that the man is dressed for height. He has a tall hat, a long coat, and his shoulders are obviously raised by padding. I think there is very little doubt that he is our man."

"It must be a dull job," I remarked, "hanging about by the hour to see a man come out of a house."

"Very," Thorndyke agreed. "I am quite sorry for the worthy person, especially as we are going to play him a rather shabby trick presently."

"What are we going to do?" I asked.

"We are going to let him in for one of the longest waits he has ever had, I am afraid. Perhaps I had better give you the particulars of our modus operandi. First, I shall send down to the stand for a hansom, which will draw up opposite the club; and thereupon I have no doubt our friend will hurry down to the cab-stand to be in readiness. At any rate, I shall let him get down to that end of the street before I do anything more. Then I shall take the liberty of putting on your coat and hat and go out to the cab with your suit-case in my hand; I shall stand on the kerb long enough to let our friend get a good view of my back, I shall get into the cab, give the driver the direction through the trap to drive to the hospital, and pay the fare in advance."

"Why in advance?" I asked.

"So that I shall not have to turn round and show my face when I get out at the hospital entrance. I assume that your friend will follow me in another hansom. Also that he will alight at the outer gates, whereas I shall drive into the courtyard right up to the main entrance, so that he will merely see your hat, coat and suit-case disappear into the building. Then, as I say, he will be in for an interminable vigil. I have a lecture to give this afternoon, and, when I have finished, I shall come away in a black overcoat and tall hat (which are at this moment hanging up in the curator's room), leaving your friend to wait for the reappearance of your coat, hat and suit-case. I only hope he won't wait too long."

"Why?"

"Because he may wear out the patience of my assistant. I have a plain-clothes man keeping a watch from the window above. If your friend sets off in pursuit of your garments, as I anticipate, the plain-clothes man will go straight to the hospital and take up his post in the porter's lodge, which, as you know, commands the whole street outside the gates."

"And what have I got to do?"

"First of all, you will put your tooth brush in your pocket—never mind about your razor—and let me try on your hat, in case we have to pad the lining. Then, when you have seen your friend start off in pursuit and are sure the coast is clear, you will make straight for my chambers and wait there for me."

"And supposing the chappie doesn't start off in pursuit? Supposing he twigs the imposture?"

"Then the plain-clothes man will go out and threaten to arrest him for loitering with intent to commit a felony. That would soon move him on out of the neighbourhood, and the officer might accompany him some distance and try to get his address. Meanwhile, you would be off to King's Bench Walk."

"But wouldn't it be simpler to run the Johnnie in, in any case? Then we should know all about him."

"No, it wouldn't do. The police wouldn't actually make an arrest without an information; and, if they did proceed, they would want me to appear. That wouldn't suit me at all. Until we obtain some fresh evidence, I don't want this man to get any suspicion that the case is being investigated. And now I think the time has come for a move. Let us go to the cloakroom and see if your hat fits me sufficiently well."

It was not a good fit, being just a shade small; but, as it was a soft felt, this was not a vital defect. The overcoat fitted well enough, though a trifle long in the sleeves, and when Thorndyke was fully arrayed in this borrowed plumage, his back view, so far as I could judge, was indistinguishable from my own.

"If you will take out your toothbrush and hand me your suit-case," said he, "I will send for a hansom, and then we will watch the progress of events from the dining-room window."

I handed him the green canvas case and we returned to the dining-room and there, when he had ordered the cab, we took up a position at the window, screened from observation by the wire blinds.

"Our friend," said Thorndyke, "was walking towards the right hand end of the street when we saw him last. As the cabstand is at the left hand end, we may hope to look upon his face once again."

As he spoke, the air was rent by the shriek of the cab-whistle, and the leading hansom began immediately to bear down on the club. It had hardly come to rest at our door when a figure appeared from the opposite direction, advancing at a brisk walk on our side of the road. I recognized him instantly as the man to whom Thorndyke had directed my attention, and watched him closely, as he approached, to see if I could identify him with the man who had shadowed Sylvia and me at the picture gallery;

but, though he passed within a few yards of the window, and I felt no doubt that he was the same man, I could trace no definite resemblance. It is true, that while actually passing the club, he averted his face somewhat; but I had a good view of him within an easy distance, and the face that I then saw was certainly not the face of the man at the gallery. The skillfulness of the make-up— assuming it to be really a disguise—was incredible, and I remarked on it to Thorndyke.

"Yes," he agreed, "a really artistic make-up is apt to surprise the uninitiated. And that reminds me that Polton has instructions to make a few trifling alterations in your own appearance."

I stared at him aghast. "You don't mean to say," I exclaimed, "that you contemplate making me up?"

"We won't discuss the question now," he replied a little evasively. "You talk it over with Polton. It is time for me to go now, as our quarry has considerately acted up to our expectations. He little knows what confusion of our plans he would have occasioned by simply staying at the other end of the street."

The spy had, in fact, now halted opposite the cabstand and was apparently making some notes in a pocket-book, facing, meanwhile, in our direction. With a few parting instructions to me, Thorndyke picked up the suit-case and hurried out, and I saw him dart down the steps-with his face turned somewhat to the right-and stand for a few seconds at the edge of the pavement with his back to the cabstand, but in full view, looking at his watch as if considering some appointment. Suddenly he sprang into the cab and, pushing up the trap, gave the driver his instructions and handed up the fare. At the same moment I saw the unknown shadower hail a hansom, and, scrambling to the footboard, give some brief directions to the driver. Then Thorndyke's cabman touched his horse with the whip, and away he went at a smart trot; but hardly had the cab turned the first corner when the second hansom rattled past the club in hot pursuit.

I was about to turn away from the window when a tall, well-dressed man ran down the steps and immediately signalled to the cabstand with his stick. Thinking it probable that this was the plain-clothes policeman, I stopped to watch; and when I had seen him enter the cab and drive off in the same direction as the other two, I decided that the show was over and that it was time for me to take my departure; which I did, after stuffing a couple of envelopes into the lining of Thorndyke's hat, to prevent it from slipping down towards my ears.

That my arrival at number 5A, King's Bench Walk was not quite unexpected I gathered not only from the fact that the "oak" stood wide open, revealing the inner door, but from the instantaneous way in which this latter opened in response to my knock; and something gleeful and triumphant in Mr. Polton's manner as he invited me to enter, stirred my suspicions and aroused vague forebodings.

He helped me out of my—or rather Thorndyke's—overcoat, and; having taken the hat from me, peered inquiringly into its interior and fished out the two envelopes, which he politely offered to me. Then, having disposed of his employer's property, he returned to confront me, and, wrinkling his countenance into a most singular and highly corrugated smile, he opened his mouth and spoke.

"So you have come, sir, the Doctor tells me, to take sanctuary for a time with us from the malice of your enemies."

"I don't know about that," I replied; "but there is a cockeyed transformationist who seems to be dodging about after me, and Dr. Thorndyke thinks I had better give him the go-by for the present."

"And very proper, too, sir. Discretion is the better part of valour, as the proverb says—though I really could never see that it is any part at all. But no doubt our forefathers, who made the proverb, knew best. Did the Doctor mention that he had given me certain instructions about you?"

"He said that I was to talk over some question with you, but I didn't quite follow him. What were his instructions?"

Polton rubbed his hands, and his face became more crinkly than ever. "The Doctor instructed me," he replied, looking at me hungrily and obviously making a mental inventory of my features, "to effect certain slight alterations in your outward personality."

"Oh, did he," said I. "And what does he mean by that? Does he mean that you are to make me up as an old woman or a nigger minstrel?"

"Not at all, sir," replied Polton. "Neither of those characters would be at all suitable. They would occasion remark, which it is our object to avoid; and as to a negro minstrel, his presence in chambers would undoubtedly be objected to by the benchers."

"But," I expostulated," why any disguise at all, if I am to be boxed up in these chambers? The chappie isn't likely to come and look through the keyhole."

"He wouldn't see anything if he did," said Polton. "I fitted these locks. But, you see, sir, many strangers come to these chambers, and then, too, you might like to take a little exercise about the inn or the gardens. That would probably be quite safe if you were unrecognizable, but otherwise, I should think, inadmissible. And really, sir," he continued persuasively, "if you do a thing at all you may as well do it thoroughly. The Doctor wishes you to disappear; then disappear completely. Don't do it by halves."

I could not but admit to myself that this was reasonable advice. Nevertheless, I grumbled a little sulkily. "It seems to me that Dr. Thorndyke is making a lot of unnecessary fuss. It is absurd for an ablebodied man to be sneaking into a hiding-place and disguising himself like a runaway thief."

"I can offer no opinion on that, sir," said Polton; "but you're wrong about the Doctor. He is a cautious man but he is not nervous or fussy. You would be wise to act as he thinks best, I am sure."

"Very well," I said; "I won't be obstinate. When do you want to begin on me?"

"I should like," replied Polton, brightening up wonderfully at my sudden submission, "to have you ready for inspection by the time that the Doctor returns. If agreeable to you, sir, I would proceed immediately."

"Then in that case," said I, "we had better adjourn to the green-room forthwith."

"If you please, sir," replied Polton; and with this, having opened the door and cautiously inspected the landing, he conducted me up the stairs to the floor above, the rooms of which appeared to be fitted as workshops and laboratories. In one of the former, which appeared to be Polton's own special den, I saw my watch hanging from a nail, with a rating table pinned above it, and proceeded to claim it.

"I suppose, sir," said Polton, reluctantly taking it from its nail and surrendering it to me, "as you are going to reside on the premises and I can keep it under observation, you may as well wear it. The present rate is plus one point three seconds daily. And now I will trouble you to sit down on this stool and take off your collar."

I did as he bade me, and, meanwhile, he turned up his cuffs and stood a little way off, surveying me as a sculptor might survey a bust on which he was at work. Then he fetched a large cardboard box, the contents of which I could not see, and fell to work.

His first proceeding was to oil my hair thoroughly, part it in the middle and brush it smoothly down either side of my forehead. Next he shaved off the outer third of each eyebrow, and, having applied some sort of varnish or adhesive, he proceeded to build up, with a number of short hairs, a continuation of the eyebrows at a higher level. The result seemed to please him amazingly, for he stepped back and viewed me with an exceedingly self-satisfied smirk.

"It is really surprising, sir," said he, "how much expression there is in the corner of an eyebrow. You look a completely different gentleman already."

"Then," said I, "there's no need to do any more. We can leave it at this."

"Oh, no we can't, sir," Polton replied hastily, making a frantic dive into the cardboard box. "Begging your pardon, sir, it is necessary to attend to the lower part of the face, in case you should wish to wear a hat, which would cover the hair and throw the eyebrows into shadow."

Here he produced from the box an undeniable false beard of the torpedo type and approached me, holding it out as if it were a poultice.

"You are not going to stick that beastly thing on my face!" I exclaimed, gazing at it with profound disfavour.

"Now, sir," protested Polton, "pray be patient. We will just try it on, and the Doctor shall decide if it is necessary."

With this he proceeded to affix the abomination to my jowl with the aid of the same sticky varnish that he had used previously, and, having attached a moustache to my upper lip, worked carefully round the edges of both with a quantity of loose hair, which he stuck on the skin with the adhesive liquid and afterwards trimmed off with scissors. The process was just completed and he had stepped back once more to admire his work when an electric bell rang softly in the adjoining room.

"There's the Doctor," he remarked. "I'm glad we are ready for him. Shall we go down and submit our work for his inspection?"

I assented readily, having some hopes that Thorndyke would veto the beard, and we descended together to the sitting-room, where we found that Jervis and his principal had arrived together. As to the former, he greeted my entrance by staggering back several paces with an expression of terror, and then seated himself on the edge of the table and laughed with an air of enjoyment that was almost offensive; particularly to Polton, who stood by my side, rubbing his hands and smiling with devilish satisfaction.

"I assume," Thorndyke said, gravely," that this is our friend Jardine."

"It isn't," said Jervis. "It's the shopwalker from Wallis's. I recognized him instantly."

"Look here," I said, with some heat, "it's all very well for you to make me up like Charley's Aunt and then jeer at me, but what's the use of it? The fifth of November's past."

"My dear Jardine," Thorndyke said, soothingly, "you are confusing your sensations with your appearance. I daresay that make-up is rather uncomfortable, but it is completely successful, and I must congratulate Polton; for the highest aim of a disguise is the utterly common-place, and I assure you that you are now a most ordinary-looking person. Fetch the looking-glass from the office, Polton, and let him see for himself."

I gazed into the mirror which Polton held up to me with profound surprise. There was nothing in the least grotesque or unusual in the face that looked out at me, only it was the face of an utter stranger; and, as Thorndyke had said, a perfectly common-place stranger, at whom no one would look twice in the street. Grudgingly, I acknowledged the fact, but still objected to the beard.

"Do you think it is really necessary, sir, in addition to the other disfigurements?"

"Yes, I do," replied Thorndyke. "It is only a temporary expedient, because, in a fortnight, your own beard will have grown enough to serve with a little artificial re-enforcement. And," he continued, as Polton retired with a gratified smile, "I am anxious that your disappearance shall be complete. It is not only a question of your safety—although that is very urgent, and I feel myself responsible for you, as we are not appealing to the police. There are other issues. Assuming, as we do assume, that some crime has been committed, the lapse of time must inevitably cause some of the consequences of that crime to develop. If the man whose body you saw at Hampstead was really murdered, he must presently be missed and enquired for. Then we shall learn who he was and perhaps we may gather what was the motive of the crime. Then, your secret enemy will be left unemployed and may produce some fresh evidence—for he can't wait indefinitely for your reappearance. And finally, certain enquiries which I am making may set us on the right track. And, if they do, you must remember, Jardine, that you are probably the sole witness to certain important items of evidence; so you must be preserved in safety as a matter of public policy, apart from your own prejudices in favour of remaining alive."

"I didn't know that you were actually working at the case," I said. "Have you been following up that man Gill of the mineral water works?"

"I followed him up to the vanishing-point. He has gone and left no trace; and I have been unable to get any description of him."

"Then," said I, "if it is allowable to ask the question, in what direction have you been making enquiries?"

"I have been interesting myself," Thorndyke replied, "in the other case; that of your patient Mr. Maddock, as the attacks on you seemed to be associated with his neighbourhood rather than with that of Hampstead. I have examined his will at Somerset House and am collecting information about the persons who benefited by its provisions. Especially, I am making some enquiries about a legatee who lives in New York, and concerning whom I am rather curious. I can't go into further details just now, but you will see that I am keeping the case in hand, and you must remember that, at any moment, fresh information may reach me from other sources. My practice is a very peculiar one, and there are few really obscure cases that are not, sooner or later, brought to me for an opinion."

"And, meanwhile, I am to eat the bread of idleness here and wait on events."

"You won't be entirely idle," Thorndyke replied. "We shall find you some work to do, and you will extend your knowledge of medico-legal practice. You write shorthand fairly well, don't you?"

"Yes; and I can draw a little, if that is of any use."

"Both accomplishments are of use, and, even if they are not, we should have to exercise them for the sake of appearances. It will certainly become known that you are here, so we had better make no secret of it, but find you such occupation as will account for your presence. And, as you will have to meet strangers now and again, we must find you a name. What do you think of 'William Morgan Howard'?"

"It will do as well as any other," I replied.

"Very well, then William Morgan Howard let it be. And, in case you might forget your alias, as the crooks are constantly doing, we will drop the name of Jardine and call you Howard even when we are alone. It will save us all from an untimely slip."

To this arrangement also I agreed with a sour smile, and so, with some physical discomfort in the neighbourhood of the lower jaw, and a certain relish of the novelty and absurdity of my position, I placed myself, under the name of Howard, on the roster of Thorndyke's establishment.

16
ENTER FATHER HUMPERDINCK

ON the day following my–and Thorndyke's–masterly retreat from Salter's Club, the plain-clothes officer called to make his report; and even before he spoke, I judged from his rather sheepish expression that he had failed. And so it turned out. He had waited in the porter's lodge, he told us, until midnight keeping a watch on the watcher, who, for his part, lurked in the street, always keeping in sight of the hospital, and whiling away the time by gazing into the shop windows. The spy had evidently failed to recognize Thorndyke, for when the latter left the hospital in company with one of the physicians, he had given only a passing glance at the open carriage in which the two men sat.

After the shops had shut, the persevering shadower had occupied himself with a sort of dismal sentry-go up and down the street, disappearing into the darkness and reappearing at regular intervals. Once or twice, the plain-clothes man went out and followed his quarry in his perambulations, but, not considering it prudent to expose himself too much to view, he remained mostly in the Lodge. It was after one of these sallies that the mischance occurred. Returning to the Lodge, he saw the spy pass the gates and disappear up the dark street; he looked, after the usual interval, for him to reappear. But the interval passed and there was no reappearance. Then the officer hurried out in search of his quarry, but found only an empty street. Even the apparently inexhaustible patience of the spy had given out at last. And so the quest had ended.

I cannot say that Thorndyke impressed me as being deeply disappointed; in fact, I thought that he seemed, if anything, rather relieved at his emissary's failure. This was Jervis's opinion also, and he had no false delicacy about expressing it.

"Well," Thorndyke replied, "as the fellow thrust himself right under my nose, I could hardly do less than make some sort of an attempt to find out who he is. But I don't particularly want to know. My investigations are proceeding from quite another direction; and you see, Jervis, how awkward it might have been to have this person on our hands. We could only charge him with loitering with felonious intent, and we couldn't prove the intent after all; for we can't produce any evidence connecting this man with the three attempted murders. He may not be the same man at all. And I certainly don't want to go into the witness box just now, and still less do I want my new clerk, Mr. Howard, put into that position. I don't want to take any action until I have the case quite complete and am in a position to make a decisive move."

"The truth is," said Jervis, addressing me confidentially in a stage whisper, "Thorndyke hates the idea of spoiling a really juicy problem by merely arresting the criminal and pumping his friends. He looks on such a proceeding much as a Master of Foxhounds would look on the act of poisoning a fox."

Thorndyke smiled indulgently at his junior. "There is such a thing," said he, "as failing to poison a fox and only making him too unwell to leave his residence. A premature prosecution is apt to fail; and then the prisoner has seen all the cards of his adversaries. At present I am playing against an unseen adversary, but I am hoping that I, in my turn, am unseen by him, and I am pretty certain that he has no idea what cards I hold."

"Gad!" exclaimed Jervis," then he is much the same position as I am." And with this the subject dropped.

The first week of my residence in Thorndyke's chambers was quite uneventful, and was mainly occupied in settling down to the new conditions. My letters were sent on by Mrs. Blunt to the hospital whence they were brought by my principal—as I may now call my quondam teacher—with the exception of Sylvia's; which we had agreed were to be sent to the chambers enclosed in an envelope addressed to Thorndyke.

At first, I had feared that the confinement would be unendurable; but the reality proved to be much less wearisome than I had anticipated. A horizontal bar rigged up by Polton in the laboratory, gave me the means of abundant exercise of one kind; and in the early mornings, before the gates of the inn were opened, I made it my daily practice to trot round the precincts for an hour at a time, taking the circuit from our chambers through Crown Office Road to Fountain Court and back by way of Pump Court and the Cloisters, to the great benefit of my health and the mild surprise of the porters and laundresses.

Nor was I without occupation in the daytime. Besides an exhaustively detailed account of all the remarkable experiences that had befallen me of late which I wrote out at Thorndyke's request, I had a good deal of clerical work of one kind and another, and was frequently employed, when clients called, in exhibiting my skill as a stenographer; taking down oral statements, or making copies of depositions or other documents which were read over to me by Thorndyke or Jervis.

It was the exercise of these latter activities that introduced me to a certain Mr. Marchmont, and through him to some new and rather startling experiences. Mr. Marchmont was a solicitor, and, as I gathered, an old client of Thorndyke's; for, when he called one evening, about ten days after my arrival, with a bagful of documents, he made sundry references to former cases by which I understood that he and Thorndyke had been pretty frequently associated in their professional affairs.

"I have got a lot of papers here," he said, opening the bag, "of which I suppose I ought to have had copies made; but there hasn't been time and I am afraid there won't be, as I have to return them to-morrow. But perhaps, if you run your eye over them, you will see what it is necessary to remember and make a few notes."

"I think," said Thorndyke, "that my friend, Mr. Howard, will be able to help us by taking down the essentials in shorthand. Let me introduce you. Mr. Howard is very kindly assisting me for a time by relieving me of some of the extra clerical work."

Mr. Marchmont bowed, and, as we shook hands, looked at me, as I thought, rather curiously; then he extracted the papers from his bag, and, spreading them out on the table, briefly explained their nature.

"There is no need," said he, "to have copies of them all, but I thought you had better see them. Perhaps you will glance through them and see which you think ought to be copied for reference."

Thorndyke ran his eye over the documents, and, having made one or two brief notes of the contents of some, which he then laid aside, collected the remainder and began to read them out to me, while I took down the matter verbatim, interpolating Marchmont's comments and explanations on a separate sheet of paper. The reading and the discussion occupied a considerable time, and, before the business was concluded, the Treasury clock had struck half-past nine.

"It's getting late," said Marchmont, folding the papers and putting them back in the bag. "I must be going or you'll wish me at Halifax, if you aren't doing so already."

He snapped the fastening of the bag, and, grasping the handle, was about to lift it from the table, when he appeared to recollect something, for he let go the handle and once more faced my principal.

"By the way, Thorndyke," said he, "there is a matter on which I have wanted to consult you for some time past, but couldn't get my client to agree. It is a curious affair; quite in your line, I think; a case of disappearance—not in the legal sense, as creating a presumption of death, but disappearance from ordinary places of resort with a very singular change of habits, so far as I can learn. Possibly a case of commencing insanity. I have been wanting to lay the facts before you, but my client, who is a Jesuit and as suspicious as the devil, insisted on trying to ferret out the evidence for himself and wouldn't hear of a consultation with you. Of course he has failed completely, and now, I think, he is more amenable."

"Are you in possession of the facts, yourself?" asked Thorndyke.

"No, I'm hanged if I am," replied Marchmont. "The case is concerned with a certain Mr. Reinhardt, who was a client of my late partner, poor Wyndhurst. I never had anything to do with him; and it unfortunately happens that our old clerk, Bell–you remember Bell–who had charge of Mr. Reinhardt's business, left us soon after poor Wyndhurst's death, so there is nobody in the office who has any personal knowledge of the parties."

"You say it is a case of disappearance?" said Thorndyke.

"Not exactly disappearance, but–well, it is a most singular case. I can make nothing of it, and neither can my worthy and reverend client, so as I say, he is now growing more amenable, and I think I shall be able to persuade him to come round with me and take your opinion on such facts as we have. Shall you be at home to-morrow evening?"

"Yes, I can make an appointment for to-morrow, after dinner, if you prefer that time."

"We won't call it an appointment," said Marchmont. "If I can overcome his obstinacy, I will bring him round and take the chance of your being in. But I think he'll come, as he is on his beams ends; and if he does, I fancy you will find the little problem exactly to your liking."

With this Mr. Marchmont took his departure, leaving Thorndyke and me to discuss the various legal aspects of disappearance and the changes of habit and temperament that usher in an attack of mental alienation. I could see that the solicitor's guarded references to an obscure and intricate case had aroused Thorndyke's curiosity to no small extent, for, though he said little on the subject, it evidently remained in his mind, as I judged by the care with which he planned the disposal of his time of the following day, and the little preparations that he made for the reception of his visitors. Nor was Thorndyke the only expectant member of our little establishment. Jervis also, having caught the scent of an interesting case, made it his business to keep the evening free, and so it happened that when eight o'clock struck on the Temple bell, it found us gathered round the fire, chatting on indifferent subjects, but all three listening for the expected tread on the stairs.

"It is to be hoped," said Jervis, "that our reverend friend won't jib at the last moment. I always expect something good from Marchmont. He doesn't get flummoxed by anything simple or common place. I think we have had most of our really thrilling cases through him. And seeing that Jardine has laid in two whole quarto note-blocks and put those delightful extra touches to his already alluring get-up —"

"There is no such person here as Jardine," Thorndyke interrupted.

"I beg his pardon. Mr. Howard, I should have said. But listen! There are two persons coming up the stairs. You had better take your place at the table, Ja-Howard, and look beastly business-like, or the reverend gentleman will want you chucked out, and then you'll lose the entertainment."

I hurried across to the table and had just seated myself and taken up a pen when the brass knocker on our inner door rattled out its announcement. Thorndyke strode across and threw the door open, and as Mr. Marchmont entered with his client I looked at the latter inquisitively. But only for a single instant. Then I looked down and tried to efface myself utterly, for Mr.

Marchmont's client was none other than the cleric with whom I had travelled from Folkestone to London. The solicitor ushered in his client with an air of but half-concealed triumph and proceeded with exaggerated geniality to do the honours of introduction.

"Let me make you known to one another, gentlemen," said he. "This is the Very Reverend Father Humperdinck. These gentlemen are Dr. Thorndyke, Dr. Jervis and Mr. Howard, who will act, on this occasion, as the recording angel to take down in writing the particulars of your very remarkable story."

Father Humperdinck bowed stiffly. He was evidently a little disconcerted at finding so large an assembly, and glanced at me, in particular, with undisguised disfavour, while I, my oiled hair, deformed eyebrows and false beard notwithstanding, perspired with anxiety lest he should recognize me. But however unfavourably the reverend father may have viewed our little conclave, Mr. Marchmont, who had been watching him anxiously, gave him no chance of raising objections, but proceeded to open the matter forthwith.

"I have not brought any digest or precis of the case," said he, "because I know you prefer to hear the facts from the actual parties. But I had better give you a brief outline of the matter of our inquiry. The case is concerned with a Mr. Vitalis Reinhardt, who has been closely associated with Father Humperdinck for very many years past, and who has now, without notice or explanation, disappeared from his ordinary places of resort, ceased from communication with his friends, and adopted a mode of life quite alien from and inconsistent with his previous habits. Those are the main facts, stated in general terms."

"And the inquiry to which you referred to?" said Thorndyke.

"Concerns itself with three questions," replied Marchmont, and he proceeded to check them off on his fingers.

"First, is Vitalis Reinhardt alive or dead? Second, if he is alive, where is he? Third, having regard to the singular change in his habits, is his conduct such as might render it possible to place him under restraint or to prove him unfit to control his own affairs?"

"To certify him as insane, if I may put it bluntly," said Thorndyke. "That question could be decided only on a full knowledge of the nature of the changes in this person's habits, with which, no doubt, you are prepared to furnish us. But what instantly strikes me in your epitome of the proposed inquiry is this: you raise the question whether Mr. Reinhardt is alive or dead, and then you refer to certain changes in his habits; but, since a man must be alive to have any habits at all, the two questions seem to be mutually irreconcilable in relation to the same group of facts."

Father Humperdinck nodded approvingly. "Zat is chust our great diffigulty," said he. "Zome zings make me suspect zat my friend Reinhardt is dead; zome ozzer zings make me feel certain zat he is alife. I do not know vich to zink. I am gombletely buzzled."

"Perhaps," said Thorndyke, "the best plan would be for Father Humperdinck to give us a detailed account of his relations with Mr. Reinhardt and of the latter gentleman's habits as they are known to him; after which we could discuss any questions that suggest themselves and clear up any points that seem to be obscure. What do you say, Marchmont?"

"It will be a long story," Marchmont replied doubtfully.

"So much the better," rejoined Thorndyke. "It will give us the more matter for consideration. I would suggest that Father Humperdinck tells us the story in his own way and that Mr. Howard takes down the statement.

Then we shall have the principal data and can pursue any issue that seems to invite further investigation."

To this proposal Marchmont agreed, a little reluctantly, fortifying himself for the ordeal by lighting a cigar; and Father Humperdinck, having cast a somewhat disparaging glance at me, began his account of his missing friend, which I took down verbatim, and which I now reproduce shorn of the speaker's picturesque but rather tiresome peculiarities of pronunciation.

"My acquaintance with Vitalis Reinhardt began more than forty years ago, when we were both schoolboys in the Jesuit's house at Louvain. But I did not see much of him then, as I was preparing for the novitiate while he was on the secular side. In spite of his German name, Vitalis was looked upon as an English boy, for his father had married a rich English lady and was settled in England; and Vitalis, being the only child, had very great expectations. When he left school I lost sight of him for some years, and it was only after the war had broken out between Germany and France that we met again. I had then just been ordained and was attached as chaplain to a Bavarian regiment; he had come out from England as a volunteer to attend the sick and wounded; and so we met, soon after the battle of Saarbrück, in the wards of a temporary hospital. But our career in the field was not a long one. Less than a month after Saarbrück, our little force met a French division and had to retreat, leaving a number of men and guns and all the wounded in the hands of the enemy. Both of us were among the prisoners, and Vitalis was one of the wounded, for, just as the retreat began, a French bullet struck him in the right hip. We were both taken to Paris with the rest of the prisoners, and there, in the hospital for wounded prisoners, I was allowed to visit him.

"His wound was a severe one. The bullet had entered deeply and lodged behind the bone of the hip, so that the repeated efforts of the surgeons to extract it not only failed but caused great pain and made the wound worse. From day to day poor Vitalis grew thinner and more yellow, and we could see plainly that if no change occurred, the end must come quite soon. So the doctors said and so Vitalis himself felt.

"Then it came to me that, if the skill of man failed us, we should ask for help from above. It happened that I possessed a relic of the blessed Saint Vincent de Paul, which was contained in a small gold reliquary, and which I had been permitted by the Father General to keep. I proposed to Vitalis that we should apply the relic and make a special appeal to the saint for help, and also that he should promise to dedicate some part of his great possessions to the service of God.

"He agreed readily, for he had always been a deeply pious man. Accordingly he made the promises as I had suggested, we offered up special prayers to the saint, and, with the permission of the surgeons, I attached the reliquary to the dressings of the wound, praying that it should avail to draw out the bullet."

"And did it?" asked Marchmont in a tone which evidently did not escape the observant Jesuit, for that noble-witted gentleman turned sharply on the lawyer and replied with severe emphasis:

"No, sir, it did not. And why? Because there was no need. The very next day after the reliquary was applied, when the dressings were changed, a small shred of filthy cloth came out of the wound. That was the cause of the trouble, not the clean metal bullet. The saint, you see, sir, knew better than the surgeon."

"Evidently," said Marchmont, glancing quickly at me, and the expression that I caught in the eye of that elderly heathen suggested that he had actually contemplated a wink and then thought better of it.

"As soon as the piece of cloth was out of the wound," Father Humperdinck resumed, "all the trouble ceased. The fever abated, the wound healed, and very soon Vitalis was able to get about, none the worse for his mishap.

"It was natural that he should be grateful to the saint who had saved his life, for though we look forward to the hereafter, we do not wish to die. Also was it natural that he should feel a devotion to the holy relic which had been the appointed instrument of his recovery. He did, and to gratify him, I obtained the Father General's permission to bestow it on him, which gave him great joy, and thenceforth he always carried the reliquary on his person."

"I hope he kept his promise to the saint," said Marchmont.

"He did; faithfully, and, indeed, handsomely. No sooner was he recovered of his wound than he proposed to me the founding of a new society of brothers of charity to attend the sick and wounded. I consulted with the Father General of my Society—the Society of Jesus—and received his sanction to act as director of the new society or fraternity which was to be affiliated to the Society of Jesus under the title of 'The Poor Brothers of Saint Joseph of Aramithea'."

"Why not Saint Vincent de Paul?" asked Marchmont.

"Because there was already a society named after that saint, and because Saint Joseph was a man of eminent charity. But I shall not weary you with a history of our society. It was founded and blessed by His Holiness, the Pope, it prospered, and it still prospers to the glory of God and to the benefit and relief of the sick, the poor, and the suffering. At first Vitalis paid all the costs, and he has been a generous benefactor ever since."

"This is all extremely interesting," said Marchmont, "but—you will excuse my asking—has it any bearing on your friend's disappearance?"

"Yes, sir, it has," replied Father Humperdinck, "as you shall berceive ven I my narradive gondinue."

Mr. Marchmont bowed, and Father Humperdinck, quite undisturbed by the interruption, "gondinued his narradive."

"Our first house was established in Belgium, near Brussels, and Vitalis came to live with us in community. He did not regularly join the society or take any vows, but he lived with us as one of ourselves and wore the habit of a lay brother when in the house and the dress of one when he went abroad. This he has continued to do ever since. Though bound by no vows, he has lived the life of a professed religious by choice, occupying an ordinary cell for sleeping and taking his meals at the refectory table. But not always. From time to time he has taken little holidays to travel about and mix—with the outer world. Sometimes he would come to England to visit his relatives, and sometimes he would spend a few weeks in one of the great cities of the Continent, looking over the museums and picture-galleries. He was greatly interested in art and liked to frequent the society of painters and sculptors, of whom he knew several; and one, in particular—an English painter named Burton, whose acquaintance he made quite recently—he seemed very much attached to, for he stayed with him at Bruges for more than a month.

"When he came back from Bruges, he told me that he purposed going to England to see his relatives and to make certain arrangements with his lawyers for securing a part of his property to our Society. I had often urged him to do this, but, hitherto, he had retained complete control of his property and only paid the expenses of the Society as they occurred. He was most generous, but, of course, this was a bad arrangement, because, in the event of his death, we should have been left without the support that he had promised. It seemed that while he was at Bruges he had discussed this matter with Mr. Burton, who was a Catholic, and that the Englishman also had advised him to make a permanent provision for the Society. It seemed that he had decided to divide his property between our community and a cousin of his who lives in England, a project of which I strongly approved. After staying with us for a month or two, he left for

England with the purpose of making this arrangement. That was in the middle of last September, and I have not seen him since."

"Did he complete the arrangements that he had mentioned?" Thorndyke asked.

"No, he did not. He made certain arrangements as to his property, but they were very different ones from those he had proposed. But we shall come to that presently. Let me finish my story.

"A few days after Vitalis left us, our oldest lay brother was taken very seriously ill. I wrote to Vitalis, who was deeply attached to Brother Bartholomew, telling him of this, and, as I did not know where he was staying, I sent the letter to his cousin's house at Hampstead. He replied, on the eighteenth of September, that he should return immediately. He said that he was then booking his luggage and paying his hotel bill; that he had to see his cousin again, but that he would try to come by the night train, or if he missed that, he would sleep at the station hotel and start as early as possible on the following day, the nineteenth. That was the last I ever heard from him. He never came and has never communicated with me since."

"You have made enquiries, of course?" said Thorndyke.

"Yes. When he did not come, I wrote to his lawyer, Mr. Wyndhurst, whom I knew slightly. But Mr. Wyndhurst was dead, and my letter was answered by Mr. Marchmont. From him I learned that Vitalis had called on him on the morning of the nineteenth and made certain arrangements of which he, perhaps, will tell you. Mr. Marchmont ascertained that, on the same day, Vitalis's luggage was taken from the cloak room in time to catch the boat train. I have made inquiries and find that he arrived at Calais, and I have succeeded in tracing him to Paris, but there I have lost him. Where he is now I am unable to discover.

"And now, before I finish my story, you had better hear what Mr. Marchmont has to tell. He has been very close with me, but you are a lawyer and perhaps know better how to deal with lawyers."

Thorndyke glanced enquiringly at the solicitor, who, in his turn, looked dubiously at the end of his waning cigar. "The fact is," said he, "I am in a rather difficult position. Mr. Reinhardt has employed me as his solicitor, and I don't quite see my way to discussing his private affairs without his authority."

"That is a perfectly correct attitude," said Thorndyke, "and yet I am going to urge you to tell us what passed at your interview with your client. I can't go into particulars at present, but I will ask you to take it from me that there are sound reasons why you should; and I will undertake to hold you immune from any blame for having done so."

Marchmont looked sharply and with evidently awakened interest at Thorndyke. "I think I know what that means," he said, "and I will take you at your word, having learned by experience what your word is worth. But before describing the interview, I had better let you know how Reinhardt had previously disposed of his property.

"About twelve years ago he got Wyndhurst to draft a will for him by which a life interest in the entire property was vested in his cousin, a Miss Augusta Vyne, with reversion to her niece, Sylvia Vyne, the only child of his cousin Robert. This will was duly executed in our office.

"After that our firm had, until quite recently, no special business to transact for Mr. Reinhardt beyond the management of his investments. The whole of his property—which was all personal—was in our hands to invest, and our relations with him were confined to the transfer of sums of money to his bank when we received instructions from him to effect such transfer. He never called at the office, and latterly there has been no one there who knew him excepting Wyndhurst himself and the clerk, Bell.

"The next development occurred last September. On the seventeenth I received a letter from him, written at Miss Vyne's house at Hampstead, saying that he had been discussing his affairs with her and that he should like to call on me and make some slight alterations in the disposal of the property. I replied on the eighteenth, addressing my letter to him at Miss Vyne's house, making an appointment for eleven o'clock on the morning of the nineteenth. He kept the appointment punctually, and we had a short interview, at which he explained the new arrangements which he wished to make.

"He began by saying that he had found it somewhat inconvenient, living, as he did, on the Continent, to have his account at an English Bank. He proposed, therefore, to transfer it to a private bank at Paris, conducted by a certain M. Desire, or rather to open an account there, for he did not suggest closing his account at his English bank."

"Do you know anything about this M. Desire?" asked Thorndyke.

"I did not, but I have since ascertained that he is a person of credit—quite a substantial man in fact—and that his business is chiefly that of private banker and agent to the officers of the army.

"Well, Mr. Reinhardt went on to say that he had become rather tired of the monotonous life of a lay brother—which he, after all, was not—and wished for a little freedom and change. Accordingly he intended to travel for a time—which was his reason for employing M. Desire—and did not propose, necessarily, to keep anyone informed of his whereabouts. He was a rich man and he had decided to get some advantage from his wealth, which really did not seem to me at all an unreasonable decision. He added that he had no intention of withdrawing his support from the Society of the Poor

Brothers; he merely intended to dissociate himself, personally, from it, and he suggested that any occasions that might arise for pecuniary assistance should be addressed to him under cover of M. Desire.

"Finally, he desired me to transfer one thousand pounds stock to his new agent seven days from the date of our interview, and gave me an authority in writing to that effect in which he instructed me to accept M. Desire's receipt as a valid discharge."

"And you did so?" asked Thorndyke.

"Certainly I did. And I hold M. Desire's receipt for the amount."

"Did you think it necessary to raise the question of your client's identity, seeing that no one in the office knew him personally?"

"No, I did not. The question did not arise. There could not possibly be any doubt on the subject. He was an old client of the firm, and our correspondence had been carried on under cover of his cousin, Miss Vyne, who had known him all his life. You remember that I wrote to him at Miss Vyne's address, making the appointment for the interview."

"And what happened next?"

"The next development was a letter from Father Humperdinck asking if I could give him Mr. Reinhardt's address. Of course I could not, but I wrote to M. Desire asking him if he could give it to me. Desire replied that he did not, at the moment, know where Mr. Reinhardt was, but would, if desired, take charge of any communications and forward them at the first opportunity. This statement may or may not have been true, but I don't think we shall get any more information out of Desire. He is Reinhardt's agent and will act on his instructions. If Reinhardt has told him not to give anyone his address, naturally he won't give it. So there the matter ends, so far as I am concerned."

"Did Vitalis make no suggestion as to altering his will?" Father Humperdinck enquired.

"None whatever. Nothing was said about the will. But," Mr. Marchmont added, after a cogitative pause, "we must remember that he has another man of business now. There is no saying what he may have done through M. Desire."

Father Humperdinck nodded gloomily, and Thorndyke addressing the solicitor, asked: "And that is all you have to tell us?"

"Yes. And I'm not sure that it is not a good deal more than I ought to have told you. It is Father Humperdinck's turn now."

The Jesuit acknowledged the invitation to resume his narrative by a stiff bow and then proceeded: "You can now see, sir, that what I said is perfectly correct. The conduct of my friend Vitalis shows a sudden and unaccountable change. It is quite inconsistent with his habits and his way of thinking. And the change is, as I say, so sudden. One day he is coming with the greatest haste to the bedside of his sick friend, Brother Bartholomew, the next he is making arrangements for a life of selfish pleasure, utterly indifferent as to whether that friend is alive or dead. As a matter of fact, the good brother passed away to his reward the day after Vitalis should have arrived, without even a message from his old friend. But now I return to my story.

"When Vitalis failed to appear, and I could get no news of him, I became very anxious; and, as it happened that the business of our Society called me to England, I determined to inquire into the matter. Circumstances compelled me to travel by way of Boulogne and cross to Folkestone. I say 'circumstances,' but I should rather say that I was guided that way by the hand of Providence, for, in the train that brought me from Folkestone to London, I had a most astonishing experience. In the carriage, alone with me, there travelled a young man, a very strange young man indeed. He was a very large man—or, I should say, very high—and in appearance rather fierce and wild.

His clothes were good, but they were disordered and stained with mud, as if he had been drunk at night and had rolled in the gutter. And this, I think, was the case, for, soon after we had started, he began to turn out his pockets on the seat of the carriage, as if to see whether he had lost anything during his debauch. And then it was that I saw a most astonishing thing. Among the objects that this man took from his pockets and laid on the seat, was the reliquary that I had given so many years ago to Vitalis.

"I could not mistake it. Once it had been mine, and I had been accustomed to see it almost dally since. Moreover the young man had the effrontery to pass it to me that I might examine it, and I found on it the very letters which I, myself, had caused to be engraved on it. When I asked him where he had obtained it, he told me that he had picked it up at Hampstead, and he professed not to know what it was. But his answers were very evasive and I did not believe him."

"Nevertheless," said Mr. Marchmont, "there was nothing improbable in his statement. Mr. Reinhardt had been at Hampstead and might have dropped it."

"Possibly. But he would have taken measures to recover it. He would not have left England until he had found it. He was a rich man, and he would have offered a large reward for this his most prized possession."

"You say," said Thorndyke, "that he habitually carried this reliquary on his person. Can you tell us how he carried or wore it?"

"That," replied Father Humperdinck, "was what I was coming to. The reliquary was a small gold object with a ring at each end. It was meant I suppose, to be worn round the wrist, or perhaps the neck, by means of a cord or chain attached to the two rings, or to be inserted into a chaplet of devotional beads. But this was not the way in which Vitalis carried it. He possessed a small and very beautiful crucifix which he set great store by, because it was given to him by one of the fathers when he left school, and which he used to wear suspended from his neck by a green silk cord. Now, when I gave him the reliquary, he caused a goldsmith to link one of its rings to the ring of the crucifix and he fastened the silk cord to the other ring, and so suspended both the reliquary and the crucifix from his neck."

"Did he wear them outside his clothing so that they were visible?" Thorndyke asked.

"Yes, outside his waistcoat, so that they were not only visible but very conspicuous when his coat was unbuttoned. It was, of course, very unsuitable to the dress of a lay brother, and I spoke to him about it several times. But he was sometimes rather self-willed, as you may judge by his refusal to settle an endowment on the Society, and, naturally, as he was not professed, I had no authority over him. But I shall return presently to the reliquary. Now I continue about this young man.

"When I had heard his explanation, and decided that he was telling me lies, I made a simple pretext to discover his name and place of abode. With the same effrontery, he gave me his card, which I have here, and which, you will see, is stained with mud, owing, no doubt, to those wallowings in the mire of which I have spoken."

He drew the card from his pocket-book and handed it to Thorndyke, who read it gravely, and, pushing it across the table to me, said, without moving a muscle of his face: "You had better copy it into your notes, Mr. Howard, so that we may have the record complete."

I accordingly copied out my own name and address with due solemnity and a growing enjoyment of the situation, and then returned the card to Father Humperdinck, who pocketed it carefully and resumed: "Having the name and address of this young man, I telegraphed immediately to a private detective bureau in Paris, asking to have sent to me, if possible, a certain M. Foucault, who makes a speciality of following and watching suspected persons. This Foucault is a man of extraordinary talent. His power of disguising himself is beyond belief and his patience is inexhaustible. Fortunately he was disengaged and came to me without delay, and, when I had given him the name and address of this young man, Jardine, and described him from my recollection of him, he set a watch on the house and found that the man was really living there, as he had said, and that he made a daily journey to the hospital of St. Margaret's, where he seemed to have some business, as he usually stayed there until evening."

"St. Margaret's!" exclaimed Marchmont. "Why that is your hospital, Thorndyke. Do you happen to know this man Jardine?"

"There is, or was, a student of that name, who qualified some little time ago, and who is probably the man Father Humperdinck is referring to. A tall man; quite as tall, I should say, as my friend here, Mr. Howard."

"I should say," said Father Humperdinck," that the man, Jardine, is taller, decidedly taller. I watched him as I walked behind him up the platform at Charing Cross, and M. Foucault has shown him to me since. But that matters not. Have you seen the man, Jardine, lately at the hospital?"

"Not very lately," Thorndyke replied. "I saw him there nearly a fortnight ago, but that, I think, was the last time."

"Ah!" exclaimed Humperdinck. "Exactly. But I shall continue my story. For some time M. Foucault kept a close watch on this man, but discovered nothing fresh. He went to the hospital daily, he came home, and he stayed indoors the whole evening. But, at last, there came a new discovery.

"One morning M. Foucault saw the man, Jardine, come out of his house, dressed more carefully than usual. From his house, Foucault followed him to a picture gallery in Leicester Square and went in after him; and there he saw him meet a female, evidently by a previous assignation. AND," Father Humperdinck continued, slapping the table to emphasize the climax of his story, "From-the-neck-of-that-female-was-hanging-Vitalis-Reinhardt's-CRUCIFIX!"

Having made this thrilling communication, our reverend client leaned back to watch its effect on his audience. I am afraid he must have been a little disappointed, for Thorndyke was habitually impassive in his exterior, and, as for Jervis and me, we were fully occupied in maintaining a decent and befitting gravity. But Marchmont–the only person present who was not already acquainted with the incident–saved the situation by exclaiming: "Very remarkable! Very remarkable indeed!"

"It is more than remarkable," said Father Humperdinck. "It is highly suspicious. You observe that the reliquary and the crucifix had been linked together. Now they are separated, and since both the rings of the reliquary were unbroken, it follows that the ring of the crucifix must have been cut through and a new one made, by which to suspend it."

"I don't see anything particularly suspicious in that," said Marchmont. "If Jardine found the two articles fixed together, and–having failed to discover the owner–wished to give the crucifix to his friend, it is not unnatural that he should have separated them."

"I do not believe that he found them," Father Humperdinck replied doggedly; "but I shall continue my story and you will see. There is not much more to tell.

"It seems that the man, Jardine, suspected Foucault of watching him, for presently he left the gallery m company with the female, and, after being followed for some distance, he managed to escape. As soon as Foucault found that he had lost him, he went to Jardine's house and waited about the neighbourhood, and an hour or two later he had the good fortune to see him coming from Hampstead towards Highgate, in company with another female. He followed them until they entered a narrow passage or lane that leads up the hill, and when they had gone up this some distance, he followed, but could not get near enough to hear what they were saying.

"And now he had a most strange and terrible experience. For some time past he had felt a suspicion that some person—some accomplice of Jardine's perhaps—was following and watching him; and now he had proof of it. At the top of the lane, Jardine stopped to talk to the female, and Foucault crept on tiptoe towards him; and while he was doing so, he heard someone approaching stealthily up the lane, behind him. Suddenly, Jardine began to return down the lane. As it was not convenient for Foucault to meet him there, he also turned and walked back; and then he heard a sound as if someone were climbing the high wooden fence that enclosed the lane. Then Jardine began to run, and Foucault was compelled also to run but he would have been overtaken if it had not happened that Jardine fell down.

"Now, just as he heard Jardine fall, he came to a broken place in the fence, and it occurred to him to creep through the hole and hide while Jardine passed. He accordingly began to do so, but no sooner had he thrust his head through the hole than some unseen ruffian dealt him a violent blow which rendered him instantly insensible. When he recovered his senses, he found himself lying in a churchyard which adjoins the lane, but Jardine and the other ruffian were, of course, nowhere to be seen.

"And now I come to the last incident that I have to relate. The assault took place on a Saturday; on the Sunday M. Foucault was somewhat indisposed and unable to go out, but early on Monday he resumed his watch on Jardine's house. It was nearly noon when Jardine came out, dressed as if for travelling and carrying a valise. He went first to a house near Piccadilly and from thence to the hospital in a cab. Foucault followed in another cab and saw him go into the hospital and waited for him to come out. But he never came. Foucault waited until midnight, but he did not come out. He had vanished."

"He had probably come out by a back exit and gone home," said Marchmont.

"Not so," replied Humperdinck. "The next day Foucault watched Jardine's house, but he did not come there. Then he made enquiries; but Jardine is not there, and the landlady does not know where he is. Also the porter at the hospital knows nothing and is not at all polite. The man Jardine has disappeared as if he had never been."

"That really is rather queer," said Marchmont. "It is a pity that you did not give me all these particulars at first. However, that can't be helped now. Is this all that you have to tell us?"

"It is all; unless there is anything that you wish to ask me."

"I think," said Thorndyke, "that it would be well for us to have a description of Mr. Reinhardt; and, as we have to trace him, if possible, a photograph would be exceedingly useful."

"I have not a photograph with me," said Father Humperdinck, "but I will obtain one and send it to you. Meanwhile I will tell you what my friend Vitalis is like. He is sixty-two years of age, spare, upright, rather tall— his height is a hundred and seventy-three centimetres —"

"Roughly five feet nine," interposed Thorndyke.

"His hair is nearly white, he is, of course, clean shaven, he has grey eyes, a straight nose, not very prominent, and remarkably good teeth for his age, which he shows somewhat when he talks. I think he is a little vain about his teeth and he well may be, for there are not many men of sixty-two who have not a single false tooth, nor even one that has been stopped by the dentist. As to his clothing, he wears the ordinary dress of a lay brother, which you are probably familiar with, and he nearly always wears gloves, even indoors."

"Is there any reason for his wearing gloves?" Thorndyke asked.

"Not now. The habit began when he had some affliction of the skin, which made it necessary for him to keep his hands covered with gloves which contained some ointment or dressing, and afterwards for a time to conceal the disagreeable appearance of the skin. The habit having been once formed, he continued it, saying that his hands were more comfortable covered up than when exposed to the air."

"Was he dressed in this fashion when he called at your office, Marchmont?" asked Thorndyke.

"Yes. Even to the gloves. I noticed, with some surprise, that he did not take them off even when he wrote and signed the note of which I told you."

"Was he then wearing the reliquary and crucifix as Father Humperdinck has described, on the front of his waistcoat?"

"He may have been, but I didn't notice them, as I fancy I should have done if they had been there."

"And you have nothing more to tell us, Father Humperdinck, as to your friend's personal appearance?"

"No. I will send you the photograph and write to you if I think of anything that I have forgotten. And now, perhaps you can tell me if you think that you will be able to answer those questions that Mr. Marchmont put to you."

"I cannot, of course, answer them now," replied Thorndyke. "The facts that you have given us will have to be considered and compared, and certain enquiries will have to be made. Are you staying long in England?"

"I shall be here for at least a month; and I may as well leave you my address, although Mr. Marchmont has it."

"In the course of a month," Thorndyke said, as he took the proffered card, "I think I may promise you that we shall have settled definitely whether your friend is alive or dead; and if we find that he is alive, we shall, no doubt, be able to ascertain his whereabouts."

"That is very satisfactory," said Father Humperdinck. "I hope you shall be able to make good your promise."

With this he rose, and, having shaken hands stiffly with Thorndyke, bestowed on Jervis and me a ceremonious bow and moved towards the door. I thought that Marchmont looked a little wistful, as if he would have liked to stay and have a few words with us alone; indeed, he lingered for a moment or two after the door was open, but then, apparently altering his mind, he wished us "good-night" and followed his client.

17
THE PALIMPSEST

IT was getting late when our friends left us, but nevertheless, as soon as they were gone, we all drew our chairs up to the fire with the obvious intention of discussing the situation and began, with one accord, to fill our pipes. Jervis was the first to get his tobacco alight, and, having emitted a voluminous preliminary puff, he proceeded to open the debate.

"That man, Jardine, seems to be a pretty desperate character. Just think of his actually wallowing in the mire—not merely rolling, mind you, but wallowing—and of his repulsive habit of consorting with females; one after the other, too, in rapid succession. It's a shocking instance of depravity."

"Our reverend friend," said Thorndyke, "reaches his conclusions by a rather short route—in some cases, at least; in others, his methods seem a little indirect and roundabout."

"Yes," agreed Jervis, "he's a devil at guessing. But he didn't get much food for the imagination out of the man, Thorndyke. Why were you so extraordinarily secretive? With what he told you and what you knew before, you could surely have suggested a line of inquiry. Why didn't you?"

"Principally because of the man's personality. I could not have answered his questions; I could, only have suggested one or two highly probable solutions of the problem that he offered and partial solutions at that. But I am not much addicted to giving partial solutions—to handing over the raw material of a promising inquiry. Certainly, not to a man like this, who seems incapable of a straight forward action."

"The reverend father," said Jervis, "does certainly seem to be a rather unnecessarily downy bird. And he doesn't seem to have got much by his excessive artfulness, after all."

"No," agreed Thorndyke; "nothing whatever. Quite the contrary, in fact. Look at his ridiculous conduct in respect of 'the man Jardine'. I don't complain of his having taken the precaution to obtain that malefactor's address; but, when he had got it, if he had not been tortuous, so eager to be cunning; if, in short, he had behaved like an ordinary sensible man, he would have got, at once, all the information that Jardine had to give. He could have called on Jardine, written to him, employed a lawyer or applied to the police. Either of these simple and obvious plans would have been successful; instead of which, he must need go to the trouble and expense of engaging this absurd spy."

"Who found a mare's nest and got his head thumped," remarked Jervis.

"Then," continued Thorndyke, "look at his behaviour to Marchmont. Evidently he put the case into Marchmont's hands, but, equally evident, he withheld material facts and secretly tinkered at the case himself. No, Jervis, I give no information to Father Humperdinck until I have this case complete to the last rivet. But, all the same, I am greatly obliged to him, and especially to Marchmont for bringing him here. He has given us a connected story to collate with our rather loose collection of facts and, what is perhaps more important, he has put our investigation on a business footing. That is a great advantage. If I should want to invoke the aid of the powers that be, I can do so now with a definite locus standi as the legal representative of interested parties."

"I can't imagine," said I, "in what direction you are going to push your inquiries. Father Humperdinck has given us, as you say, a connected story, but it is a very unexpected one, to me, at least, and does not fall into line at all with what we know—that is, if you are assuming, as

I have been, that the man whom I saw lying in Millfield Lane was Vitalis Reinhardt."

"It is difficult," replied Thorndyke, "to avoid that assumption, though we must be on our guard against coincidences; but the man whom you saw agreed with the description that has been given to us, we know that Reinhardt was in the neighbourhood on that day, and you found the reliquary on the following morning in the immediate vicinity. We seem to be committed to the hypothesis that the man was Reinhardt unless we can prove that he was someone else, or that Reinhardt was in some other place at the time; which at present we cannot."

"Then," said I, "in that case, the bobby must have been right, after all. The man couldn't have been dead, seeing that he called on Marchmont the following day and was afterwards traced to Paris. But I must say that he looked as dead as Queen Anne. It just shows how careful one ought to be in giving opinions."

"Some authority has said," remarked Jervis, "that the only conclusive proof of death is decomposition. I believe it was old Taylor who said so, and I am inclined to think that he wasn't far wrong."

"But," said Thorndyke, "assuming that the man whom you saw was Reinhardt, and that he was not dead how do you explain the other circumstances? Was he insensible from the effects of injury or drugs? Or was he deliberately shamming insensibility? Was it he who passed over the fence? And if so, did he climb over unassisted or was he helped over? And what answers do you suggest to the questions that Marchmont propounded? You answer his first question: 'Is Reinhardt alive?' in the affirmative. What about the others?"

"As to where he is," I replied. "I can only say, the Lord knows; probably skulking somewhere on the Continent. As to his state of mind, the facts seem to suggest that, in vulgar parlance, he has gone off his onion. He must be as mad as a hatter to have behaved in the way that he has. For, even assuming that he wanted to get clear of the Poor Brothers of Saint Jeremiah Diddler without explicitly saying so, he adopted a fool's plan. There is no sense in masquerading as a corpse one day and turning up smiling at your lawyer's office the next. If he meant to be dead, he should have stuck to it and remained dead."

"The objection to that," said Jervis, "is that Marchmont would have proceeded to get permission to presume death and administer the will."

"I see. Then I can only suppose that he had got infected by Father Humperdinck and resolved to be artful at all costs and hang the consequences."

"Then," said Thorndyke, "I understand your view to be that Reinhardt is at present hiding somewhere on the Continent and that his mind is more or less affected?"

"Yes. Though as to his being unfit to control his own affairs, I am not so clear. I fancy there was more evidence in that direction when he was forking out the bulk of his income to maintain the poverty of the Poor Brothers. But the truth is, I haven't any opinions on the case at all. I am in a complete fog about the whole affair."

"And no wonder," said Jervis. "One set of facts seems to suggest most strongly that Reinhardt must certainly be dead. Another set of facts seems to prove beyond doubt that he was alive, at least after that affair in Millfield Lane. He may be perpetrating an elephantine practical joke on the Poor Brothers; but that doesn't seem to be particularly probable. The whole case is a tangle of contradictions which one might regard as beyond unravelment if it were not for a single clear and intelligible fact."

"What is that?" I asked.

"That my revered senior has undertaken to furnish a solution in the course of a month; from which I gather that my revered senior has something up his sleeve."

"There is nothing up my sleeve," said Thorndyke, "that might not equally well be up yours. I have made no separate investigations. The actual data which I possess were acquired in the presence of one or both of you, and are now the common property of us all. I am referring, of course, to the original data, not to fresh matter obtained by inference from, or further examination of those data."

Jervis smiled sardonically. "It is the old story," said he. "The magician offers you his hat to inspect. You observe, ladies and gentlemen, that there is no deception. You can look inside it and examine the lining, and you can also inspect the top of my head. I now put on my hat. I now take it off again and you notice that there is a guinea pig sitting in it. There was no deception, ladies and gentlemen, you had all the data."

Thorndyke laughed and shook his head, "That's all nonsense, Jervis," he said. "It is a false analogy. I have done nothing to divert your attention. The guinea pig has been staring you in the face all the time."

"Very rude of him," murmured Jervis.

"I have even drawn your attention to him once or twice. But, seriously, I don't think that this case is so very obscure, though mind you, it is a mere hypothesis so far as I am concerned, and may break down completely when I come to apply the tests that I have in view. But what I mean is, that the facts known to us suggested a very obvious hypothesis and that the suggestion was offered equally to us all. The verification may fail, but that is another matter."

"Are you going to work at the case immediately?" I asked.

"No," Thorndyke replied. "Jervis and I have to attend at the Maidstone Assizes for the next few days. We are retained on a case which involves some very important issues in relation to life assurance, and that will take up most of our time. So this other affair will have to wait."

"And meanwhile," said Jervis, "you will stay at home like a good boy and mind the shop; and I suppose we shall have to find you something to do, to keep you out of mischief. What do you say to making a longhand transcript of Father Humperdinck's statement?"

"Yes, you had better do that," said Thorndyke; "and attach it to the original shorthand copy. And now we must really turn in or we shall never be ready for our start in the morning."

The transcription of Father Humperdinck's statement gave me abundant occupation for the whole of the following morning. But when that was finished, I was without any definite employment, and, though I was not in the least dull–for I was accustomed to a solitary life–I suppose I was in that state of susceptibility to mischief that is proverbially associated with unemployment. And in these untoward circumstances I was suddenly exposed to a great temptation; and after some feeble efforts at resistance, succumbed ignominiously.

I shall offer no excuses for my conduct nor seek in any way to mitigate the judgment that all discreet persons will pass upon my folly. I make no claims to discretion or to the caution and foresight of a man like Thorndyke. At this time I was an impulsive and rather heedless young man, and my actions were pretty much those which might have been expected from a person of such temperament.

The voice of the tempter issued in the first place from our letter-box, and assumed the sound of the falling of letters thereinto. I hastened to extract the catch, and sorting out the envelopes, selected one, the superscription of which was in Sylvia's now familiar handwriting. It was actually addressed to Dr. Thorndyke, but a private mark, on which we had agreed, exposed that naively pious fraud and gave me the right to open it; which I did, and seated myself in the armchair to enjoy its perusal at my ease.

It was a delightful letter; bright, gossipy and full of frank and intimate friendliness. As I read it, the trim, graceful figure and pretty face of the writer rose before me and made me wonder a little discontentedly how long it would be before I should look on her and hear her voice again. It was now getting into the third week since I had last seen her, and, as the time passed, I was feeling more and more how great a blank in my life the separation from her had caused. Our friendship had grown up in a quiet and unsensational fashion and I suppose I had not realized all that it meant; but I was realizing it now; and, as I conned over her letter, with its little personal notes and familiar turns of expression, I began to be consumed with a desire to see her, to hear her speak, to tell her that she was not as other women to me, and to claim a like special place in her thoughts.

It was towards the end of the letter that the tempter spoke out in clear and unmistakable language, and these were the words that he used, through the medium of the innocent and unconscious Sylvia: "You remember those sketches that you stole for me–' pinched,' I think was your own expression. Well, I have cleaned off the daubs of paint with which they had been disfigured and put them in rough frames in my studio. All but one; and I began on that yesterday with a scraper and a rag dipped in chloroform. But I took off, not only the defacing marks but part of the surface as well; and then I got such a surprise! I shan't tell you what the surprise was, because you'll see, when you come out of the house of bondage. I am going to work on it again to-morrow, and perhaps I shall get the transformation finished. How I wish you could come and see it done! It takes away more than half the joy of exploration not to be able to share the discovery with you; in fact, I have a good mind to leave it unfinished so that we can complete the transformation together."

Now, I need not say that, as to the precious sketches, I cared not a fig what was under the top coat of paint, What I did care for was that this dear maid was missing me as I missed her; was wanting my sympathy with her little interests and pleasures and was telling me, half unconsciously, perhaps, that my absence had created a

A Resurrected Press Mystery

blank in her life, as her absence had in mine. And forthwith I began to ask myself whether there was really any good reason why I should not, just for this once, break out of my prison and snatch a few brief hours of sunshine. The spy had been exploded. He was not likely to pick up my tracks after all this time and now that my appearance was so altered; and I did not care much if he did seeing that he had been shown to be perfectly harmless. The only circumstance that tended to restrain me from this folly was the one that mitigated its rashness-the change in my appearance; and even that, now that I was used to it and knew that my aspect was neither grotesque nor ridiculous, had little weight, for Sylvia would be prepared for the change and we could enjoy the joke together.

I was aware, even at the time, that I was not being quite candid with myself, for, if I had been, I should obviously have consulted Thorndyke. Instead of which I answered the letter by return, announcing my intention of coming to tea on the following day; and having sent Polton out to post it, spent the remainder of the afternoon in gleeful anticipation of my little holiday, tempered by some nervousness as to what Thorndyke would have to say on the matter, and as to what "my pretty friend," as Mrs. Samway had very appropriately called her, would think of my having begun my letter with the words, "My dear Sylvia."

Nothing happened to interfere with my nefarious plans.

On the following morning, Thorndyke and Jervis went off after an early breakfast, leaving me in possession of the premises and master of my actions. I elected to anticipate the usual luncheon time by half an hour, and, when this meal was disposed of, I crept to my room and thoroughly cleansed my hair of the grease which Polton still persisted in applying to it; for, since my hat would conceal it while I was out of doors, the added disfigurement was unnecessary. I was even tempted to

tamper slightly with my eyebrows, but this impulse I
nobly resisted; and, having dried my hair and combed it
in its normal fashion, I descended on tip-toe to the
sitting-room and wrote a short, explanatory note to
Polton, which I left conspicuously on the table. Then I
switched the door-bell on to the laboratory, and, letting
myself out like a retreating burglar, closed the door
silently and sneaked away down the dark staircase.

Once fairly outside, I went off like a lamplighter, and,
shooting out through the Tudor Street gate, made my
way eastward to Broad Street Station, where I was
fortunate enough to catch a train that was just on the
point of starting. At Hampstead Heath Station I got out,
and, snuffing the air joyfully, set forth at my best pace up
the slope that leads to the summit; and in little over
twenty minutes found myself at the gate of "The
Hawthorns."

There was no need to knock or ring. My approach had
been observed from the window, and, as I strode up the
garden path, the door opened and Sylvia ran out to meet
me.

"It was nice of you to come!" she exclaimed, as I took
her hand and held it in mine. "I don't believe you ought to
have ventured out, but I am most delighted all the same.
Don't make a noise; Mopsy is having a little doze in the
drawing room. Come into the morning room and let me
have a good look at you."

I followed her meekly into the front room, where, in
the large bay window, she inspected me critically, her
cheeks dimpling with a mischievous smile.

"There's something radically wrong about your
eyebrows," she said, "but, really, you are not in the least
the fright that you made out. As to the beard and
moustache, I am not sure that I don't rather like them."

"I hope you don't," I replied, "because, off they come at
the first opportunity—unless, of course, you forbid it."

"Does my opinion of your appearance matter so much then?"

"It matters entirely. I don't care what I look like to anyone else."

"Oh I what a fib!" exclaimed Sylvia. "Don't I remember how very neatly turned out you always were when you used to pass me in the lane before we knew one another?"

"Exactly," I retorted. "We didn't know one another then. That makes all the difference in the world—to me, at any rate."

"Does it?" she said, colouring a little and looking at me thoughtfully. "It's very-very flattering of you to say so, Dr. Jardine."

"I hope you don't mean that as a snub," I said, rather uneasy at the form of her reply and thinking of my letter.

"A snub!" she exclaimed. "No, I certainly don't. What did I say?"

"You called me Dr. Jardine. I addressed you in my letter as 'Sylvia -My dear Sylvia'."

"And what ought I to have said?" she asked, blushing warmly and casting down her eyes.

"Well, Sylvia, if you liked me as well as I like you, I don't see why you shouldn't call me Humphrey. We are quite old friends now."

"So we are," she agreed; "and perhaps it would be less formal. So Humphrey it shall be in future, since that is your royal command. But tell me, how did you prevail on Dr. Thorndyke to let you come here? Is there any change in the situation?"

"There's a change in my situation, and a mighty agreeable change, too. I'm here."

"Now don't be silly. How did you persuade Dr. Thorndyke to let you come?"

"Ha—that, my dear Sylvia, is a rather embarrassing question. Shall we change the subject?"

"No, we won't." She looked at me suspiciously for a moment and then exclaimed in low, tragical tones:

"Humphrey! You don't mean to tell me that you came away without his knowledge!"

"I'm afraid that is what it amounts to. I saw a loophole and I popped through it; and here I am, as I remarked before."

"But how dreadful of you! Perfectly shocking! And whatever will he say to you when you go back?"

"That is a question that I am not proposing to present vividly to my consciousness until I arrive on the doorstep. I've broken out of chokee and I'm going to have a good time–to go on having a good time, I should say."

"Then you consider that you are having a good time now?"

"I don't consider. I am sure of it. Am I not, at this very moment looking at you? And what more could a man desire?"

She tried to look severe, though the attempt was not strikingly successful, and retorted in an admonishing tone: "You needn't try to wheedle me with compliments. You are a very wicked person and most indiscreet. But it seems to me that some sort of change has come over you since you retired from the world. Don't you think I'm right?"

"You're perfectly right. I've improved. That's what it is. Matured and mellowed, you know, like a bottle of claret that has been left in a cellar and forgotten. Say you think I've improved, Sylvia."

"I won't," she replied, and then, changing her mind, she added: "Yes, I will. I'll say that you are more insinuating than ever, if that will do. And now, as, you are clearly quite incorrigible, I won't scold you any more, especially as you 'broke out of chokee' to come and see me. You shall tell me all about your adventures."

"I didn't come here to talk about myself, Sylvia. I came to tell you something–well, about myself, perhaps, but–er–not my adventures you know or–or that sort of thing–but, I have been thinking a good deal, since I have

been alone so much–about you, I mean, Sylvia–and–er–
Oh! the deuce!"

The latter exclamation was evoked by the warning
voice of the gong, evidently announcing tea, and the
subsequent appearance of the housemaid; who was
certainly not such a goose as she was supposed to be, for
she tapped discreetly at the door and waited three full
seconds before entering; and even then she appeared
demurely unconscious of my existence. "If you please,
Miss Sylvia, Miss Vyne has woke up and I've taken in the
tea."

Such was the paltry interruption that arrested the
flow of my eloquence and scattered my flowers of rhetoric
to the winds. I murmured inwardly, "Blow the tea!" for
the opportunity was gone; but I comforted myself with the
reflection that it didn't matter very much, since Sylvia
and I seemed to have arrived at a pretty clear
understanding; which understanding was further
clarified by a momentary contact of our hands as we
followed the maid to the drawing-room. Miss Vyne was on
this occasion, as on the last, seated in the exact centre of
the room, and with the same monumental effect; so that
my thoughts were borne irresistibly to the ethnographical
section of the British Museum, and especially to that part
of it wherein the deities of Polynesia look out from their
cases in perennial surprise at the degenerate European
visitors. If she had been asleep previously, she was wide
enough awake now; but the glittering eyes were not
directed at me. From the moment of our entering the
room they focussed themselves on Sylvia's face and there
remained riveted, whereby the heightening of that young
lady's complexion, which our interview had produced,
became markedly accentuated. It was to no purpose that I
placed myself before the rigid figure and offered my hand.
A paw was lifted automatically to mine, but the eyes
remained fixed on Sylvia.

"What did you say this gentleman's name was!" the
waxwork asked frigidly.

"This is Dr. Jardine," was the reply.

"Oh, indeed. And who was the gentleman who called some three weeks ago?"

"Why, that was Dr. Jardine; you know it was."

"So I thought, but my memory is not very reliable. And this is a Dr. Jardine, too? Very interesting. A medical family, apparently. But not much alike."

I was beginning to explain my identity and the cause of my altered appearance, when Sylvia approached with a cup of tea and a carefully dissected muffin, which latter she thrust under the nose of the elder lady; who regarded it attentively and with a slight squint, owing to its nearness.

"It's of no use, you know," said Sylvia, "for you to pretend that you don't know him, because I've told you all about the transformation—that is, all I know myself. Don't you think it's rather a clever make-up?"

"If," said Miss Vyne, "by 'make-up' you mean a disguise, I think it is highly successful. The beard is a most admirable imitation."

"Oh, the beard is his own; at least, I think it is."

I confirmed this statement, ignoring Polton's slight additions.

"Indeed," said Miss Vyne. "Then the wig—it is a wig, I suppose?"

"No, of course it isn't," Sylvia replied.

"Then," said Miss Vyne, majestically, "perhaps you will explain to me what the disguise consists of."

"Well," said Sylvia, "there are the eyebrows. You can see that they have been completely altered in shape."

"If I had committed the former shape of the eyebrows to memory, as you appear to have done," said Miss Vyne. "I should, no doubt, observe the change. But I did not. It seems to me that the disguise which you told me about with such a flourish of trumpets just amounts to this; that Dr. Jardine has allowed his beard to grow. I find the reality quite disappointing."

"Do you?" said Sylvia. "But, at any rate, you didn't recognize him; so your disappointment doesn't count for much."

The old lady, being thus hoist with her own petard, relapsed into majestic silence; and Sylvia then renewed her demand for an account of my adventures. "We want to hear all about that objectionable person who has been shadowing you, and how you finally got rid of him. Your letters were rather sketchy and wanting in detail, so you have got to make up the deficiency now."

Thus commanded, I plunged into an exhaustive account of those events which I have already chronicled at length and which I need not refer to again, nor need I record the cross-examination to which I was subjected, since it elicited nothing that is not set forth in the preceding pages. When I had finished my recital, however, Miss Vyne, who had listened to it in silence, hitherto, put a question which I had some doubts about answering.

"Have you or Dr. Thorndyke been able to discover who this inquisitive person is and what is his object in following you about?"

I hesitated. As to my own experiences, I had no secrets from these friends of mine, excepting those that related to the subjects of Thorndyke's investigations, But I must not come here and babble about what took place in the sacred precincts of my principal's chambers.

"I think I may tell you," said I, "that Dr. Thorndyke has discovered the identity of this man and that he is not the person whom we suspected him to be. But I mustn't say any more, as the information came through professional channels and consequently is not mine to give."

"Of course you mustn't," said Sylvia; "though I don't mind admitting that you have put me on tenterhooks of curiosity. But I daresay you will be able to tell us everything later."

I agreed that I probably should; and the talk then turned into fresh channels.

The short winter day was running out apace. The daylight had long since gone, and I began, with infinite reluctance, to think of returning to my cage. Indeed, when I looked at my watch, I was horrified to see how the time had fled.

"My word!" I exclaimed. "I must be off, or Thorndyke will be putting the sleuth-hounds of the law on my track. And I don't know what you will think of me for having stayed such an unconscionable time."

"It isn't a ceremonial visit," said Sylvia, as I rose and made my adieux to her aunt. "We should have liked you to stay much longer."

Here she paused suddenly, and, clasping her hands, gazed at me with an expression of dismay. "Good Heavens! Humphrey!" she exclaimed.

"Eh?" said Miss Vyne.

"I was addressing Dr. Jardine," Sylvia explained, in some confusion.

"I didn't suppose you were addressing me," was the withering reply.

"Do you know," said Sylvia, "that I haven't shown you those sketches, after all. You must see them. They were the special object of your visit."

This was perfectly untrue, and she knew it; but I did not think it worthwhile to contest the statement in Miss Vyne's presence. Accordingly I expressed the utmost eagerness to see the trumpery sketches, and the more so since I had understood that they were on view in the studio; which turned out to be the case.

"It won't take a minute for you to see them," said Sylvia. "I'll just run up and light the gas; and you are not to come in until I tell you."

She preceded me up the stairs to the little room on the first floor in which she worked, and, when I had waited a few moments on the landing she summoned me to enter.

"These are the sketches," said she, "that I have finished. You see, they are quite presentable now. I cleaned off the rough daubs of paint with a scraper and finished up with a soft rag dipped in chloroform."

I ran my eye over the framed sketches, which, now that the canvases were strained on stretchers and the disfiguring brush-strokes removed, were, as she had said, quite presentable, though too rough and unfinished to be attractive. "I daresay they are very interesting," said I, "but they are only bare beginnings. I shouldn't have thought them worth framing."

"Not as pictures," she agreed; "but as examples of a very curious technique, I find them most instructive. However, you haven't seen the real gem of the collection. This is it, on the easel. Sit down, on the chair and say when you are ready. I'm going to give you a surprise."

I seated myself on the chair opposite the easel, on which was a canvas with its back towards me.

"Now," said Sylvia. "Are you ready? One, two, three!"

She picked up the canvas, and, turning it round quickly, presented its face to me. I don't know what I had expected-if I had expected anything; but certainly I was not in the least prepared for what I saw. The sketch had originally represented, very roughly, a dark mass of trees which occupied nearly the whole of the canvas; but of this the middle had been cleaned away, exposing an under painting. And this it was that filled me with such amazement that, after a first startled exclamation, I could do nothing but stare open-mouthed at the canvas; for, from the opening in the dark mass of foliage there looked out at me, distinct and unmistakable, the face of Mrs. Samway.

It was no illusion or chance resemblance. Rough as the painting was, the likeness was excellent. All the well-known features which made her so different from other women were there, though expressed by a mere dextrous turn of the knife; the jet-black, formally-parted hair, the clear, bright complexion, the pale, inscrutable eyes; all were there, even to the steady, penetrating expression that looked out at me from the canvas as if in silent recognition. As I sat staring at the picture with a surprise that almost amounted to awe, Sylvia looked at me a little blankly.

"Well!" she exclaimed, at length, "I meant to give you a surprise, but–what is it, Humphrey? Do you know her?"

"Yes," I replied;" and so do you. Don't you remember a woman who looked in at you through the glass door of Robinson's shop"

"Do you mean that black and scarlet creature? I didn't recognize her. I had no idea she was so handsome; for this is really a very beautiful face, though there is something about it that I don't understand. Something–well eerie; rather uncanny and almost sinister. Don't you think so?"

"I have always thought her a rather weird woman, but this is the weirdest appearance she has made. How on earth came her face on that canvas?"

"It is an odd coincidence. And yet I don't know that it is. She may have been some relative of that rather eccentric artist, or even his wife. I don't know why it shouldn't be so."

Neither did I. But the coincidence remained a very striking one, to me, at least; much more so than Sylvia realized; though what its significance might be–if it had any–I could not guess. Nor was there any opportunity to discuss it at the moment, for it was high time for me to be gone.

"You will send me a telegram when you get back, to say that you have arrived home safely, won't you," said Sylvia, as we descended the stairs with our arms linked together. "Of course nothing is going to happen to you, but I can't help feeling a little nervous. And you'll go down to the station by the High Street, and keep to the main roads. That is a promise, isn't it?"

I made the promise readily having decided previously to take every possible precaution, and, when I had wished

Sylvia "good-bye" at some length, I proceeded to execute it; making my way down the well-populated High Street and keeping a bright look-out both there and at the station. Once more I was fortunate in the matter of trains, and, having taken a hansom from Broad Street to the Temple, was set down in King's Bench Walk soon after half-past six.

As I approached our building, I looked up with some anxiety at the sitting-room windows; and when I saw them brightly lighted, a suspicion that Thorndyke had returned earlier than usual filled me with foreboding, I had had my dance and now I was going to pay the piper, and I did not much enjoy the prospect; in fact, as I ascended the stairs and took my latch-key from my pocket, I was as nervous as a school-boy who has been playing truant However, there was no escape unless I sneaked up to my bed-room, so, inserting the key into the lock, I turned it as boldly as I could, and entered.

18
A VISITOR FROM THE STATES

As I pushed open the inner door and entered the room I conceived the momentary hope of a reprieve from the wrath to come, for I found my two friends in what was evidently a business consultation with a stranger, and was on the point of backing out when Thorndyke stopped me.

"Don't run away, Howard," said he. "There are no secrets being disclosed—at least, I think not. We have finished with your affairs, Mr. O'Donnell, haven't we?"

"Yes, doctor," was the answer; "you've run me dry with the exception—of your own little business."

"Then, come in and sit down, Howard, and let me present you to Mr. O'Donnell, who is a famous American detective and has been telling us all sorts of wonderful things."

Mr. O'Donnell paused in the act of returning a quantity of papers to a large attache case and offered his hand. "The doctor," he remarked, "is blowing his trumpet at the wrong end. I haven't come here to give information but to get advice. But I guess I needn't tell you that."

"I hope that isn't quite true," said Thorndyke. "You spoke just now of my little business; haven't you anything to tell me?"

"I have; but I fancy it isn't what you wanted to hear. However, we'll just have a look at your letter to Curtis and take your questions one by one. By the way, what made you write to Curtis?"

"I saw, when I inspected Maddock's will at Somerset House, that he had left a small legacy to Curtis. Naturally, I inferred that Curtis knew him and could give me some account of him."

"It struck you as a bit queer, I reckon, that he should be leaving a legacy to the head of an American detective agency."

"The circumstance suggested possibilities," Thorndyke admitted.

O'Donnell laughed. "I can guess what possibilities suggested themselves to you, if you knew Maddock. Your letter and the lawyer's, announcing the legacy, came within a mail or two of one another. Curtis showed them both to me and we grinned. We took it for granted that the worthy testator was foxing. But we were wrong. And so are you, if that is what you thought."

"You assumed that the will was not a genuine one?"

"Yes; we thought it was a fake, put up with the aid of some shyster to bluff us into giving up Mr. Maddock as deceased. So, as I had to come across about these other affairs, Curtis suggested that I should look into the matter. And a considerable surprise I got when I did; for the will is perfectly regular and so is everything else. That legacy was a sort of posthumous joke, I guess."

"Then do I understand that Mr. Curtis was not really a friend of Maddock's?"

O'Donnell chuckled. "Not exactly a friend, doctor," said he. "He felt the warmest interest in Maddock's welfare, but they weren't what you might call bosom friends. The position was this: Curtis was the chief of our detective agency; Maddock was a gentleman whom he had been looking for and not finding for a matter of ten years. At last he found him; and then he lost him again; and this legacy, I take it, was a sort of playful hint to show which hole he'd gone down."

"Was Maddock in hiding all that time?" asked Thorndyke.

"In hiding!" repeated O'Donnell. "Bless your innocent heart, doctor, he had a nice convenient studio in one of the best blocks in New York a couple of doors from our agency, and he used to send us cards for his private views. No, sir, our dear departed friend wasn't the kind that lurks out of sight in cellars or garrets. It was Maddock, sure enough, that Curtis wanted, only he didn't know it. But I guess I'm fogging you. I'd best answer the questions that you put to Curtis.

"First, do we know anything about Maddock? Yes, we do. But we didn't know that his name was Maddock until a few months ago. Isaac Vandamme was the name we knew him by, and it seems that he had one or two other names that he used on occasion. We now know that the gay Isaac was a particularly versatile kind of crook, and a mighty uncommon kind, too, the Lord be praised; for, if there were many more like him we should have to raise our prices some. He wasn't the kind of fool that make a million dollar coup and then goes on the razzle and drops it all. That sort of man is easy enough to deal with. When he's loaded up with dollars everybody knows it, and he's sure to be back in a week or two with empty pockets, ready for another scoop. Isaac wasn't that sort. When he made a little pile, he invested his winnings like a sensible man and didn't live beyond his means; and the only mystery to me is that, when he died, he didn't leave more pickings. I see from his will—which I've had a look at—that the whole estate couldn't have been above five thousand dollars. He had a lot more than that at one time."

"He may have disposed of the bulk of his property by gift just before his death," Jervis suggested.

"That's possible," agreed O'Donnell. "He'd escape the death dues that way. However, to return to his engaging little ways. His leading line was penmanship—forgery—and he did it to an absolute finish. He was the most expert penman that I have ever known. But where he had us all was that he didn't only know how to write another man's name; he knew when to write it. I reckon that the great bulk of his forgeries were never spotted at all, and, of the remainder very few got beyond the bare suspicion that they were forgeries. In the case of the few that were actually spotted as forgeries, his tracks were covered up so cleverly that no one could guess who the forger was."

"And how did you come to suspect him eventually?" Thorndyke asked.

"Ah!" said O'Donnell. "There you are. Every crook–even the cleverest–has a strain of the fool in him. Isaac's folly took the form of suspicion. He suspected us of suspecting him. We didn't; but he thought we did, and then he started to dodge and make some false clues for us. That drew our attention to him. We looked into his record, traced his little wanderings and then we began to find things out. A nice collection there was, too, by the time we had worked a month or two at his biography; forgeries, false notes, and, at least two murders that had been a complete mystery to us all. We made ready to drop on Isaac, but, at that psychological moment, he disappeared. It looked, as if he had left the States, and, as we have no great affection for extradition cases, we let the matter rest, more or less, expecting that he would turn up again, sooner or later. And then came this lawyer's letter and yours, announcing his decease. Of course Curtis and I thought he was at the old game; that it was a bit of that sort of extra caution that won't let well alone. So, as I was coming over, I thought I'd just look into the affair as I told you; and, to my astonishment, I found everything perfectly regular; the will properly proved, the death certificate made out correctly and a second certificate signed by two doctors."

"Did you go into the question of identity?" asked Thorndyke.

"Oh, yes. I called on one of the doctors, a man named Batson, and ascertained that it was all correct. Batson's eyesight seemed to be none of the best, but he made it quite clear to me that his late patient was certainly our friend Isaac, or Maddock. So that's the end of the case. And if you want to go into it any further you've got to deal with a little pile of bone ash, for our friend is not only dead; he's cremated. That's enough for us. We don't follow our clients to the next world. We are not so thorough as you seem to be."

"You are flattering me unduly," said Thorndyke. "I'm not so thorough as that; but our clients, when they betake themselves to the happy hunting-ground, usually leave a few of their friends behind to continue their activities. Do you happen to know what Maddock's original occupation was? Had he any profession?"

"He was originally an engraver, and a very skilful engraver, too, I understand. That was what made him so handy in working the flash note racket. Then he went on the stage for a time, and didn't do badly at that; but I fancy he was more clever at making-up and mimicry than at acting in the dramatic sense. For the last ten years or so he was practising as a painter—chiefly of landscape, though he could do a figure subject or a portrait at a pinch. I don't fancy he sold much, or made any great efforts to sell his work. He liked painting and the art covered his real industries, for he used to tour about in search of subjects and so open up fresh ground for the little operations that actually produced his income."

"Was his work of any considerable merit?" Thorndyke asked.

"Well, in a way, yes. It was rather in the American taste, though Maddock was really an Englishman. Our taste, as you know, runs to technical smartness and novelty of handling; and Maddock's work was very peculiar and remarkably smart and slick in handling. He used the knife more than the brush, and he used it uncommonly cleverly. In fact, he was unusually skilful in many ways; and that's the really surprising thing about him, when one considers his extraordinary-looking paws."

"What was there peculiar about his hands?" asked Thorndyke. "Were they noticeably clumsy in appearance?"

"Clumsy!" exclaimed O'Donnell. "They were more than that. They were positively deformed. A monkey's hands would be delicate compared with Maddock's, They were short and thick like the paws of an animal. There's some jaw-twisting name for the deformity that he suffered from; bronchodaotilious, or something like that."

"Brachydactylous." suggested Thorndyke.

"That's the word; and I daresay you know the sort of paw I mean. It didn't look a very likely hand for a first-class penman and engraver of flash notes, but you can't always judge by appearances. And now as to your other questions: You ask what Maddock was like in appearance. I can only give you the description which I gave to Batson and which he recognized at once."

"Had he noticed the peculiarity of the hands?" enquired Thorndyke.

"Yes. I asked him about it and he remembered having observed it when he was attending Maddock. Well, then, our friend was about five feet nine in height, fairly broad and decidedly strong, of a medium complexion with grey eyes and darkish brown hair. That's all I can tell you about him."

"You haven't got his finger-prints, I suppose?"

"No. He was never in prison, so we had no chance of getting them."

"Was he married?"

"He had been; but some years ago his wife divorced him, or he divorced her. Latterly he has lived as a bachelor."

"There is nothing else that you can think of as throwing light on his personality or explaining his actions?"

"Nothing at all, doctor. I've told you all I know about him, and I only hope the information may be more useful than it looks to me."

"Thank you," said Thorndyke; "your information is not only useful; I expect to find it quite valuable. Reasoning, you know, Mr. O'Donnell," he continued, "is somewhat like building an arch. On a supporting mould, the builder lays a number of shaped stones, or voussoirs; but until all the voussoirs are there, it is a mere collection of stones, incapable of bearing its own weight. Then you drop the last voussoir–the keystone–into its place, and the arch is complete; and now you may take away the supports, for it will not only bear its own weight, but carry a heavy superstructure."

"That's so, doctor," said O'Donnell. "But, if I may ask, is this all gratuitous wisdom or has any particular bearing?"

"It has this bearing," replied Thorndyke. "I have myself been, for some time past, engaged, metaphorically, in the building of an arch. When you came here tonight, it was but a collection of shaped and adjusted stones, supported from without. With your kind aid, I have just dropped the keystone into its place. That is what I mean."

The American thoughtfully arranged the papers in his case, casting an occasional speculative glance at Thorndyke.

"I'd like to know," he said presently, "what it was that I told you. It doesn't seem to me that I have produced any startling novelties. However, I know it's no use trying to squeeze you, so I'll get back to my hotel and have a chew at what you've told me."

He shook hands with us all round, and, when Thorndyke had let him out, we heard him bustling downstairs and away up King's Bench Walk towards Mitre Court.

For a minute or more after his departure none of us spoke. Thorndyke was apparently ruminating on his newly-acquired information, and Jervis and I on the statement that had so naturally aroused the detective's curiosity.

At length Jervis opened the inevitable debate. "I begin to see a glimmer of daylight through the case of Septimus Maddock, deceased," said he; "but it is only a glimmer. Whereas, from what you said to O'Donnell, I gather that you have the case quite complete."

"Hardly that, Jervis," was the reply. "I spoke metaphorically, and metaphors are sometimes misleading. Perhaps I overstated the case; so we will drop metaphor and state the position literally in terms of good, plain, schoolboy logic. It is this: we had certain facts presented to us in connection with Maddock's death. For instance, we observed that the cause of death was obscure, that the body was utterly destroyed by cremation and that Jardine, who was an unofficial witness to some of the formalities, was subsequently pursued by some unknown person with the unmistakable purpose of murdering him. Those were some of the observed facts; and the explanation of those facts was the problem submitted to us; that is to say, we had to connect those facts and supply others by deduction and research, so that they should form a coherent and intelligible sequence, of which the motive for murdering Jardine should form a part.

"Having observed and examined our facts, we next propose a hypothesis which shall explain them. In this case it would naturally take the form of a hypothetical reconstruction of the circumstances of Maddock's death. That hypothesis must, of course, be in complete agreement with all the facts known to us, including the attempts to murder Jardine. Then, having invented a hypothesis which fits our facts completely, the next stage is to verify it. If the circumstances of Maddock's death were such as we have assumed, certain antecedent events must have occurred and certain conditions must have existed. We make the necessary inquiries and investigations, and we find that those events had actually occurred and those conditions had actually existed. Then it is probable that our hypothesis is correct, particularly if our researches have brought to light nothing that disagrees with it.

"With our new facts we can probably amplify our hypothesis; reconstruct it in greater detail; and then we have to test and verify it afresh in its amplified and detailed form. And if such new tests still yield an affirmative result, the confirmation of the hypothesis becomes overwhelmingly strong. It is, however, still only hypothesis. But perhaps we light on some final test which is capable of yielding a definite answer, yes or no. If we apply that test–the 'Crucial Experiment,' of the logicians– and obtain an affirmative result, our inquiry is at an end. It has passed out of the region of hypothesis into that of demonstrative proof."

"And are we to understand," asked Jervis, "that you have brought Maddock's case to the stage of complete demonstration?"

"No," answered Thorndyke. "I am still in the stage of hypothesis; and when O'Donnell came here tonight there were two points which I had been unable to verify. But with his aid I have been able to verify them both, and I now have a complete hypothesis of the case which has been tested exhaustively and has answered to every test. All that remains to be done is to apply the touchstone of the final experiment."

"I suppose," said Jervis," you have obtained a good many new facts in the course of your investigations?"

"Not a great many," replied Thorndyke; "and what new data I have obtained, I have, for the most part, communicated to you and Jardine. I assure you, Jervis, that if you would only concentrate your attention on the case, you have ample material for a most convincing and complete elucidation of it."

Jervis looked at me with a wry smile. "Now Jardine-Howard." said he; "why don't you brush up your wits and tell us exactly what happened to the late Mr. Maddock

and why some person unknown is so keen on your vile
body. You have all the facts, you know."

"So you tell me," I retorted; "but this case of yours
reminds me of those elaborate picture puzzles that used
to weary my juvenile brain. You had a hatful of irregular-
shaped pieces which, if you fitted them together, made a
picture. Only the beggars wouldn't fit together."

"A very apt comparison," said Thorndyke. "You put
the pieces together, and, if they made no intelligible part
of a picture, you knew you were wrong, no matter how
well they seemed to fit. On the other hand, if they seemed
to make parts of a picture you had to verify the result by
finding pieces of the exact shape and size of the empty
spaces. That is what I have been doing in this case; trying
the data together and watching to see if they made the
expected picture. As I have told you, O'Donnell's visit
found me with the picture entire save for two empty
spaces of a particular shape and size; and from him I
obtained two pieces that dropped neatly into those spaces
and made the picture complete. All I have to do now is to
see if the picture is a true representation or only a
consistent work of imagination."

"I take it that you have worked the case out in pretty
full detail," said Jervis.

"Yes. If the final verification is successful I shall be
able to tell you exactly what happened in Maddock's
house, what was the cause of death—and I may say that it
was not that given in the certificates—who the person is
who has been pursuing Jardine and what is his motive,
together with a number of other very curious items of
information. And the mention of that person reminds me
that our friend has been disporting himself in public,
contrary to advice and to what I thought was a definite
understanding."

"But surely," I said, "it doesn't matter now. We have
given that spy chappie the slip, and, even if he hasn't
given up the chase as hopeless, we know that he is quite
harmless."

"Harmless!" exclaimed Thorndyke. "Why, my dear fellow, he was your guardian angel. Didn't you realize that from Father Humperdinck's statement? He shadowed you so closely that no attack on you was possible; in fact, he actually caught a rap on the head that was apparently meant for you. You were infinitely safer with him at your heels than alone."

"But we've given the other fellow the slip, too," I urged.

"We mustn't take that for granted," said Thorndyke. "The French detective, you remember, came on the scene quite recently, whereas the other man has been with us from the beginning. He probably saw Jervis and me enter the mineral water works on the night of the fire, for he was certainly there; and he may even have followed us home to ascertain who we were. There are several ways in which he could have connected you with us and traced you here; so I must urge you most strongly not to venture out of the precincts of the Temple for the next few days, in fact, it would be much wiser to keep indoors altogether. It will be only a matter of days unless I get a quite unexpected set back, for I hope to have the case finally completed in less than a week; and when I do, I shall take such action as will give your friend some occupation other than shadowing you."

"Very well," I said. "I will promise not to attempt again to escape from custody. But, all the same, my little jaunt today has not been entirely without result. I have picked up a new fact, and a rather curious one, I think. What should you say if I suggested that Mrs. Samway was the wife of that eccentric artist who used to paint on the Heath? The man, I mean, who always worked in gloves?"

"I have assumed that she was in some such relation to him," replied Thorndyke, "but I should like to hear the evidence."

"Mrs. Samway," Jervis said in a reflective tone; "isn't that the handsome uncanny-looking lady with the mongoose eyes, who reminded me of Lucrezia Borgia?"

"That is the lady. Well, I met with a portrait of her today which was evidently the work of the man with the gloves," and here I gave them a description of the portrait and an account of the odd way in which it had been disinterred from the landscape that had been painted over it, to which they both listened with close attention.

"It's a queer incident," said Thorndyke, "and quite dramatic. If one were inclined to be superstitious one might imagine some invisible agency uncovering the tracks that have been so carefully hidden and working unseen in the interests of justice. But haven't you rather jumped to your conclusion? The existence of the portrait establishes a connection, but not necessarily that of husband and wife."

"I only suggested the relationship; but it seemed a likely one as the portrait had been painted over and thrown into the rubbish box."

Jervis laughed sardonically; and even Thorndyke's impassive face relaxed into a smile. "Our young friend," said the former, " doesn't take as favourable a view of the married state as one might expect from a gay Lothario who breaks out of his cage to go a-philandering. But we'll overlook that, in consideration of the very interesting information that he has brought back with him. Not that it conveys very much to me. It is obviously a new piece to fit into our puzzle, but I'm hanged if I see, at the moment, any suitable space to drop it into."

"I think," said Thorndyke, "that if you consider the picture as a whole, you will soon find a vacant space. And while you are considering it, I will just send off a letter, and then we had better adjourn this discussion. We have to catch the early train to Maidstone to-morrow, and that, I hope, will be the last time. Our case ought to be disposed of by the afternoon."

He seated himself at the writing-table and wrote his letter, while Jervis stared into the fire with a cogitative frown. When the letter was sealed and addressed, Thorndyke laid it on the table while he went to the lobby to put on his hat and coat, and, glancing at it almost unconsciously, I noted that the envelope was of foolscap size and was addressed to the Home Office, Whitehall. The name of the addressee escaped me, for, suddenly realizing the impropriety of thus inspecting another man's letter, I looked away hastily; but even then when Thorndyke had taken it away to the post, I found myself speculating vaguely on the nature of the communication and wondering if it had any relation to the mysterious and intricate case of Septimus Maddock.

19
TENEBRAE

THE resigned composure with which I accepted Thorndyke's sentence of confinement within doors was not entirely attributable to discretion or native virtue. My resolution to follow scrupulously my principal's very pointed advice was somewhat like the ascetic resolutions formed by the gourmet as he rises replete from the banquet table; for, just as the latter is in a peculiarly favourable condition for the unmoved contemplation of a—temporary—abstinence from food, so I, having enjoyed my little dissipation, could now contemplate with fortitude a brief period of retirement. Moreover, the weather was in my favour, being—as Polton reported, when he returned, blue-nosed and powdered with snow, with a fresh supply of tobacco for me—bitterly cold, with a threatening of smoky fog from the east.

Under these circumstances it was no great hardship to sit in a roomy armchair with my slippered feet on the kerb and read and meditate as I basked in the warmth of a glowing fire; though, to be sure, my reading was perfunctory enough, for the treatise of "The Surface Markings of the Human Body," admirable as it was, competed on very unfavourable terms with other claimants to my attention. In truth, I had plenty to think about even if I went no farther for matter than to the events of the previous day. There was my visit to Sylvia, for instance. I had not said much to her, but what I had said had pledged me to a life-long companionship; which was a solemn thing to reflect upon even though I looked forward to the fulfilment of that pledge with nothing but hopeful pleasure. The dice were thrown. Of course they would turn up sixes, every one; but still–the dice were thrown. From my own strictly personal affairs my thoughts rambled by an easy transition to the singular episode of the buried portrait, and thence to the subject of that strange palimpsest. Viewed by the light of Mr. O'Donnell's revelations, Mrs. Samway's position was not all that could have been desired. She and her husband had unquestionably been closely associated with Maddock; but Maddock was, it seemed, a habitual criminal. Could this fact have been known to the Samways? Or was it that the cunning forger and swindler had sheltered himself behind their respectability. It was impossible for me to say.

Then there was the strange and perplexing case of the man Maddock, himself. I could make nothing of that, had not, indeed, been aware that there had been a "case", until Thorndyke's investigations had put me in possession of the fact. And even now I could see nothing on which to base any suspicion, apart from the attempts on my life, which we were assuming to be in some way connected with events that had occurred in Maddock's house. The cause of death was apparently not "Morbus Cordis"; which might easily enough be, seeing that the diagnosis of heart disease was a mere guess on Batson's part. But if not Morbus Cordis, what was it? Thorndyke apparently knew, and seemed to hint that it was something other than ordinary disease. Could there have been foul play? And, if so, were the Samways involved in it in any way? It seemed incredible, for had not Maddock himself suspected that he was in a dangerous state of health. There was certainly one possibility which I considered with a good deal of distaste; namely, that Maddock had been in a hypochondriacal state and that the Samways had taken advantage of his gloomy views as to his health to administer poison. The thing was actually possible; but I did not entertain it; for, even if one assumed that poison had been administered, at any rate, the cremation of the body was not designed to hide the traces of the crime. The Samways had nothing to do with that; the cremation had been adopted in preference to burial by Maddock's own wish.

So my thoughts flitted from topic to topic, with occasional interludes of Surface Markings, through the lazy forenoon until Polton came to lay my solitary luncheon. And after this little break in the comfortable monotony, another spell of meditative idleness set in. Polton was busy upstairs in the laboratory with some photographic copying operations and I was disposed to wander up and look on; but my small friend politely but very firmly vetoed any such proceeding. On some other occasion he would be delighted to show me the working of the great copying camera, but, just now, he had a big job in hand, and, as he was working against time, he would prefer to be alone. He even suggested that I might attend to any stray callers and make my own tea on the gas-ring so as to avoid interrupting his work; and when I had agreed to relieve him to this extent, he thanked me profusely and retired and I saw no more of him.

For some time after his departure, I stood at the window looking out across the wide space at Paper Buildings and the end of Crown Office Bow. It was a wretched afternoon. The yellow, turbid sky brooded close down upon the houseroofs and grew darker and more brown moment by moment, as if the invisible sun had given the day up in despair and gone home early.

A comfortless powdering of snow filtered down at intervals and melted on the pavements, along which depressed wayfarers hurried with their coat collars turned up and their hands thrust deep into their pockets. I watched them commiseratingly, reflecting on the superior advantages of being within doors and forbidden to go out; and then, having flung another scoopful of coal on the fire, I betook myself once more to the armchair, the Surface Markings and idle meditation.

It was some time past four when my reflective browsings had begun to proceed in the direction of the teakettle, that I heard a light footstep on the landing as of someone wearing goloshes. Then a letter dropped softly into the box, and, as I instantly pushed back my chair to rise, the footsteps retreated. I crossed the room quickly and opened the door; but the messenger had already disappeared down the dark staircase, and had gone so silently on his rubber soles that, though I listened attentively, I could hear no sound from below.

Having closed the door, I extracted the letter from the box and took it over to the window to examine it, when I was not a little surprised to find that it was addressed to W. M. Howard, Esq. This was the first communication that I had received in my borrowed name, and my surprise at its arrival was not unreasonable, for, of the few persons who knew me by that name, none—with the exception, perhaps, of Mr. Marchmont—was in the least likely to write to me.

But, if the address on the envelope had surprised me, the letter itself surprised me a good deal more; for though the writer was quite unknown to me, even by name, he seemed to be in possession of certain information concerning me which I had supposed to be the exclusive property of Thorndyke, Jervis, Polton and myself. It bore the address, 29, Fig-tree Court, Inner Temple, and ran thus:

"DEAR SIR,
I am taking the liberty of writing to you to ask for your assistance as I happen to know that my friends, Drs. Thorndyke and Jervis, are away at Maidstone and not available at the moment, and I understand that you have some acquaintance with medical technicalities.
The circumstances are these. At half-past five today I shall be meeting a solicitor to advise as to action in respect

*of a case in which I am retained; and the decision as to
our action will be vitally affected by a certain issue on
which I am not competent to form an opinion for lack of
medical knowledge. If Dr. Thorndyke had been within
reach I should have taken his opinion; as he is not, it
occurred to me to ask if you would fill his place on this
occasion, it being, of course, understood that the usual fee
of five guineas will be paid by the solicitor. If you should
be unable to come to the consultation, do not trouble to
reply, as I am now going out and shall not be returning
until five-thirty, the time of the appointment. I am,*
    Yours faithfully,
    ARTHUR COURTLAND."

The contents of this letter, as I have said, surprised
me more than a little. How, in the name of all that was
wonderful, had this stranger, whose very name was
unknown to me, come to be aware that I had any
knowledge of medicine? Not from Thorndyke, I felt
perfectly sure; nor from Jervis, who, notwithstanding a
certain flippant facetiousness of manner, was really an
extremely cautious and judicious man. Could it be that
my principal was overseen in his trusted laboratory
assistant? Was it conceivable that the suave and discreet
Polton had moments of leakiness, when, in unofficial talk
outside, he let drop the secrets of which his employer's
unbounded confidence had made him the repository? I
could not believe it. Not only did Polton appear to be the
very soul of discretion; there was Thorndyke himself; he
was not the man to give his confidence to anyone until
after the most exhaustive proof of the safety of so giving
it. Nor was he a man who was likely to be deceived; for
nothing escaped his observation, and nothing that he
observed was passed over without careful consideration.
    My lethargy having been shaken off, I addressed
myself to the task of preparing tea; and, as I listened to
the homely crescendo of the kettle's song, I turned the

matter over in all its bearings. By some means this Mr. Courtland had become aware that I was either a doctor or a medical student. But by what means? Was it possible that he had merely inferred from the circumstance of my being associated with Thorndyke that I was of the same profession? That was just barely conceivable; but, if he had, then, as Jervis had said of Father Humperdinck, he must be "a devil at guessing."

As I made the tea and subsequently consumed it, I continued to ruminate on the contents of that singular letter. No answer to it was required. Then what was Mr. Courtland going to do if I did not turn up? He admitted that the issue, which seemed to be an important one, was beyond him, and yet he had to give an answer to the solicitor. And he was prepared to pay five guineas for the advice of a man of whom he–presumably–knew nothing. That was odd. In fact, the whole tone of the letter, with its inconsistent mixture of urgency and casual trusting to chance, seemed irreconcilable with the care and method that one expects from a professional man.

And there was another point. The time of the consultation was half-past five. Now within an hour of that time Thorndyke would be back–or even sooner if he came by the earlier train as he had done on the previous day–as Mr. Courtland must have known, since he knew whither my principal had gone, and he must have often attended assizes himself. Could he not have waited an hour? And again; had this business been sprung upon him so suddenly that he had had no time to get Thorndyke's opinion? And, yet again, why had be written at all, instead of dropping in at our chambers with the solicitor, as was so commonly done by Thorndyke's clients?

All of which were curious and puzzling questions which I put to myself, one by one, and had to dismiss unanswered. And then I came to the practical question, to which I had to find an answer, and which was: Could I, under the existing circumstances, accede to Mr.

Courtland's request? To go outside the precincts of the Inn was, I recognized, absolutely forbidden; but I had given no actual promise to remain in our chambers, nor had I been positively forbidden to leave them. Thorndyke had advised me to remain indoors, and his advice had been given so pointedly and with so evident a desire that it should be followed that I had not hitherto even thought of leaving our premises. But this was an unforeseen contingency; and the question was, did it alter my position in regard to Thorndyke's advice?

I think I have never been so undecided in my life. On the one hand, I was strongly tempted to keep the appointment. The prospect of triumphantly handing to Thorndyke a five-guinea fee which I had earned as his deputy appealed to me with almost irresistible force. On the other hand, my knowledge of Thorndyke did not support this appeal. I knew him to be a man to whom a principle was much more important than any chance benefit gained by its abandonment, and my inner consciousness told me that he would be better pleased by a strict adherence to our understanding than by the increment of five guineas.

So my thoughts oscillated, to and fro, now impelling me to risk it and earn the fee, and now urging me to keep to the letter of my instructions; and, meanwhile, the time ran on and the hour of the consultation approached What decision I should have reached, in the end, it is impossible to say. As matters turned out, I never reached any decision at all, for, just as the Treasury clock struck a quarter past five, I heard a light, quick step on our landing and immediately after a soft but hurried knock at the door.

I strode quickly across the room and threw the door open. And then I started back with an exclamation of astonishment. For the visitor—who stood full in the light of the landing-lamp—was a woman; and the woman was Mrs. Samway.

As I stood gazing at her in amazement, she slipped past me into the room and softly shut the door. And then I saw very plainly that there was something amiss, for she was as pale as death, and had a dreadful, frightened, hunted look which haunts me even now as I write. She was somewhat dishevelled, too, and, though it was a bitter evening, her plump, shapely hands were ungloved and cold as ice, as I noted when I took them in mine.

"Are you alone?" she asked, peering uneasily at the door of the little office.

"Yes. Quite alone," I replied.

She gazed at me with those strange, penetrating eyes of hers and said in a half-whisper: "How strange you look with that beard. I should hardly have known you if I had not expected —"

She stopped short, and, casting a strange, scared glance over her shoulder at the dark windows, whispered: "Can they see in? Can anyone see us from outside?"

"I shouldn't think so," I replied; but, nevertheless, I stepped over to the windows and drew the curtains.

"That looks more comfortable, at any rate," said I. "And now tell me how in the name of wonder you knew I was here."

She grasped both my wrists and looked earnestly-almost fiercely-into my eyes.

"Ask me no questions!" she exclaimed. "Ask me nothing! But listen. I have come here for a purpose. Has a letter been left here for you?"

"Yes," I replied.

"Asking you to go to a place in Fig-tree Court?"

"Good God!" I exclaimed. "How on earth—"

She shook my wrists impatiently in her strong grasp. "Answer me!" she exclaimed; "Answer me!"

"Yes," I replied. "I was to go there at half-past five."

Again her strong grasp tightened on my wrists. "Humphrey," she said, in a low, earnest voice, "you are not to go. Do you hear me? You are not to go."

And then, as I seemed to hesitate, she continued more urgently; "I ask you–I beg you to promise me that you won't."

I gazed at her in sheer amazement; but some instinct, some faint glimmer of understanding, restrained me from asking for any explanation.

"Very well," I said. "I won't go if you say I'm not to."

"That is a promise?"

"Yes, it's a promise. Besides, it's nearly half-past already, so if I don't go now, the appointment falls through."

"And you won't go outside these rooms tonight. Promise me that, too."

"If I don't go to this lawyer, I shan't go out at all."

"And to-morrow, too. Give me your word that you won't let any sort of pretext draw you out of these rooms to-morrow, or the next day, or, in fact, until Dr. Thorndyke says you may."

For a few moments I was literally struck dumb with astonishment at her last words, and could do nothing but gaze at her in astounded silence. At length, recovering myself a little, I exclaimed: "My dear Mrs. Samway–," but she interrupted me.

"Don't call me by that horrible name! Give me my own name, Letitia; or," she added, a little shyly and in a soft, coaxing tone, "call me Lettie. Won't you, Humphrey, just for this once? You needn't mind. You wouldn't if you knew. I should like, when I think of my friend–the only friend that I care for–to remember that he called me by my own name when he said good-bye. You'll think me silly and sentimental, but you needn't mind indulging me just once. It's the last time."

"The last time!" I repeated. "What do you mean by that, Lettie, and by speaking of our saying good-bye? Are you going away?"

"Yes, I am going away. I don't suppose you will ever see me again. I am going out of your life."

"Not out of my life, Lettie. We are always friends, even if we never see one another."

"Are we?" she said, looking up at me earnestly, "Perhaps it is so; but still, this is good-bye. I ought to say it and go; but O God!" she exclaimed with sudden passion, "I don't want to go—away from you, Humphrey, out into the cold and the dark!"

She buried her face against my shoulder, and I could feel that she was sobbing though she uttered no sound.

It was a dreadful situation. Instinctively certain though I was that her grief had a real and tragic basis, I could offer no word of comfort. For what was there to say? She was going, clearly, to a life of wretchedness without hope of any relief or change and without a single friend to cheer her loneliness. That much I could guess, vaguely and dimly. But it was enough. And it wrung my heart to witness her passion of grief and to be able to offer no more than a pressure of the hand.

After a few seconds she raised her head and looked in my face, with the tears still clinging to her lashes.

"Humphrey," she said, laying her hands on my shoulders, "I have a few last words to say to you, and then I must go. Listen to me, dearest friend, and remember what I say When I am gone, people will tell you things and you will come to know others. People will say that I am a wicked woman, which is true enough, God knows. But if they say that I have done or connived at wickedness against you, try to believe that it was not as it seemed, and to forgive me for what I have done amiss. And say to yourself, 'This wicked woman would have willingly given her heart's blood for me.' Say that, Humphrey. It is true. I would gladly give my life to make you safe and happy. And try to think kindly of me in the evil report that will reach you sooner or later. Will you try, Humphrey?"

"My dear Lettie," I said," we are friends, now and always. Nothing that I hear shall alter that."

"I believe you," she said," and I thank you from my heart. And now I must go–I must go; and it's good-bye–good-bye, Humphrey, for the very last time."

She passed her arms around my neck and pressed her wet cheek to mine; then she kissed me, and, turning away abruptly, walked across to the door and opened it. On the landing, in the light of the lamp, she turned once more; and I saw that the hot blush that had risen to her cheek as she kissed me, had faded already into a deathly pallor, and that the dreadful, frightened, hunted look had come back into her face. She stood for a moment with her finger raised warningly and whispered: "Good-bye, dear, good-bye! Shut the door now and shut it quietly," and then she passed into the opening of the dark staircase.

I closed the door softly and turned away towards the window; and, as I did so, I heard her stumble slightly on the stair a short way down and utter a little startled cry. I was nearly going out to her, and did, in fact, stand a moment or two listening; but, as I heard nothing more, I moved over to the window, and, drawing back the curtain, looked down on our doorstep to see her go out. My mind was in a whirl of confused emotions. Profound pity for this lonely, unhappy, warm-hearted woman contended with amazement at the revelation of her manifest connection with the mystery that surrounded me; and I stood bewildered by the tumult of incoherent thought, grasping the curtain and looking down on the great square stone that I might, at least, catch a farewell glance at this poor soul who was passing so unwillingly out of my life.

The seconds passed. A man came out of our entry and, turning to the left, walked at a rapid pace towards the Tudor Street gate. Still she did not appear. Perhaps she had heard him on the stairs and was waiting to pass out unnoticed. But yet it was strange.

Nearly a minute had elapsed since she started to descend the stairs. Could I have missed her? It seemed impossible, since I had come to the window almost immediately. A vague uneasiness began to take possession of me. I recalled her white face and frightened eyes, and as I stared down at the door-step with growing anxiety, I found myself listening-listening nervously for I knew not what.

Suddenly I caught a sound–faint and vague, but certainly a sound. And it seemed to come from the staircase. In a moment I had the door open and was stealing on tip-toe out on the landing. The house was profoundly silent. No murmur even penetrated from the distant streets. I crept across the landing, breathing softly and listening. And then, from the stillness below, but near at hand came a faint, whispering sigh or moan. Instantly I sprang forward, all of a tremble and darted down the stairs.

At the first turn I saw, projecting round the angle, a hand–a woman's hand, plump and shapely and white as marble. With a gasp of terror I flew round the turn of the staircase and–

God in Heaven! She was there! Huddled limply in the angle, her head resting against the baluster and one hand spread out on her bosom, she lay so still that she might have been dead but for the shallow rise and fail of her breast and the wide-staring eyes that turned to me with such dreadful appeal, I stooped over her and spoke her name, and it seemed to me that a pitiful little smile trembled for a moment on the bloodless lips, but she made no answer beyond a faint, broken sigh, and it was only when she moved her hand slightly that the overwhelming horror of the reality burst upon me. Then when I saw the crimson stain upon her fingers and upon the bosom of her dress, the meaning of that horrible pallor, the sharpening features and strange, pinched expression flashed upon me with a shock that seemed to arrest the very blood at my heart. Yet, stunned as I was, I realized instantly that human skill could avail her nothing; that I could do nought for her but raise her from the sharp edge of the stair and rest her head on my arm. And so I held her, whispering endearments brokenly, and looking as well as I might through the blinding tears into those inscrutable eyes, that gazed up at me, no longer with that stare of horror but with a vague and childlike wonder. And, even as I looked, the change came in an instant. The wide eye-lids relaxed and drooped, the eyes grew filmy and sightless, the hand slipped from her breast and dropped with a thud on the stair, and the supple body in my arms shrank of a sudden with the horrible limpness of death.

Up to this point my recollection is clear, even vivid, but of what followed I have only a dim and confused impression. The awfulness–the unbelievable horror of this frightful thing that had happened left me so dazed and numb that I recall but vaguely the passage of time of what went on around me in this terrible dream from which there was to be no waking. Dimly I recollect kneeling by her side on the silent staircase-but how long I know not–holding her poor body in my arms and gazing incredulously at the marble-white face–now with its drowsy lids and parted lips, grown suddenly girlish and fragile–while the hot tears dropped down on her dress; choking with grief and horror and a fury of hate for the foul wretch who had done this appalling thing, and who was now far away out of reach. I see–dimly still–the livid marks of accursed fingers lingering yet on the whiteness around the mouth to tell me why no cry from her had reached me, and the dreadful, red-edged cut in the bodice mutely demanding vengeance from God and man.

And then of a sudden the silence is shattered by rushing feet and the clamour of voices. Someone–it is Jervis–leads me forcibly away to our room and places me in a chair by the table. Presently I see her lying on our sofa, drowsy-eyed, peaceful, like a marble figure on a tomb. And I see Thorndyke, with a strange, coppery flush and something grim and terrible in the set calm of his face, showing the letter, which I had left on the table, to a tall stranger, who hurries from the room. Anon come two constables with heads uncovered carrying a stretcher. I see her laid on the sordid bier and reverently covered. The dread procession moves out through the doorway, the door is shut after it, and so, in dreadful fulfilment of her words, she passed out of my life.

20
THE HUE AND CRY

THE silence of the room remained unbroken for a quite considerable time after the two bearers had passed out with their dreadful burden. My two friends sat apart and, with a tact of which I was gratefully sensible, left me quietly undisturbed by banal words of consolation, to sustain the first shock of grief and horror and get my emotion under control. Still dazed and half-incredulous, I sat with my elbows on the table and my teeth clenched hard, looking dreamily across the room, half unconsciously observing my two friends as they silently examined the fatal letter. I saw Thorndyke rise softly and take a small bottle from a cabinet, and watched him incuriously as he sprinkled on the paper some of the dark-coloured powder that it contained. Then I saw him blow the powder from the surface of the paper into the fire and scan the letter closely through a lens. And still no word was spoken. Only once, when Jervis, in crossing the room, let his hand rest for a moment on my shoulder, did any communication pass between us; and that silent touch told me unobtrusively–if it were needful to tell me– how well he understood my grief for the woman who had walked open-eyed into the valley of the shadow, had offered her heart's blood that I might pass unscathed.

In about a quarter of an hour the tall stranger returned, bringing with him an atmosphere of bustling activity that at once dispelled the gloomy silence. His busy presence and brisk, matter-of-fact speech, though distressing to me at the moment, served as a distraction and brought me out of my painful reverie to the grim realities of this appalling catastrophe.

"You were quite right, sir," said he. "The chambers were an empty set. Mr. Courtland left them about six weeks ago, so they tell me at the office. I've looked them over carefully, and I think it is pretty clear what this man meant to do."

"Did you go in?" asked Thorndyke.

"Yes. Mr. Polton went with me and picked the lock, so I was able to go right through the rooms. And it is evident that this villain was not acting on the spur of the moment. He'd made a very neat plan, and I should say that it was pretty near to coming off. He had selected his chambers with remarkable judgment, and uncommonly well suited they were to his purpose. In the first place, they were the top set—nothing above them; no chance strangers passing up or down; and they were the only set on that landing. Then some previous tenant had made a little trap or grille in the outer door, a little hole about six inches square with a sliding cover on the inside. That was the attraction, I fancy. The landing lamp was alight—he must have lighted it himself, as the landing was out of use—and I fancy he meant to watch through the grille for your friend to come and shoot him as he knocked at the door."

"That would be taking more risk than he usually did," said Thorndyke.

"You mean that the report of the shot would have been heard. Perhaps it might. But these modern, small-bore, repeating pistols make very little noise, though they are uncommonly deadly, especially if you open the nose of the bullets."

"But," objected Thorndyke, "if he had been heard, there he would have been, boxed up in the chambers with no means of escape."

Our acquaintance shook his head. "No," said he; "that's just what he wouldn't have been, and there is where he had planned the affair so neatly. These chambers are a double set. They have a second entrance that opens on the staircase of the next house. You see the idea. When he's fired his shot and made sure that it was all right–or all wrong, if you prefer it–he would just have slipped through to the other entrance, let himself out, shut the door quietly and walked down the stairs. Then, if the shot had been heard, there was he, coming out of the next house to join the crowd and see what was the matter. It was a clever scheme, and, as I say, it might very well have come off if this poor young lady hadn't given it away. So that's all about the chambers; and now"–here he cast a glance in my direction–"I must ask for a few particulars." He produced a large, black-covered notebook and, opening it on the table, looked at me inquiringly.

"This," said Thorndyke, "is Mr. Superintendent Miller of the Criminal Investigation Department. He has charge of this case, so you must tell him exactly what happened. And try, Jardine, to be as clear and circumstantial as possible."

The Superintendent looked up sharply. "I had an impression," said he, "that this gentleman's name was Howard."

"He has used the name of Howard since he has been staying here, for reasons which no longer exist but which I will explain to you later. His name is Humphrey Jardine, and he is a bachelor of medicine."

Mr. Miller entered these particulars in his book and then said: "I suppose it is not necessary to ask if you were actually present when this poor lady was murdered?"

"No, I was not."

"And I presume you did not see the murderer?"

"I saw a man, whom I believe to have been the murderer, come out of our entry and walk quickly towards the Tudor Street Gate. But I can give you no description of him. I saw him from the window and by the light of the entry lamp."

The Superintendent wrote down my answer and reflected for a few moments. "Perhaps," said he, "you had better just give us an account of what happened and we can ask you any questions afterwards. It's very painful for you, I know, but it has to be, as you will understand."

It was more than painful; it was harrowing to reconstitute that hideous tragedy, step by step, with the knowledge that the poor murdered corpse was still warm. But it had to be, and I did it, haltingly, indeed, and with many a pause to command my voice; but in the end, I gave the superintendent a full description of the actual occurrences, though I withheld any reference to those words that my poor dead friend had spoken for my ear alone. When I had read through and signed my statement, Mr. Miller studied his note-book with an air of dissatisfaction and then turned to Thorndyke.

"This is all quite clear. Doctor," said he, "and just about what you inferred from that letter. But it doesn't help us much. The question is. Who is this man? I've an inkling that you know, Doctor."

"I have a very strong suspicion as to who he is," replied Thorndyke.

"That will do for me," said Miller. "Your strong suspicion is equal to another man's certainty. Do you know his name, sir?"

"He has recently passed under the name of Samway," replied Thorndyke. "What his real name is, I think I shall be able to tell you later. Meanwhile, I can give you such particulars as are necessary for making an arrest."

The Superintendent looked narrowly at Thorndyke as the latter pressed the button of the electric bell. "Apparently, Doctor," said he, "you have been making some investigations concerning this man, and, as it was not in connection with this crime, it must have been in connection with something else."

"Yes," replied Thorndyke, "you are quite right, Miller, and it will be a matter of the deepest regret to me to my dying day that circumstances have hindered those investigations as they have. The delay has cost this poor woman her life. A few more days and my case would almost certainly have been complete, and then this terrible disaster would have been impossible."

As Thorndyke finished speaking, the door opened quietly and Polton entered with a small, neatly-made parcel in his hand.

"Ah!" said Thorndyke, "you guessed what I wanted, and guessed right, as you always do, Polton. How many are there in that parcel?"

"Three dozen, sir," replied Polton.

"That ought to be enough for the moment. Hand them to the Superintendent, Polton. If you want any more, Miller, we can let you have a further supply, and I am having a half-tone block made which will be ready to-morrow morning."

"Are these portraits of the man you suspect?" asked Miller.

"No, I haven't his portrait, unfortunately, but on each card is a photograph of three of his finger-prints, which are all I have been able to collect, and on the back is a description which will enable you easily to identify him. You can post them off to the various sea-ports and telegraph the description in advance; and I would recommend you especially to keep a watch on Dover and Folkestone, as I know that he has been in the habit of using that route."

"Speaking of finger-prints," said Miller, "have you tried that letter for them?"

"Yes," replied Thorndyke, "I powdered it very carefully, but there is not a single trace of a fingerprint. He must have realised the risk he was taking and worn gloves when he wrote it."

The Superintendent pocketed the parcel with a thoughtful air, and, after a few moments' cogitation, turned once more to Thorndyke.

"You've supplied me with the means of arresting the man, Doctor," said he, "but that's all. Supposing I find him and detain him in custody? What then? I don't know that he murdered this poor woman. Do you? Dr. Jardine can't identify him, and apparently no one else saw him. I have no doubt that you have substantial grounds for suspecting him, but I should like to know what they are."

Thorndyke reflected for a moment or two before replying. "You are quite right. Miller," he said, at length, "you ought to have enough information to establish a prima facie case. But I think, that on this occasion, I can say no more than that, if you produce the man, you can rely upon me to furnish enough evidence to secure a conviction. Will that do?"

"It will do from you, sir," replied Miller, rising and buttoning his overcoat. "I will get this description circulated at once. Oh—there was one more matter; the name of the deceased lady was Samway—the same as that of the suspected murderer. What was the relationship?"

"She passed as—and presumably was—his wife."

"Ah!" said Miller. "I see. That was how she knew. Well, well. She was a brave woman, to take the risk that she did, and she deserved something very different from what she got. But we are taught that there is a place where people who suffer injustice and misfortune in this world get it made up to them. I hope it's true, for her sake—and for his," he added abruptly with a sudden change of tone.

"Naturally you do," said Thorndyke, "but, meanwhile, our business is with this world. Spread your net close and wide, Miller. I shall never forgive you if you let this villain slip. It is our sacred duty to purge the world of his presence. You do your part, Miller, and be confident that I will do mine."

"You can depend on me to do my best, sir," said Miller, "though I am working rather in the dark. I suppose you couldn't give me any sort of hint as to what you've got up your sleeve. You've no doubt, for instance, that it was really the man Samway who committed this murder?"

Thorndyke, according to his usual habit, considered the Superintendent's question for awhile before answering. At length he replied: "I don't know why I shouldn't take you into my confidence to some extent, Miller, knowing you as I do. But you will remember that this is a confidence. The fact is that I am proposing to proceed against this man on an entirely different charge. But I am not quite ready to lay an information; and I want you to secure his person on the charge of murdering his wife while I complete the other case."

"Is that another case of murder?" asked Miller.

"Yes. The facts are briefly these. A certain Septimus Maddock, who was living with the Samways, died some time ago under what seem to me very suspicious circumstances. He was nursed by Samway and his wife and by no one else. The cause of death given on the certificate was, in my opinion, not the true one, and I am proceeding to verify my theory as to what was the real cause of death."

"I see," said Miller. "You are applying for an exhumation of the body?"

"Well, hardly an exhumation. The man Maddock was cremated."

"Cremated!" exclaimed Miller. "Then we've done. There isn't any body to exhume."

"No," agreed Thorndyke, "there is no body, but there are the ashes."

"But, surely," said Miller, "you can't get any information out of a few handfuls of bone ash?"

"That remains to be proved," replied Thorndyke. "I have applied for an authority to make an exhaustive examination of those ashes, and, if my opinion as to the cause of death is correct, I shall be able to demonstrate its correctness; and that will involve a charge of murder against this man Samway. It will also support a charge against him of attempts to murder Dr. Jardine, and furnish strong evidence connecting him with the horrible crime that has just been committed. So you see, Miller, that the important thing is to get possession of him before he has time to escape from this country, and hold him in custody, if necessary, while the evidence against him is being examined and completed. And I must impress on you that no time ought to be lost in getting the description circulated."

"No, that's true," said Miller. "I'll go and telegraph it off at once, and I'll send one or two of our best men to watch the likely seaports."

He shook hands with us all round, and, when we had all most fervently wished him success he took his departure.

As soon as he was gone, Jervis turned to his senior, and, looking at him with a sort of puzzled curiosity exclaimed: "You are a most astounding person, Thorndyke! You really are! I thought I had begun to see daylight in that Maddock case, and now I find that I was all abroad. And I can't, for the life of me, conceive what in the world you expect to discover by examining a few pounds of calcined phosphates. Suppose Maddock was poisoned, what evidence will be obtainable from the ashes? Of the poisons which could possibly have been used under the known circumstances, not one would leave a trace after cremation. But, of course, you've thought of all that."

"Certainly, I have," replied Thorndyke, "and I agree with you that the ashes of a body that has been cremated are highly unpromising material for a primary investigation. But, does it not occur to you that, in a case where certain circumstantial evidence is available, excellent corroborative data might be obtained by the examination of the ashes?"

"No," replied Jervis, "I can't say that it does."

"It is not too late to consider the question," said Thorndyke. "I shall probably not get the authority for a day or two, so you will have time to turn the problem over in the interval. It is quite worth your while, I assure you, apart from this particular case, as a mere exercise in constructive theory. You can acquire experience from imaginary cases as well as from real ones, as I have often pointed out; in fact, much of my own experience has been gained in this way. I think I have mentioned to you that, in my early days, when I had more leisure than practice, it was my custom to construct imaginary crimes of an elaborately skilful type, and then–having, of course, all the facts–to consider the appropriate procedure for their detection. It was a most valuable exercise, for I was thus able to furnish myself with an abundance of problems of a kind that, in actual practice, are met with only at long intervals of years. And since then a quite considerable number of my imaginary cases have presented themselves, in a more or less modified form, for solution in the course of practice, and have come to me with the familiarity of problems that have already been considered and solved. That is what you should do, Jervis. Try the synthetic method and then consider what analytical procedure would be appropriate to your result."

"I have," Jervis replied, gloomily. "I have worked at this confounded case until I feel like a rat that has been trying to gnaw through a plate-glass window. Still, I'll have another try. By the way, where are you going to make this examination?"

"I think I shall do it here. I had thought of handing the ashes over to one of the more eminent analysts, but it will be only a small operation, well within the capacity of our own laboratory. I think of asking Professor Woodfield to come here and carry out the actual analysis. Polton will give him any help that he may want and, of course, we shall be here to give any further assistance if he should need it."

"Why not have made the analysis yourself?" asked Jervis. "Is there anything specially difficult or intricate about it?"

"Not at all," replied Thorndyke. "But, as the case will have to go into Court on a capital charge–that is, assuming that my hypothesis turns out to be correct–I thought it best to have the analysis made by a man whose name as an authority on chemistry will carry special weight. Neither the judge nor the jury are likely to have much special knowledge of chemistry, but they will be able to appreciate the fact that Woodfield is a man with a world-wide reputation, and they will respect his opinion accordingly."

"Yes," agreed Jervis, "I think you are quite right. A well-known name goes a long way with a jury. I hope your experiment will turn out as you expect, and I hope, too, that some of Miller's men will manage to lay that murderous devil by the heels. But I'm afraid they'll have their work cut out. He is a clever scoundrel; one must admit that. How do you suppose he contrived to track Jardine here?"

"I think," replied Thorndyke, "that he must have seen us on one of the two occasions when we went to the mineral water works and followed us here. Then, when Jardine disappeared from his lodgings, he would naturally look for him here, this being, in fact, the only place known to him in connection with Jardine, excepting Batson's house, on which he also probably kept a watch."

"But how would he have discovered that Jardine actually was here?"

"There are a number of ways in which he might have ascertained the fact. A good many persons knew that we had a new resident. We could not conceal his presence here. Many of our visitors have seen him, and the porter and hangers-on of the inn will have noticed him taking his exercise in the morning. Samway, himself, even, may have seen him, and he would easily have penetrated the disguise if he saw him out of doors, for there is no disguising a man's stature. He might have made enquiries of one of the porters or lamp-lighters, or he might have employed someone else to make enquiries. The fact that someone was staying here and that his name was Howard could not have been very difficult to discover, while, as for ourselves, we are as well known in the inn as the griffin at Temple Bar. From the circumstance that he knew of our attendance at the Maidstone Assizes, it seems likely that he had subsidized some solicitor's clerk who would know our movements."

"And I suppose," said I, "as he is gone now, I may as well go back to my lodgings."

"Not at all," replied Thorndyke. "In the first place, we don't know that he is gone, and we do know that he is now absolutely desperate and reckless. And you must not forget, Jardine, that whether we charge him with murder in the case of Maddock, with the murder of poor Mrs. Samway, or the attempted murder of yourself, in either case you are the chief witness for the prosecution. You are the appointed instrument of retribution in this man's case, and you must take the utmost care of yourself until your mission is accomplished. He knows the value of your evidence better than you do, and it is still worth his while to get rid of you if he can. But you, I am sure, are at least as anxious as we are to see him hanged."

"I'd sooner twist his neck with my own hands," said I.

"I daresay you would," said Thorndyke, "and it is perfectly natural that you should. But it is not desirable. This is a case for a few fathoms of good, stout, hempen rope, and the common hangman. The private vengeance of a decent man would be an undeserved honour for a wretch like this. So you must stay here quietly for a few days more and give us a little help when we need it."

Thorndyke's decision was not altogether unwelcome. Shaken as I was by the shock of this horrible tragedy, I was in no state to return to the solitude of my lodgings. The quiet and tactful sympathy of my two friends—or I should rather say three, for Polton was as kind and gentle as a woman–was infinitely comforting and their sober cheerfulness and the interest of their talk prevented me from brooding morbidly over the catastrophe of which I had been the involuntary cause. And, dreadful as the associations of the place were, I could not but feel that those of my older resorts would be equally painful. For me, at present, the Heath would be haunted by the figure of poor Letitia, walking at my side, telling me her pitiful tale and so pathetically craving my sympathy and friendship. And the Highgate Road could not but wring my heart with the recollection of that evening when we had walked together up the narrow lane–all unconscious of a black-hearted murderer stealing after us and foiled only by that futile spy–when, as we said good-bye I had kissed her and she had run off blushing like a girl.

Moreover, if Thorndyke's chambers were fraught with terrible and gloomy associations, they were also pervaded by an atmosphere of resolute, relentless preparation which was itself a relief to me; for, as the first shock of horrified grief passed, it left me possessed by a fury of hatred for the murderer and consumed by an inextinguishable craving for vengeance. Nor by the time of suspense so long as we had anticipated, as the very next morning a letter arrived from the Home Office containing the necessary authority to make the proposed examination and informing Thorndyke that on the following day the police would take possession of the ashes, which would be delivered to him by an officer who would remain to witness the examination and to resume possession of the remains when it was concluded.

I saw very little more of Thorndyke that day, but gathered that he was busy making the final arrangements for the important work of the morrow and clearing off various tasks so as to leave himself in from engagements. Nor did I enjoy much of Jervis's society, for he, too, was anxious to have the day free for the "Crucial Experiment," which was–we hoped–to solve the mystery of Septimus Maddock's death and explain the villain Samway's strange vindictiveness towards me.

Left to myself, and by no means enamoured of my own society, I wandered up to the laboratory to see what Polton was doing and to distract my gloomy thoughts by a little gossip with him on the various technical processes of which he possessed so much curious information. I found him arrayed in a white apron, with his sleeves turned up, busily occupied with what I took to be a slab of dough, which he had spread on a pastry board and was levelling with a hard-wood rolling-pin. He greeted me, as I entered with his queer, crinkly smile, but made no remark; and I stood awhile in silence, watching him cut the paste in halves, sprinkle it with flour, fold it up and once more roll it out into a sheet with the wooden pin.

"Is this going to be a meat pie, Polton?" I asked, at length.

His smile broadened at my question–for which I suspect he had been waiting. "I don't think you'd care much for the flavour of it, if it was, sir," he answered. "But it does look like dough, doesn't it. It's moulding-wax; a special formula of the Doctor's own."

"I thought that white powder was flour."

"So it is, sir; the best wheaten flour. It's lighter than a mineral powder and more tenacious. You have to use some powder to reduce the stickiness of the wax, especially in a soft paste like this, which has a lot of lard in it."

"What are you going to use it for?" I asked.

"Ah!" exclaimed Polton, pausing to give the paste a vicious whack with the rolling-pin, "there you are, sir. That's just what I've been asking myself all the time I've been roiling it out. The Doctor, sir-God bless him-is the most exasperating gentleman in the world. He fairly drives me mad with curiosity, at times. He will give me a piece of work to do–something to make, perhaps–with full particulars–all the facts, you understand, perfectly clear and exact, with working drawings if necessary. But he never says what the thing is for. So I make a hypothesis for myself–whole bundles of hypotheses, I make. And they always turn out wrong. I assure you, sir," he concluded with solemn emphasis, "that I spend the best part of my life asking myself conundrums and giving myself the wrong answers."

"I should have thought," said I, "that you would have got used to his ways by now."

"You can't get used to him," rejoined Polton. "It's impossible. He doesn't think like any other man. Ordinary men's brains are turned out pretty much alike from a single mould, like a batch of pottery. But the Doctor's brain was a special order. If there was any mould at all, that mould was broken up when the job was finished."

"What you mean is," said I, "that he has a great deal more intelligence than is given to the rank and file of humanity."

"No, I don't," retorted Polton. "It isn't a question of quantity at all. It's a different kind of intelligence. Ordinary men have to reason from visible facts. He doesn't. He reasons from facts which his imagination tells him exists, but which nobody else can see. He's like a portrait painter who can do you a likeness of your face by looking at the back of your head. I suppose it's what he calls constructive imagination, such as Darwin and Harvey and Pasteur and other great discoverers had, which enabled them to see beyond the facts that were known to the common herd of humanity."

I was somewhat doubtful as to the soundness of Polton's views on the transcendental intellect, though respectfully admiring of the thoughtfulness of this curious little handicraftsman; accordingly I returned to the more concrete subject of wax.

"Haven't you any idea what this stuff is going to be used for?"

"Not the slightest," he replied. "The Doctor's instructions were to make six pounds of it, to make it soft enough to take a squeeze of a stiff feather if warmed gently, and firm enough to keep its shape in a half-inch layer with a plaster backing, and to be sure to have it ready by to-morrow morning. That's all. I know there's an important analysis on to-morrow and I suppose this wax has got something to do with it. But, as to what moulding wax can have to do with a chemical analysis, that's a question that I can't make head or tail of."

Neither could I, though I had more data than Polton appeared to possess. Nor could Jervis, to whom I propounded the riddle when he came in to tea. We went up to the laboratory together and inspected, not only the wax, but the exterior of three large parcels addressed to Professor Woodfield, care of Dr. Thorndyke, and bearing the labels of a firm of wholesale chemists. But neither of us could suggest any solution of the mystery; and the only result of our visit to the laboratory was that Polton was somewhat scandalized by the conduct of his junior employer, who consoled himself for his failure by executing with the wax, a life-sized and highly grotesque portrait of Father Humperdinck.

21
THE FINAL PROBLEM

AT exactly half-past eleven in the following forenoon, Professor Woodfield arrived, bearing a massive cowhide bag which he deposited on a chair as a preliminary to taking off his hat and wiping his forehead. He was a big burly, heavy-browed man, sparing of speech and rather gruff in manner.

"Stuff arrived yet?" he asked when he had brought his forehead to a satisfactory polish.

"I think it came yesterday morning," replied Thorndyke.

"The deuce it did!" exclaimed Woodfield.

"Yes. Drapers—Three parcels from Townley and—"

"Oh, you're talking of the chemicals. I meant the other stuff."

"No; the officer hasn't arrived yet, but I expect he will be here in a few minutes. Superintendent Miller is a scrupulously punctual man."

The professor strode over to the window and glared out in the direction of Crown Office Row. "That man of yours got everything ready?" he asked.

"Yes," answered Thorndyke; "and I have looked over the laboratory myself. Everything is ready. You can begin the instant the ashes are delivered to us."

Woodfield expressed his satisfaction—or whatever he intended to express—by a grunt, without removing his eyes from the approach to our chambers.

"Cab coming," he announced a few moments later. "Man inside with a parcel. That the officer?"

Jervis looked out over the professor's shoulder. "Yes," said he, "that's Miller; and, confound it! Here's Marchmont with old Humperdinck. Shall we bolt up to the laboratory and send down word that we're all out of town?"

"I don't see why we should," said Thorndyke. "Woodfield won't be inconsolable if we have to leave him to work by himself for a while."

The professor confirmed this statement by another grunt, and, shortly afterwards, the clamour of the little brass knocker announced the arrival of the first contingent, which, when I opened the door, was seen to consist of the solicitor and his very reverend client.

"My dear Thorndyke!" exclaimed Marchmont, shaking our principal's hand; "what a shocking affair this is—this murder, I mean. I read about it in the paper. A dreadful affair!"

"Yes, indeed," Thorndyke assented; "a most callous and horrible crime."

"Terrible! Terrible!" said Marchmont. "So unpleasant for you, too, and so inconvenient. Actually on your own stairs, I understand. But I hope they'll be able to catch the villain. Have you any idea who he is?"

"I have a very strong suspicion," Thorndyke replied.

"Ah!" exclaimed Marchmont, "I thought so. The rascal brought his pigs to the wrong market. What? Like doing a burglary at Scotland Yard. He couldn't have known who lived here. Hallo! Why here's Mr. Miller. Howdy-do, Superintendent!"

The officer, for whom I had left the door ajar, entered in his usual brisk fashion, and, having bestowed a comprehensive salutation on the assembled company, deposited on the table an apparently weighty parcel, securely wrapped and decorated with a label bearing the inscription "This side up."

"There, sir," said he, "there's your box of mystery; and I don't mind telling you that I'm on tenterhooks of curiosity to see what you are going to make of it."

"Professor Woodfield is the presiding magician," said Thorndyke, "so we will hand it over to him. I suppose the casket is sealed?"

"Yes; it was sealed in my presence, and I've got to be present when the seals are broken."

"We'll break the seals up in the laboratory," said Woodfield, "but we may as well undo the parcel here."

He produced a solid-looking pocket knife, fitted with a practicable corkscrew, and, having cut the string, stripped off the wrappings of the parcel.

"God bless my soul!" exclaimed Marchmont, as the last wrapping was removed; "why, it's a cremation urn! What in the name of Fortune are you going to do?"

Miller tapped the lid of the urn with a dramatic gesture. "Dr. Thorndyke," said he, "is going, I hope, to extract from the ashes in this casket an instrument of vengeance on the murderer of Mrs. Samway."

"Ach!" exclaimed Father Humperdinck, "do not speak of vengeance in ze bresence of zese boor remains of a fellow greature. Chustice if you laig, but not vengeance. 'Vengeance is mine, eaiz ze Lordt!'"

"M'yes," agreed Miller, "that's perfectly true, sir, and we quite understand your point of view. Still, we've got our job to do, you know."

"But," said Marchmont, "I don't understand. What is the connection? These appear to be the remains of Septimus Maddock, whoever he may have been, and he seems to have died last November. What has he to do with the murder of this poor woman, Samway?"

"The connection is this," replied Thorndyke; "the man who murdered Mrs. Samway murdered the man whose ashes are in this urn. That is my proposition; and I hope, with the skilful aid of my friend Professor Woodfield, to prove it."

"Well," said Marchmont, "it is a remarkable proposition and the proof will be still more remarkable. I certainly thought that a body that had been cremated was beyond the reach of any possible inquiry."

"I am afraid that is so, as a rule," Thorndyke admitted. "But I hope to find an exception in this case. Shall we go upstairs and commence the examination?"

Woodfield having agreed with gruff emphasis, Miller picked up the casket and we all proceeded to the laboratory, where Polton, like a presiding analytical demon, was discovered amidst his beloved apparatus. The casket was placed on a table, the seals broken and the cover removed by Woodfield, whereupon we all, with one accord, craned forward to peer in at what looked like a mass of fragments of snowy madrepore coral.

"Ach!" exclaimed Father Humperdinck, "bot it is a solemn zought zat zese boor ashes vas vunce a living man chust like ourselves."

"Yes," said Marchmont, "it is, and I suppose we shall all be pretty much alike by the time we reach this stage. Cremation is a leveller, with a vengeance. Still, I will say this much, these remains are perfectly unobjectionable in every way, in fact they are almost agreeable in appearance; whereas, an ordinary disinterment after this lapse of time would have been a most horrid business."

"Yes, indeed," agreed Thorndyke; "I have had to make a good many examinations of exhumed bodies, and, as you say, they were very different from this. If I were not a practitioner of legal medicine—in which exhumation often furnishes crucial evidence—I should say that this cleanly and decent method of disposing of the dead was incomparably superior to any other. Unfortunately it has serious medico-legal drawbacks. I think, Woodfield, that we will turn, the ashes out on that sheet of paper on the bench, and then, with your permission, I will pick out the recognizable fragments and examine them while you are working on the small, powdery portions."

He took up the urn—which was an oblong, terracotta vessel some fourteen inches in length—and very carefully inverted it over the large sheet of clean white paper.

Then, from the dazzling, snowy heap, he picked out daintily the larger fragments–handling them with the utmost tenderness–for, of course, they were excessively fragile–and finally transferring them, one by one, to another sheet of paper at the other end of the bench.

The appearance of the remains was not quite as I had expected. Among the powdery debris was a quite considerable number of larger fragments, most of which were easily recognizable by the anatomical eye, while some of the larger long bones almost gave the impression of having been broken to enable them to be placed in the urn, and suggested that a partial reconstitution, for the purpose of determining the stature or other peculiarities of the skeleton was by no means as impossible as I had supposed. But, large and small alike, the pieces were strangely light and attenuated, like the ghosts of bones or artificial counterfeits in porous, spongy coral.

When Thorndyke had picked out such of the fragments as he wished to examine, Professor Woodfield glanced casually over the collection, but suddenly he paused and, stooping over a large piece of the right innominate bone, narrowly inspected a somewhat shiny yellow stain on its inner surface.

"Looks as if you were right, Thorndyke," he said in his laconic way, "qualitatively, at any rate. We shall see what the quantitative test says."

I pored over that dull yellow stain-as did Jervis also-but could make no guess at its nature or conceive any explanation of its presence. What interested me more was a small depression or cavity in the bone at the centre of the stain. That it was not the result of cremation was obvious from the fact that it was surrounded by a small area of sclerosed or hardened bone, which was quite plainly distinguishable on the spongy background, and which clearly pointed to some inflammatory change that had occurred during life. But of its cause, as of that of the stain itself, I could think of no intelligible explanation.

"Have you enough of the small fragments to go on with for the present, Woodfield?" Thorndyke asked.

"Plenty," replied Woodfield.

"Then," said Thorndyke, "I will get on with my side of the inquiry. I shall want the whole-plate camera first, Polton."

While his assistant was preparing the camera, he laid several of the fragments on a baize-covered board and secured them in position by threads attached to wooden-headed pins like diminutive bradawls. When the fragments were fixed immovably, he placed the board in a vertical position on a stand in a good light, by which time Polton was ready to make the exposure.

Meanwhile, Professor Woodfield was proceeding-under the horrified supervision of Father Humperdinck-with his part of the investigation. He was a matter-of-fact man, a chemist to the backbone, and to him it was evident that the late Septimus Maddock was simply so many pounds of animal phosphates. Quite composedly he shovelled up a scoopful of the ashes, which he emptied into the pan of a spring-balance, and, having weighed out a pound and a quarter, shot the contents of the pan into a large mortar and forthwith began to grind the fragments to a fine powder, humming a cheerful stave to the ring of the pestle. But his next proceeding scandalized the worthy Jesuit still more deeply. Having weighed out certain quantities of charcoal, sodium carbonate and borax, he pulverized each in a second mortar, mixed the whole together and shot the mixture into the first mortar, which contained the ash, stirring the entire contents up into a repulsive-looking grey powder.

"But, my dear sir!" exclaimed Father Humperdinck. "You are destroying ze remains!"

Woodfield looked at him from under his beetling brows, but went on stirring. "Matter is indestructible," he replied stolidly; and with this he tipped the contents of the mortar on to a sheet of paper and transferred them to a large fireclay crucible.

"Now, Polton," said he, "is the furnace ready?"

Polton disengaged himself for a moment from the camera, and took up a position by the side of the big fireclay drum with his hand on the gas cock. Then Woodfield, having dropped three or four large iron nails into the crucible, carried the latter over to the furnace and lowered it into the central cavity. The cock was turned on by Polton and a match applied, whereupon a great purplish flame shot up with a roar from the mouth of the furnace; and even when this had been confined by the dropping on of the massive cover, the ironcased cylinder continued to emit a muffled, sullen growl.

While the crucible was heating, I transferred my attention to Thorndyke. The photographic operations were now concluded and the moulding wax had just been produced from a warmed incubator. Polton's curiosity–and mine–was about to be satisfied.

Thorndyke began by laying a thick slab of the warm and pliable wax on the middle of a smooth plate of varnished plaster, at each corner of which was a small, hemispherical pit, and dusting powdered French chalk sparingly over the level surface of the wax. Then he took the large fragment of bone, which bore the mysterious yellow stain, and laid it on the wax with the stained side uppermost, pressing it very gently until it gradually sank into the soft, pasty mass. Next, he took a somewhat smaller slab of wax and, having dusted its surface with French chalk, laid it on the fragment of bone, pressing it on gently but firmly, especially in the neighbourhood of the stain. Having squeezed some irregular-shaped lumps of wax on the back of the top slab, he fastened a strip of india-rubber round the edge of the plaster plate, so that it formed an upright rim, and turned to Polton.

"Now mix a bowl of plaster–and mix it extra stiff, so that it will set quickly and hard."

With a soft brush he painted a thin coat of oil on the exposed portion of the plaster plate, up to the edges of the wax, and including the little circular hollows. By the time he had done this, Polton reappeared from the workshop with a basin of liquid plaster, which he was beating up with a spoon as if preparing a custard or batter pudding. As soon as the plaster began to thicken, he poured it on the wax and the oiled slab until it formed a level mass, nearly flush with the top of the india-rubber rim. In a surprisingly short time, the smooth, creamy liquid solidified into a substance having the appearance of icing-sugar, and when Polton had stripped away the india-rubber rim, exposing the edge of the new plaster slab, this part of the process was finished.

"We will put this mould aside for the plaster to harden while we make the other mould," said Thorndyke.

"Aren't you going to make moulds of all the fragments?" asked Jervis.

"No," Thorndyke answered; "the photographs of the rest will be sufficient, and I don't think we shall want even those; in fact, what I am doing now is merely by way of extra precaution. We are obliged to destroy the fragments in order to make the analysis, so I am just putting their appearance on record. You never know what an ingenious defending counsel may spring on you."

As Polton produced a second plate of varnished plaster and Thorndyke began to prepare the wax for the next mould, I turned my attention once more to Professor Woodfield. He had now deserted the mortar—in which he had been preparing a further supply of "the stuff"—and taken up a position by the furnace, with a long pair of crucible-tongs in his hand. On the bench, hard by, was an iron plate, and on this an oblong block of iron in which were six conical hollows.

Presently Woodfield glanced at his watch, turned off the gas-cock, removed the cover of the furnace with his tongs, and, reaching down into the glowing interior, lifted out the nearly white-hot crucible. Instantly Marchmont, Humperdinck and Jervis gathered round to watch, and even Thorndyke left his mould to come and see the result of the first trial.

Having stood the crucible on the iron plate while he picked out the large nails, one by one, Woodfield lifted it and steadily poured its molten contents into the first hollow in the iron block, which they soon filled, and overflowing ran along the iron plate in glowing streams that soon grew dull from contact with the cold surface. I noticed that, as the crucible was slowly tilted, Thorndyke kept his eyes fixed on its interior, as also did Jervis and Woodfield; and, watching closely, I saw just as the vessel was nearly empty, what looked somewhat like a red-hot oil-globule floating in the last of the glowing liquid. This passed out as the crucible was tilted further, and disappeared into the iron mould; when Woodfield, having exchanged a quick, significant glance with Thorndyke, proceeded forthwith, in his matter-of-fact way to fill up the still red-hot vessel with another pound and a quarter of the late Septimus Maddock.

"I suppose," said Marchmont," it is premature to ask you what is the final object of these very interesting operations?"

"It's no use asking me," replied Woodfield, "because I don't know. I am searching for traces of a particular substance, but what may be the significance of its presence, I haven't the slightest idea. You'd better ask Dr. Thorndyke–and he won't tell you."

"No, I know," said Marchmont. "Thorndyke will never tell you anything until he can tell you everything. By the way, will the remains be completely destroyed or will it be possible to recover them?"

"They are not destroyed at all," replied Woodfield. "They are all in the slag that came out of the crucible. We shall simply put the slag in the urn. There is a little charcoal, soda and borax added, but nothing is taken away."

I could see that to the unchemical mind of Father Humperdinck, this was far from satisfactory, and I observed him poring, with obvious disapproval, over the dark-coloured, glassy masses of slag on the iron plate. "Ashes to Ashes" was an intelligible formula, but "ashes to slag" was quite another matter, for which no provision had been made in any known ritual.

After a rather hurried luncheon, the wax moulds were carefully opened and the fragments of bone picked out, when it was seen that each fragment had left a perfect impression on the wax surface into which it had been pressed. These hollow impressions were now filled with liquid plaster, and, when the latter had thickened sufficiently, the two halves of each mould were quickly fitted together and kept in close contact by a weight.

During the interval which was necessary to allow of the plaster setting quite firmly, I had leisure to note that Professor Woodfield had filled two more of the cavities in the iron mould. Now that the furnace was thoroughly hot, he was able to work rather more quickly, and he had economized time by leaving a crucible to heat while we were at lunch. He was preparing to take the fourth charge from the furnace when I observed Polton removing the weight from one of the moulds and hurriedly transferred my patronage to his part of the entertainment. The mould on which he was operating was the one bearing the impressions of the stained fragment of the innominate bone, and when he separated the two halves and exposed the newly-made cast inside one might have thought that the actual bone had been left in, so perfectly did the snowy plaster cast reproduce the dazzlingly-white calcined bone. But, naturally, the stain did not appear in the cast, a defect which Thorndyke proceeded at once to remedy by making a tracing of the exact position and extent of the coloured patch and transferring it to the cast. Then, and not till then, Thorndyke regretfully handed the original fragment to Professor Woodfield, who impassively dropped it into the mortar and pounded it into a mere characterless powder.

After the opening of the second mould and the removal of the casts, the interest of the investigation lapsed for a time. Woodfield's operations were, doubtless, the most important part of the procedure, but they were not thrilling to look on at. In fact they became by unvarying repetition, decidedly tedious, and when the last charge-containing the uttermost crumb of ash-had been placed in the furnace and there was nothing to do but stare at the great fireclay drum, Marchmont and Humperdinck began to yawn in the most portentous manner. I rather wondered that they did not go, for the investigation was no business of theirs, and there was little entertainment in gazing at the outside of the furnace or watching Polton and the Superintendent gather up the masses of slag from the plate and drop them into the casket. But I supposed that they, like myself, were consoling themselves for the tedium of the chemist's manipulations by the prospect of satisfying their curiosity as to the final result of the experiment.

When at length, the last charge was ready, Woodfield withdrew the white-hot crucible from the furnace and stood it on the iron plate. But this time he did not pour out the contents. Instead, he tilted the iron mould, and, picking out the conical masses of slag that it contained, one by one, lowered them with his tongs into the hot crucible. Then, having thrown in a little fresh flux, he returned the crucible to the furnace.

"Why didn't he pour out the melted stuff this time?" Marchmont asked.

"Because," Thorndyke replied, "I want, for certain reasons, to have the total result of the analysis in a single mass. Each of those little cones of slag contains the result from a sixth part of the ash; the crucible now contains the matter extracted from the whole of the ashes. For my purposes this is more suitable, as you will see in a few minutes–for we shall not have to leave the crucible in the furnace so long this time."

"I'm glad of that," said Marchmont, "though this has been a most interesting, and I may say, fascinating experience. I am delighted to have had an opportunity of witnessing these most instructive and–er–aw –"

The rest of the sentence was rendered somewhat obscure by a colossal yawn; but very soon the interest of the proceedings was revived by Woodfield, who approached the furnace with a determined air and removed its cover with somewhat of a flourish.

"Now we shall see, Thorndyke," said he, turning off the gas and reaching down into the glowing cavity with his tongs. He lifted out the crucible and, standing it on the iron plate, took out the nails, tapping each on the side of the pot as he withdrew it.

"Do you want me to pour it out, or shall I break the pot?" asked Woodfield.

"That rests with you," replied Thorndyke.

"Better break the pot, then," said Woodfield.

This entailed a further spell of expectant waiting, and we all stood round, gazing impatiently at the crucible as it slowly faded from bright red to dull red and from this to its natural dull drab. It was quite a long time before Woodfield considered it cool enough to be broken, indeed I half suspected him of prolonging our suspense with deliberate malice. At length he took up a peculiarly-shaped hammer which Polton had handed to him, and, laying the crucible on its side, struck it sharply near the bottom with the pointed beak; then he turned the pot over and struck a similar blow on the opposite side; upon which the bottom of the crucible broke off cleanly, exposing the mass of dark, glassy slag, and, embedded in it, a bright button of metal.

"What metal is that?" Jervis demanded eagerly.

The professor struck the button smartly with the hammer, whereupon it detached itself from the slag and rolled on to the plate.

"Lead," said he. "I don't vouch for its parity, but it is undoubtedly lead."

Jervis turned to Thorndyke with a puzzled look. "You can't be suggesting," said he, "that this was a case of acute lead poisoning. The circumstances didn't admit of it, and besides, the quantity of lead is impossibly large."

"I should suppose," interposed Miller, "that the doctor was suggesting a most particularly acute form of lead poisoning, only that it is impossible to imagine that a cremation certificate would be granted in a case where a man had been killed by a pistol shot."

"I am not so sure of that," said Thorndyke; "though it is not likely that a cremation certificate would be applied for under those circumstances. But I am certainly not suggesting lead poisoning."

"What do you say is the weight of this button, Thorndyke?" the professor asked.

"That," replied Thorndyke, "depends on its relation to the total content of lead in the ashes. What percentage do you suppose has been lost in the process of reduction?"

"Not more than ten per cent. I hope. You may take this button as representing ninety per cent of the total lead; perhaps a little more."

Thorndyke made a rapid calculation on a scrap of paper. "I suggest," said he, "that the total lead in the ashes was three hundred and eighty-six grains. Deducting a tenth, say thirty-eight and a half grains, we have three hundred and forty-seven and a half grains, which should be the weight of this button."

Woodfield picked up the button and striding over to the glass case which contained the chemical balance, slid up the front, and, placing the button in one pan, put the weight corresponding to Thorndyke's estimate, in the other. On turning the handle that released the balance, it was seen that the button was appreciably heavier than Thorndyke had stated, and Woodfield adjusted the weights with a small pair of forceps until the index stood in the middle of the graduated arc.

"The weight is three hundred and forty-nine and a half grains," said Woodfield. "That means that my assay was rather better than I thought. You were quite right, Thorndyke, as you generally are. I wonder what the object was that weighed three hundred and eighty-six grains. Are you going to tell us?"

Thorndyke felt in his waistcoat pocket. "It was an object," said he," very similar to this."

As he spoke, he produced a rather large, dark-coloured bullet, which he handed to Woodfield, who immediately placed it in the pan of the balance and tested its weight.

"Just a fraction short of three hundred and eighty-seven grains," said he.

The Superintendent peered curiously into the balance-case, and, taking the bullet out of the pan, turned it over in his fingers.

"That's not a modern bullet," said he. "They don't make 'em that size now, and they don't generally make 'em of pure lead."

"No," Thorndyke agreed. "They don't. This is an old French bullet; a chassepot of about 1870."

"A chassepot!" exclaimed Humperdinck, with suddenly-awakened interest.

"Yes," said Thorndyke; "and this button,"—he picked it up from the floor of the balance-case as he spoke,—"was once a chassepot bullet, too. This, Father Humperdinck," he added, holding out the little mass of metal towards the Jesuit, "was the bullet which struck your friend, Vitalis Reinhardt, near Saarbrück more than thirty years ago."

The priest was thunderstruck. For some seconds, he gazed from Thorndyke's face to the button of lead, with his mouth agape and an expression of utter stupefaction. "But," he exclaimed, at length, "it is impossible! How can it be, in the ashes of a stranger!"

"I take it," said Marchmont, "that Dr. Thorndyke is suggesting that this was the body of Vitalis Reinhardt."

"Undoubtedly I am," said Thorndyke.

"It sounds a rather bold supposition," Marchmont observed, a little dubiously. "Isn't it basing a somewhat startling conclusion upon rather slender data? The presence of the lead is a striking fact, but still, taken alone –"

"But it isn't taken alone," Thorndyke interrupted. "It is the final link in a long chain of evidence. You will hear that evidence later, but, as it happens, I can prove the identity of these remains from facts elicited by the examination that we have just made. Let me put the argument briefly.

"First, I will draw your attention to these plaster casts, which you have seen me make from the original bones, Take, to begin with, these small fragments. Dr. Jervis will tell you what bones they are."

He handed the small casts to Jervis, who looked them over–not for the first time–and passed them to me. "I say that they represent two complete fingers and the first, or proximal, joint of a right thumb. What do you say, Jardine?"

"That is what I had already made them out to be," I replied.

"Very well," said Thorndyke. "That gives us an important initial fact. These remains contained two complete fingers and the first joint of a thumb. But these remains profess to be those of a man named Septimus Maddock. Now this man is known to have had deformed hands, of the kind described as brachydactylous. In such hands all the fingers are incomplete–they have only two joints instead of the normal three–and the first, or proximal joint of the thumb is absent. Obviously, then, these remains cannot be those of Septimus Maddock, as alleged.

"But, if not Maddock's remains, whose are they? From certain facts known to me, I had assumed them to be those of Vitalis Reinhardt. Let us see what support that assumption has received. Reinhardt is known to have been wounded in the right hip by a chassepot bullet, and the bullet was never extracted. Now I find, among these remains, a considerable portion of the right hip-bone. In that bone is a mark which plainly shows that it has been perforated and the perforation repaired, and there is a cavity in which a foreign body of about the size of a chassepot bullet has been partly embedded. The chemical composition of that foreign body is plainly indicated by a stain which surrounds the cavity; which stain is evidently due to oxide of lead. Clearly the foreign body was composed of lead, which will have melted in the cremation furnace and run away, but left a small portion, in the cavity, which small portion, becoming oxidized, the oxide will have liquefied and become soaked up by the absorbent bone-ash, thus producing the stain.

"Finally, we find by assay, that this foreign body actually was composed of lead and that its weight was—within a negligible amount of error—three hundred and eighty-six grains, which is the weight of a chassepot bullet.

"I say that the evidence, from the ashes alone, is conclusive. But this is only corroborative of conclusions that I had already formed on a quite considerable body of evidence. Are you satisfied, Marchmont? I mean, of course, only in respect of a prima facie case."

"Perfectly satisfied," replied Marchmont. "And now I understand why you insisted on my being present at this investigation and bringing Father Humperdinck; which, I must admit, has been puzzling me the whole day. By the way, I rather infer, from what you said, that there has been foul play. Is that so?"

"I think," replied Thorndyke, "there can hardly be a doubt that Reinhardt was murdered by Septimus Maddock."

Father Humperdinck's face suddenly turned purple. "And zis man Maddock," he exclaimed fiercely, "zis murderer of my poor friendt Vitalis, vere is he?"

"He is being sought by the police at this moment," replied Thorndyke.

"He must be caught!" Father Humperdinck shouted in a furious voice, "and ven he is caught he must be bunished as he deserves. I shall not vun moment rest until he is hanged as high as Haman."

Here I caught a quick glance from Marchmont's eyes and seemed to hear a faint murmur which framed the words "Vengeance is mine."

"But," the Jesuit continued, after a momentary pause, in the same loud, angry tone: "Zis villain has a double grime gommitted; he has murdered a goot, a chenerous, a bious man; and he has robbed ze boor, ze suffering and ze unfortunate."

"How has he done that?" asked Marchmont.

"By murdering ze benefactor of our zoziety," was the answer.

"Yes, to be sure," agreed the solicitor. "I hadn't thought of that. Of course, the original will in favour of Miss Vyne probably stands without modification."

At this point Superintendent Miller interposed. "You were saying, sir, that the man Maddock is now being sought by the police. Do you mean under that name?"

"No," answered Thorndyke. "I mean under the name of Samway. Septimus Maddock, alias Isaac Van Damme, is written off as deceased. But Samway, alias Maddock, alias Burton of Bruges, alias Gill, is his re-incarnation, and, as such, I commend him to your attention; and I hope, Miller, you will be able to produce him shortly, in the flesh. The evidence, as you see, is now ready, and all that is lacking is the prisoner."

"He shan't be lacking long, sir, if any efforts of mine can bring him to light. I see a case here that will pay for all the work that we can put into it; and now, with your permission, doctor, I will take possession of this urn and get off, to see that everything necessary is being done."

The Superintendent, as so often happens with departing guests, infected our other two visitors with a sudden desire to be gone. Father Humperdinck, especially, seemed unwilling to lose sight of the police officer–who was correspondingly anxious to escape–and, having wished us a very hasty adieu, hurried down the stairs in his wake, followed, at a greater interval, by his legal adviser.

22
THORNDYKE REVIEWS THE CASE

WHEN Professor Woodfield, having deliberately packed his bag and–to my great relief and Jervis's– declined Thorndyke's invitation to stay and take tea with us, presently took his departure, we descended to the sitting-room, whither Polton followed us almost immediately with a tea-tray, having, apparently, boiled the kettle in the adjacent workshop while the final act of the analysis was in progress. He placed the tray on a small table by Thorndyke's chair, and, evidently, anticipating the inevitable discussion on the results of the analysis, made up the fire on a liberal scale and retired with unconcealed reluctance.

As soon as we were alone, Jervis opened the subject by voicing his and my joint desire for "more light."

"This has been a great surprise to me, Thorndyke," said he.

"A complete surprise?" Thorndyke asked. "No, I can't say that. The solution of the problem was one that I had proposed to myself, but I had rejected it as impossible; and it looks impossible still, though I now know it to be the true solution."

"I quite appreciate your difficulty," said Thorndyke, "and I see that if you did not happen to light on the answer to it, the difficulty was insuperable. That was the really brilliant feature in Maddock's plan. But for a single fact which was almost certain to be overlooked, the real explanation of the circumstances would appear utterly incredible. Even if suspicion had been aroused later and the true explanation suggested, there seemed to be one fact with which it was absolutely irreconcilable."

"Yes," agreed Jervis; "that is what I have felt."

"The truth is," said Thorndyke, "that this crime was planned with the most diabolical cleverness and subtlety. We realize that when we consider by what an infinitely narrow margin it failed. Indeed, we can hardly say that it did fail. As far as we can see, it succeeded completely, and if the criminal could only have accepted its success, there seems to be no reason why any discovery should ever have taken place. Looking back on the case, we see that our experience has been the same as O'Donnell's; we had no clue whatever expecting the one that was furnished by the criminal himself in his unnecessary efforts to obtain even greater security. Suppose Maddock, having carried out his plan successfully, had been content to leave it at that, who would have known, or even suspected, that a crime had been committed? Not a soul, I believe. But instead of that he must needs do what the criminal almost invariably does; he must tinker at the crime when all is going well and surround himself by a number of needless safeguards by which, in the end, attention is attracted to his doings. He knows, or believes he knows, that Jardine has in his possession certain knowledge of a highly dangerous character; he does not ask himself whether Jardine is aware that he possesses such knowledge, but, appraising that knowledge at what he, himself, knows to be its value, he decides to get rid of Jardine as the one element of danger. And that was where he failed. If he had left Jardine alone, the whole affair would have passed off as perfectly normal and its details would soon have been lost sight of and forgotten. Even as it was, he missed complete success only by a hair's breadth. But for the most trivial coincidence, Jardine's body might be lying undiscovered in that cellar at this very moment."

"That's a comfortable thought for you, Jardine," my younger colleague remarked.

"Very," I agreed, with a slight shudder at the recollecting of that horrible death-trap. "But what was the coincidence? I never understood how you came to be in that most unlikely place at that very opportune moment."

"It was the merest chance," replied Thorndyke. "I happened to have called in at the hospital that evening, and, having an hour to spare, it occurred to me to look in at Batson's and see if you were getting on quite happily in your new command. As I had induced you to take charge, I felt some sort of responsibility in the matter."

"It was exceedingly kind of you, sir," said I.

"Not in the least," said Thorndyke. "It was just the ordinary solicitude of the teacher for a promising pupil. Well, when I arrived at the house, I found that excellent girl, Maggie, standing on the doorstep, looking anxiously up and down the street. It seemed that, on reflection, she was still convinced that the works were untenanted, and the oddity of the whole set of circumstances had made her somewhat uneasy. I waited a few minutes and disposed of one or two patients, and then, as you did not return, after what seemed an unaccountably long absence, I very easily induced her to show me where the place was; and when we arrived there, the deserted aspect of the building and the notice board over the gate seemed rather to justify her anxiety.

"I rang the bell loudly, as I daresay you know, but I did not wait very long. When I failed to get any response, I too, became suspicious, and proceeded without delay to pick the lock of the wicket–and it is most fortunate that the wicket was unprovided with a bolt, which would have delayed me very considerably. You know the rest. When I shouted your name you must have tried to answer, for I caught a kind of muffled groan and the sound of tapping, which guided me and Maggie to your prison. But it was a near thing; for, when I opened the cellar door, you fell out quite unconscious and accompanied by a gush of carbon dioxide that was absolutely stifling."

"Yes," said I, "it was touch and go. A few minutes more and it would have been all up with me. I realised that as soon as I recovered consciousness. But I couldn't, for the life of me understand why anybody should want to murder me, and I am not so very clear on the subject now. I really knew nothing about Maddock."

"You knew more than anyone else knew, and he thought you knew more than you did. But perhaps it would be instructive to review the case in detail."

"It would be very instructive to me," said Jervis, "for I don't, even now, see how you managed to bridge over those gaps that stopped me in my attempts to make a hypothesis that covered all the circumstances."

"Very well," said Thorndyke, "then we will begin at the beginning; and the beginning, for me, was the finding of Jardine, as I have described it. Here was a pretty plain case of attempted murder, evidently premeditated and apparently committed by some person who had access to these works; evidently, also, conceived and planned with considerable knowledge, skill and foresight, though with how much foresight I did not realize until I had heard Jardine's story. When I had Jardine's account of the affair, I saw that the crime had been planned with quite remarkable ingenuity and judgment; in fact, the circumstances had been so carefully considered, and contingencies so well provided for that, but for a single tactical error the plan would have succeeded. That error was in making the pretended emergency a surgical injury. If the letter to Jardine had stated that a man was in a fit, instead of suffering from a wound, our friend would have had no need to call at the surgery for appliances but would have gone straight to the works. And there, in all probability, his body would still be lying, for no one would have known whither he had gone; and even if his body had been accidentally discovered, all traces of the means by which he had been killed would probably have been removed. There would have been nothing to show that he had not strayed into the deserted factory and turned on the gas himself; indeed, it is pretty certain that matters would have been so arranged as to convey that impression to the persons who made the discovery."

"There was the letter," said I. "That would have given things away to some extent."

"But you would have had it in your pocket, from which he would, of course, have removed it. We may be sure that he had not overlooked the letter. It was the need for surgical appliances that he had overlooked; but, in spite of this error, the plan was ingenious subtle, and clearly not the work of an ignorant man.

"And here I would point out to you that this latter fact was one of great importance in searching for the solution of the mystery. We knew something of our man. He was subtle, resourceful, and absolutely ruthless. Noting this, I was prepared, in pursuing the case, to find his other actions characterized by subtlety, resourcefulness and ruthlessness. His further actions were not going to be those of a dullard or an ignoramus.

"But this was not all the information that I had concerning the personality of this unknown villain. Jervis and I looked over the cellars that same night within an hour and a half of the rescue and before anything had been moved. We were then in a position to infer that the unknown was probably a somewhat tall man and above the average of strength, as shown by the weight, position and arrangement of the iron bottles. Moreover, since there was no faintest trace of a finger-print on any of them, it followed that some precaution against them— such as gloves—had been adopted; which again suggested either a professional criminal or a person well acquainted with criminal methods.

"So much for the man. As to the rest of the information that I obtained by looking into the cellar, it seemed, at the time meagre enough; and yet, when considered by the light of Jardine's statement, it turned out to be of vital importance. You remember what it was, Jardine? That cellar contained certain objects. They seemed very unilluminating and commonplace, but, according to my invariable custom, I considered them attentively and made a written list of them. Do you remember what they were?"

"Yes, quite well. There were ten empty cylinders, a spanner, a packing-case —"

"What were the dimensions of the case?" Thorndyke interrupted. "Seven feet long by two and a half wide and deep. Then there were a couple of waterproof sheets and a quantity of straw. That is the lot, I think, and I'll be hanged if I can see what any of them—excepting the three cylinders that were used for my benefit—have to do with the case. Can you, Jervis?"

"I'm afraid I can't," he replied. "They are all such very ordinary objects."

"Ordinary or not," said Thorndyke, "there they were; and I made a note of them on the principle—which I am continually impressing on my students—that you can never judge in advance what the evidential value of any fact will be, and on the further principle that, in estimating evidence, there is no such thing as a commonplace fact or object.

"Until I had heard Jardine's account of the affair there was not much to be gained by thinking about the possibilities that it presented. There was, however one point to be settled, and I dealt with it at once. My slight inspection of the works had shown that no business was being carried on in them; and the question was whether they were completely untenanted or whether there was some person who had regular access to them. My enquiries resulted, as you know, in the unearthing of the mysterious Mr. Gill, but what his relation to the affair might be I was not, at the moment, in a position to judge.

"Then came our talk with Jardine, from which emerged the fact that the ordinary motives of murder apparently did not exist in this case, and that the crime appeared to have its origin in circumstances that had arisen locally and recently. And, on our proceeding to search for such conditions as might conceivably generate an adequate motive, we lighted on a case of cremation.

"Now, it is my habit, whenever I have to deal with death which has been followed by cremation, to approach the case with the utmost caution and scrutinize the circumstances most narrowly. For, admirable as is this method of disposing of the dead regarded from a hygienic standpoint, it has the fatal defect of lending itself most perfectly to the more subtle forms of murder, and especially to the administration of poison. By cremation all traces of the alkaloids, the toxines and the other organic poisons are utterly destroyed, while of the metals, the three whose compounds are most commonly employed for criminal purposes—arsenic, antimony and mercury—are volatilized by heat and would be more or less completely dissipated during the incineration of the body. It is true that the most elaborate precautions in the form of examination and certification are prescribed—and usually taken, I presume—before cremation is performed; but, as every medical jurist knows, precautions taken before the event are useless, for, to be effective, they would have to cover every possible cause of death, which would be impracticable. Hence, as suspicion, in case of poisoning, commonly does not arise until some time after death, I always give the closest consideration to the antecedent circumstances in cases where cremation has been performed.

"But in this case of Jardine's it was at once obvious that the circumstances called for the minutest inquiry and that no inquiry had been made. On the face of it the case was a suspicious one; and the curious incident that Jardine described made it look more suspicious still and, moreover, suggested a possible motive for the attempt on his life. Apparently he had seen, or was believed to have seen, something that he was not desired to see; something that it was not intended that anyone should see.

"Now what might that something have been? Apparently it was connected with the hand or with the part of the arm adjacent to the hand. I considered the possibilities; and at once they fell into two categories. That something might have been a wound, an injury, a hypodermic needle-mark; something, that is to say, related to the cause of death; or it might have been a mutilation, a deformity, a finger-ring, a tattoo-mark; something, that is to say, related to the identity of the deceased. And it followed that the cremation might have been made use of to conceal either the cause of death or the identity of the body. But all this was purely speculative. The case looked suspicious; but there was not a particle of positive evidence that anything abnormal had occurred.

"At this point Jardine exploded on us his second mystery; that of the dead cleric at Hampstead. This gave us, at once, an adequate motive for getting rid of him; for it had every appearance of a case of murder with successful concealment of the body, and Jardine was the only witness who could testify to its having occurred. On hearing of this I was for a moment disposed to dismiss the cremation case; to consider that the suspicious elements in it had been magnified by our imaginations in our endeavours to find an explanation of the assault on Jardine. Moreover, since we now had a sufficient motive for that assault the cremation case appeared to be outside the scope of the inquiry.

"But there was a difficulty. It was now six weeks since Jardine had encountered the body in the lane, and during that time he had been entirely unmolested. The assault had occurred on his moving into a new neighbourhood, to which he had come unexpectedly unannounced. Moreover, the assault had been committed by some person who either had access to the factory or was, at least, well acquainted with it and who, therefore, seemed to be connected with the new neighbourhood; and it was committed within a few days of the cremation incident. Furthermore, the assault was manifestly premeditated and prepared; but yet the circumstances–namely, Jardine's recent and unexpected appearance in the neighbourhood–were such as to make it certain that the crime could have been planned only a day or two before its execution. Which again seemed to connect it with the cremation case rather than with the Hampstead case.

"There were two more points. We have seen that Jardine's would-be murderer was a subtle, ingenious, resourceful and cautious villain. But a crime adjusted, to the conditions of cremation is exactly such a crime as we should expect of such a man; whereas the Hampstead crime–assuming it to be a crime–appeared to have been a somewhat clumsy affair, though the successful concealment of the body pointed to a person of some capacity. So that the former crime was more congruous with the known personality of the would-be murderer than the latter.

"The second point was made on further investigation. The day after our consultation I looked round the neighbourhood with the aid of a large-scale map; when I discovered that the yard of the factory in Norton Street backed on the garden of the Samways' house in Gayton Street. This, again, suggested a connection between the cremation case and the assault on Jardine; and the suggestion was so strong that once more the cremation incident assumed the uppermost place in my mind.

"I considered that case at length. Assuming a crime to have been committed, what was the probable nature of that crime? Now, cremation, as I have said, tends to destroy two kinds of evidence, namely; that relating to the cause of death and that relating to the identity of the body; whence it follows that the two crimes which it may be used to conceal are murder and substitution.

"To which of these crimes did the evidence point in the present instance? Well we had the undoubted fact that cremation had been performed pursuant to the expressed wishes of Septimus Maddock, the man who was alleged to have been cremated. But if it was a case of murder, the crime must have been hurriedly planned a few days before the man's death–that is, after the execution of the will; for we could assume that Maddock would not have connived at his own murder; whereas, if it was a case of substitution Maddock, himself, was probably the actual agent. Considering the circumstances–the inexplicable, symptomless illness and the unexpected death–the latter crime was obviously more probable than the former. The illness, in that case, would be a sham illness deliberately planned to prepare the way for the introduction of the substituted body.

"Moreover, the attendant circumstances were more in favour of substitution than of murder. Of the three doctors who saw the body, only one had seen the living man; and that one, Batson, was more than half blind and wholly inattentive and neglectful. For the purpose of substitution, no more perfectly suitable practitioner could have been selected. The identity of the body was taken for granted-naturally enough, I admit–and no verification was even thought of. Then, as to Jardine's experience. The hand or wrist is not at all a likely region on which to find either a fatal injury or the trace of a hypodermic injection; whereas it is a most important region for purposes of identification. The hand is highly characteristic in itself even when normal; and there is no part of the body that is so subject to mutilation or in which mutilations and deformities are so striking, so conspicuous, and so characteristic. Lost fingers, stiff fingers, webbed fingers, supernumary fingers, contracted palm, deformed nails, brachydactyly and numerous other abnormal conditions are not only easily recognized, but–since the hand is usually unclothed and visible–their existence will be known to a large number of persons.

"The evidence, in short, was strongly in favour of substitution as against murder.

"If, however, the body which was cremated was not that of Maddock, then it was the body of some other person; that is to say that the theory of substitution left us with a dead body that was unaccounted for. And since a dead body implies the death for some person, the theory of substitution left us with a death unaccounted for and obviously concealed; that is to say, it raised a strong presumption of the murder of some unknown person. And here it seemed that our data came to an end; that we had no material whatever for forming any hypothesis as to the identity of the person whose dead body we were assuming to have been substituted for that of Septimus Maddock.

"But while I was thus turning over the possibilities of this cremation case, the other–the Hampstead case– continued to lurk in the background of my mind. It was much less hypothetical. There was positive evidence of some weight that a crime had been committed. And the circumstances offered a fully adequate motive for getting rid of Jardine. Thus it was natural that I should raise the question. Was it possible that the two cases could be in any way connected?

"At the first glance, the suggestion looked absolutely wild.. But still I considered it at length; and then it looked somewhat less wild. The two cases had this in common, that if a crime had been committed, Jardine was the sole witness. Moreover, the supposition that the two cases were connected and incriminated the same parties, greatly intensified the motive for making away with Jardine. But there was another and much stronger point in favour of this view. If we adopted the theory of substitution, it was impossible, on looking at the two cases, to avoid being struck by the very curious converseness of their conditions. In the Hampstead case we were dealing with a body which had suddenly vanished, no one could say whither; in the Maddock case we were dealing with a body which had suddenly appeared, no one could say whence.

"When I reflected on this very striking appearance of relation it was inevitable that I should ask myself the question. Is it conceivable that these two bodies could have been one and the same? That the body which was cremated could have been the body which Jardine saw in the lane?

"Again, at the first glance, the question looked absurd. The first body was seen by Jardine more than six weeks before the alleged death of Maddock; and the body which he saw at the Samways' house was that of a man newly dead, with rigor mortis just beginning. It was, indeed barely conceivable that the Hampstead body was not actually dead and that the man might have lingered on alive for six weeks. But this suggestion failed to fit the known facts in two respects, In the first place, the body which Jardine saw in the lane was, from his description, pretty unmistakably a dead body, and, in the second, the sham illness of Maddock and the elaborate, leisurely preparations suggest a complete control of the time factor, which would be absent if those preparations were adjusted to a dying man who might expire at any moment.

"Rejecting this suggestion, then, the further question arose. Is it possible that the body that was seen in the lane could, after an interval of six weeks, have been produced in Gayton Street, perfectly fresh and in a state of incipient rigor mortis? And when the question was thus fairly stated, the answer was obviously in the affirmative. For, is it, not a matter of common knowledge that the bodies of sheep are habitually brought from New Zealand to London, traversing the whole width of the Tropics in the voyage, and are delivered, after an interval of more than six weeks, perfectly fresh and in a state of incipient rigor mortis? The physical possibility was beyond question.

"But if physically possible, was such preservation practicable? Well, how are the bodies of the sheep preserved? By exposing them continuously to intense cold. And how is that intense cold produced? Roughly speaking, by the volatilization of a liquified gas-ammonia, in the case of the sheep. But behold! The very man whom we are suspecting of being the agent in this crime is a man who has command of large quantities of a liquefied gas, and who has hired a mineral water factory for no apparent reason and put the premises to no apparent use."

At this point Jervis brought his fist down with a bang on the arm of his chair.

"Idiot!" he exclaimed. "Ass, fool, dolt, imbecile that I am! With those cylinders staring me in the face, too! Of course, it was that interval of six weeks that brought me up short. And yet I had actually heard Jardine describe the cloud of carbon dioxide snow that fell on his face! Don't you consider me an absolute donkey, Thorndyke?"

"Certainly not," replied Thorndyke. "You happened to miss a link and, of course, the chain would not hold. It occurs to us all now and again. But, do you see, Jardine, how 'the stone which the builders rejected has become the head of the corner'? Don't you understand how, when I reached this point, there rose before me the picture of that cellar with the commonplace objects that it contained? The case, seven feet by two and a-half–so convenient for preserving a body in a bulky packing; the two waterproof sheets–so well adapted to holding a mass of carbon dioxide snow in contact with the body; the mass of straw–one of the most perfect non-conductors–so admirably fitted for its use as a protective packing for the frozen body; and lastly, those ten empty cylinders, of which seven had been used for some purpose unknown to us? Let this case be a lesson to you, Jardine, not only in legal medicine but in clinical medicine, too, to take the facts as you find them–relevant or irrelevant, striking or commonplace—note them carefully and trust them to find their own places in the inductive scheme."

"It has been a most instructive lesson to me," said I; "especially your analysis of the reasoning by which you identified the criminal."

"Hum," said Thorndyke. "I didn't know I'd got as far as that."

"But if the body was preserved in a frozen state, there could not be much doubt as to who had preserved it."

"Possibly not," Thorndyke agreed. "But I had not proved that it had been so preserved, but only that it was possible for it to have been; and that the supposition of its having been so preserved was in agreement with the known circumstances of the case. But I must impress on you that up to this point I was dealing in pure hypothesis. My hypothesis was perfectly sound, perfectly consistent in all its parts, and perfectly congruous with all the known facts, but it did not follow therefore that it was true. It was entirely unverified; for hitherto I had not one single item of positive evidence to support it.

"Nevertheless, the striking agreement between the hypothesis and the known facts encouraged me greatly; and, as it was evident that I had now exhausted the material yielded by the cremation incident, I decided to take up the clue at the other end; to investigate the details of the Hampstead affair. To this end I called on Jardine, who very kindly went over the case with me afresh. And here it was that I first came within hail of positive evidence. On his wall was pinned an oil sketch, and on that sketch was a distinct print of a right thumb. It was beautifully clear; for the paint having been dry on the surface but soft underneath, had taken the impression as sharply as a surface of warm wax.

"Now, you will remember that I took possession of the letter which summoned Jardine to the mineral water works and I may now say that I tested it most carefully for finger-prints. But paper is a poor material on which to develop invisible prints owing to its absorbent nature and

I had very indifferent success. Still, I did not fail entirely. By the combined use of lycopodium powder and photography I obtained impressions of parts of two finger-tips and a portion of the end of a right thumb. They were wretched prints but yet available for corroboration, since one could see part of the pattern on each and could make out that the ridge-pattern of the thumb was of the kind known as a 'twinned loop.'

"Bearing this fact in mind, you will understand that I was quite interested to find that the print on the sketch—also that of a right thumb—had a twinned loop pattern. I noted the fact as a coincidence, but, of course, attached no importance to it until Jardine told me that the artist who painted the sketch habitually worked in gloves; and even then I merely made a mental note that I would ascertain who and what the artist was.

"I need not go over our examination of the scene of the crime. I need only say that I was deeply interested in following the track along which the body had been carried because I was on the look-out for something; and that something was a house or other building in which the body might have been temporarily deposited.

"My hypothesis seemed to demand such a building. For, since the body was quite fresh and rigor mortis was only beginning when Jardine saw it at Gayton Street, it must have been frozen very shortly after death. Now, it obviously could not have been carried from Hampstead to Gayton Street on a man's back; the alternative is either a vehicle waiting at an appointed place—and necessarily not far away—or a house or other building to which the body could be taken. But the vehicle would, under the circumstances be almost impracticable. It would hardly be possible to make an appointment with any exactness as to time; and the presence of a waiting or loitering vehicle would, at such an hour—it was about midnight, you will remember—be almost certain to arouse suspicion and inquiry.

"On the other hand, a house to which the body could be conveyed would meet the conditions perfectly. When once the body was deposited there, the danger of pursuit would be practically at an end; and it would be quite possible to have a supply of the liquid gas ready for use on its arrival. This is assuming long premeditation and very deliberate preparation; an assumption supported by Gill's peculiar tenancy of the factory.

"I, therefore, kept a sharp look-out for a likely house or building; and, as Jardine and I came out of Ken Wood by the turnstile, behold! a house which answered the requirements to perfection. It was a solitary house; there was no other house near; and it lay right on the track along which the body had apparently been carried. Instantly, I decided to investigate the recent history of that house and its tenants; but Jardine saved me the trouble. From him I learned that, at the time of the assumed murder, it had been inhabited by the artist whom he had mentioned, but that it had now been empty for a week or two.

"Here were news indeed! This artist, who habitually wore gloves and whose right thumb-print was a twinned loop, had been living in this house at the time of the assumed murder, but had been living elsewhere at the time of the cremation! It was a striking group of facts, and I eagerly availed myself of the opportunity of looking over the house.

"At first, the examination was quite barren and disappointing. The man's habits, as shown by the few discarded articles of use or other traces, were of no interest to me-and still less to Jardine; and of traces of his personality there were none. I searched all the rejected canvases and every available scrap of paper in the hope of collecting some fresh finger-prints, but without the smallest result. In fact, the examination looked like being an utter failure up to the very last, when we entered the stable-loft; but here I came upon one or two really significant traces of occupation.

"The first of these was a smooth, indented line on the floor, as if some heavy, metallic object had been dragged along it, with other, rougher lines, apparently made by a heavy wooden case. Then there was a quantity of straw, not new straw such as you might expect to find in a stable-loft, but straw that had evidently been used for packing. And, finally, there was a pair of canvas pliers which appeared to have been strained by a violent effort to rotate from right to left some hard, metallic body, three quarters of an inch wide, with sharp corners and apparently square in section; some body, in fact, that in shape, in size and apparently in material, was identical with the square of the cock on one of the liquid gas bottles; which appeared to have been connected with a screw thread and had clearly required great force to turn it with this inadequate appliance.

"The evidence collected from the loft, suggesting that a large case had been moved in and out and that a gas cylinder had been opened, you will say was of the flimsiest. And so it was. But the effects of evidence are cumulative. To estimate the value of these observations made in the loft, you must add them to the facts just obtained concerning the artist himself, the position of his house and the date on which he vacated it; and these coincidences and agreements must be added to–or, more strictly, multiplied into–the body of coincidences and agreements which I have already described.

"But the evidence collected at the house was the least important part of the day's 'catch.' On returning to Jardine's rooms I ventured to borrow the sketch and took it home with me; and when I compared the thumb-print on it with the photograph of the thumb-print on the letter–employing the excellent method of comparison that is in use at Scotland Yard–there could be no possible doubt (disregarding for the moment, the chances of forgery) that they were the prints of one and the same thumb.

"Here, then, at last I had stepped out of the region of mere hypothesis. Here was an item of positive evidence, and one, moreover, of high probative value. It proved, beyond any reasonable doubt, the existence of some connection between the house on the Heath and the factory in Norton Street; and it established a strong presumption that the artist and the man at the factory were the same person; the weak point in this being the absence of proof that the thumb-print on the painting was made by the artist.

"And here, Jardine, I would draw your attention to the interesting way in which, when a long train of hypothetical reasoning has at length elicited an actual, demonstrable truth, that truth instantly reacts on the hypothesis, lifting it as a whole on to an entirely different plane of probability. I may compare the effect to that of a crystal, dropped into a super-saturated solution of a salt, such as sodium sulphate. So long as it is at rest, the solution remains a clear liquid; but drop into it the minutest crystal of its own salt, and, in a few moments the entire liquid has solidified into a mass of crystals.

"So it was in the present case. In the instant when it became an established fact that the house at Hampstead and the factory in Norton Street had been occupied by the same person, the entire sequence of events which I had hypothetically constructed sprang from the plane of mere conceivability to that of actual probability. It was now more likely than unlikely that the unknown cleric had been murdered, that his body had been conveyed to the artist's house, that it had there been frozen, transferred to the factory, preserved there for some weeks, passed over the wall to the Samways' house, and finally cremated under the name of Septimus Maddock.

"All that now remained to be done was the verification and identification of the body. As to the first, I examined the will at Somerset House and found it, as the American detectives suspected, a mere notification to the New York authorities that Septimus Maddock was dead. I wrote to the detective agency and in due course came O'Donnell with the answers to my questions; from which we learned for certain that the artist was Septimus Maddock and that the assumed peculiarity of the hands consisted of brachydactyly. And then came the good Father Humperdinck to enable us to give a name to the body and to furnish us with that unlocked for means of identification. Henceforward, all was plain sailing with only one possible source of failure; the possibility that the bullet might have been subsequently extracted. But this was highly improbable. We knew that the wound had healed completely, and it was pretty certain that the bullet was lying quietly encysted or embedded in the bone. Still, I will confess that I have never in my life been more relieved than I was when my eyes lighted on that dent in the ilium with the stain of lead oxide round it."

"So I can imagine," said Jervis. "It was a triumph; and you deserved it. I have never known even my revered senior to work out the theory of a crime more neatly or with less positive matter to work from. And I suppose you have a pretty clear and connected idea of the actual sequence of events."

"I think so," replied Thorndyke, "although much of it is necessarily conjectural. I take it that Maddock, while hiding in Bruges under the name of Burton, made the acquaintance of Reinhardt, and saw in the rich, friendless, eccentric bachelor a suitable subject for a crime which he had probably already considered in general terms. I should think that they were probably somewhat alike in appearance and that the idea of personation was first suggested by the circumstance that they both wore gloves habitually. Maddock will have learned of Reinhardt's intended visit to England and immediately begun his preparations. His scheme—and a most ingenious one it was, I must confess—was clearly to cause Reinhardt to disappear in one locality and produce his body after a considerable interval in another at some distance; and the house on the Heath was apparently taken with this object and to be near Reinhardt's haunts. I take it, that on the night of the murder, Reinhardt had an appointment to visit him at that house, but that, having learned at Miss Vyne's of the sudden illness of Brother Bartholomew, he suddenly altered his plans and refused to go. Then Maddock–who had probably waited for him on the road–seeing his scheme on the point of being wrecked, walked with him as he was going home and took the risk of killing him in Millfield Lane. The risk was not great, considering the time of night and the solitary character of the place, and the distance from the house was not too great for a strong man, as Maddock seems to have been, to carry the body.

"Death was almost certainly produced by a stab in the back; and Maddock was probably just about to carry the body away when destiny, in the form of Jardine, appeared. Then Maddock must have lurked, probably behind the fence which had the large hole in it, until Jardine went away, when he must instantly have picked up the body, carried it down the lane, pushed it over the fence–detaching the reliquary as he did so–carried it away to the house, stripped it and proceeded at once to freeze it, having provided a bottle of the gas in readiness.

"The next morning he will have gone to Marchmont's office, probably dressed in Reinhardt's clothes, from thence to Charing Cross, and, with Reinhardt's luggage, gone straight on to Paris, leaving the body packed in an abundance of the carbonic acid snow. At Paris he will have made his arrangements with Desire and then disappeared, returning in disguise to England to carry out the rest of the plan. And a wonderfully clever plan it was, and most ingeniously and resolutely executed. If it had succeeded–and it was within a hair's breath of succeeding–the hunted criminal, Maddock, would have been beyond the reach of Justice for ever, and the fictitious Reinhardt might have lived out his life in luxury and absolute security."

As Thorndyke concluded, he rose from his chair, and, stepping over to a cabinet, drew from some inner recess a cigar of melanotic complexion and repulsive aspect. Jervis looked at it and chuckled. "Thorndyke's one dissipation," said he. "At the close of every successful case he proceeds, as a sort of thanksgiving ceremony, to funk us out of these chambers with the smoke of a Trichinopoly cheroot. But listen! Don't light it yet, Thorndyke. Here comes some harmless and inoffensive stranger."

Thorndyke paused with the cigar in his fingers. A quick step ascended the stairs and then came a sharp, official rat-tat from the little brass knocker. Thorndyke laid the cigar on the mantelpiece and strode over to the door. I saw him take in a telegram, open it, glance at the paper and dismiss the messenger. Then, closing the door, he came back to the fireside with the "flimsy" in his hand.

"There, Jardine," said he, laying it on my knee; "there is your order of release."

I picked up the paper and read aloud its curt message. "Maddock arrested Folkestone now in custody Bow Street. Miller."

"That means to say," said Thorndyke," that the halter is already around his neck. I think I may light my Trichinopoly now."

And he did so.

There is little more to tell. This has been a history of coincidences and one more coincidence brings it to a close. The very day on which my formal engagement to Sylvia was made public, chanced to be the day on which the execution of Septimus Maddock was described in the papers. On that day, too, the portrait of poor Letitia, painted by that skilful and murderous hand, was placed in the handsome ebony frame that I had caused to be made for it. As I write these closing words, it hangs before me, flanked on either side by the little jar of violets that are renewed religiously from day to day by my wife or me. The pale, inscrutable eyes look out on me, her friend whom she loved so faithfully and who so little merited her love; but as I look into them, the picture fades and shows me the same face glorified, waxen, pallid, drowsy-eyed, peaceful and sweet—the dead face of the woman who gave her heart's blood as the price of my ransom, and who was fated then to pass—out of my life indeed, but out of my heart's shrine and my most loving remembrance, never.

THE END

Other Resurrected Press Mysteries from the Dr. John Thorndyke Series

Dr. John Thorndyke - Lecturer on Medical Jurisprudence and Forensic Medicine. Before Bones, before CSI, before Quincy, M.E – there was Dr. John Thorndyke solving the most baffling cases of Edwardian London using the latest tools of medical science. Read about his cases in:

The Eye of Osiris
John Bellingham, noted Egyptologist has vanished not once but twice in the same day. Now Dr, Thorndyke must unravel the tangled claims on his estate, solve the riddle of the missing man and find the "Eye of Osiris".

The Mystery of 31 New Inn
When Dr. Jervis is whisked away in a coach with no windows to an unknown location to treat a man in a coma from undivulged causes it is Dr. Thorndyke who must come up with the solution.

The Red Thumb Mark
The first of Dr. Thorndyke's cases finds him trying to prove the innocence of a young man accused of being a diamond thief despite the fact that his finger print was found at the scene of the crime.

John Thorndyke's Cases
More cases of medical mysteries as told by his trusted assistant Jervis, M.D. Eight stories of crime and deduction in Edwardian London.

Visit www.resurrectedpress.com

Other Resurrected Press Mysteries

Mysteries on a Train

Before the Orient Express there was:

The Rome Express by Arthur Griffiths
A man is found dead in his first class sleeping compartment on the express from Rome to Paris. Who was his murderer? The Countess? The English General? His brother the clergy man? The maid who has disappeared? Is the French justice system up to solving the crime? Read about it in The Rome Express.

The Passenger from Calais by Arthur Griffiths
Colonel Basil Annesley finds he is the only passenger on the train from Calais to Lucerne. That is until a mysterious woman shows up at the last minute to book a compartment. Who is after her? What is her secret? Is she a criminal or a victim? Read about it in The Passenger from Calais

Visit us at www.resurrectedpress.com

Now from the Resurrected Press

The Hampstead Mystery

High Court Justice Sir Horace Fewbanks found shot dead in his Hampstead home, a butler with a criminal past, a scorned lover and a hint of scandal. These are the elements of the *Hampstead Mystery* that Detective Inspector Chippenfield of Scotland Yard must unravel with the assistance of the ambitious Detective Rolfe. But will he be able to sort out the tangled threads of this case and arrest the culprit before he is upstaged by the celebrated gentleman detective Crewe. Follow the details of this amazing case at it plays out across Hampstead, London and Scotland until it reaches a stunning conclusion in the courts of the Old Bailey.

The Hampstead Mystery
by John R. Watson & Arthur J. Rees
RPM -101

Visit www.resurrectedpress.com to order now.

Now from the Resurrected Press

The Mystery of the Downs

When Harry Marsland was caught in a sudden down pour he sought shelter at Cliff Farm. Met at the door by a young woman clearly expecting someone else he is only too glad to get inside to wait out the storm. When they hear a noise upstairs in the deserted house they investigate only to discover the body of the farm's owner, Frank Lumsden, dead of a gunshot wound. Who then, killed Lumsden, and why? Who was the woman expecting and did she have any roll in the murder? These are the questions that private detective Crewe must answer in The Mystery of the Downs.

The Mystery of the Downs
by John R. Watson & Arthur J. Rees

Visit www.resurrectedpress.com to order now.

The Fictional Detective
by Greg Fowlkes

Who killed Ezekial O. Handler?

A beautiful dame, a hard-boiled private eye – and a dead body.

It started like any other case. When a famous writer dies in a mysterious car crash, private detective Frank Slade is called in to find answers, but all he finds is more questions. Who killed Ezekial Handler? Who is Janet Nielsen and why is she so interested in finding out? Who is leaving the neatly typed clues? And as Slade tries to find answers to these questions he starts to wonder if the ultimate answer will threaten his very existence.

Read about it in
The Fictional Detective

Visit www.thefictionaldetective.com

About Resurrected Press

A division of Intrepid Ink, LLC, Resurrected Press is dedicated to bringing high quality, vintage books back into publication. See our entire catalogue and find out more at www.ResurrectedPress.com.

About Intrepid Ink, LLC

Intrepid Ink, LLC provides full publishing services to authors of fiction and non-fiction books, eBooks and websites. From editing to formatting, from publishing to marketing, Intrepid Ink gets your creative works into the hands of the people who want to read them. Find out more at www.IntrepidInk.com.

Made in the USA
Coppell, TX
08 October 2021

63757520R00197